NEW STORIES
FROM THE SOUTH

The Year's Best, 2001

*The editor wishes to thank Kathy Pories, Dana Stamey,
and Anne Winslow, colleagues whose talent, skill, patience,
and tact are essential to this anthology.*

Edited by
Shannon Ravenel

with a preface by Lee Smith

NEW STORIES
FROM THE SOUTH

The Year's Best, 2001

Algonquin Books of Chapel Hill

Published by
ALGONQUIN BOOKS OF CHAPEL HILL
Post Office Box 2225
Chapel Hill, North Carolina 27515-2225

a division of
WORKMAN PUBLISHING
708 Broadway
New York, New York 10003

ISSN 0897-9073
ISBN 1-56512-311-5

CONTENTS

PREFACE: DRIVING MISS DAISY CRAZY; OR, LOSING THE
MIND OF THE SOUTH
   by Lee Smith   vii

Moira Crone, WHERE WHAT GETS INTO PEOPLE COMES FROM   I
From *Ploughshares*

James Ellis Thomas, THE SATURDAY MORNING CAR WASH CLUB   18
From *The New Yorker*

Christie Hodgen, THE HERO OF LONELINESS   29
From *Meridian*

Elizabeth Tippens, MAKE A WISH   48
From *Harper's*

Ingrid Hill, JOLIE-GRAY   69
From *The Southern Review*

Linda Wendling, INAPPROPRIATE BABIES   102
From *River Styx*

Jane R. Shippen, I AM NOT LIKE NUÑEZ   118
From *Meridian*

George Singleton, PUBLIC RELATIONS   139
From *The Georgia Review*

William Gay, THE PAPERHANGER   154
From *Harper's*

Robert Love Taylor, PINK MIRACLE IN EAST TENNESSEE   173
From *The Ohio Review*

Jim Grimsley, JESUS IS SENDING YOU THIS MESSAGE   194
From *Ontario Review*

Marshall Boswell, IN BETWEEN THINGS   206
From *The Missouri Review*

Nicola Mason, THE WHIMSIED WORLD   226
From *Epoch*

Madison Smartt Bell, TWO LIVES   234
From *Meridian*

Carrie Brown, FATHER JUDGE RUN   246
From *The Oxford American*

Edith Pearlman, SKIN DEEP   269
From *The Antioch Review*

Kurt Rheinheimer, SHOES   279
From *The Nebraska Review*

Stephen Coyne, HUNTING COUNTRY   296
From *The Southern Review*

John Barth, THE REST OF YOUR LIFE   306
From *TriQuarterly*

APPENDIX   327

PREVIOUS VOLUMES   335

Lee Smith

PREFACE:
DRIVING MISS DAISY CRAZY;
OR, LOSING THE MIND OF
THE SOUTH

I want to start by introducing you to Miss Daisy. Chances are, you already know her. She may be your mother. She may be your aunt. Or you may have your own private Miss Daisy, as I do: a prim, well-educated maiden lady of a certain age who has taken up permanent residence in a neat little room in the frontal lobe of my brain. I wish she'd move, but as she points out to me constantly, she's just no trouble at all. She lives on angel food cake and she-crab soup, which she heats up on a little ring right there in her room.

Miss Daisy was an English teacher at a private girls school for forty-three years, back in the days when English was English — before it became Language Arts. She was famous for her ability to diagram sentences, any sentence at all, even sentences so complex that their diagrams on the board looked like blueprints for a cathedral. Her favorite poet is Sidney Lanier. She likes to be elevated. She is still in a book club, but it is not Oprah's book club. In fact, Miss Daisy is not quite sure who Oprah is, believing that her name is *Okra* Winfrey, and asking me repeatedly what all the fuss is about. Miss Daisy's book club can find scarcely a thing to elevate them these days, so they have taken to reading *Gone with the Wind* over and over again.

Miss Daisy's favorite word is *ought,* as in, "You ought to go to church this morning." She often punctuates her sentences with "you know," as in, "Lee Marshall, you *know* you don't believe that!" or, "Lee Marshall, you *know* you don't mean it!" She believes it is *true* about the two ladies who got kicked out of the Nashville Junior League: one for having an orgasm, and the other for having a job.

In fact, Miss Daisy reminds me of another lady I encountered many years ago, when I moved down to Alabama to become a reporter for the *Tuscaloosa News.* The former editor of the ladies page of the paper had just retired. "Thank God!" everybody said, since for many years she had ceased to write up events in the paper the way they actually happened, preferring instead to write them up the way she thought they *should* have happened.

Pat Conroy has said that the South runs on denial. I think this is true. We learn denial in the cradle and carry it to the grave. It is absolutely essential to being a lady, for instance. I myself was sent from the mountains of southwest Virginia, where I was growing up, down to Birmingham every summer to stay with my Aunt Gay Gay, whose task was to turn me into a lady. Gay Gay's two specialities were Rising to the Occasion and Rising Above It All, whatever "it" happened to be. Gay Gay believed that if you can't say something nice, say nothing at all. If you don't discuss something, it doesn't exist. She drank a lot of gin and tonics and sometimes she'd start in on them early, winking at my Uncle Bob and saying, "Pour me one, honey, it's already dark underneath the house." Until she died, I never knew that another of my aunts had had a previous marriage. It had been edited right out of the family, in the same way all pictures of that husband had been removed from the family albums.

Denial affects not only our personal lives, but also our political lives, our culture, and our literature. In her book *Playing in the*

Dark: Whiteness and the Literary Imagination, Toni Morrison talks about a kind of denial she sees operating in American literature and criticism; she chides liberal critics for what she calls their "neglect of darkness." She says that "the habit of ignoring race is understood to be a graceful, even generous, liberal gesture . . . but excising the political from the life of the mind is a sacrifice that has proven costly. . . . A criticism that needs to insist that literature is not only 'universal' but also 'race-free' risks lobotomizing that literature, and diminishes both the art and the artist." Morrison suggests that Black characters in classic American novels have been as marginalized as their real-life counterparts.

But back to Miss Daisy. I'm taking her out to lunch today. Miss Daisy claims she "just eats like a bird," not deigning to confess to anything as base as hunger or even appetite, but she *does* like to go out to lunch. And while she's making her final preparations — that is, clean underwear in case we are in a wreck, gloves, money safely tucked in her bra in case her purse is stolen — let me tell you about this restaurant we're going to.

You may be surprised to learn that I actually *own* this restaurant, and that it is actually a sushi bar. But, hey! It's the New South, remember? And actually, my sushi bar (named Akai Hana and located in Carrboro, North Carolina) presents a little case study in the New South.

The land Akai Hana stands on today, at 313 N. Main St, was farmland not so very long ago, when Carrboro was a dusty, sleepy little farm village on the old road from Chapel Hill to Greensboro. This was an open field, with a tenant house at the end of it. Then Carr Mill came in, and mill houses sprouted up in neat little rows, like beans, to house the families that worked at Carr Mill. As the university grew, Chapel Hill grew, too, spreading outward toward Carrboro, which gradually became a service adjunct of Chapel Hill. This was the place you came to buy your grass seed or to get your tires fixed at the Chapel Hill Tire Company, right across the street from us. Carrboro was mostly black then, and all poor. Miss Daisy never came here except to pick up her cook. Every business in

Carrboro closed at noon on Wednesday, because everybody went to church on Wednesday night. And nothing was open on Sunday.

The first restaurant to occupy our brick building here, constructed in the early fifties, was a popular, locally owned café named the Elite Lunch, which featured Southern cooking and lots of it. It had two dining rooms, one for white and one for colored. In the early sixties it was superseded by Pizza Villa, whose name alone testifies to Chapel Hill's — and Carrboro's — increasing sophistication. By now, plenty of graduate students and even some professors lived in Carrboro. The mill had closed, and those mill houses were affordable.

By the mid-seventies, when an outrageously colorful chef took over and turned it into Avanti, Carrboro was coming of age. The mill became Carr Mill Mall, filled with trendy boutiques. A cooperative health-food grocery named Weaver Street opened up. Artists moved in. Carrboro started calling itself "The Paris of the Piedmont."

Avanti's chef hung paintings by his artist friends. He stuck candles in wine bottles on each of his artfully mismatched tables. He opened the patio for outdoor dining. He made soup with forty cloves of garlic. Then, even Avanti was superseded by the truly gourmet Martini's. The owner's wife's mother came from Italy to run the kitchen, while her homemade pasta dried on broomsticks upstairs. My first husband and I had some memorable meals there, and my present husband remembers that he was eating polenta in this very gazebo when a former girlfriend gave him the gate. Ah, what sweet revenge it is now to own that gazebo, which we have (of course) transformed into a pagoda.

But back to our narrative. The owner died in a wreck, Martini's closed, and the restaurant underwent a total transformation before opening again, for breakfast and lunch only, as a bakery and café, very French, with a marble floor and lace curtains at the windows. Pre-Starbucks, it served muffins accompanied by the first good coffee in Carrboro.

We bought the place from the muffin ladies. Why? You might well ask. Have I always had a burning desire to go into the sushi business? No, actually, my own attitude toward raw fish is closer to Roy Blount's poem about oysters:

> I prefer my oysters fried
> Then I know my oyster's died.

It was my husband's idea. He calls my son the "Samurai step-son," and their favorite thing to do together has always been to go out for sushi. The closing of the only sushi bar in town coincided with this son's recovery from a severe bipolar disorder. New medications made it possible for him to have a regular life, and what better job could a Samurai stepson get than in a sushi bar? (I can hear Miss Daisy saying in my ear, "Now Lee Marshall, *you know* you shouldn't have told that!" But I am telling it anyway.) We held long conferences with Bob, the sushi chef. We met with the muffin ladies and with the bank. We hired a designer and a construction firm. We were under way, even though nobody except us thought this was a good idea. Our accountant was horrified. The guys from the tire shop across the street kept coming over to ask, "How's the bait shop coming along?"

Now we've been open for a little over four years. Let me introduce you around.

Bob, manager and head chef, hails from the coastal North Carolina town of Swansboro. At college in Chapel Hill, he wrote poetry and played guitar until his wanderlust led him to California, where he eventually became an ardent convert of the Reverend Moon and joined the Unification Church. He married his Japanese wife, Ryoko, in a ceremony of twenty-five thousand couples in Madison Square Garden. They are still happily married, with six beautiful children.

Under Bob's direction, Akai Hana employs people from diverse backgrounds, including Hispanic, Burmese, Thai, Japanese, Filipino, Chinese, Korean, African American, and African. Meet Rick, for instance, who heads the kitchen in back (yes, we *do* have cooked food, for people like Miss Daisy, who is enjoying some grilled teriyaki chicken right now). Anyway, both Rick and his wife, a beautician, are Chinese Filipinos who have been in this country for eighteen years, sending for their siblings one by one. Their son, a physician, is now completing his residency in Seattle. Their daughter, who recently earned her doctorate in public health, works for a world health organization in L.A. Rick's nephew Brian, one of our wait staff, plays saxophone in the UNC jazz band.

Ye-tun, a cook and a former Burmese freedom fighter whose nickname is "Yel," proudly showed me a picture of himself coming through the jungle dressed in camo, carrying an AK-47. Now my husband calls him the "Rebel Yell," but nobody gets it.

Okay: Bob, Ryoko, Brian, Helen Choi, Ye-tun, Miguel, Jose, Genita, Mister Chiba, and Mister Choi — these people are Southerners. We are all Southerners. Akai Hana is a Southern restaurant, just like Miss Pittypat's or Hardee's.

Judging merely from our lunch at Akai Hana, we are going to have to seriously overhaul our image of the South, and of Southerners, for this millennium.

I called up John Shelton Reed, over at the university, to get some statistics:

My little piece of land in Carrboro is typical. The South was two-thirds rural in the 1930s. Now it is over two-thirds urban. One half of all Southerners were farmworkers in the thirties; now that figure is at 2 percent. And out of those farmworkers in the thirties, one half were tenant farmers. Now we have no tenant farmers, but migrant workers instead.

As the largest metro areas continue to attract people and jobs, the viability of rural life comes increasingly into question. One half of all the new jobs in this country are being created in the South, with nine out of ten of them in Texas, Florida, and a dozen metropolitan areas, including the Research Triangle here in North Carolina, where Carrboro is located.

Our Southern birth rate, which used to be famously *above* the national average, is now below it. This means that immigration is defining the South's population. Ten years from now, Texas will have a 57 percent nonwhite population. Florida will have a 54 percent nonwhite population. Some of the "big nine" states that now contain half the U.S. population will be eclipsed by the "New South": Georgia, North Carolina, and Virginia. Among African Americans, there was a great migration out of the South in the twenties, the thirties, and on into the fifties. But in the 1970s more blacks started moving *to* the South — in many instances, back to the South — than leaving it. That trend has now accelerated.

Well, all these statistics have given Miss Daisy a headache. She just doesn't have a head for figures, anyway. She'd like some dessert, but Akai Hana serves only green tea ice cream, which is too weird to even think about, in Miss Daisy's opinion. So we pay up and drive around the block to Dip's Country Kitchen, where Dip Council, Miss Daisy's former cook, has opened her big, fancy new restaurant. She's published a cookbook, too. She's been written up by Calvin Trillin and Craig Claiborne; she's been on TV. She's an entrepreneur now. Miss Daisy orders the lemon chess pie. I go for the peach cobbler myself.

Some things never change. Some Southern food will never go out of style, no matter how much it may get *nouveau*ed. And large parts of the South still look a lot like they used to — the Appalachian coal country where I'm from, for instance, and the old Cotton Belt. As a whole, we Southerners are still religious, and we are still violent. We'll bring you a casserole, but we'll kill you, too. Southern women, both black and white, have always been more likely than Northern women to work outside the home, despite the image projected by such country lyrics as "Get your biscuits in the oven and your buns in the bed, this women's liberation is a-going to your head." It was not because we were so liberated; it's because we were so poor. This, too, is changing: now our per capita income is at 92 percent of the national average.

With all these changes, what should I tell my student, one of my very favorite students, who burst into tears after we attended a reading together at which Elizabeth Spencer read her fine short story entitled "Cousins." "I'll *never* be a Southern writer!" my student wailed. "I don't even *know* my cousins!" Raised in a military household, relocated many times, she had absolutely no sense of place, no sense of the past, no sense of family. How did she spend her childhood? I asked. In the mall in Fayetteville, North Carolina, she tearfully confessed, sneaking cigarettes and drinking Cokes.

I told her she was lucky.

But she was also right. For a writer cannot pick her material any more than she can pick her parents; her material is given to her by the circumstances of her birth, by how she first hears language. And if she happens to be Southern, these given factors may already be trite, even before she sits down at her computer to begin. Her neurasthenic, fragile Aunt Lena is already trite, her mean, scary cousin Bobby Lee is already trite, her columned, shuttered house in Natchez is already trite. Far better to start out from the mall in Fayetteville, illicit cigarette in hand, with no cousins to hold her back, and venture forth fearlessly into the New South.

I once heard George Garrett say that the House of Fiction has many rooms. Well, the House of Southern Fiction is in the process of remodeling. It needs so many more rooms that we've got brand-new wings shooting out from the main house in every direction. It looks like one of those pictures of the sun as drawn by a second-grader. In fact, that's the name of it—the House of the Rising Sun—which is right over here by the interstate. I'll run you by it as we drive Miss Daisy home.

Look—there's my student right now, knocking on the door, suitcase in hand. She doesn't know yet that once she takes a room in there, she can never come out again. She doesn't understand that she's giving up her family and her home forever, that as soon as she writes about these things she will lose them, in a way, though she will mythologize them in her work, the way we all do, with all our little hometowns of the heart.

Allan Gurganus has called ours "the literature of nostalgia," pointing out that many of the great anthems of the South are written from a position of exile such as "Way down upon the Swanee River"; "I wish I was in the land of cotton"; James Taylor's "going to Carolina in my mind"; or "Country roads, take me home."

The writer puts herself in exile by the very act of writing. She will feel guilty about leaving, and for the rest of her life, she will write, in part, to expunge this guilt. Back home, they will be embarrassed by what she's become, wishing that she'd married a surgeon and joined the Country Club instead. Mostly, they just won't mention it, sticking to safer subjects.

Miss Daisy and I sit in the car watching my student, who keeps banging on the door, trying to get in there. "Honey, don't do it!" Miss Daisy rolls down her window and cries across the grass. "Go back home! It's not too late to stop!" But of course it is. Now my student is trying to peer in a window, shading her eyes with her hand.

Oh, I remember when I was that age myself, desperate for a room in the House of the Rising Sun. You think you'll pay for it out of your day job, and maybe you will for a while, but you'll whore out, too, eventually. We all do. The House of the Rising Sun is full of desperate characters. Some of us are drinking ourselves to death quietly, in our rooms, or loudly, at MLA. A lot of us are involved in secret affairs and unseemly couplings — we'd be real embarrassed if everybody knew who we're sleeping with. Some of us just can't do it anymore, but we put on our makeup anyway, and sit at the window all dressed up, and *talk* about doing it.

Look! The door is opening, just a crack. It's the Madam herself, but she stands just far enough back in the shadows so you can't really see who she is — maybe it's Shannon Ravenel, or maybe it's Okra.

My student slips inside. She does not look back.

"Well, I *never!*" Miss Daisy announces before falling over into a dead faint on the seat beside me.

But I know she'll be all right. I know she'll be herself again by the time I get her back to her room, and she'll be talking about what's happened to my student, and she'll make a big story out of it, and *she will never, ever, shut up.*

This is the main thing that has not changed about the South, in my opinion — that will never change. We Southerners love a story, and will tell you *anything*. Narrative is as necessary to us as air. We use the story to transmit information as well as to while away the time. In periods of stress and change, the story becomes even more important. In the telling of it we discover or affirm who we are, why we exist, what we should do. The story brings order and delight. Its form is inherently pleasing, and deeply satisfying to us. Because it has a beginning, middle, and end, it gives a recognizable shape to the muddle and chaos of our lives.

Just look at Miss Daisy now. She's already sitting back up on the seat fanning herself and going on and on about what happened to that poor girl, which reminds her of another awful thing that happened to her niece Margaret's daughter, not the Margaret I know that lives in Atlanta, but the other one that lives in middle Tennessee who was never quite right in the head after that terrible automobile accident that happened when she was not but six, when Cousin Dan was driving in that open car, you know he was such an alcoholic. . . .

NEW STORIES
FROM THE SOUTH

The Year's Best, 2001

Moira Crone

WHERE WHAT GETS INTO PEOPLE COMES FROM

(from *Ploughshares*)

Lily Stark's mother had just said the facts of the murder were too horrible to repeat. But Lily's father insisted a story as awful as how Mr. Sam was slaughtered would teach Lily something about this world.

"I don't care about the world you even mean," Lily said. For a long time Lily had been looking for a cause for her wildness. She'd just found it. So she felt like she could tell her father off. And they were in front of neighbors, so he wouldn't slap her.

It was the day of Mr. Sam's funeral. The man *had* been murdered in the most degrading way imaginable. There were thirty or forty people standing around, some in line with the Starks, waiting for the coconut cake, others over with Methodist ladies in navy-blue crepe dresses pulling out their small handkerchiefs, giving condolences to the Cobbs' living children. There were men and boys in between, staring out, eating deviled eggs off glass plates. It was 1967, a small town in eastern North Carolina. Lily Stark was fifteen. She could hardly stand being alive.

Earlier that day at the Cobbs' plot, Lily had noticed the headstone of Mr. Sam's first son, Archie, who had died the day she was born. August 19th, 1952. When he was twenty-seven years old. Lily had lived next door to the Cobbs her whole life, but she had never known there was an Archie.

As soon as they had come back to the home, Lily had gone to ask Zachary, who had been hired for the day to serve the food for the mourners and wash up. Zachary worked freelance: bartending, butlering, throwing weddings and funerals. He knew things that went on in white people's houses. He said that when Archie Cobb got home from the war back in 1948, he took a job at a state hospital outside of town "to be near the dope." By and by Archie fell for a nurse, who saw his withered thigh where he'd found the veins. She wouldn't have him. "And he could not be consoled by the Lord or any person, so Archie took his mother's Nash to the Cliffs of the Neuse, drove off the edge, and crashed it to tiny pieces. Died like that. It was August, over a hundred degrees."

"I was born then," Lily said.

"I know," Zachary said.

Archie must have had a second thought as his momma's car was tumbling down to the river, and he came flying out, spirit only, flesh doomed, and there was my mother, pregnant in that heat, sitting outside in a hammock only a few yards away from the Cobbs' back porch. Archie dove right into my girl baby body. I have his soul, so Lily thought.

If somebody had offered her morphine that spring, she would not have thought twice about trying it. Archie had been a reckless man. She herself was a reckless girl. He just wanted to get out. He hadn't made it. So it was Lily's destiny to leave: she'd known this since she was little. This even explained why her mother couldn't stand her—her mother always said the Cobbs were low. And Lily had no respect for the solid things in life, to hear her father tell it, but Lily could appreciate the flight of Archie's soul over town because of the terribleness of lost love, hoping to leave and looking to land at the same time. She adored the image of poor Archie overhead, she could even feel how the sky felt, the soft heat of the heavens. Then she told her father what she thought of the world he meant.

He said: "Listen to me. You mind what can be seen, touched, counted otherwise—"

"What?" she asked, not really caring to know, not anymore. "Why didn't anybody ever tell me about Archie Cobb, how he died? The day I was born? Nobody ever tells me what *I need to know.*"

"You want to end up like Sam Cobb? Or his son?"

Lily refused to see the parallel. She stood there, in line for the coconut cake. She knew what she knew. What mattered.

In eastern North Carolina the land appears at first too low and dull for any feature as remarkable as a deep river and a steep drop, so the Cliffs of the Neuse are a shock. But when you follow the folds of the plain from where the Neuse River starts to its destination—the Cape Fear, the Atlantic—it's clear that what at first seems overly-dramatic for that landscape in truth cannot be helped.

Fayton was a town like other towns on that plain, so small all kinds of people were close at hand. There were twelve houses total on the block of Winter between Park and Locust, one mansion, several proud Queen Annes with towers, and the rest little houses, like the Starks' place and the Cobbs'. People lived in each other's porches and backyards and parlors then. Their was some vigilance, but sooner or later every secret saw the light.

Lily's father's house and the Cobbs' right beside it started out in the twenties as plain bungalows, white frame and mute, raised on piers with seven stairs up the front and thick half-brick pillars that supported the roof of the porch. They each had two gumball trees in their yards, and across the street from both of them were the brick walls of finer houses with generous gardens, which were opened every spring so everyone else could peep into them, and wish.

When he was young, Sam Cobb was slender but muscled, dark, considered handsome. In high school in the early twenties, he liked to act in plays. Eventually he became a salesman. He bought the house on Winter after he married in 1921. This was during the days when people thought the town of Fayton would amount to something: a ten-story building was put up, two five-and-dimes were built, then a hotel with an imposing lobby. There was a bus station, a train station with a train that came into it and left for Danville, Virginia, and three cab companies. Mr. Sam was excitable, but he was a working man. Up to a certain point in his life, he was an Elk, a Methodist, a fair earner, a charmer, a good father.

Mrs. Geneva, his wife, was a practical nurse, a kind woman with a sweet tooth, stout, and a great baker. Her specialty was big white cakes. She used boiled icing, the kind that hardens and makes a cake a monument. The hair about her head was cotton candy. There were burst veins in cheeks. Archie was Mrs. Geneva's first son, born 1925, and the best looking. His hair was dark and slightly curly. His chin had a dimple. Raleigh, who came much later, in 1937, was stout, after his mother's side. His whole life he would never get rid of the name Rolley. The third boy, Jimbo, was born during the Second War, 1944. Wild red hair. Soon as he was walking, all of Winter Street said there was something wrong with him.

In 1954, when he was seventeen, after his brother died, after his daddy set out upon his second life, Rolley Cobb eloped with Isabel Odom, runner-up to homecoming queen, who was pregnant. Her people were upstanding, but they'd lost everything in the thirties. Everybody still thought she had married down. So she got Rolley to make her promises.

Rolley's worst flaws were his weakness for his mother's cakes and the fact he went after his living brother with whatever was near at hand—a belt, a big shoe, a plank of wood. He believed in the beating. Jimbo had to be tamed, it was true—anything in the world might get into him. The boy shot at birds with BBs from his own little blind in the backyard, and he missed, killing squirrels, terrorizing the neighborhood dogs and cats. He came sneaking around after Lily Stark and her friends in the yard with a garter snake dangling from the handle of a hoe. Mrs. Geneva never intervened, on either side, Rolley or Jimbo. That was what living with men was like, she said. Stop them from one thing they will do something else, pretend it is the opposite, but it will be just as bad.

Through the early years, the fifties, due to her father's efforts and her mother's demands, Lily Stark's family's bungalow took on dormers, and wrought iron like people had in New Orleans so it didn't match Mrs. Geneva's exactly anymore. Her mother got creeper with little leaves to cover the grassless yard because she said she couldn't stand the sad sight of that white East Carolina soil. It wasn't even soil. It was sand.

All this time the Cobbs' got shabbier. It sorely needed paint, repairs to the porch. But it turned out that the fact that the two houses looked less and less alike had no effect whatsoever upon Sam Cobb and his ways.

Long after midnight one night when she was four years old, Lily came downstairs for water and saw the front door was open. Rolley Cobb was standing just beyond the screen under the yellow bug light. It was a summer without air-conditioning, only fans. The Starks didn't keep their windows closed or their doors locked. Nobody did. Lily's father finally let Rolley in, but still for a while they stood there looking at something, not doing anything. Rolley's striped pajamas were turned over at the waist. She could see the exhausted elastic. He had stubble on his round face, and ashy hair that fell into his wide blue eyes. Rolley had moles. All the Cobbs had moles.

Eventually Lily put her head around to see what the two men saw: on her mother's slipcovered couch against the wall lay Sam Cobb half-curled up in a ball, his head thrown back at an angle, his mouth open, snot puddled on his upper lip. Her mother was going to be furious, furious. Rolley, who was large so people assumed he was strong, assumed he could play football well, for example, when the fact was he couldn't, made the first move. He lifted his daddy's head, then reached under the arms and dragged him down, causing the body to unfurl on her mother's wall-to-wall carpet. Mr. Sam would wake up, Lily hoped. She came out from hiding, and her daddy didn't see her, but Rolley looked right at her. He was in awful pain, she could see that. Rolley was married, but he was not a real daddy like Lily's, he was not one who had been through the war, seen action in the Pacific, suffered, bled, saved people's lives and had his life saved. Rolley didn't have a store like Lily's daddy did. Rolley was a teenage father with barely a job and a father in the wrong living room, and he lived in a tired house the shame of the neighborhood, and in his face even Lily could see how terrible he felt even to exist.

Finally Lily's father stepped forward and took Mr. Sam's limp ankles. With Lily's father moving forwards, Rolley going backwards, they carried Mr. Sam, whose arms hung down on his sides, across the porch, down the stairs, over her mother's creeper, across the Cobbs' dirt yard. At the other end Mrs. Geneva was holding the door open. For all the disturbance nobody said very much. The next morning Lily's father said Mr. Sam didn't care anymore about who he was or what he was, didn't give a damn, always had been a dreamer. Now he was worse.

After Dora, Isabel had a son, Beverly, people called Bit. They still all lived in that house. Rolley went to work selling cars.

In 1958 Lily's mother hired one of the brilliant gardeners who worked across the street to set in rows of bulbs in her backyard that took turns blooming, and azaleas, and behind them flowering plum trees. They built an arbor for grapes. In March, Isabel invited herself over with Dora and Bit to sit on a blanket, and Lily joined them. It felt like everybody's garden. Lily was conscious of spring, of the beauty. She said to herself, I am alive. I am six years old.

Isabel seemed proud Rolley had started moonlighting doing home additions, small jobs. He paid a crew to paint his parents' house. Crisp, sharp white. Green shutters. Wood houses were white then; it was like a law. You didn't have anything too grand, too gaudy; it might make people covet. Rolley was finally making some money.

When she was about eight, Lily started wondering about God, what He could possibly have been thinking. Her father's father had been a preacher, a poor man, some people said crazy. Her mother said crazy. Her father always took her to church. Her mother wouldn't go. Lily was bored by most of the ceremonies and the sermon, but there was something about praying.

Every so often Mr. Sam would still stumble into the Starks' in the middle of the night, and Lily's daddy would call next door. When Rolley came over, that was all Lily saw of Rolley. He was selling cars or he was doing renovations those days. Eventually Rolley put in a walkway of slate around the side of the Cobbs' house leading to the rear, and installed a light. After that, Mr. Sam slept it off on the back porch, not in the Cobbs' house proper. He mostly stopped showing up at the Starks'.

When Lily was nine, Rolley took a few lots at the edge of Fayton, next to nothing, cheap land, other side of the train tracks, and built three little houses on speculation. They were all alike, with choppy yards and few trees. People bought them right up.

Mr. Sam took up drinking with white cab drivers whose records were so bad they could only work for the colored cab company. He went with the men who ran numbers and moonshine and made deliveries for the homegrown gangsters, men left over from Prohibition, white men and Indian men and light-colored colored men who wore boots and hats even inside a store. Sometimes they wore their old striped suits from the thirties, so they looked like people in the TV show *The Untouchables*. Everybody had a TV by that time, although some had been quite reluctant. Many said it was a fad and would pass, not to take it to heart.

Lily started walking to the library by herself when she was nine. It was in an old house way downtown. She read about religions there. She liked the Christian heresies. She read she lived in a fallen world. The ones who made it hadn't got it right, and they were falling or fallen, too, and terribly sorry about it. She could see that. She read how everything has its cause in the soul's life. She practically memorized *The Encyclopedia of Superstition:* in Bohemia when a person is dying they open a window. Let the ghost get where it's going. In the Baltic countries it is widely believed that animals always see the spirits of the dead.

The fall she was ten, Lily could hear the Cobbs arguing if she lay awake at night. Isabel wanted to find a bigger house. Everybody could move, Mrs. Geneva, and Jimbo, the whole crowd. Mrs. Geneva said absolutely no. In the end they didn't do it. Isabel was furious. Rolley had to make it up to everybody. He bought his mother a dog, Cookie, whom Lily soon fell in love with. He promised Isabel a new brick house, just for her, himself, and the kids, in a subdivision he was going to start, out across the highway. Everything spanking. He said he would borrow the money. Become a real developer. Then they would move. Isabel said if he didn't keep his word she wasn't sure what she would do.

Christmas 1963, Mrs. Cobb sent over three pounds of pecan divinity in a tin, so Lily's father said they were calling on them. Her mother wouldn't go. Nothing was good enough that year for her mother. She'd gotten a Cadillac and didn't like driving it.

For a long time at the Cobbs', it was just Rolley and Lily's daddy, and Mrs. Geneva and Isabel and the children, and of course Jimbo there impersonating a human being, Lily thought, a short clip-tie on, a jacket with the sleeves too short. Jimbo was a topic all over Fayton by that time. He kept failing tenth grade, held the record, for one thing. He showed up in the middle of the night in people's yards, howling, sticking his face in their windows.

It was as if nobody thought of Mr. Sam as missing until he appeared in the archway by the dining room. He made a slow, tentative entrance. He had on a shirt and a coat as if he'd been to church—Lily knew he hadn't. He began looking around and saying sweet things to his grandchildren, whom he reached for, but didn't truly touch. In the center was the tree with so many gifts Rolley had bought underneath. Mr. Sam said nothing, but there was a place for him on the couch, as far away from the tree as possible, and he seemed grateful for it. Mr. Sam took a chocolate Millionaire Lily's father had brought and chewed it with his mouth open, the way even older people did tobacco. Seeing Mr. Sam and how his clothes hung off of him made Lily notice Rolley had become a real fat man. Lily had heard at Sunday School that Mr. Sam was drinking with the hands from the bright leaf tobacco warehouses who came through in August. He drank with oyster shuckers and flounder cleaners from the fish market, with men who worked around the bus station, which still did a fair business.

The train had stopped stopping in Fayton, but Lily figured this out that following summer: you could get on a bus in Fayton and get off the very same one in New York City. It started in Savannah as a local, and it went all the way. After Richmond, it was even an express. But whenever Lily charted it out, made plans to run away, something told her it couldn't be. Fayton was the sort of town, when you were in it, there was no way out. People you met believed this even though they would agree a person might leave if you asked them twice. The truth made no difference in the long run, though, to what people believed. No difference at all.

In seventh grade, she made a new plan. Boarding school. She was rough, she needed finishing. They weren't going to send her, so she could shut up, her mother said. I'll finish you, her mother said.

Rolley and Isabel were building their dream home by then, something other people thought was a marvel. Lily's mother was thinking about one, too, and on Sundays they'd drive out into the country, and look at land to buy.

The year Lily became a teenager, something went right. The Army took Jimbo. After that Rolley and Isabel and Bit and Dora moved across the highway, into their mansion, which was up on a clay rise in Rolley's new subdivision. People were amazed by it: a huge brick negotiation between a ranch and a Georgian with a wide yard and large rooms all on one floor. Lily went to see it. The kitchen had thick-doored cabinets, all milled and built up and stained, not painted. There were exposed brick walls in the den, and a new sort of wood floor, plastic-shiny, and central air conditioners, not in the windows, outside the house. The inside Formica was inspiring in its way, as was the sunken pit for watching the TV. Dora told Lily her grandmother couldn't ever leave that house in town because she was worried her grandpa wouldn't find his way home if she moved. Dora thought this was a secret.

After six months, the Army sent Jimbo back. Mrs. Geneva took him in. She had Cookie, she said. He'd never do anything to his mother. He was worse than ever, wrecking cars, spending time with dangerous people. When he was bored he ran outside naked in the daytime holding his BB gun, doing a rebel yell: it took a lot to get Lily's attention by the time she was in eighth grade. She went over and told Mrs. Geneva to get him to stop. Mrs. Geneva's lips trembled a little—she was trying to keep from smiling. Lily could not imagine what was in Mrs. Geneva's mind, behind her little teeth. Rolley tried putting Jimbo in an apartment, but Jimbo came home to his mother after a few weeks. What was he going to eat?

Lily heard tales from the wild boys she french-kissed and went half the way with. Mr. Sam was riding the rails, camping out with the hobos, carrying on. As far as Lily knew, Mrs. Geneva never filed a report on her husband. She never kicked him out formally. She never refused to let him come to his hammock.

Once, Mr. Sam stayed gone for two months straight. Then, it was a morning in January, when Lily went to get Cookie to take a walk, that the old man shocked her, more a ghost by then than a person, nearly bald and long-jawed, sleeping on the floor of the back porch. She sat there, listening to his thready breathing, watching him so long he started to look innocent. She was fourteen then, nearly grown. She remembered him that way, after.

When Mr. Sam woke he saw Rolley's workmen fixing the door screen. He told them to go to hell. What was the use, he said. He always cursed his son's crews. Nevertheless, piece by piece, Rolley had completely renovated the exterior of the house. He had destroyed the original front porch on piers and lowered it to the ground. Instead of the half-brick California bungalow pillars, he put up plain, stained wood columns. He had painted the house Williamsburg green, which was daring. He paved the entry area with flat aged bricks, and sealed it. The whole front looked rather stately. Even Lily's mother admitted it: Rolley had managed to make Mrs. Geneva's house seem older, and also newer, and larger, and more imposing, than Lily's house. But when you were inside, nothing had changed: Mrs. Geneva's afghans and her old kitchen stove.

That next summer Lily's mother announced they were really going to get away from that place. She had two decorators, an architect. Start over from scratch. A new life. Where? Lily asked, full of hope. They'd go out in the country, away from it all, into the most expensive subdivision. Moving, which everybody was doing, was a piss-poor excuse for getting out, she said to her mother. Her mother told her to get out of her sight. Let me go, Lily said. Let me go really go.

The next April, Jimbo had got a girl pregnant. She was gritting her teeth and marrying him, so Jimbo took a job banging nails into two-by-fours for his rich brother. Mrs. Geneva had found out she had diabetes—she had to stop baking. Cookie barked at things that weren't there, because he was blind, people thought.

Mr. Sam had been away one of his extra-long stretches. It was a day right after Easter, around noon, that Cookie, who was sleeping on the new brick front porch where it was cool, suddenly woke up and went around the back of the house in the waddling way he had been walking lately. He started barking at Mr. Sam's empty hammock. Mrs. Geneva opened the door for him. But Cookie didn't come into the kitchen to eat, his custom. Neither Mrs. Geneva nor Lily could get him off the subject of the hammock for the longest time.

Two days later the police found Samuel Cobb's body in a warehouse in the oldest part of downtown, near the abandoned train station. His companion had risen up and beat Sam Cobb about the head until he died.

This took many blows, with a heavy weapon. When people heard the story, what was peculiar to them was that Mr. Sam hadn't run home, when he was only twelve blocks from his own house. The coroner said he'd been awake for the first five or ten hits. And he was dehydrated, but not drunk.

Sam Cobb's companion left him there to die, in that makeshift encampment where they were living to drink. He took to the rails. They found him in Wilmington by the docks. Every name he gave was an alias.

The weapon was one detail Lily's father held on to. He came back to the murder, that night, after the funeral, after Lily had already told him off once, demanding to hear about Archie the suicide. Her father said the murder was evidence of how far a man could fall, and evidence of this sort, that was ubiquitous when he was a boy, had become rarer and rarer in those days. This was the sixties, and everybody was losing their way. Mr. Sam's murder illustrated that ruin could be just blocks away from you—her father wanted Lily to see this point. Something had gone so terribly wrong with her. He'd worked hard to keep misery from her, but that had drawn her to it: she was talking to crazy people, seeing the wrong boys, smoking cigarettes, being moody and lazy, planning to run off soon as she could.

She didn't need her father to serve her some misery, she said. Everything she saw in Fayton by then broke her heart. Like that girl going ahead and marrying Jimbo. Everybody, everybody, desperate to get out, incapable of leaving, of even seeing over the lip of this tiny, binding world.

Look at it, how bad it can get: a once handsome and lively man with a wife and three sons ends up killed the way someone might kill a cockroach, with the same sort of everyday and kitchen sort of instrument, a rather female instrument. The humiliation. It was a touchstone, a cautionary tale. Lily needed a dose of reality. Here it was. The man gave up, he gave in, he was swallowed. It can happen.

Lily said to her father, "Do you know what was in his mind?"

"His mind was gone," her father said. "What difference does his mind make?"

"He sat there for it. The coroner said so," she said.

"Look at it. In the face. The man failed at life," he said.

"How do you know?" she said.

"You have to have something to live for," he said.

"But all of this you put store by is going asunder sometime. The vain things, things of this world. Mr. Sam knew that. You made me read that."

"You going to make that drunk a hero? Wise?"

"There must be something else," Lily said.

"Well, what is it? What is it?" her father said.

"Was everybody wrong before, to say there was something more?" she said. "What about your daddy?"

Her father looked at her as if she'd shot him.

The day Sam Cobb was going to die, the man who was with him asked for three dollars and twenty-eight cents for liquor. Sam had two dollars and a nickel. The man decided to take it out on him, the one dollar and twenty-three cents, so he picked up a cast-iron coffee pot lying there, and he hit him, again and again.

Early on, the pain got to be too much, so Sam let himself fly right out of his body, out a window, it felt like. He sort of watched the pain as it continued to come to him as a neutral phenomenon, a feeling of a certain density and shape and breadth, but the fact that he was being hurt was something he couldn't identify with anymore. Instead he saw his second son, Rolley, his house up on that red knoll above the highway, attracting other big houses, and money like a magnet. And he saw Jimbo, a baby coming now, would he finally get himself attached to this earth, to practical life. He took a good long stare into that baby's face, the one who hadn't been born yet, Jimbo's child inside that poor girl. He tried to bless him. It occurred to Sam Cobb he was dying then, because he could see many things quite well, past and future, and he knew that in ways his family would be relieved to see him go, and he didn't fault them for that, since he had failed so utterly, for so very long, to show his love for them by any other means.

With every one of the later blows, he saw a wider pattern, the Starks next door, the fussy creeper in their yard, that house away from it all they had decided to build. He saw all the other people in Fayton—how the ones who were different were so close to the ones who weren't. He could hear Cookie barking then, loudly, full of mourning. The second to last one he saw was his wife, the light behind her, standing in the kitchen door, which opened into that house Rolley had so cruelly disguised. So Sam let it be back the way it started in the twenties, just a bungalow, modest and white, Geneva in the middle of everything, the source of everything, there holding one of her high white stiff cakes. And then he turned around and saw something more, and beautiful, a place completely hidden from the ordinary world. He hadn't expected this, but soon as he saw it, he was sure it was where his first and dearest son had tried to coax the morphine to take him. Archie had made an error—it had never been a judgment. A glimpse of this, and Sam let that go, finally, finally, finally, that burden he'd borne so long, his belief that his son had thrown away the life Sam had given him, because he found it worth so little. And then Mr. Sam paused, he had to pause, because of the sweetness, the sorrow, the relief—

These days, Rolley's project is complete. To find the residents of Fayton you have to circle around the edges, and seek out cul-de-sacs, and hidden grounds of his subdivisions, which form a defense against the old town, the abandoned, rotten parts. Hardly anybody, of any class or race, lives downtown anymore.

Lily Stark turned out to be exactly what her father didn't want her to be. Except she was not a suicide, but she thought of it in her twenties. She tried something else, and then something else, and then something else. Nothing practical, usually nothing expected. She turned her back, she invented herself new more than once. She never could take the tangible life very seriously, even while she longed for comfort. In part, she had been happy.

When she got the call and had to go home, she knew she would grieve, but she didn't know it would feel like drowning. She kept remembering the way her father's face fell that day they buried Mr. Sam, the day she heard about Archie.

"You just want an escape," her father said to her finally after he recovered from looking like he'd been shot.

That was true. He had that right. "And what do you really want? Why do you always turn it into things?"

"Your mother wants them," he said.

"You have spent your whole life on them," she said. "Every hour."

"Why are you so cruel?" he said. "What made you like this?"

"You," she said.

Her father said nothing.

"Talk to me."

He wouldn't.

She slammed the door to her room, to contemplate the soul of Archie Cobb the suicide.

After the ceremony she went back and stood in front of those two old bungalows on Winter Street, both of them faded, with peeling paint, windows broken, no grass, no creeper in the yards, and she remembered how she felt like dying for winning that day with her father, but it had been her father who died first.

Someone who came to the funeral told her that lately a few of the people who live in the developments have been saying something must be missing, maybe they should go back and live downtown. Maybe they could be inside each other's lives, and dwell in each other's secrets, share each other's living rooms and gardens, the way people say they used to do. As if they were kin. She recognized him. He was Jimbo's boy, a sane, and decent man, impossibly.

"Maybe we shouldn't have ever left," he said.

"There never was any leaving, never is," she said, but he didn't understand her, because she was speaking of her dreams: when they were serious she was always in Fayton, even though she was forty-five years old, with her own history, she was still in that garden, where whatever she was before she was born came into her girl baby body. She was with her family or with Mrs. Geneva or Cookie or Dora or Mr. Sam or Rolley or Zachary or with the wild boys she used to try to get to love her. Just the night before, Archie had appeared to her. He was hovering above, invisibly tethered to the garden, which he gazed upon with a longing that was the last thing he'd ever thought he'd feel, so it held him. He gestured toward the lands beyond the town's limits, the Cliffs, the rushing Neuse, the Cape Fear, the ocean. Then he came so close he touched her shoulder, turned her around. What he showed her then startled her, woke her up: both their fathers staring back at them, inconsolable and amazed.

Moira Crone, a native of North Carolina tobacco country, directs the M.F.A. program at Louisiana State University in Baton Rouge. She is the author of three books of fiction, the most recent being *Dream State*. She edits the fiction series for the University Press of Mississippi and is on the faculty of the Prague Summer Seminars. She has received grants from the National Endowment for the Arts, the Bunting Institute at Radcliffe, and the National Endowment for the Humanities for her writing and teaching. This is her third appearance in *New Stories from the South*.

JIM ZIETZ

For a very long time I have been dealing with the question of what to do with the stories that surrounded me when I was very young—stories of people I knew well, people I knew before I could make any judgments about people, people who defined for me, in my earliest years, what living with other human beings means. I take these original events as the book that I am always, very deep in my consciousness, reading and rereading—not in language, always, but deeper than that. It was probably these stories, and the job of their interpretation, that made me start writing in the first place.

This particular story has a level of reality to it, as well as many fictions. The facts are these: I was raised in a small town on the coastal plain of North Carolina, and in my childhood I knew some people who committed suicide, a few more who attempted to. I knew some very violent, scary people; some who were, I guess you would say, wanton. In those days it was common to be aware of the inner secrets of the families who lived nearby in a way that seems to me to be very unusual today.

And then there was a belief for so long that somehow a suburban house would cure things. I'm not sure what; I suppose the fetters of relatedness, of knowing what really goes on. The whole suburban thing is a kind of internal migration—towns playing hide-and-seek with themselves, trying to forget what is unforgettable, basically, willed amnesia. What got into some people. What they did, to each other, or to you.

Southerners my age have this in common: we were raised in a pre-psychological age. We come from the past.

James Ellis Thomas

THE SATURDAY MORNING CAR WASH CLUB

(from *The New Yorker*)

To be sixteen on a July Saturday was heaven. Our neighborhood really showed out in the summer. Chumps who dragged ass to work all week leaped out of bed on Saturday mornings — it was the best way to cheat the heat. A lawnmower, a grill, a chair beneath a shade tree, anything that involved making something out of nothing powered their need to rise. Even the ne'er-do-wells started early on a Saturday. You'd see guys who hadn't caught a weather report in years strolling about like businessmen, on their way to trade chat with their down-the-block neighbors. My mother always said that Pig and Sammy Sam, our local hopheads, liked to get out early on a Saturday because then no one could tell them to go get a job. "It's Saturday!" Pig would say. "Unemployment office closed on Saturday!"

Most fellas between sixteen and married spent their weekend mornings at the Saturday Morning Car Wash Club. Actually, it wasn't really a club, just a rundown, semi-automated car wash two blocks up from Cedar Heights. The structure itself was ugly. Faded, cracked, and tornado-abused, it looked like a pistol-whipped tin man, surrounded by kudzu and non-biodegradables from the Burger King uphill. It was green. The hoses all had leaks in them. The vacuum cleaners were from the seventies, and the change machine was still chewing on the counterfeit five that Pig had fed it two years ago. Yet this did not stop the solitary ride from pulling up to the car wash every Saturday.

Around eight o'clock, the solitary ride, the first car, would roll in and park beside a vac-bot. There'd be a good jam on the stereo. Nothing loud, no need for excessive bass this early. The passenger side would be vacuumed first, then the floorboard, the seat, the back, then the driver's side. Soda-straw wrappers and six-day-old French fries would fly into the garbage can like dirt from a dog's hole. For breaks, this first Saturday Morning Car Wash Club member would look up and down the highway for cars he might recognize. Then back to work. Sweeping the crack where the seats folded forward, he would finally hear a beep-beep, and then another, and then a honk and a thump of bass. And for the next six hours he would go on cleaning and washing his car, watching the parade of incoming vehicles. As soon as the second Saturday Morning Car Wash Club member asked the first one for a quarter, the meeting officially commenced.

"Man, stop playin' around," I said, as the hooptie chugged closer and closer to the car wash. "You wanna get your ass beat this early?"

Chester had failed to tell me the whole truth about helping him wash his car. "Let's clean the machine," he'd said. I thought we were going to park it in his front yard and break out the water hose and the lemon-fresh Joy. I had no problem with that. What I did have a problem with was the fact that I was now riding in Chester's ugly brown rustmobile, his hooptie, his lemon, his clunker—in other words, his 1978 AMC Pacer.

I wasn't a big fan of the hooptie. Aside from the more obvious reasons for disliking Chester's ride, I charged the car with the most heinous variety of crime: a crime against childhood. Chester and I no longer watched cartoons. When the hooptie's first oil stains appeared on Chester's driveway our toon watching was over. Tools replaced the toons, motor oil replaced the milk in our Froot

Loops, and the Bat Signal was answered by a super-inflated Michelin Man, hellbent on avenging bad front-end alignments. Chester's ugly brown rustmobile had killed Saturday morning cartoons forever, and it was about to kill us as well. We were heading toward the one place where ugly brown rustmobiles were chastised on a regular basis—the Saturday Morning "Back That Hunk of Junk Out of Here" Club. We were motorvating toward an early grave.

"Apollonia needs washin'," said Chester. "That's why I'm takin' her to the car wash. What's wrong with that?"

I jumped around beneath my seat belt. "What's wrong with that? Tommy, Buck, Mann, Leon. All of those fools hang out up there."

Chester strummed his fingers against the steering wheel; last week, he'd wrapped it with duct tape. He said it was for the grip, but I had never once seen Chester drive with anything more than a rotating palm.

"You're trippin'," he said, taking a wide right turn around a slow-moving cat. "I'm grown. Everybody know me, everybody know you. It's the same fools at the car wash that be around the neighborhood." He turned and looked at me; I saw my reflection in his silver, mirrored shades. "You act like you're scared," he said.

"I ain't scared."

"You act like it."

The engine suddenly dropped, idled down, then shrieked back up three times louder. A fat little Vietnamese kid, playing in his front yard, picked up a stick and made as if to throw it at us. He ducked when the engine backfired.

"Do you know what they call this thing?" I asked.

"Apollonia," said Chester, stroking the dashboard.

"Doo-Doo Brown, man, they call your car Doo-Doo Brown. I was out at the pool yesterday, and as soon as I jumped in, everybody got out because they said they'd seen me riding around in the Doo-Doo-Mobile. What's up with that, man?"

Chester grinned. "That's all right, though. I see you ain't walkin' anywhere. Punks about fifty years old still ridin' the bus to school, ignorant. This is luxury."

I craned my head toward the roof of the car. Pockets of uphol-
stery sagged down like small bellies against my face.

"I just don't feel like getting my ass beat this early, that's all," I
said.

"Well, don't worry about it. Damn it." "Damn it" was the cuss
of the moment. We'd been cussing since way back when, but the
new thing that summer was to try to cuss like Eddie Murphy's
father, or the way Eddie Murphy sounded when he impersonated
his father—a drunken slur with attitude. Chester's Vernon was
pretty good. Mine, on the other hand, sounded like me trying to
sound like Chester trying to sound like Eddie Murphy trying to
sound like his father.

"For real, though, man," said Chester. "This is where the ladies
hang out."

"Oh yeah," I said. "The ladies."

"That's right. 'The ladies,'" said Chester. "But anyway, I know
you don't want to walk up to the car wash with no car."

I thought about that for a second. The Saturday Morning Car
Wash Club loomed just a few turns away from our current position. Apollonia's rattle was loud enough to be heard in Botswana.
Meanwhile, there I was, afraid to put pressure against the passenger-
side door for fear of tumbling out. Maybe walking wasn't such a
bad idea.

"Doo-Doo Brown, huh?" said Chester, palming us into another
turn. "We'll see what they call it when we ride off with all the sweet
potatoes!" He laughed for a bit, and I would've laughed with him
if he hadn't punched the speedometer in order to get the needle to
move.

While Apollonia was revving herself into a fit, we slowly approached the hill between us and the car wash. Not a steep hill, if
you were riding in anything other than a hooptie, but we were, of
course, hooptienauts. Apollonia took to the incline like a pushcart
on a roller-coaster track. When we finally crested the hill, I could
see that the Saturday Morning Car Wash Club was already in
session, at least it was until Apollonia backfired, frightening the

members and a war-torn village or two somewhere in the Middle East. Chester looked at me. I looked at Chester. We rolled downhill in a prolonged, gear-grinding lurch.

"Luxury," I said.

"The ladies," said Chester. "Sweet potatoes! I told you they'd be here!"

If only my friend had taken off his shades and looked at his own reflection. There he was, practically kissing the windshield, grinning as we approached the car wash—and the ladies. Meanwhile, his right foot was hammering on the brakes, cheating Apollonia out of a sweet-potato massacre. The only thing more embarrassing than riding downhill in Chester's stalled car was riding downhill in Chester's stalled car toward every single girl that I'd ever planned on asking out. To this day, I firmly believe that Apollonia did more to steady the course of my virginity than my mother, my pastor, or those homemade Converse hightops that my cousin Meat Meat sold to me back in seventh grade. A true struggle buggy, a true hooptie, forms a clamp around the rider's crotch like some kind of pig-iron codpiece. I groaned as Apollonia shuddered to a halt.

"My hair look all right to you?" asked Chester.

It was barely nine o'clock, and already the Saturday Morning Car Wash was packed and vibrant. Not counting Apollonia, there were fifteen vehicles parked at various angles around the lot. Six of them sat inside the wash-and-wax bays. As usual, the guys who were washing their cars felt the need to go shirtless while they soaped. It didn't matter if they were muscular or not—something about a long black hose shooting chemically treated water urged them to work bare-topped. I could understand it if you were in your front yard with your toes in the grass, airing your car and the funk of your labor at the same time. But these jokers were flexing their pecs inside veritable saunas of industrial-strength detergent. You knew they were showing off for the benefit of the ladies, while the ladies were paying attention to anything but the soap operas.

All that wax-o-wax and gunk-o-gunk repelled the females faster than drugstore-brand cologne. The guys never noticed. Most of them were too busy trying to scrape lovebugs off their headlights.

Six girls were at the car wash when Chester and I rolled in. Twice as many fellas were hovering around them. Most of these guys were older than we were, dropouts and two-time seniors, people who seemed to have owned rides all their lives. Some of the girls had their own cars. For the most part, they drove sporty, bright, quick-trip Civics, or Camrys, or whatever looked good behind an airbrushed vanity plate, and they brought them to the club for their boyfriends, or some other shirtless wonders, to give them a wash. Every one of these guys would treat his girlfriend's ride as if it were Cinderella's stagecoach. They'd use illicit waxes, controversial sponges, and forbidden emollients to rub, butter, and caress the various paint jobs. The only no-no was fooling around under the hood. The girls never allowed it. I don't know if it was Daddy's orders or suspicion of shade-tree mechanics, but rarely would you see a guy working on the engine of a girl's car. Their own cars, of course, they butchered no end.

"What's up, Chester?"

"Leon."

"What's up, Lorenzo?"

"Leon."

We'd barely got out of the car when Leon slid up with three of his *stank*-breath friends, all of them with towels around their necks soaking up the juice from their hairdos. Leon was already smirking.

"I like the ride, man," said Leon.

"Yep," said Chester.

"My sister got one just like it." Every time Leon opened his mouth, his boys would snicker. It was too early for an ass beating, and too hot. Leon was only three years older than us, but he'd been handing out ass beatings in Cedar Heights ever since I was old enough to walk to the playground by myself. I was tired of Leon. Maybe if somebody else had beaten my ass for a change, things would have been different, but Leon tended to bogart Cedar Heights ass like a demented Santa Claus who came every day except Christmas. He was a rusty-necked, two-toothed, head-cheese-eating bastard, and he always wore a mesh jersey with nothing underneath and thick gold-rope chains with foreign-car emblems hanging from them.

"Yeah, man, that's a smooth ride," said Leon. "What kind of gas you use?"

"I don't know," said Chester. "Gas."

Leon and his boys started laughing. I didn't get the joke. I looked over at Chester, and I could tell that he was becoming upset. The most vicious tool that the bad guys had was always their laughter. Leon had never uttered a funny phrase in his life, but he didn't really have to. His portable laughtrack took care of the rest.

I leaned back against Apollonia. Lime-green engine fluids fanned across the asphalt.

"Damn Doo-Doo Brown!" yelled Leon, affecting "the Vernon." "Doo-Doo Brown!"

Chester folded his arms. "I came here to wash my car, man, dang. Why ya'll always got to be messin' with people? Why don't you go worry about your own car?"

"Shoot, my car clean," said Leon, gesturing back to his black Camaro. "I'm worried about Doo-Doo Brown. That junk start a rustquake, you gonna be washin' every car out here!"

He chortled. I knew what was coming before he could even say it, but he said it anyway. "I hate to tell you this, cuz, but your car is kinda messed up—for real, though. I ain't tryin' to be funny or nothin', but damn. It look like King Kong wiped his ass with a can of Pepsi. Look like a truckload of toe jam had an accident. Look like a roll of pennies with a damn steerin' wheel. I hate to tell you."

But, of course, he told us anyway. At one point or another, Leon compared Chester's car to a three-thousand-year-old foot, *stankin'* dried-up alligator balls, one roller skate being squeezed through somebody's ass, and two roller skates giving dried-up alligator balls a ride to the liquor store. Chester remained silent.

The more Leon and his boys laughed, the more attention they gathered. Music that had been pounding from the cars was turned down. Hoses were placed back on their hooks. Vacuums were switched off, and, most unfortunately, the girls drew near. No one had said the word "fight," but that's what everyone had heard, and that's what everyone expected. Leon had gained an audience. He'd hyped, he'd promoted, and he'd thoroughly teased; now all that was left was the main event.

"There ain't no room to wash that piece of doo-doo, no way," said Leon. "Why don't you ask your mama for a damn water hose, with those damn stupid shades. It look like you busted up a mirror to make that junk. *Ooh wee,* let me hold them shades, cool breeze!"

Before Leon raised his left hand to grab the sunglasses from Chester's face, I noticed two things about the crowd that had gathered around us. First, not everyone was amused by Leon's antics. Second, there was a girl standing off to the side whom I had not seen here before. Her name was Le Ly, and she was the one girl in the neighborhood that Chester always got quiet about whenever her name came up in conversation. She seemed out of place, but then again, I hardly ever saw her hanging out anywhere. When Leon raised his hand, I glimpsed her gazing at Chester. I intervened. With my right hand, I caught Leon's rising left.

"You better get yo' hand offa me!" roared Leon. "Walrus-lookin' punk, I'll punch you in yo' damn throat!"

My damn throat gulped. Holding his ashy wrist in my grip, I could feel the tendons wiggling into fist mode. "Do something!" the tendons were saying, wiring me like a traitor from within Leon's flesh. "Do something, man, don't just stand there feeling me up! This is the same fist that de-toothed the entire after-school chess program! Run! Run right now!"

"Race," I said, as Leon wrenched his had free. "That messed-up hunk of rat turds you got can't beat this ride here. My man Chester says he'll race you for a spot."

"Shut up," said Leon. To my surprise, he stomped off toward the Camaro, boys in tow, towels dropped in their wake. I'd expected a punch or, at least, a smack. Foolish suggestions often drew smacks. With no smack to be had, the audience became a tense, buzzing mob of color commentators. "They crazy" was their main catchphrase.

"I know I didn't hear you say that," said Chester, turning to me with a frown. He removed his sunglasses and threw them inside the car. "Lorenzo, man, let's just go home."

"Why?" I asked. "Leon's already at home. Leon lives in Cedar Heights, too."

"Yeah, but—"

"Just get in the car, man." I opened the door and stood there until he got in. Making my way around the back of the car, I scanned the crowd for Le Ly. She had moved farther away, but her eyes were focussed on the hooptie.

"You'll thank me for this someday," I said, lowering myself into the seat. It took me a moment, while I slammed and re-slammed the door, to realize that Chester had placed his head on the steering wheel. He was crying.

"They're always messin' with me," he said, sobbing between gasps of air. "What did I do? They're supposed to be grown. How come grown folks always messin' with kids, man?"

I placed my hand on his shoulder. "Be cool," I said.

"Naw, bump that!" He raised his head up and faced the windshield. "Yeah, that's right, chumps!" he yelled, scowling at the onlookers, wiping snot on his sleeves. Leon's engine could be heard in the background. It sounded like an idling tractor: *Bow! Zugga zugga. Bow! Zugga zugga.*

"I can't race that fool," said Chester. "My mama will kill me if I wreck this car. My auntie gave me this car, man, I don't know what you're thinking about."

"Roll up your window," I said. "Nah, forget that. Just lean your ear over."

"What?" asked Chester.

"Just listen, man. I think I know what to do."

• • •

It was the oldest trick in the book. With spectators on either side, both Leon and Chester revved their engines. They faced away from the car wash, toward the hill that led to it, the strip being the open road. I stood among the crowd, listening to the protests and disbelief. The general suspicion was that Chester was going to end up in the hospital.

"Let's get this mother gone!" yelled a friend of Leon's. A girl in a pair of pink hot pants stepped in between the two cars. Overhead, the blazing sun made jewels of the rocks in the asphalt. Apollonia seethed. Blue smoke billowed from every pipe.

"Dead man!" shouted Leon, leering from his dark ride.

"Ain't nothin' but a *thang,*" said Chester, grinning behind the mirrored sky of his sunglasses. "Here come the sweet potatoes!"

The girl shrieked a countdown. Leon's car launched on "two," taking the hill and then vanishing in a thick fog of exhaust. People were still knocking the dust from their clothes when the first few giggles could be heard in Leon's wake.

"He calls that 'fast'?" said Chester, still sitting in the same position as before the countdown. "That's why his mama got sent to jail for stealin' hot sauce on Christmas."

The crowd had seen it coming. The six-day-old French fries had seen it coming. With the roar of the black Camaro receding in the distance, guffaws and loud talk arose from the spectators. "Told you!" they shouted to each other. "Told you!" and "Damn it!" and "I'll be dogged!" and, most vehemently, "Where my two dollars at?" Apollonia, whose engine was still running, slowly went into reverse, easing herself into the carwash bay made vacant by Leon's haste. Simply put, the hare had hauled tail and now the tortoise was taking up shack in the rabbit's hole. It was a Saturday morning cartoon. The Car Wash Club was hip, but not too hip for cartoons. They laughed and they cackled and they shook their heads. Even Leon's boys were making fun of his skid marks.

"What are we supposed to do when he comes back?" asked Chester, stepping out of the car.

"Pop the hatch," I said.

"Pop the hatch? What's that supposed to do?"

I smiled, glancing around to make sure Le Ly was still there. "It's supposed to open up the back, so I can get the cleaning stuff out. What's wrong with you, man? I thought we came here to wash Apollonia?"

"Oh, yeah," said Chester. A thousand words should have been pouring from my best friend's mouth. This was his hour. People were shaking his hand, but I knew who was really racing his heart.

"Nice sunglasses," she said, eyeing her own reflection.

James Ellis Thomas is a graduate of the University of Alabama. He received an M.F.A. from the University of Notre Dame and is currently working on a novel.

CHRISTOPHER MARTIN

*E*veryone should own a junky car at some point *in life. It should be a rite of passage. I'm hoping "The Saturday Morning Car Wash Club" will start a movement, an excruciatingly powerful movement that will lift people up out of their chairs and send them running toward enlightenment. It probably won't, but if someone gets a cheap yuk out of it, that's cool. In my mind, I was hearing Chuck Berry while picturing a trickster fable—nothing too deep, no big whoop. Cheap yuks are funny that way.*

Christie Hodgen

THE HERO OF LONELINESS

(from *Meridian*)

Seventeen years ago our town suffered an invasion of gypsy moths. The moths—which were not yet moths but still inch-long worms, fat and black, with red spots and a coating of soft fur—made prisoners of the polite upper class, whose grand houses lined the edge of a forest of ancient oaks. Efforts were made to prevent the inevitable. Orange nets were draped over the branches of every tree. And so in the same way circuses pitch their bright tents at the edges of respectable towns, threatening whole neighborhoods of decency and good taste, the moths marked their arrival. They thrived, crawled out of the forest and blanketed the streets. It was nearly impossible to drive. Soon the worms began to climb up the sides of houses. Women leaned from windows and poured pots of boiling water on the offending troops.

My mother went into labor when the infestation was at its exact worst. The way my brother Ephram tells it, my mother's safe arrival at the hospital, and therefore my safe delivery into the world, was nearly thwarted by the worms that were so thick in the streets that my father struggled to steady the car. Ephram says it was like driving on wet leaves, and that as he sat in the backseat of the car that morning he heard—even louder than the sound of my mother's heavy breathing—the sibilant squashing of worms under the tires. By the time I arrived home all of the neighborhood trees had been scalped, every leaf savaged.

Seventeen years later, the worms plotted their return, and once again our town began its futile preparation. Canopies of orange nets were placed over the trees, and rumors started to circulate about a secret fleet of single-engine planes scheduled to fly low over our houses each night, leaving the neighborhood in a dreamy cloud of pesticide. As for Ephram, news of the returning gypsy moths prompted him to prepare for his escape from our town, an event that had been pending since his graduation from high school five years prior. Ephram purchased his first car, a refurbished 1972 Firebird with a brand-new silver paint job, and he vowed to leave upon sight of the first moth. Shortly after Ephram purchased the car, he spotted the forerunner of doom wriggling on the front steps.

When Ephram announced his departure, it was the end of the hottest summer in fifty years. I was tired and nervous from a series of weekend trips in the backseat of my parents' car, staring out the window, bored as a grazing cow, touring a dozen of New England's tulip-lined college campuses, any of which might have harbored me as I became a younger version of my parents—a future lawyer and golfer, a future home shopper, a driver of expensive cars, a carrier of calfskin briefcases. The morning that Ephram told me he was leaving, headed to points south by way of Graceland, I wanted nothing more than escape.

"Wait for me," I said. I'd instantly calculated the pros and cons of the decision, like my father taught me. If I had to argue the point to him, I would mention first and foremost the boredom of our privileged hometown—with its population of quaintly decaying historic homes and its constellation of white churches and automatic lawn-sprinkler systems—and the dainty, deadening girlishness all of this was fostering in me. Secondly, there was the mystery of the South, which I had never visited but often imagined, with its tall glasses of lemonade and its front-porch swings, with its rabid dogs hobbling down unpaved streets and its bright red

square-dance barns. Needless to say there was Graceland, the lav-
ish monument that a once-poor country boy had dedicated to
himself. And finally there was Ephram, and the absolute certainty
that he would never return.

"Shift it in gear," Ephram said, and headed toward his car,
slouched under the weight of his backpack. "You got five minutes
to pack." I had been certain that Ephram would leave me behind. I was a seventeen-year-old Catholic schoolgirl, a knee-sock-
wearing class president, a sullen book-reader, an overly tall and
horribly pale teenager with few friends, a person who had never
once disobeyed her parents. In three minutes I heard the Firebird's
magnificent and impatient horn. I ran down the stairs and out to
the car without stopping to water the plants, to slide a coaster
beneath the water glass I had left on the dining-room table, to
scratch the dog behind his ear, to write a note.

In only twenty minutes we were at the edge of town, and also
at the edge of the longest conversation we had had since I was
twelve. For the last few years Ephram had been a stranger, and riding next to him was like riding with a character from a TV show
that I had watched many years back, before it went off the air.

"I'm surprised at you," said Ephram, and he punched me in the
arm. "My little fucking sister."

"How's it been going?" I said, and Ephram scoffed. I always
managed to forget that he didn't partake in small talk.

"The weather, the Red Sox, everything's great," he said, in a deep
and formal and falsely optimistic voice, an exact imitation of our
father.

"Dad's gonna kill me," I said. "Dead."

"Agnes Mildred Clayson," Ephram said, looking at me over the
top of an imaginary pair of half-glasses. "You're a grave disap-
pointment, young lady. I had nothing when I was your age. Rats
used to crawl under my bed at night."

We laughed. Ephram was speeding up the on-ramp to the interstate, and we were caught in the force of the steep curve that was
turning us away from home. Our arms hung casually out the

window, our fingers threading through the wind. This was living, I thought. This was what people did.

For the first few hours Ephram and I disclosed our particular objections to life in the Clayson household. It turned out that we had shared for the last five years, unbeknownst to one another, a mutual hatred for our parents. The Claysons were, in short, ex-liberals who had traded their Volkswagen Beetles for Volvos. First we discussed our mother, Muriel, a tax attorney who had recently begun the practice of adopting children at the rate of two a month by calling toll-free numbers on the television screen and pledging her support of four-hundred dollars per year. She was an insomniac who stayed up late into the night drinking gin and tonic, abusing the remote control, scrolling through the channels so fast that they blurred.

Then there was our father, Alden, of particular offense to Ephram. Our father was also a tax attorney, a man who worked six days a week and who couldn't stand the sight of himself in a mirror. He even refused to consult the rearview while driving, and had risked many an accident for the sake of avoiding his own reflection. Sometimes our father couldn't stand to look at other people. There were days that he refused to wear his glasses, and he reveled in the fog of nearsightedness. He prowled the house in a haze, looking at his family without ever seeing the intricacies of our expressions, whether we were sad or curious or sarcastic. Our father was the kind of rich man who had grown up poor and had never managed to forgive himself for amassing his fortune. His children were of particular concern. We were growing up rich and spoiled, and he snapped at us, exploding in fits of rage when we neglected to practice the piano or feed the dog or make good on a college scholarship. He was increasingly strange and he knew it. His beard was turning gray, and his tongue was brown from drinking coffee and smoking cigarettes. His teeth were edged in black. He barely opened his mouth to speak, as if there was something terrible running through him that might escape.

When Ephram and I exhausted the topic of our parents there

was little left to discuss. We were into the trip's third hour, and the joy of flight was fading. There were long stretches of silence and sighing, and staring out the window at the cornfields and the desolate scarecrows that were nothing more than tattered clothes decaying on crosses.

In the middle of Pennsylvania, as we were driving through the mountains, Ephram pulled off for gas. The exit ramp was paved, but the road soon deteriorated to gravel, and it wound tightly down a woodsy hill. The road went on and on. It seemed that the car would lose control and we would slip off the road at any moment, crashing headlong into a thicket. "I don't like this," I said, but Ephram was paying his usual silent attention to the road, and he didn't answer. Finally we came to a crossroads, which was the center of a small town. There was a hand-painted wooden sign nailed to a telephone pole. WELCOME TRAVELERS TO OUR VILLAGE, it read.

"Oh my God," I said. "We're in a village."

There were three buildings positioned around the crossroads. One was a tall, three-story house with a giant porch that wrapped around all sides. The other was a shack, squat and windowless, that had been painted a brilliant pink. A giant sign was propped on the roof. "Look!" I said, pointing. "The Sugar Shack. Nude Girls!" Ephram ignored the shack and pulled up to the third building, a rambling general store that looked as though it had been built from the salvaged lumber of an ancient shipwreck. There was a single gas pump standing in the front parking lot of the store. Ephram pulled up and pumped gas, and then headed into the store to pay. I followed.

The store was something from a dream. One side was an old-fashioned ice-cream counter, with chrome detailing and red vinyl stools. The other half of the store sold, as a sign indicated, "notions." There was a glass case of antiques, including jewelry and silverware and porcelain dolls. But the main feature of the shop was a collection of antique medical equipment. There were stethoscopes with colorful fabric cords, and miniature metal saws, and glass thermometers and peculiar, U-shaped clamps made of ivory. Strangest of all was a framed, poster-sized mosaic that depicted a doctor in the process of bloodletting a Pygmy. The doctor was standing over the Pygmy, holding a knife. There was a red gash in the Pygmy's arm, and his blood was flowing into a large bowl. "God Bless Missionaries" was spelled out across the sky in white tiles.

I walked around the store, examining everything, but Ephram was unmoved. He simply walked to the counter and paid the woman who was standing there, so still she at first looked like another curiosity, a wooden statue of a country woman in a plain yellow dress. The woman did not speak to Ephram when she rang him up, not even to announce his total. He held out the money and she tapped the counter with her finger, indicating that he should leave it there. She placed the change on the counter and stepped away from Ephram, looking away, shaking slightly, like a caught rabbit.

In the lot, Ephram's car was reflecting so much of the sun's glare that it was nearly invisible. We didn't notice that there was a stranger sitting in the back until we had settled into our seats. The stranger was bald, and he wore wire-framed glasses with small circular lenses. He wore a gray suit with a white shirt and a red tie. Nothing fit him quite right. The man's tie was looped in a messy amateur's knot, and the suit jacket was too narrow to button. Nevertheless the man gave off an air of frightening formality. He had a long and serious face, like the farmer from *American Gothic*. His hands were folded neatly in his lap.

"May I help you?" said Ephram.

"Just need a ride up the hill," said the man, as though Ephram were a chauffeur.

I was surprised when Ephram started up the hill without protest, without a moment's concern with the stranger. I leaned my head against Ephram's arm and glanced at the man through a veil of hair. The stranger sat perfectly still, staring straight ahead.

He had impeccable posture. He kept a slight smile on his face, like he was holding in a secret.

Ephram stopped at the top of the hill to let the stranger out. As we started to drive off, the man called out. "You're a sinner," the man yelled to Ephram. "May God have mercy on your soul." The stranger held his hand out in a blessing and backed away, starting on foot up the ramp to the highway, due east, away from us. I watched Ephram's face in the rearview. His eyes seemed out of focus, occupied with some far-off thought or vision. He didn't speak for hours, and I busied myself with an inventory of roadside terrors: rusted mobile homes; clotheslines strung between trees, spotted with pink nightgowns and men's overalls and children's shorts pinned up to dry; tarpaper shacks and their accessory satellite dishes, their giant faces turned skyward, and cars without wheels or doors, and bicycles left on their sides in the yard; a preponderance of litter, fast food cups, and paper bags; dead birds and possum decaying under a haze of flies and the sickening circling of vultures. All of these horrors dimmed with the setting of the sun, and soon there was nothing to behold but darkness, the oncoming headlights of eastbound traffic, a row of cars and their drivers headed toward an infinite variety of destinations. Ephram was enthralled by this, I could tell, by the possibilities of a life outside of his familiar circle. He looked dreamily at each exit sign, wondering what might be in store for him in towns named Sunnyville, Peytona, Salt Lick.

We spent the night at a rest stop. It was late August but the night was chilly and I woke shivering. I reached for Ephram, who was slumped away from me, his head resting against the window. He was cold. I sat up and looked at him. We had parked under a lamppost and the light was good. This was the first time since childhood I had really watched him up close. Ephram hated to be watched. He always spoke with his head down. Because he had two different colored eyes, one gray and one amber, and because he was shy about such a magnificent feature, Ephram hardly ever looked anyone in the eye. His right eyelid didn't entirely shut, and there was a gap where his eyeball was visible even as he slept. The eye roamed, and I flinched when I saw the iris roll across the gap. I thought for a moment that he could see me, and that he would wake when he sensed himself watched. But he was truly asleep. I reached over and touched his hair.

Cars pulled up periodically. Couples emerged, hobbling toward the restrooms on stiff legs. The couples did not touch or speak to each other. They parted ways, using the restrooms and the telephones separately, buying snacks from the vending machines. They walked separately back to their cars, slamming the doors and looking out the windows. The travelers were tired of each other.

Insects buzzed against the overhead light, flapping their wings and knocking their heads against the glass, making terrible, futile sounds. By the time Ephram woke, many of the insects had succeeded in killing themselves.

Ephram is a heartbreak of a brother, a failure, a sulker and a creep. He is obsolete. Strange as a telegram, a phonograph, an inkwell.

Ephram is adopted, and my ties to him have always been fragile. My parents took him in as a foster child when he was two. When they eventually adopted him he became the first black resident of our small suburb. My parents raised him with every advantage, and he thrived. During his junior year of high school he earned a perfect score on the SATs. When he was offered a scholarship to Harvard the following year, he shocked the entire town by turning it down. He refused to go to college altogether.

Since then I have endured the sight of Ephram at countless menial jobs, first at the grocery—hunchbacked, slicing blocks of meat at the deli, a paper hat anchored to his afro with bobby pins. I have watched him mop the floor behind countless counters, rowing the handle in sensuous circles. I have seen him standing on the street corner handing out circulars, shivering in his signature army coat, his arm extended, the cheap yellow paper of the circulars flapping in the coldest of winds. I have seen him working at summer church bazaars, standing over a grill lined with sausage links, or perched on the high seat of the dunking booth, staring solemnly at the horizon, ignoring the line of teenaged pitchers hoping to sink him. I have seen him go under, dropped in the filthy vat of warm water, and I have seen him emerge, stoic as ever, to take his seat again. Most recently Ephram has settled at a new job as a nighttime gas-station attendant, and I see him now and then glassed away, sitting alone in the small bulletproof booth at the center of the rows of gas pumps. When I walk past the station at night he is reading, always reading, his back turned. This is my brother, the family's chagrin. He is the mess hidden in the garage — the wooden tennis racket, the rusted lawn chair, the mateless croquet mallet, the empty aquarium, the red plastic jug filled with spare gasoline.

I bear all of this knowing it is the life Ephram has chosen, one he prefers to the atmosphere of Ivy League schools, with their monogrammed sweater vests and their upscale pubs and their green-shaded desk lamps. Ephram has lived in the basement of my parents' house for years, reading and educating himself in utter isolation. This is the life he designed, and it has failed him slowly. He has searched this whole time for an acceptable version of himself. As a boy he took to reading biographies, and many times he adopted the personality of whoever he studied. He took up juggling after reading about W. C. Fields, and he worked on his technique for years until he was able to handle bowling pins and knives and telephone books. When Ephram read about Muhammad Ali, he studied Islam, and he hung a punching bag from rafters in the basement. When he read about Richard Pryor, he developed a language of profane criticism so intricate and hilarious that it sparked, for one brief week, a trend in our otherwise humorless household that allowed us to point out each other's every Goddamn motherfucking flaw.

A year ago Ephram stopped eating with the family. He let his hair grow into an outrageous afro, six inches tall. He grew painfully thin and did nothing but work at the gas station and watch old movies in his room, working his way through every black-and-white feature available at the video store. Recently he had stumbled on the films of Elvis Presley. Soon he began to commute to a small record store in Boston, the last place on Earth where you could still buy an LP. Ephram paid good money for a stack of Elvis hits on 45s, and he listened to them for weeks. There was something about Elvis he couldn't let go of.

For the entire summer I was the last member of our family that Ephram spoke to. And even then it was subtle and silent, done in signals and glares. Ours was the language of umpires and third-base coaches, of pitchers and catchers, the winks and nods and tugging of ears. "I'm black," Ephram said to me once, "but I've never been black." He said this as he was walking past the dinner table, where my parents and I were eating a silent meal. He walked on by. He was shirtless, and I saw the intricate bones of his spine. He was so thin, fragile as a fossil.

We drove without stopping and crossed into Memphis the following morning. Ephram hadn't planned. He wasn't sure where Graceland was, and we hadn't brought a map. In North Memphis, there were signposts without signs. We were lost, driving past a series of housing projects. Some of the buildings had been devastated by fire. There were windowless windows, and frames without doors. The bricks at the edges of windows and doors were stained with soot. People still lived in these buildings. They sat on the steps, and they roamed around the dirt courtyard whose grass had been burned out by the worst heatwave in fifty years. The people moved slowly, suffering in the heat. Children played in the courtyard. They seemed ghostly, unsupervised, invisible to the adults around them.

"Don't these people have jobs?" I said. "It's a Tuesday afternoon. What are they all doing just standing around like that?"

Ephram didn't respond. He was having trouble driving. Broken stoplights hung from their posts, the lights burnt out. At intersections, there were no rules of traffic.

"What if we break down," I kept saying. "This is crazy." I had never seen people like this, and I alternated between gawking and looking away. I knew that Ephram still recalled some of his childhood, before he had been adopted. He had spoken about it once, when we were teenagers, when we first began drifting apart. Ephram had said he remembered running down a long hallway of an apartment building, lit only by the red glow of the exit sign. He remembered crouching down to run his fingers against the slats of a heating vent. This was his earliest memory. The Claysons had adopted him when he was two. He had never really learned what his life had been like beforehand, except that it was so depraved that he had become a ward of the state.

"What if we break down? What if we keep circling around and around and we can't get out?" I said. I looked pleadingly at Ephram. He glanced at me, annoyed. "What would we do?"

"Shut up, you baby," he said.

"That's all you've said this whole trip!" Tears welled up in my eyes and streamed down my face, but I resisted sobbing or gasping or even sniffling. Ephram had once complimented me on the way I cried. "If you have to do it," he had said, "at least you keep it to yourself."

"What should we do?" I said.

"What should we do?" Ephram mocked, using his best falsetto. "I'll show you what we'll do." He pulled the car to the side of the road and got out, and he started walking toward a group of men who were standing in the parking lot of a boarded-up gas station.

"Ephram!" I yelled. "Come back!" But he continued walking. I rolled up the windows and locked the doors of the car. Ephram approached the men, who at first stood with their arms folded. But soon the men relaxed, joking and laughing. Ephram was animated, moving his arms and talking loudly. I had never seen him like that, and something startled me about the ease with which he had slipped into character. Eventually Ephram led the men toward the car. They gathered around, all talking at once.

"This is classy," one of the men exclaimed, and Ephram beamed. When the men walked off, Ephram came around to the side of the car and pulled at the door handle, but it was locked.

"Open up," he yelled, "you baby." I waited until the men were a safe distance away before opening the door.

"Graceland," Ephram said brightly, after he settled in the car. "Two miles."

"Oh thank God," I said. "Thank God, thank God."

"Have some faith," Ephram told me.

We parked, paid for tickets, and waited for the shuttle that would take us to Graceland. It was so hot that my clothes clung to me, and I kept wiping sweat from my forehead. Ephram seemed in a perfect state of comfort. He held his face up to the sun and basked. When the shuttle driver arrived and opened the door he was wearing a long-sleeved wool uniform. He also wore a black hat embellished with lengths of gold braid, and a leather glove on one hand. He smiled at me and Ephram, showing a gold front tooth and the flinty resilience of a person who had smiled professionally at tourists for several years.

"Welcome to Graceland," he said, speaking into a hand-held microphone. "The most beautiful place on Earth." The driver had said this so many times that there was no longer any feeling left. It was a phrase so familiar and personal to him, like a phrase mumbled during sleep, that it was difficult for others to decipher.

All kinds of people were seated on the shuttle—middle-aged housewives in polyester pants and flip-flops, cameras strapped around their necks; black-clad teenagers, their hair oily and dark, their skin horrifically pale; men dressed like cowboys, the brims of their white hats soaked with sweat, their tight jeans tucked into snakeskin boots; rich New Yorkers with their expensive bags and manicures, and their high-heeled shoes and giant sunglasses. No one spoke. It was a short trip to the mansion and the driver barely had time to inform his passengers that the house had been owned by Elvis Presley and occupied by him, his friends, and his family during the greatest years of their lives.

I first saw the house through the shuttle window as we were waiting for the crowd to file out. The house was much smaller than I had imagined. It was beautifully kept, with a glistening paint job and fine landscaping, but it looked no bigger than a regular home. I felt strange, suddenly, going into another person's house to look around. It was the first time that I had thought of Elvis, or any celebrity, as a person.

"You look just like Judy Garland," a woman said to me. "Did you know that?"

"No," I said. "But thanks." I smiled at the woman, who was short and fat and wore a T-shirt decorated with a cartoon sketch of a litter of poodles.

"I like your bag," said the woman.

"Thank you," I said, though my bag was an ordinary backpack.

"See my bag?" said the woman, holding it up. It was decorated all over with poodles. "I love poodles," said the woman. "Did you know poodles are prone to seizures?" she said.

"No!" I said, in feigned astonishment.

"Well they are." The woman smiled. Her lips were painted tulip pink. Just above her lip was a dark mole in the shape of Florida.

"Do you like poodles," the woman said to Ephram, who had put a protective arm around me. Ephram simply stared at the woman, fixing his strange eyes on her, and she backed away.

The tour guide was a cheery blonde girl with a thick Southern drawl. She wore her hair in a high ponytail that was tied with a bow, and she managed to look like someone who had stepped straight out of the fifties. She began the tour with the story of Elvis's birth, explaining that Elvis had been a twin. Jesse Presley had been stillborn. Elvis had lived. Surprised members of the tour clucked their tongues and turned to whisper to each other. Others nodded gravely, lowering their heads in respect, for they had known for the majority of their lives the first thing there was to know about Elvis, what they considered the initial victory and tragedy of his life.

The tour guide showed the group through several rooms, each

with its own decorative theme. One room was filled with animal-skin furniture and rugs. There was a recording studio, an exercise room where Elvis performed martial arts in front of his admiring friends, and the kitchen, where Elvis's staff would cook whatever he wanted, whenever he wanted it, even if it was a six-week-long, non-stop craving for meatloaf.

On the tour there was a man dressed like a cowboy. He was tall and thin, and he had a habit of perching one foot up on seats or railings or benches, and lunging while he spoke. He stroked his long moustache and talked constantly throughout the tour of the famous people he had brushed shoulders with. He told how he had once seen Jerry Lewis in the Dallas Airport. In the days before the success of the PTL Network, he had seen Tammy Faye Bakker sing at a revival. Most impressive of all, the man said, was his relation by marriage to Hank Williams's embalmer. "My cousin Jody got the call early that morning when Hank had his accident," the man said. "'Jody,' they says to him, 'You'd better come on into work. It's Hank Williams himself down here.'" The cowboy was speaking to no one in particular, but the whole lot of us, as if we were friends by virtue of a shared tour. "My cousin Jody said it didn't even look like Hank there at the morgue. Looked nothing like him. Jody had his work cut out, he said." The cowboy scanned his audience, looking for an attentive face. "Hank Williams was the best," the cowboy said to me. "But Elvis did alright too, I guess."

The tour moved downstairs to the basement, which was the saddest part of the house. The walls were unfinished, made of concrete blocks. The blocks had been detailed with a painted lightning bolt and Elvis's trademark letters, T.C.B., which, the tour guide explained, stood for "taking care of business." The tour filed through the basement to a small museum that housed some of Elvis's accumulated trophies—platinum records, awards, gold statuettes, and a variety of expensive costumes, including a magnificent white cape that was decorated with hundreds of gold beads formed into a spread-winged eagle. It was in this museum that the tour guide first spoke of Elvis in the past tense. "It was prescription drugs," she said, "that killed Elvis. Prescription. He was in a great deal of pain," she said sadly, "and his doctors couldn't manage to help him."

The poodle lady began sobbing, clutching her bag to her chest, and the blonde tour guide bowed her head. The tour guide seemed to be accustomed to these outbursts. There were a million poodle ladies who flocked to Graceland, who had once been bee-hived teenagers screaming up at the stage, their arms outstretched, wanting, wanting to touch the cuff of Elvis's pants, to move their hips with him, to sway sensually in their poodle skirts. The poodle lady must have lived as a young woman with the torture of that terrible mole, and all of her fantasies about Elvis falling in love with a stout, ugly girl from the country were sometimes all that kept her going. She had been young once and she was crying about this more than anything, it was clear.

Suddenly everything was awful. I glimpsed my life with Ephram as a high school dropout, a vagrant Southerner. I imagined our lives as residents of trailer parks—toasting hot dogs on sticks, watching our clothes spin despondently in the dryers of coin laundries, eating at all-night diners, choosing slices of glazed fruit pies from rotating glass cases and listening to the life stories of down-and-out truck drivers.

I once read an article in *Time* about a boy who was working the grill at a restaurant when lightning struck an antenna on the roof of the building. The shock had come through the stove and the spatula the boy was holding, and it ran up his arm and out his shoulder. He had explained in the interview how he still gave off a warmth from that arm that you could feel just by standing next to him. There was some kind of current still running through him, the reporter confirmed, even months after the accident. This was the kind of experience I wanted, something thrilling and dangerous that would mark me forever without altogether changing my life. I wanted to go home. I didn't know how to tell this to Ephram.

Something different was happening to Ephram. He was at

home here. He loved the heat, the ache of everything. He loved sleeping in the car. He loved the way train tracks crossed his path, and he loved watching the boxcars bang past, some with open doors. He loved the possibility of it, a ride in a direction you weren't even sure of.

I realized this during the last minutes of the Graceland tour. The poodle lady was sobbing violently, and everyone on the tour was hushed. We all looked at our feet and thought private thoughts, and I believe that at the very same moment Ephram and I knew we had reached our last hour together.

We walked sullenly to the shuttle, which dropped us off at the Graceland gift shop. I'm not sure when I lost track of Ephram. The cowboy had started a story about his great, great uncle, who had married a girl who had known Billy the Kid in the Biblical sense. I've always been enthralled by a good lie. Before I knew it I was standing at a counter in the gift shop, still listening to the cowboy and absently shaking a Graceland snow globe, and it was then I realized that Ephram was gone.

By that time Ephram was driving out of town, stuck behind an old wagon that he couldn't see around. The wagon was tall and boxy, trailing thick exhaust. The body of the wagon had been handmade out of wooden slats, and Ephram strained to see through the cracks. The worst smell he had ever known was coming from the wagon. Something was rotting in the heat, and Ephram felt a nauseous quiver in the back of his throat each time he took a breath. He tried to go around the wagon, but he couldn't pass. Then something flew from the truck, swirled in the air and flattened against his windshield. It was a feather, a dirtied white feather, and Ephram knew then he was following a chicken truck, that these animals were on their way to slaughter, and that what he smelled in some part was their shit and their fear.

Ephram remembered a birthday party he had attended when he was young, at which his friend had been given a live chicken for a pet. The boy's parents owned a house on a two-acre lot, and they had already made presents of a sheep and three geese. Ephram had shown up to that birthday party wearing a dress. At the time, our mother was a feminist who encouraged everyone to question the conventional. When Ephram had admired a denim jumper in a storefront window, our mother had bought it for him. Every grown man, she thought, should count among his experiences at least one public appearance in drag. There was a picture from that party, a group of children in triangular paper party hats, sitting around a table, admiring a sheet cake. Ephram was the only black child. He was wearing the blue jumper over a white turtleneck, and he was looking away from the camera.

At the party, the chicken had walked unnoticed around the house, exploring, stopping here and there to peck at chair legs and balls of wrapping paper. By the end of the party the chicken had wandered off, and the guests had searched the house and grounds, finding nothing. The birthday boy had taken the chicken's disappearance in stride. He was the kind of rich kid who knew from an early age that most everything could be replaced.

Ephram couldn't pass the truck. He followed it for miles, waiting for the road to diverge. As soon as he got out from behind the truck, Ephram thought, he would let go of this memory from his former life, the absurdity of it, the strangeness of the people he had known. He would take whatever exit presented itself, and follow it without looking back.

How I know this about Ephram and his trip out of town is difficult to explain. I wasn't there in the car with him, really. It might just be too difficult to say out loud the truth of all of this, that I, Agnes Mildred Clayson, never really existed, that my mother and Ephram's mother, Mrs. Clayson, delivered a two-pound daughter the day that the gypsy moths were doing their worst, that I died within hours, that Ephram was allowed only the briefest glance of his sister struggling in an incubator, that he had pressed his hand against the plastic dome that separated us, and that after I was buried, and after a few years when nearly everyone had forgotten me, I was still growing in his mind, becoming his sister, his only friend in the world and only ally in a household so quiet that the only sounds at the dinner table were the ticking of the grandfather clock and the terse proclamations of Dan Rather. It is hard to say now that my whole life has been imagined by Ephram in the most intricate detail, that my brother has been the only person to know and love me, and that after all this time he is ready to let me go, that he is leaving home for good and starting a new life, and I am not coming along for the ride. Ephram will think of me less and less as he wanders the streets of Tuscaloosa or Galveston or Green Bay, juggling on street corners for spare change, sleeping on park benches and stables and in the basements of university buildings, touring the South by bus, trading yard work for home-cooked meals, taking the occasional job harvesting fruit or working behind the counter of small diners that ask no questions and pay cash at the end of the week. He will be the hero of loneliness. Soon he will remember me as one remembers a character in a book or movie, and the remembrance will be vague, reduced to a slight rush of feeling, warmth or sorrow or nausea.

Meanwhile I've been abandoned in the Graceland gift shop. This is where he left me. In his mind I am simply a tall, pale girl standing at a counter examining souvenirs, perhaps shaking a snow globe, watching Graceland in miniature, watching the white flakes settle over that magnificent white house, and over the pink Cadillac parked out front, the snow falling so softly and peacefully. A nice dream, though we all know it never snows in Memphis. I stand fixed in his mind, twirling a rack of postcards, gazing at those beautiful black-and-white pictures of Elvis as a young man. The only images for sale in the gift shop are of Elvis while he was still young and newly rescued from poverty, still surprised to have his picture taken and to be dressed in such fine, tailored suits. What sells is the memory of someone young and promising, someone whose troubles haven't found him yet, someone who can't see the future for what it is.

Christie Hodgen's fiction has appeared in *Scribner's Best of the Fiction Workshops 1999*, the *Greensboro Review*, the *Bellingham Review*, the *Notre Dame Review*, *Meridian*, and the *Texas Review*. She is a graduate of the University of Virginia and Indiana University. Her stories have been awarded first prize in the 2000 Tobias Wolff Award for Fiction and the 1995 Ernest Hemingway Days Festival Short Story Contest. She lives in Columbia, Missouri.

BART PATENAUDE

This is the last in a series of stories about Ephram and Agnes. They are stories about loneliness and imagination, about the ways people choose to distract themselves from solitude. I think of Graceland as just such a distraction. When I visited the house, it seemed like a failed attempt at happiness, stability, immortality. I thought it would be fitting for Ephram to stop there on his way to a solitary life.

Elizabeth Tippens

MAKE A WISH

(from *Harper's*)

Y OU ARE HERE.

Or so it says on the Level 2 directory.

I wear bright red lipstick and no other makeup until another sales associate, a girl named Bailey, tells me that my eyes, and not my lips, are the feature I should accentuate. Bailey is not the kind of girl I would have been friends with in high school. She uses expressions like "Sweetie" and "P.S." But here, now, on Level 2, things are not high school. Things are different.

"Sweetie, I could tell you stories," Bailey says. And then she does.

Bailey is a one-girl FBI who has accumulated massive amounts of personal information about the employees of Level 2, like which employees shoplift, who's gay (male and female), who's a slut (male and female), who's a parking-lot whore, who just looks like one but is really a nice person, who binges and purges, who's listening to Prozac, who isn't but should be, who's about to get fired, promoted, demoted, engaged, dumped, cheated on, stabbed in the back, used for sex, or taken away from all this by a very rich customer, which has happened, according to Bailey. And abortions. Bailey can tell who is even a little bit pregnant, and then, two days later, who is not anymore.

"P.S., try dark black eyeliner and just a little bit of clear lip gloss," she tells me.

I do. I try this.

When mornings are slow Bailey tells me all about her sex life with her boyfriend, Duff. Now I know so much about what Bailey likes Duff to do to her, and what Duff likes to do to Bailey, that I feel as though I have had sex with both of them. Duff has a motorcycle.

Bailey and I arrange the accessories rack, straightening out a tangled mess of ugly belts and cheap scarves. She gives me advice like, when a guy is hazardous to your health, watch, and the little hairs on your arms will stand up straight.

Bailey has a chubby little stomach, but because she wears a navel ring and cropped-off sweaters, it took me forever to make this simple observation. That's something I've noticed here on Level 2. If a girl markets herself as cute, if by wearing a navel ring, for instance, she telegraphs her own belief in the attractiveness of her stomach, there will be a lag time before reality hits the eye of the beholder. If it ever does.

The store manager, a short, wired woman named Robin, has no marketing strategy for herself. What she does have is a lack of personal style. Her outfits are anti-personal, like somebody's boxy, generic uniform, passed along apathetically from one employee to the next. Robin is a corporate misfit who believes in misguided sales techniques she invents herself, like, "Disco sells clothes." Does this mean that disco makes customers more inclined to buy, or that with disco hammering at our brains we are more inclined to sell? The answer, like everything else lately, lies in the realm of Divine Mystery.

I heard somebody say, Burn baby burn, Disco inferno, Burn baby burn. It plays over and over. "An endless loop of disco madness," Bailey calls it.

Robin puts Bailey and me up front to sell coats.

Who could have guessed that I would actually excel at something like this? My ability to sell coats has come crashing out of nowhere, meteorlike, and has nothing to do with any previously known talent of mine, or with my actual personality, which is what you would call introverted. It all happens in a kind of trance. While this new, outgoing coat-selling girl works the floor, I seem to disappear altogether. Later, when my impressively high sales are tallied, I have no clear memory of what I could have said that was so persuasive and convincing. It's a blur. With disco.

My mother and I just bought the exact same ones! One night, right before I was about to fall asleep, I remember saying this. Apparently I will say anything at all to sell a coat. I appear to be a genius at the mother/daughter double sale.

I sell a lot of coats.

The president of the company sends me a congratulatory letter, which leaves me, and even Bailey, nearly speechless in its pathetic enthusiasm.

"P.S., you can't even make fun of something this banal," says Bailey.

I win a prize.

For lunch I insist on eating the exact same thing every day: a very large, very sweet wedge of cheese Danish, and an extra-tall cup of coffee with extra cream and sugar. I get my Danish and coffee in the Food Court at a small store called Alpenhaus.

Just to get their German-Swiss-Austrian-whatever theme across to the one last mall customer who might have missed it, Alpenhaus has hired a dwarf to parade back and forth outside its entrance wearing an Alpenhaus sandwich board, lederhosen, and a little green Alpine hiking hat. With a feather. And I have to pass by this reeking medieval indignity in order to get my Danish and coffee. But this is how badly I want my Danish and coffee. It is my one and only pleasure of the day, and while I actually do care that it is sickening and unhealthy and causes an intense sugar/caffeine rush/crash, and that I have to witness human debasement in order to get it, I feel physically incapable of ordering anything else.

Once I have made it past the dwarf, a relief you can't believe, I

MAKE A WISH 51

get to see the boy behind the counter. I find his hostility refreshing after a morning of being NICE to the general public. I find it bubbly, like Sprite. His ears, his eyebrows, and his nose are all pierced. He will be the one to inflict the pain here, NOT YOU. He is the boy who hates everything. He is a little younger than me, and very tall, with big feet and hands, like a puppy. He acts bored and tired, and he speaks softly, forcing the customers to crane their necks to hear what he is saying. But the boy who hates everything likes me. It's the kind of acknowledgment you shouldn't feel honored by, but you do anyway. We have a mental crush on each other, which you can actually feel the purity of. Each day we have a brief yet satisfying conversation.

"Will you be dining *in* today?" he asks.

Together we eye the dining conditions. One sticky plastic table and two metal folding chairs.

"I believe I'll be dining *out* today," I answer.

This portion of my daily routine is what you would call a highlight.

The mall is a space station. No day. No night. A synthetic habitat of regulated, piped-in weather. I eat on a white bench by a fake pond with a fountain that drips down onto copper lily pads. If someone sits down beside me on the bench while I am eating my cheese Danish and drinking my coffee, my lunch is ruined.

I listen to the persistent sound of water hitting copper as it echoes everywhere. It is an open, hollow sound. Children come by with their mothers to throw coins into the fountain.

Make a wish.

After lunch I usually go by Pop Cowboy to visit my boots. My boots are beautifully constructed from dark red leather, and not something I would actually be able to afford, not with my pathetic paycheck. But the boots and I have a relationship anyway. They sing to me from their little perch behind the glass window, ditties about the open trail, which are not their real personality but pseudo-cowboy junk they have picked up at the pseudo-cowboy store, and sung with a scary, forced enthusiasm, alarming if you're not expecting it. Like pick-up lines. The boots can be obnoxious, but they are so pretty you can overlook it most days. They are always Happy Trails.

For one strange, exhilarating moment not one customer is in the store.

"Oh, Miss. Miss sales*gal,* can you help me?" Bailey screams, pulling up her tartan skirt and twirling around in a circle. She's got on men's underwear, the white Jockey kind with the blue line around the waistband.

"Wa-hooooo," she shouts, "excuse me while I kiss the sky."

I love her for this.

Later, when the gate is pulled down and Robin is vacuuming in her tight black skirt and stocking feet, and Bailey is hand-steaming wrinkled skirts with her Walkman on, and I can't remember what I said that made all those women buy all those coats, I become extremely tired, shy again, more or less who I consider myself to actually be, wordlessly folding sweaters into perfect squares and stacking them into neat, fluffy piles. It is somehow satisfying to look at a neat stack of things, any things, that are all the exact same color. I linger over this tiny study in order and perfection. Then I go home.

"Mind if I sit down?" he says.

My lunch, and therefore my entire day, is in danger of being ruined by a man in a big white cowboy hat. That is, if I'm seeing things right. I mean, I know I am, but you have to question a hat like that. You just have to.

"It's a free whatever," I say.

"A free country?"

"That too."

I've seen this guy around the mall, strolling the lower levels in his unsullied cowboy boots, lurking noticeably, in that big hat, in the background of things. His mustache is thick and bushy, but carefully combed, well manicured, like a lawn. He wears clean jeans and a good leather belt, its big silver buckle coiled into the shape of a sleeping snake.

"I'm trying to guess which store you work at," he says. I keep seeing you on this bench."

Someone from another level drops a penny into the fake pond.

"I bet you work at Paraphernalia," he says. "Or The Sox Box."

"Wrong," I say.

"Then I bet you work at Talbots. No," he says, "Laura Ashley. You're the Laura Ashley type. The classic type. The good-bone-structure type."

"Wrong," I say.

"You tell me then, beautiful girl."

"If you must know, I work at Steinway," I say. "I play the pianos so the customers can hear how the instruments sound. It's not really that fun, but I'm working my way through college on a music scholarship, and they really pay a lot."

"Really?" he says.

"Uh-huh."

"How come I don't believe you?"

"I don't know," I say, shrugging.

"I bet you really work at one of those little shitholes for minimum wage and no benefits," he says.

"I guess you're a real cowboy, then," I say.

"Darlin', there are no more real cowboys," he says, "only outlaws in cowboy hats."

"Is that what you are?"

"What's your name?" he asks me.

Once, Bailey wore a nametag that said PURPLE HAZE. Jimi Hendrix is her hero, the guitar god for all time. Five days went by before Robin noticed and delivered a hyperactive lecture on acting more professional. Before that, though, the two of us were giddy, almost free.

"Bailey," I tell him.

"What's your real name?"

"Why can't Bailey be my real name?" I say.

"Because it's not the truth," he says. "Why can't I be Willie Nelson?"

"You're not?" I say.

I look, but I can't see his eyes behind the dark gray lenses of his glasses, the aviator kind.

I am surprised by how much time goes by while my car spins around and around on the frozen road. I've hit an ice patch on the exit ramp, coming off of the highway. In the movies, action of this kind takes place so quickly, but here, in real life, there appears to be plenty of time to think about things, like, Can this really be happening? Am I really here? I have enough time to become totally aware of the darkness of the highway, the absence of other vehicles, of drivers, of people, of anything but frozen road, my car, and me. Driver's ed, taken in summer school, comes back to me. There is that kind of time. Time to recall a whole summer with friends two years ago, and driving around on the blacktop, bashing into bright orange cones and laughing like maniacs. Take your foot off the brake, I think. Isn't that what you're supposed to do on ice? And finally the spinning stops, and I begin a strange, silent drift, sliding off of the road and onto the ramp's shoulder, where I sit completely unharmed and singing to myself the same song I was singing before the wheels of my mother's old VW Rabbit hit the ice and began to spin.

"Carrie," they shriek.

I try to get away from them by hiding behind one of the round coatracks. I keep circling, around and around, but the little stalkers circle, too.

"Carrie?" They are still shrieking.

"Carrie, it's *us,*" one of them says. They have me sandwiched in between them, trapped, like bologna.

I find I can't remember their names. For some reason I think that they must all be named the same thing. Either they are all named Ashley or Amber, or Ashley-Amber with a hyphen.

"From last year. From Senior Choir." Then all together, "From *high school*," they say, laughing.

"We heard about your mother," says Ashley-Amber, her mood suddenly solemn.

"Heard what?" I say.

"Well, that she died."

"You heard that?"

"Well, yeah," one of them says softly.

"She didn't die at all," I say. "She almost died. She was sick. She had cancer. But she recovered with a combination of macrobiotic food and chemotherapy. She had a radical mastectomy, but she's doing really great. She's getting total reconstructive surgery, but in the meantime, she and I went shopping for all these new bathing suits and bras with falsies in the front. Then we bought a bunch of matching stuff, like coats. Now she and my dad are on vacation, like a second honeymoon, in the Caribbean."

"Which island?" asks one of the girls.

"Ashley," another says, hitting her.

"St. Barth's," I say.

"Well, that's so great, then," one of them says gently. They like the word "great." I remember that, how much they liked the word "great."

"God, I'm, like, so glad," says another. "That's so *great*."

"So, where are you going to college?" It's the same one who asked which island.

"My parents wanted me to go away, but I decided to stay home and help them out."

They just stare at me.

"What does that mean?" one of them asks. Bailey has me wearing a nametag that says FOXY LADY, which Robin is too freaked out by her incoming shipment of hideous sweaters to have noticed yet.

"It's like a joke," I say. "Jimi Hendrix."

They all stare at the joke.

"Who's Jimi Hendrix?" they ask.

"A famous architect," I say. "He built this mall."

"Great."

"I've got to go," I say. "I've got to go unlock a dressing room."

I back away from them, calling out how great they all look. How totally great. And wasn't it great to run into each other? Everything is so unbelievably *great*.

I unlock the dressing-room door and stand in there with my forehead resting against the cold smooth mirror. My legs go, and I let myself slide against the carpeted wall to the floor. Robin is out there, pounding on the door. Are you in there? What is going on in there? I am definitely wearing too much eye makeup. Black mascara and black eyeliner hollow out my eyes and make my skin look pale. I can no longer seem to tell what looks good. As opposed to what looks bad.

I need a marketing strategy.

P.S., my skin is breaking out.

I close my eyes and listen to the sound of drizzling water as it echoes inside the mall. It's like water inside a cave. When I open my eyes he will be there.

"Wake up," he says. He's there. *He's there.*

"Do I look like I'm asleep?" I say.

"Yeah, you do," he says. "Sleeping Beauty takes a nap."

He sits down on the bench beside me.

"Do you know that it ruins my day completely if someone sits down on this bench while I'm eating my lunch?"

"You call that shit lunch?"

I notice how pointy his snakeskin boots are. He is short, and those little stacked heels give him a slight boost in height, not that cowboy boots on short guys ever really fool anyone. I notice things I didn't notice before, things you can't notice when you are bombarded with the big picture. Or the big hat. Now I notice details, like the small size of his hands, and the rings. He's got on silver rings. One ring is a cat's face with tiny rubies for eyes.

"If I didn't work here," I tell him, "I'm pretty sure I wouldn't be hanging around on this bench criticizing what the salespeople eat."

"I'm rich," he tells me.

"So," I say.

"So, rich is nothing to sneeze at."

"Do I look like I'm going to sneeze?"

"You could sneeze," he says. "That's a good name for you, Sneezy."

"That's amazing," I say, "because Sneezy really is my name. See, it says so right here on my nametag."

Actually, my nametag is missing again. I keep losing them. Today my nametag says LaShonda Brown, the name of an employee who was fired for having sex in the bathroom at the Food Court. "It may say Sneezy, or it may say Sleeping Beauty," he says.

"Can't you read?" I say.

"No ma'am," he answers. I can't read or write, but I can pay someone to do it for me. Muhammad Ali said that," he tells me.

"I think Muhammad Ali had dyslexia," I say.

"There's something real special about you," he says.

"I bet you say that to all the girls," I say, taking a large sip of coffee.

"I don't need to say it to all the girls," he says. "I'm saying it to you because I can see you're different."

I am sure this guy is known among the salesgals of this world as one gigantic joke, something to laugh about later with Bailey.

"Can I give you a ride home after work?" he asks.

"Of course," I say. "I'll meet you in the parking lot at nine."

"I'm serious," he says.

"I'm not," I say.

"Why not?"

"First of all, I have my own car," I say. "And besides, my mother says never to take a ride with a stranger."

"Do you always do what Mama says?"

I take the last sips from the bottom of my cup, which is basically crystals of coffee-soaked sugar. In high school I used to drink carrot juice.

"What if you got to know me?" he says.

"You say there are no more real cowboys, right?" I say.

"That's right, darlin'," he says.

"So if there are no more real cowboys, then soon there will be no more pseudo cowboys, right? I mean, who are all the pseudo cowboys going to imitate?"

"Darlin', I'm afraid we're on the very verge of extinction," he says, holding up his small hand and pointing it at me like a gun. He smiles a little, like a smirk. "Pow," he says. "You better get it while you can."

I visit my boots. They are mute today. Not in the mood for little songs.

The store is just about to open, and Robin decides to give a panicked motivational speech that she calls "Selling to the Upscale Customer."

"No woman is ever just looking," she tells us. "She's looking to buy. Now, let's have the best sales week ever."

She raises a lame little power fist. She looks especially anemic today.

Within an hour, Bailey and I are buttoning up blouses and picking up sweaters that the upscale customer has strewn all over the dressing-room floors.

"Could this be more like vomit?" she says, holding up a white silk sweater that's been smeared around the collar with punch-pink lipstick.

"Gross," I say, as though that would even begin to express it.

Here he comes, big, fake cowboy, into the store, looking not at all red in the face to be touching girls' things, running his fingers up and down the arms of a silk sweater. Bailey throws a gum wrapper at my head. She cannot believe what she is seeing. Bailey cannot believe her good luck, because she is always waiting for exactly this kind of walking spectacle.

He's wearing a black Harley-Davidson T-shirt, which fits tight across his small, muscular chest and arms. His jeans are black and tight, and he rolls when he walks, from his heels through to the pointy toes of his cowboy boots.

Bailey's way of snickering is to way over-smile at things. She laughs behind a huge, fake smile, which makes her peace-sign earring shake. She marches right up to him and, smiling hugely, asks if she can help him find something nice for his wife or his girlfriend today. Then she starts asking rude questions about the authenticity of the hat, and he lets her try it on, and she shouts ya-hoo and any other cowboy thing she can think of. He has his own way of snickering, which is to barely smile at all.

Bailey checks herself out in the mirror.

"I'm starting to like this. It's fresh," she says.

"Hey, cowgirl," he says.

Bailey is playing with him, but he is playing with her, too, and it surprises me that she thinks she's the only one having fun.

He circles around the store a few more times, rolling on his boots, taking his time on his way out. He is like a time bomb in here, something waiting to go shooting off. Robin is watching him now, glaring from behind the cash register.

"I knew I'd find you," he whispers. His breath hits my ear, and a flash of heat shoots down my neck and into my spine, where it sits in the small of my back, like a guy's hand while you're dancing.

Bailey comes bouncing over, full of a good time. "What did he say?" she asks.

"I don't know," I say. "He's crazy."

"He likes you," Bailey says, poking me in the arm. "He was staring at you the whole time."

"He likes *you*," I say.

"Secret boyfriend, secret boyfriend," she says, clapping her hands and jumping.

"That's right," I say, relieved to see him go, "he's my secret boyfriend."

"He's a drug dealer," Bailey says, leaning her body out into the mall to see where he's gone. "The sluts at the Food Court buy coke off him. And that's not all they do."

Robin is marching across the floor, coming right for us.

"He's got a good bod," Bailey says. "He wouldn't be so bad without all the cowboy paraphernalia." She leans out even farther. "Come back, secret boyfriend," she calls, "come back."

Robin grabs Bailey's arm and physically pulls her back into the store.

"I was *leaning* out," complains Bailey. "My feet were still inside the store. Carrie can testify on my behalf. My feet were in. My feet were in."

What passes for fun, here on Level 2, is now over, and Bailey and I return to the task of picking up clothes other women have decided it was okay to throw on the floor. I zip up pants and hang them back on hangers while I think about the boys I slept with in high school. There was one boy who said I love you, but then I found out he loved everyone. Boys, some of them with beautiful long hair in ponytails and soccer-team legs—boys, but not one man. I have never kissed anyone with small creases around his eyes and actual pick-up lines and in his head Willie Nelson singing the soundtrack to the movie of his life. I've never kissed anyone with such a fully realized mustache. I look down and see the faint imprint of his boot in the carpeted floor. I put my foot inside the impression. His boots were my boots, my red boots from Pop Cowboy, the ones that sang to me and made me delirious with "consumer lust." Bailey's term, but I've already made it my own.

Bailey gets a personal call and comes back out onto the floor with black mascara tears running down her bright pink face. I watch while Robin, in defense mode, crosses her arms over her chest. I listen while Bailey pleads with her for the rest of the day off.

"I just can't let you go," Robin says.

"Jesus Christ," says Bailey, sobbing.

"I really wish I could," says Robin, "but the store. I have no one covering the back of the store."

"My boyfriend crashes his bike into a fucking telephone pole and all you care about is the back of the store."

"The back of the store is my job," says Robin, who is sobbing now, too.

"You think I'm going to stand around in the back of the store while Duff lies there in a coma?"

"I'm sorry about your boyfriend, but I just can't let you out, not this afternoon."

"Fuck you," Bailey screams. "You people are heartless. Fucking pigs."

Bailey storms into the back to get her stuff out of her locker. On her way out of the store she stops by the coats to give me a big hug in her little rabbit-fur jacket, so soft, so helplessly soft.

"Duff will be all right," I say. I never know what to tell people, except to repeat all the things people said to me.

"Oh, sweetie," Bailey says, clinging to me. Her tears are all over me. Her tears are all over my face.

Later, I watch a girl about my age shoplift a thin pink belt, which is missing its plastic antitheft device. I lean against the coat-rack, watching, while she rolls it neatly around her hand and stashes it away inside her backpack.

Saturdays are the busiest days of the week. Sales associates are required to arrive two hours prior to opening in order to attend various seminars with titles like "Sweater Folding," "Accessorizing," and "Staying Psyched." Without Bailey to stand behind Robin and make faces, the seminars are in danger of being taken even the tiniest bit seriously. My eyes are already burning from the dry air and fluorescent lighting, and the fact that it is way too early in the morning.

"Purple is to be referred to as 'Eggplant,'" Robin says. She is twitchy in her scuffed high heels, which you can tell were cheap to start with, shifting her weight nervously from one leg to the other. "There is no *purple* in this store," she says. "Got it?"

"Is this 'Sweater Folding' or 'Staying Psyched?'" asks a girl named Breck. She is new and takes notes.

Robin looks as tired as the rest of us, fueled by nothing more substantial than coffee and sugar, burning out before our eyes.

"Pantyhose. Pantyhose," she repeats, unaware that she is caught up in the middle of an incoherent rant about a pair of pantyhose so dirty they will stand up by themselves.

Near tears, Robin says, "Some people don't even have three minutes to wash out a pair of pantyhose."

I whisper to Breck, "It's good to have role models."

Outside it has begun to snow. I know this only because thick hair goes bushy, thin hair goes flat, and everybody complains that they have the wrong kind of hair. *How about a new coat? How about a new coat on sale? Burn baby burn.*

Now it is just me up front, selling coats to snowed-on women. Cheap, trendy coats that are not well made, that are not anything substantial, not anything that is going to last or hold up. Coats that will lose buttons and stays and little tacked-on velvet bows. Coats that will unravel. In my mind I can see them all unravel.

Last night, on my way upstairs to my bedroom, I passed by my mother's old room. My father doesn't sleep in there anymore. He sleeps downstairs on the couch with all of the lights on. When I looked in, I noticed that white powder from a blue box of hers had spilled all over the bureau and mingled with the dust. I wondered if my father opened the blue box, trying to remember the way she smelled when she was still here, and when she still used those things. From the doorway I could see the glass bottles of perfume. They sat untouched. Other things she threw away in a fit of disgust at things of beauty, at life, at the world, but these she left to turn old and dark from time and heat and too much light.

Robin is clapping her hands in front of my face.

"Wake up," she says.

People keep telling me this.

"It's the busiest day of the week and you're standing around here daydreaming," she says.

I'm looking at Robin, thinking, She has got to stop using brown mascara, because it smudges, and then all it does is make her face look dirty.

"I put you up front to sell coats," she snaps. "Now if you don't want to stand in the back, you better WAKE UP."

"Robin, you need a day off," I tell her.

"I need some salespeople," she says, snapping her fingers at me. "Now, let's wake up and *smell* some coats."

"You mean, sell some coats," I say, correcting her.

"Listen," she tells me, "your sales have gone way downhill lately. You better get it together, girl."

"I don't think you want that coat," I tell a woman whose huge hat hair is wild with static electricity. "It's a total waste of money," I tell her. "The style is over. It will look like a joke next fall."

The woman looks angry, as if she suspects she's being tricked.

"Can't you see it's not well made?" I say. "Can't you see that?"

"Is there a coat in this store you could recommend?" she asks, gesturing sarcastically.

I shake my head no.

"I appreciate your honesty," the woman says, "but I still want the coat. *I* like it."

"Take it, then," I snap. "Who's stopping you?"

"What?" she says.

"Panty-Ho," I call her. I have just made this up, and I start laughing.

"You're being abusive," she says. "Where is the manager? I want the manager."

"Still want the coat?" I ask.

"I like it," she says, clutching it to her chest. I watch her scurry across the sales floor to the register.

Burn baby burn. Maybe disco does sell clothes.

No cheese Danish today. I can no longer face the dwarf, the sight of him standing there in the sandwich board. I don't feel like a witness anymore. I feel like, just seeing him, I am part of the crime. And the boy who hates everything, his wrists with their jagged purple scars, zigzags, and small dots that look unreal, drawn on in Magic Marker. I no longer want to look or know or care or imagine. I don't want to have little conversations anymore.

I fall in with a group of mall walkers, old people dressed like fuzzy babies in pastel pink and blue. People brush up against me with their big bags. Purchases. The boy who hates everything passes me, loping along, and we nod, one mall employee to another. His T-shirt says GRAVITY SUCKS. I turn and watch him walk through the mall until it's just the top of his half-shaved head, disappearing down the escalator.

My mother floats up the escalator, at her worst, with no vanity left in her, tubes in her nose and her arms, colorless tufts of hair on her head, big, vacant eyes staring out at a spot on the wall. She seems to be watching something that no one else can see. My father is sitting on the end of my bed. The phone rang at an odd hour, and I knew to try and stay asleep as long as I possibly could. Later, my father came into my room, which he never did, because it was a girl's room and embarrassed him. I knew he was sitting there, and he knew I was only pretending now to be asleep, postponing hearing it for as long as I could. We froze like this for hours, I think.

I walk through the big department store, hoping to hear her voice there. *Ladybugs bring you luck,* she might say in her low, breathless voice, rough and soft, like tiny grains of sand pouring through your open fingers. I wonder where the sound of her voice might be, because for a while it lingered here and there. For a while you could catch a trace of it, a faint half whisper at the cosmetics counter, near the perfume. You could catch a trace of it. It lingered. I swear.

I let the women run their smooth, cool fingers over my eyelids, contouring my eyes, they tell me, with three different shades of beige. I inhale the smell of expensive perfumes. Flowery, lemony, cinnamon smells. I wait in the makeover chair for what could be hours. I wait until the white-coated women look annoyed, then concerned. I wait until a plainclothes security guard (good suit/bad shoes) approaches me, asking if everything is all right.

"Just waiting for someone," I tell him.

"Looks like that person is a no-show," he says.

But for a while it lingered right here.

"Guess so," I say.

On my way out to my car I see the dwarf and the boy who hates everything getting high behind a giant orange Dumpster.

In the underground parking lot I hear his voice. It echoes, ricocheting off of parked cars.

"Hey, girl, can I give you a ride home?" Bing, bing, bing, and bing, and it's everywhere.

"No," I say, looking around, wondering how long I have been sitting in my car, running my hairbrush through my hair.

He is in the shadows, behind a concrete pole that says LEVEL 2 in huge blue letters.

I lock my doors.

I sit with the key in the ignition, wishing I could remember certain things that I have forgotten, but I can't even seem to remember what to remember. I rest my forehead on the steering wheel and accidentally blow my car horn.

He appears at the window in his absurd white hat, and I realize that a joke doesn't have to be funny to still be a joke.

"Unlock the door," he says through the window.

"Go away," I say.

"Go ahead, unlock the damn door."

I do. I do this.

He opens the car door, pulling it hard because it sticks badly. He tosses a bunch of empty Diet Coke cans into the back seat and slides in beside me. He is wearing the warmest-looking coat I have ever seen, a thick, shearling-lined jacket made of soft tan leather, a coat too good to ever unravel.

He stretches out in the seat beside me and blows on his hands for warmth.

"Sometimes life gives you shit," he says.

"What are you talking about?" I say.

"You know what I'm talking about, since you drive this shitty car."

"Does it make you feel superior to criticize everything?"

"I want to show you something," he says.

"Like what?" I answer.

"Like my fish," he says. "Each one of my fish is named for a character on *All My Children*."

"You're a drug dealer," I say.

"You're a little liar," he says.

"I really did work at the piano store," I say, "but I changed jobs because they wouldn't let me off work when my boyfriend crashed his motorcycle. I lost it and started screaming at the manager what a heartless pig he was, and then I stormed out of the store and never went back."

"What happened to your boyfriend?" he asks.

"He died," I say, feeling unexpectedly satisfied by the sound of it.

"Really?" he asks.

"Yes, really," I say. "He was this incredibly gifted person whose life was completely wasted."

"I want to know your real name," he says.

"Aren't you missing *All My Children*?" I ask.

"It's Saturday," he says.

"What about weekdays?"

"I tape," he says. "Where's your coat at?"

"I lost it," I say. I can see my breath, and I realize how cold I am, and that I will never see my coat again because my coat is hanging in the locker room in the back of the store and I have just decided that I am never going back. "I won my coat in a contest," I say, "a coat-selling contest."

He takes off his coat and wraps it around my shoulders. It is heavy and smells of sheared wool and expensive leather.

"I don't do drugs," I say.

"Tell me your name."

"Drugs bore me. Cocaine is passé. You should sell heroin."

"If I knew your name, I could name a fish in your honor."

"Won't I have to join the cast of *All My Children*?"

I want to settle into the coat, pull it tightly around me, give in to its soft, thick lining, but I let it sit, resting stiffly on my back.

"You're pretty enough to," he says.

"Right," I say.

"You shouldn't be running yourself down," he says. "I don't like to hear you running yourself down."

"It's *so* none of your business what I do."

"I want to touch your hair," he says. "Right now, in my mind, I'm touching your hair."

"Get out of my car," I say.

"Do you want to see my fish?"

"Are you high or just insane?"

"None of the above," he says, reaching toward me. "Now, go ahead and take my hand."

A flash of silver rings, of ruby cat's eyes.

"Go ahead, take it."

I reach to turn the key in the ignition, but he grabs my wrist and pulls me toward him.

"Get out of my car," I say.

"Your teeth are chattering," he says. "You're shaking all over."

He gathers the coat by its lapels and pulls me, wrapped up in it, toward him.

Even so, there is still time to put a stop to stupid compliments and all of the rest of it, none of which makes any sense in the world. I know I could still get out of the car. I could turn, I could walk, I could run, before his mouth becomes the only warmth in the world.

Elizabeth Tippens is the author of the novel *Winging It.* Her short stories have appeared in *Harper's Magazine, Ploughshares, Mademoiselle,* and elsewhere, and her nonfiction has been published in *Rolling Stone* and *Playboy.* She lives in New York City with her husband and son.

TESS STEINKOLK

Simultaneous impulses were at work in the creation of this story. I was interested in the idea of a story in which a person with normally good sense overrides not only her good sense, but her true instinct, out of a need for love. That's the girl, Carrie. And she had to have a predator. That's the mall cowboy. He is a man who lives in my own head; he's my own natural predator, but he's also based on a real person I once knew. Over the years the real person has slipped farther and farther away. He shows up in my dreams and will probably show up in my work again. He's dangerous.

I also wanted to write about the time I sold coats in a mall, which I did as a teenager in Maryland. I found I was frighteningly good at selling coats, but it was a sort of hysteria, and it caused me to have a small nervous breakdown. Unlike the girl in the story, I had a mom who called in sick for me, sort of permanently, as I recall. The mall itself began as just background for the story but quickly became a crucial element, an overheated, claustrophobic environment, a hellish realm unto itself.

This story is one that went through many, many drafts. Including one in which I thought it might be a novel. It stretched out like a rubber band, then finally, it went boing, *contracting back into place. Finally, I got what I wanted.*

Ingrid Hill

JOLIE-GRAY

(from *The Southern Review*)

The real reason Jolie-Gray Boisseneau has come up to New Orleans to stay with the Marshes on Esplanade Avenue—her father, Gray, calls them "your mother's high-and-mighty relations"—is that nobody down in Grand Isle can stand her. The explanation is that simple.

It is the Depression, and though the Grand Isle Boisseneaus are by Esplanade Avenue standards just *bougalie* white trash, they eat from what later will be called Depression glass plates every day. They know nothing else.

In Grand Isle, near the mouth of the Mississippi, on the margins of civilization, nothing seems different from what it was before or will be afterward. No one there remembers the days, a quarter-century before, when the finest people came down from New Orleans, even sometimes from as far away as St. Louis, in summer-white suits and batiste dresses, straw hats all around, to take their recreation, to drink mint juleps on verandas that have since disappeared—the days when Grand Isle was grand.

Jolie-Gray's mother has fretted and whined about Jolie-Gray's impossibility for over two years. It is a whine that rises to a wheedle and then to a keen, with an undertone of ravening roar, like a waterfall in a deep cave. But there are neither caves nor waterfalls anywhere around, only the Delta, and cottonmouth moccasins sticking their heads up out of the river, pale-brown as too-milky coffee, and slithering s-shaped back down again. There are only dried grass, and parched dirt, and rusting Nehi signs on the road.

Several matters are involved, are—to put it one way—under Bertille Boisseneau's skin, or—as she puts it—are "stuck in her craw." Jolie-Gray involuntarily imagines her mother as a white leghorn pecking about in the straw, nipping up pieces of oyster shell. Jolie-Gray has nicknamed one of the best laying hens, "Madame Sniffee," because of her high-stepping chicken hauteur, her seeming almost to flare her little beak-nostrils when Jolie-Gray goes out back past the wire fence in her red rubber boots to strew corn for the flock. Madame Sniffee has, the previous month, swallowed the string from a feed sack. Jolie-Gray's father had to get out the sheep-dip and the single-edged razor and surgically extract the string, with its little metal tag-end, from the soft pouch of skin at the base of the hen's throat.

She deletes the memory of Madame Sniffee's cut-open crop, and her father extracting that string, pulling it out, and out, and out, so many feet of it, an interminable snake of string, and she deletes that unsummoned imagining of her mother, who says she herself has something stuck in her craw. That picture just will not do.

Nonetheless, in Bertille Boisseneau's acerbic and self-assured framing of matters, Jolie-Gray just does not listen to anyone. Bertille has said it again and again: Jolie-Gray seems to think she's a star, as if she expects somebody to send her a telegram and a train ticket to Hollywood so she can plop her hand in the cement by that Chinese theater alongside Errol Flynn's.

Jolie-Gray's eyes invariably contract—small wild purple touch-me-nots, shutting down and pulling back—when her mother's voice swoops its long, buzzard-black arc in the air. She wants nothing more than her mother's love. Her father's is steady and sure, but her mother's? Jolie-Gray thinks hard and seriously about the matter.

She walks all the way to Saint Clothilde's to pray about this, to do a more thorough examination of conscience before the Blessed

Sacrament itself, exposed on the side altar for twenty-four hours. The blindingly white wafer is stuck up there—smack!—in the gold, lollipop-shaped monstrance, sandwiched between little round windows, with all of its gold curlicues radiating.

Sister Felicitas has said—and she did go to college way up at the motherhouse and does know the facts of this—that the jewels embedded in those filigreed arms include seventeen actual pearls from the Sea of Japan, brought up by native divers, and eight genuine rubies dug out of the earth in Ceylon. Jolie-Gray wonders why there are seventeen pearls, not sixteen, not eighteen; the rays of the monstrance, after all, spread out in bilateral symmetry.

Jolie-Gray imagines the church in deep night, after the pink neon sign at Aucoin's Bar down the street is shut off, and the Gendrons' porchlight, and the single bare bulb in the Comeauxs' rear kitchen that sways every time someone walks on the rickety floor. Profound darkness. She tries to imagine the silence. She wonders if mice come out then, whether there might be scurrying sounds. She imagines a pearl popping out of the monstrance and clittering across the floor. She can see the mouse rolling that pearl to its hole in the sacristy, invisible under the shelf where Father Matherne keeps the unconsecrated hosts.

Jolie-Gray puts on her silk bandanna with the cherry blossoms, the stamped picture so detailed that the pink flowers' pistils and stamens look real, photographic. She bought this on a trip to New Orleans and has been saving it for some special time, she could not figure what. When she ties the knot under her chin, the blossoms clump up together and lose themselves in the beige silk. She prays in the last pew, in shadow. She begs for enlightenment. What is it she keeps doing to rile her mother so? No answer comes.

One thick candle in its red glass cylinder burns near the monstrance. The light dances over the gold rays, and flickers, and almost seems to make a whooshing sound, like mystic wind. The lit candle is meant to direct all eyes to itself, to the fact that Jesus is *here,* and not in the tabernacle as He usually is.

For a split second, Jolie-Gray's mind tells itself that the leaping, cavorting red light—there is a wind coming through the side door that leads to the priests' yard—resembles Hell, perhaps seems to be coming from Hell. She crosses herself. That will not do, either. The gold-filigree doors of the empty tabernacle gape open. There is something eerie about this, and somehow obscene, as if Jesus—looking just like a pale Necco wafer—were naked there in the flesh, tiny as a pink King Cake baby, sandwiched in glass, on the side altar. Jolie-Gray squashes that thought quickly and prays three Hail Marys for penance, and then seven more. Ten should do it. No wonder her mother says she is a horrid thing, she thinks. Where could such a thought come from but Hell itself?

One Saturday afternoon, someone has left a pamphlet containing a novena to Saint Jude, patron saint of the impossible, on the dark, rubbed-silken wood of the pew she slips into. Jolie-Gray prays the whole nine days of the novena without fail—all three densely printed pages of the pamphlet—asking for enlightenment, but she never can figure out what it is that she keeps doing wrong. She decides—but only for now; she'll go back and retry it—that perhaps understanding the thing is itself impossible.

So what is the job of Saint Jude, then, thinks Jolie-Gray? To preside over Impasse? She squints at the little flame over his head, like the curly topknot of a baby in some cartoon. She remembers the tiny back burner on the stove where her father, when he leaves for the shop, sets the coffee pot to warm while her mother sleeps, and the smell of the coffee grows denser, more chicoried, staler, all morning. She wonders whether Saint Jude, like the stove, had his head piped for natural gas.

The priest who came for the annual Mission had put almost everyone to sleep—the church was so hot, and he droned some long story about visiting the lepers at Carville. Almost everyone had tuned him out. Jolie-Gray, though, was enamored of one thing he'd preached. He said: Saint Augustine held that miracles are not contrary to nature, just contrary to *what we know of nature*.

Did Saint Jude preside, then, over openings-up of what we know of nature, crocuses of possibility that had been there all the time but to which our human minds, like crabbed wet pink cerebral intestines, had been heretofore blind?

The little girl in the mountains in France who regrew a leg that had been amputated by the wheels of a train: this had happened, most certainly, because Jolie-Gray had heard that it did, and had seen an artist's rendition of the girl standing, radiant, two-legged, in a courtyard. But a starfish could do that. So clearly, then, what we know of fish-nature might just be applied in the human sphere, and be called miracle.

She waggled her head as if to shake off the silly, irreverent thought. Other times when Jolie-Gray had done this—had had a thought so intense she became unaware there were others around her—her mother had seen her shake her head this way and been outraged. Jolie-Gray was, in her estimation, incalculably vain, and at that moment was—obviously!—displaying her hair, which, inexplicably, considering that both parents' hair was plain Cajun brown, danced in unruly corkscrews of strawberry blond. It sprang up the moment it dried after being washed, like small cool phosphorescent tongues of foxfire.

"As if!" her mother would say, unprompted, at any time at all. "Always showing off, no matter where you are. Parading around at school—you and your prissy straight A's, everybody just *making* over you. So prideful!" She rode that long *i* like a slick silver chute-the-chute. "Polishing up the whites of your saddle oxfords like you were going to be curtseying for the Pope! Or . . ." She tried to think of a charge more extreme. ". . . getting canonized! Cleaning the kitchen as if you were trying for some sort of prize—polish, polish, Miss Betty Crocker of Grand Isle!" Her mother made a sound of disgust. "You make me sick," she added, in case there was any doubt, seeming to choke on the string or the tag or the oyster shell and to threaten to upchuck.

When Bertille wrote to her cousin Lucette Thibodeaux Marsh, on Esplanade Avenue, she did not say these things. Instead, she wrote, licking the lead of her pencil and rehearsing the words out loud in a tone she thought sounded genteel: "Jolie-Gray is fifteen now and a lovely girl. I would appreciate it if she could stay with you to finish high school in the city, and I am sure that in return she could be of assistance to you with the children." She misspelled *fifteen* and *appreciate* and *assistance*.

Lucette had been the third-prettiest girl in Grand Isle in her day. Bertille Boisseneau looked up from the note she was writing, in some surprise, blinking in the dust motes that danced in the over-bright light through the window, realizing how quickly, in some ways, these nineteen years had passed. Lucette had left Grand Isle to marry the skinny optometrist she had met in the Maison Blanche department store when he fitted her for glasses.

Bertille remembered how glad she had been at first that Lucette, the beauty, was not going to have to wear glasses, and the glaucous, glazed envy she'd felt, that Lucette was—instead of becoming a bespectacled old maid—getting out of Grand Isle, and marrying someone she thought to be money and class.

Three years later, rejoicing that at least she would have her own moment of glory, have a pretty wedding in springtime, with bridesmaids in mint-green organdy, Bertille had married Gray Boisseneau, son of Clement Boisseneau, who owned the gasoline station. Gray repaired small engines. He had a clear forehead and very brown eyes and big muscles that bulged in the sleeves of his work-shirts.

Within the year, Jolie-Gray was born. She became her father's darling. Bertille found she was not fond of that. Her cousin Lucette, however, had been unable to conceive, and Bertille found that some small compensation.

One day when she came back from the doctor's, Bertille told Gray that she had a heart condition and they should not be sleeping together. She was hanging up her coat when she said this, so he could not see her face. She said something about palpitations, and murmurs, and little green pills. Gray blinked mildly, gathered his brows in a furry rosette for a second, and acceded. The little green pills never did appear.

The ease of this bothered Bertille. It made her wonder whether he had something else going on. Perhaps the barmaid from Aucoin's, or the girl with the harelip who did the shop's books. That would be just like him, she thought.

Just before Easter the year she moved away from Grand Isle, Lucette had showed Bertille a picture of herself with the doctor the day they got engaged, an overexposed snapshot taken in Audubon Park in New Orleans. Behind the pair was the lagoon, where a couple of paddleboats were docked. They almost seemed to rock in the water. On either side Spanish moss draped languidly from the live oaks' low branches.

Had it been several decades later, the snapshot might have been in color, filled in with myriad shades of green. Instead, the picture was black, white, and gray. Lucette's face and the optometrist's— his name was Lamberton Marsh—had their features flattened by the harsh sunlight. Lucette's right hand tried to shade her eyes and seemed to fail. The optometrist looked for all the world like old photographs of James Joyce (a man born twenty years before Lamberton Marsh), with a thin, bony face, hats that made him look thinner and bonier, spectacles thick as the bottoms of Courvoisier bottles. A maker of glasses so that other people might read, though no reader himself, Dr. Marsh did not know and would never know James Joyce, or that he resembled him almost as a twin. This Lamberton Marsh, standing next to Lucette in her pale cotton dress, peered out of the photograph in a sort of daz- zlement, as if he were struck stock-still by something more than that bright sunlight. All around them the grass grew, in black and white.

Lucette and Lamberton Marsh finally had two babies, a boy and a girl, after going all the way to Minnesota to some clinic—What, *Minnesota?* asked people; what would they possibly have in *Minnesota* that we don't have here?—and taking some pills, then shots, and then giving up. Bertille heard the news and felt smug.

People in Grand Isle to whom Bertille told this made spitting sounds and said, "That's what she gets, trusting those Yankee crook doctors. She gets nothing! *Rien!*"

Six months later, folded into Lucette and Lamberton's Christmas card (which had a Dalmatian in a stocking cap on the front and their names inside in gilt Old English lettering, printed by an actual printer's shop), came a note with the news: Lucette was expecting.

She said she had prayed to Saint Jude, the patron saint of impossible causes. She said Saint Jude was the brother of Jesus and thus very special.

"What!" said Bertille out loud, reading the back of the card in her living room, all alone. "The brother of Jesus!" This was what Protestants said. Lucette must have met some Protestants up in Minnesota, was all she could think. Catholics called Mary "ever Virgin," and so when the Bible said Jesus had *brothers and sisters* it really meant *friends*. It meant *cousins*. It spoke metaphorically. But then Protestants thought everything the Bible said was flat-out literal.

Bertille went on reading: It seemed, Lucette wrote, that Saint Jude had been neglected so long, all these centuries, with no one praying to him, because of his name, you see. His name was so much like *Judas,* the betrayer, that everyone shunned poor old Jude. So a couple of people—she didn't know where this had happened, but somewhere—prayed to him to make him feel good, and wouldn't you know but he did some spectacular miracles out of gratitude at being noticed. This made good human sense to Lucette, and she thought, Even in heaven we'll be human.

Lucette said she was going to place an ad in the *New Orleans Times-Picayune*—humbly, no name attached—that said *Thank You, Saint Jude* and gave clear prayer-instructions so more people would know how to pray to him. The ad would have a picture of Saint Jude, with his little flame topknot, and Old English lettering because this would get people's attention. She put in parentheses the price of the ad. It was the cost of two weeks' groceries in Grand Isle, with gasoline for Gray's truck thrown in.

Jolie-Gray knows none of this when, a full decade later, she comes upon the Saint Jude novena leaflet in the pew. She prays independently. Saint Jude is new to her.

When, months after that, Jolie-Gray leaves for the Marshes', she carries a black Gladstone bag that Bertille had rummaged for in the garage rafters. It is old and cracked, so Jolie-Gray has rubbed the leather with boot salve until it is soft and lustrous. Bertille passes by while Jolie-Gray is sitting with her legs hanging over the knobby footboard of her bed, rubbing ointment into the dark leather. Bertille clicks her tongue; she sighs a dramatic sigh; she shakes her head side to side. There is no mistaking her dissatisfaction. This is precisely what she cannot stand about Jolie-Gray: *Nothing satisfies the ridiculous girl*. She can't just *take* the Gladstone bag; she has to gussy it up. It is a good thing Bertille does not know that Jolie-Gray has rubbed down the interior, too, and made several sachets to put into the bag to disperse the mold smell. The girl's excesses are beyond reason.

Lucette Marsh is pleased to see what a fine, cheerful girl her sour cousin has produced. She will be a wonderful sitter for little Vincent and Cara Nell, and from the letter the girl sent, introducing herself with great politeness, Lucette has seen that she writes a fine Palmer hand, with seagull-wing *r*'s, and exquisitely looped capital *W*'s. Jolie-Gray will be a godsend to help the children with their homework. Furthermore, Bertille wrote in her own letter that the girl baked a fine pecan pie and made excellent gumbo. Bertille did not mention that she got very tired of hearing the neighbors' compliments on Jolie-Gray's skills, nor that she herself deemed the pie far too sweet and the gumbo so thick that she wanted to gag on it.

When Bertille tells Jolie-Gray again and again that *no one* in Grand Isle can stand her, she is leaving out the neighbors, the nuns, and the girl's father. Jolie-Gray knows this at some level, but it does not matter, really. Her own mother just does not love her.

Now it is the first week after the end of school. Summer started in April, and by late morning daily the heat rises wavery, whoofty, implacable, off the tall-oak-shaded avenue.

Before Jolie-Gray came to New Orleans, Vincent and Cara Nell were by late morning irritable and bored. But now Jolie-Gray takes them on streetcar rides all over town. The fare is only five cents. Lucette keeps a penny jar next to the Luzianne coffee-can of congealed bacon grease, there on the enamel-topped vitrine that stands next to the stove. The penny jar is always full.

On the olive-green trolley with its shiny, hard wooden seats, they can ride and ride. After they have transferred twice and ridden a couple of hours, they can get off at Plum Street and walk three blocks to the snowball stand, buy three snowballs—strawberry, spearmint, and coconut. Cara Nell says, "Red," and then Vincent says, "Green," and then Jolie-Gray says, "Coconut." Then they window-shop in the Oak Street stores, go to the library, stop at the wading pool. After this there is the endless trolley-ride back. The children come home happy, ready to go to bed early, before it is even dark.

Lucette feels relieved by Jolie-Gray's able assistance, but also, now, faintly puzzled and useless.

Jolie-Gray seems not to tire of these travels. Whenever they pass a church, she and the children tiptoe into its coolness. She takes out a little white-lace handkerchief for herself and one for Cara Nell. They balance them carefully atop their heads, because God frowns on bareheaded women, or priests do, and then the three kneel in the shadows.

Jolie-Gray prays to Saint Jude that her mother might love her, that she might be pleasing to her, that she might understand what she has been doing all this time to be so odious and unacceptable. Vincent, slipped down in the seat so that he is half-sitting on his neck, plays with a Mexican tricolored straw monkey-finger-trap that Jolie-Gray has bought him at Woolworth's. Cara Nell draws a mustache on a pamphlet about Saint Thérèse of Lisieux, the tubercular Little Flower of the Carmelites, then adds a fat cigar. Its penciled smoke spirals heavenward through the printed shower of rose petals.

Lucette, in her fifth-wheelness, is beginning to think there is something sinister in the girl, that Bertille sent the girl here to make her unhappy. Jolie-Gray made crawfish étouffée the previous Sunday afternoon, and Dr. Marsh remarked on its smoothness, its perfectly seasoned savor. Lucette rearranged her shoulders, discomfited, and listened to her spine make cellophane crackling sounds. She did not like the tone of his voice. She looked at his brandy-bottle glasses and could not see where his eyes were focused.

One afternoon the thermometer on the porch reads a hundred. Even in the shade it is in the high nineties. This is no day for a trolley-ride. Lucette has gone in a taxicab to Pearl Rouilleaux's salon, which the woman runs from the rear of her house, to have her hair chestnut-rinsed and marcelled. Then she will have been driven, in a different cab, to the Fontainebleau Ladies' Social Club, where there are dozens of ceiling fans, tall potted palm trees curving over the white-linened tables, bottomless vats of cracked ice for mint tea and shrimp cocktails, and shiny black maids, two to a table, waving gilt-flowered folding fans.

Jolie-Gray and the children sit in front of the big window fan in the kitchen and let the hot breeze hit their faces. They pretend to be cool, but really the sweat is just drying and cracking. Jolie-Gray teaches Vincent and Cara Nell to play bourrée. There is the sound of the cards slapping down, slick against the enamel of the table-top, the sound of the cards sliding into and out of the spreads in their hands, the sound of the deck being shuffled expertly and smoothly by Jolie-Gray. Sighing sounds; sounds as they slurp their tea, whose ice has melted completely away. No one talks. It is just too hot.

After an hour or so, Cara Nell begins rubbing her eyes. Within moments she falls asleep curled where she sits, on a soft chair she has carried into the kitchen. It barely fit through the door, and Lucette would likely be horrified to find it there, but the chair as well as the secret will be safe. Vincent lays his head gently, as if it were injured, on the cool edge of the enamel table and does not move. He rolls his eyes at Jolie-Gray like a silly dog.

"Do you want a nap, too?" she asks. He shakes his head slowly, emphatically, no. He is playing at being a mute. He seems to have become a dog. They sit staring out through the fan's rotating blades. In the street, they hear the tinny clamor of Eskimo Eddie's ice-cream truck. The strange ding-a-ling sound flattens out and deforms as it twists through the fan blades.

"Do you want an Eskimo Pie, then?" Jolie-Gray says. She can hear voices of children shaping themselves around the noise of the vendor's bell. There are half a dozen children hidden behind the façades of these grand houses. Hot days, often no one comes outdoors at all until the silver tintinnabulation heralds the truck's coming. Then they stand sighing, waiting in line without shoving—it is just too hot—staring at the somehow scary grin of Pierre, Pierre, the Polar Bear, the picture on the side of the truck.

Vincent, now a basset hound, nods his doggy head: *Yes, oh, yes, doggy want Eskimo Pie.* Vincent pants a dog-pant, his tongue hanging out pink and child-perfect, and drags himself toward the kitchen.

"Vincent?" calls Jolie-Gray. "I am going to take a shower, OK? I am so hot."

She picks up a pie pan that sits in the dish-drain and fans herself with it. The air scarcely moves. She says, "Whew!" and puts the pan back into the drying rack. The air seems to have turned thick with the heat, as if summertime had been cooking down progressively, day after day, like a brown sugar caramelizing, until it has reached its limit and threatens to transform into something else—dangerous, poisonous—or to consume the pan, or to catch fire.

She turns to walk, barefoot, enjoying the feel of the smooth Esplanade Avenue waxy-wood floors, to the bathroom she and the children use. Lucette and her husband have their own bathroom, at the other end. Its water-lily wallpaper makes the room look—if not feel—green and cool as underwater, and it smells of Lucette's loose face-powder. As she passes the little ceramic gas heater in the living room, she is astonished to remember winter's existence at all: She remembers the little blue flames in the open gas heaters at home and how she used to watch them, when she was a child, after she was supposed to be sleeping.

Cara Nell will sleep through. The house in the heat, with her father at work and her mother at the Fontainebleau Ladies' Club, is quiet, and Cara Nell's thick post-bourrée sleep is impervious to the tinklings of Eskimo Eddie's bell.

"Just eat your Eskimo Pie in the kitchen, please. Not in the living room. You know your mama," says Jolie-Gray.

Vincent angles his head and gives her another basset-hound look; even his ears seem to droop. Then he runs heavily, slowly, despite his little-boy lightness, as if he is fighting Jupiter gravity, toward the ice-cream man's tinkling bell. Everything is moving so lugubriously today that Jolie-Gray is certain Eddie will wait. Surely the truck is trapped too in this tarry heat.

Jolie-Gray turns on the faucet in the big claw-footed bathtub. The pipes make a great deal of noise before they will release their water. A second's lurch of brownish rust-water precedes the clear, and then the noise dissipates. Jolie-Gray sweeps the brown water down the drain with the heel of her hand and jams the white rubber plug into the hole.

Outside, the bell has stopped jangling. Eddie is helping the children to Dixie cups, popsicles, Eskimo pies, taking their nickels and dimes. He is telling the children that he bribed the weatherman so he could have this good business today. They smile, but they don't understand what he means, or that this is a joke. Adults always say odd things like this.

The bathroom is an ad hoc, awkward thing, an afterthought made of space stolen from adjacent rooms. It is shaped like a railroad car. The house was built, Lucette says, not long after the "War between the States." It seems to Jolie-Gray that Lucette puts it this way to minimize the South's loss, as if it were a generalized skirmish, with various states throwing pots and pans and rolling pins, then everyone going home to cool their tempers.

Jolie-Gray unbuttons her sundress and steps out of it. Then she realizes that she ought to shut the two doors, one at each end of the railroad-car bathroom—Vincent will be back quickly—so she shuts first one, then the other.

Over the sound of the running water, she hears the front door close heavily. Outside, there is still the clamor of children's voices. Jolie-Gray tugs the pink shower curtain with its fat gardenias around the ring overhead, to close it, and turns on the shower, spraying her hair just a little. She reaches for her shower cap on the wall peg and slips it over her head. Her springy hair fights the confinement. Some tendrils escape.

She climbs into the tub and pulls the curtain around herself. She feels the elastic of the shower cap biting into her forehead. She leans to turn the faucets to make the water hotter; then she will have the further pleasure of cooling off afterward.

She feels music rising in her throat. The week before, she went with the senior Marshes to the opera at the Municipal Auditorium, to Verdi's *Aïda*. Dr. Marsh had the tickets, and there was a dinner beforehand, so Jolie-Gray took the trolley and met them there. Lucette had the colored girl who did the ironing stay with the children. Jolie-Gray does not know Italian, of course, so she is garbling made-up words into the shower and humming in between, but she has the pure, clear, joyous melody of the funeral march firmly in memory, and she is singing it: *bum-bum, ba-pa-da bum bum, deedle ee bum-bum*.

The near door bursts open, and she shrieks and grabs the shower curtain around herself. "Blam-blam-blam!" shouts Vincent. He is an outlaw now—she can tell from the handkerchief he has across his mouth, like the outlaws in Saturday serials at the Paris Theatre—with a white-handled silvery gun, and he is chasing another cowboy, in a silly straw hat, a boy from down the street. Clearly the ice cream has not lasted long in this heat.

"Vincent!" says Jolie-Gray, laughing through the gap in the curtain. She is holding the semi-transparent curtain around herself, and it sticks to her skin, half-outlining her form. "You and John-Lloyd get *out* of here! My word!" She composes her face, getting rid of the laugh, calculating whether there is any way she can recapture her dignity. "You *do* know better than this."

Vincent, mischievous, knowing his advantage, aims his gun straight at her heart behind the pink curtain. "Blam!" he shouts. "You are so so so dead!" Then he careens out the other end of the bathroom, after the neighbor boy, slamming the door behind him.

Jolie-Gray sighs and climbs out, dripping a clear pool onto the black-and-white floor tile, and shuts the near door again, heavily, then climbs back into the tub.

The pleasure of the water is exquisite. She lets the heat seep into every pore, turning the white ceramic C handle totally off now. She soaks the fat sea-sponge with fruit-smelling, rose-amber shampoo, and she slathers herself. She is singing into the spray. Aïda is marching right into the tomb, and the whole chorus's voices uphold her.

Suddenly the door bursts open once more, and here come Vincent and John-Lloyd, yelling, shrieking, blubbering, wanting attention.

"Oh, boys!" Jolie-Gray says. "I am ashamed of you!" They run out the far door, and before she can even call after them, they are back in, through the near door. "You are going to wake up your sister, and *then* you'll be sorry! She'll whine and tag after you! Shame!"

"Blammity-blam-blam!" yells Vincent. This time he is the sheriff. He is wearing the star on the sweaty button-front shirt Lucette insists he wear—he must on no account go shirtless, like riffraff, despite the thermometer. John-Lloyd, by contrast, is shirtless: There's nowhere to pin a star.

"No fa-a-a-ir!" shouts Jolie-Gray. She is, after all, only fifteen.

The boys are gone, and it is quiet. But she does not trust this. It seems the enterprise of her shower is near-hopeless. She pulls off the cap and hangs it back on its peg with a sigh. She climbs out of the tub once more, careful not to slip and fall in the chain of lakes her drips have made on the tile. She closes the far door, then goes to the near door.

She peers out to make sure the boys are not sneaking up on her. as she leans into the four-in-the-afternoon sun of the bedroom, the light falls on her hair, fresh-sprung out of its shower cap, as if light had just been reinvented, falls on her body in such a way that any painter would stand breathless. A beaded drop gathers at her collarbone and rolls down, down, to the tip of her perfect, fresh, gravity-defying fifteen-year-old right breast, and quivers there. Her ribs beneath the thin skin pinked by the heat of the shower are outlined with breathtaking delicacy. She has grabbed a towel to her middle, and she wads it at her cleft, for some infinitesimal shred of protection or privacy in this invasion.

Then she sees him: Dr. Marsh, in his black suit and hat, standing next to the chaise longue with its bright peony-print slipcovers, staring. She has no doubt, despite his thick glasses, where his eyes are resting. In her shock, she involuntarily drops the towel. The skin of her thighs is white, and the hair at their tops that same strawberry hue, half-dried by the press of the towel and now springing up in the light. She tries to vanish back into the bathroom's semi-shadow, half-slips in a puddle, catches herself on the doorjamb, says, "Oh!"

Two seconds have passed.

She is staring directly at Dr. Marsh's face, and he is staring directly at her naked body. Around the corner come John-Lloyd and Vincent. The two boys stop dead, looking first at Jolie-Gray and then at Dr. Marsh.

Four seconds have passed.

Vincent says, "Oops," in a tone that is the strangest Jolie-Gray has ever heard, delighted, terrified, wretched, flippant. John-Lloyd just stands looking straight at the tips of Jolie-Gray's breasts. He cannot understand why they are so different from his mother's.

Five seconds have passed.

Dr. Marsh takes off his hat and holds it in front of him, at the height of the hang of his hands, for what reason Jolie-Gray, rooted to the spot, two seconds more, cannot comprehend: It is as if he were *honoring* her, and still he stands staring. Is the stare *bold*? Is it *stunned*? Is it simply *slow to react*?

She steps back into the bathroom and closes the door, saying nothing. She is shaking. The shower keeps pouring, splat-sounds on the porcelain tub, blat-sounds on the curtain. On the other side of the door, no one says anything. There is a sound of the floor creaking slightly—someone or everyone going away.

For nearly a quarter-hour Jolie-Gray sits on the tub's edge this way, in silence. It is as if everyone had vaporized instantaneously. The shower keeps pouring, splat-blat, until finally Jolie-Gray notices and turns it off.

She puts her dress on and wipes the tile floor with the towel. She is telling herself stories: *Dr. Marsh came home early because . . . because . . .* She cannot think of a reason, but there is a reason. *Dr. Marsh was coming after the boys, with their noise, because he had seen Cara Nell sleeping. He did not know Jolie-Gray was in the shower.* But then *what*? And *what*?

She wants the weather to have cooled off while she was in the bathroom, enough that she can put on three layers of clothing, be wrapped up, invisible. This has not happened. She has been charged with readying dinner this evening, so she puts one foot in front of the other and heads to the blood-smelling butcher's for veal wrapped in white paper to make pepper steak.

Where are the boys? Where is Dr. Marsh? Irrelevant. She must make dinner. Lucette is not home yet. Cara Nell sleeps like a drugged cat in the chair, curled up tight.

No one appears until six o'clock, and then they all appear simultaneously. Cara Nell wakes, unfurling slowly in amazement, her face wrinkled and sweaty and squashed. Lucette notices that the soft chair has been moved into the kitchen, but there is so much else at the forefront that the chair is no issue at all.

Jolie-Gray is perspiring and salty again from an hour of cooking. The green peppers that cling to the steak in its pan are cooked to the perfect softness Dr. and Mrs. Marsh are so fond of. She tries not to look at either of them, but she feels Dr. Marsh's eyes, through their thick lenses, trying to catch hers. Is he trying to calm her or warn her, or what is he trying to do? No one speaks. Cara Nell looks blinking from one face to the next. Vincent plays with his little soft pieces of green pepper, lining them up like a train on the rim of his plate.

Jolie-Gray says, "I have a headache," and indeed she does. She thinks she may throw up. She goes to her room. On her prickly bedspread, she lies facedown. She does not cry. She does not know when she falls asleep, but she hears the door open and sits upright. It is almost dark, so it must be past nine. It is Lucette, and Jolie-Gray can tell from her face that she knows. But what does she know?

"Jolie-Gray," says Lucette, her voice tight. "Vincent told me what happened."

Jolie-Gray sits trying to gather her wits. "What happened," she echoes. She blinks. She frowns.

"He said . . . he was in the wrong," Lucette says. She has this Grand Isle probity: Someone is always right, someone is always wrong, and both must be very clear. "That he and his little friend ran through the bathroom."

"Oh, ma'am," says Jolie-Gray. "They're just kids. Children. Please, don't punish him."

"But I understand that there is more," Lucette says.

"Yes ma'am," says Jolie-Gray docilely. She wonders if Lucette has similar categories for the doctor, if he too must be either in the right or in the wrong, and if he is in the right, whether that puts Jolie-Gray in the wrong.

"That Dr. Marsh had come home because of the power failure at the store, and that you came out of the bathroom stark naked and stood right in front of him. Displaying your body. Pushing your little pink titties at him."

"No ma'am," Jolie-Gray says. She hears her voice rising in pitch. She tries not to be rude. She flushes. "Who said that?" she asks, and she knows instantly that she cannot be anything but in the wrong in this whole interaction.

"No one *said* that," says Lucette. She is smoothing her dress, standing straight in the doorway, in shadow. "I'm not stupid."

"No ma'am, you're not," Jolie-Gray agrees. She feels as if something, a weight, has let loose in her, that she is a balloon and will drift away, up over Esplanade Avenue, all the way to the river, then follow the current into the Gulf, follow a fish that has swum all the way from Minnesota and will lose itself in the Caribbean, looking around in the green depths, its fishy mouth opening, shutting, and opening. Then she *prays* she will drift away like a balloon.

"What did you *think* you were doing?" Lucette says. Jolie-Gray hears her mother's edge in Lucette's voice. "What the *hell* did you think you were doing?"

Jolie-Gray feels a defense rise and pushed it down. There is too much at stake here. High school is at stake. High school in New Orleans. Her honor. She almost laughs at this last: How can she think she has honor to lose?

"I thought I was closing the door," Jolie-Gray says, mildly, "That's all, ma'am." She pauses a moment. "I had no idea that Dr. Marsh would be . . ." she tries to think how to say it. "I had no idea Dr. Marsh was, umm, home, or that I, umm, and then there he was, with . . . his eyes . . ." She trails off into stupid slack mumbling. Yes, there is no way to be right.

"Are you going to blame Dr. Marsh?" Lucette demands, her voice shriller now.

"No ma'am," says Jolie-Gray. "No ma'am. It all was an accident." She flushes, with rage, with despair. That word *all* was so stupid. She just wants to take it back. There was not enough *anything* to call it "all."

She wants Vincent to explain it better, but poor little boy, he is only nine, *he* does not understand. She wants Dr. Mash to exonerate her, but he will not, because someone must be right, and a clear explanation would make him wrong. But then, she thinks, *that* is not quite right either. He has the power here, and all he would have to do is to explain to Lucette. But perhaps it is not that simple. She remembers his eyes in the kitchen: exhorting her, pleading, colluding?

"I certainly hope not," says Lucette. Jolie-Gray tries to remember what she hopes *not*. "Well." The word comes down hard, like a rock landing in soft grass: no damage, but definite impact. "Well. I suppose these last weeks have been a silly illusion for me, Jolie-Gray. I did trust you."

"Yes ma'am," says Jolie-Gray. "And you can."

Before Jolie-Gray sees the back of Lucette's hand, it hits, with the hard little knuckles, the marcasite ring with its multiple, intricate onyx and diamond-chip surfaces, flat across Jolie-Gray's mouth. She tastes blood with the tip of her tongue. Her eyes widen and well up. She tries not to cry. A subtler and more complex response seems called for.

"I cannot imagine how I can avoid telling this to your mother," Lucette says, exasperated. She is looking at the pale blue hydrangeas in the wallpaper, which are gray in the dusk. She is looking at Jolie-Gray's Sunday hat on the hat stand. She is looking at her own hands and thinking that they are beginning to freckle, or age, or change somehow else. "It will break her heart."

"Yes ma'am," says Jolie-Gray, meaning not *It will break her heart,* because Jolie-Gray knows Bertille would be gladdened by this even though she would know Lucette's charges as false. She means, instead, *I expect you will tell her whatever you choose.*

"I suppose if you were simply to vanish, I could tell her you ran away, without giving details of what happened here," Lucette says.

Jolie-Gray says, "Ma'am? Vanish?"

"You know the word," Lucette says, her tones cane-syrupy with condescension. "Disappear. *Poof.*"

"Vanish, ma'am?"

Lucette sighs at her denseness. "I can provide you with a minimal severance pay . . . oh, a *generous* severance . . . if you will leave tonight." She looks out at the purpling sky and says, expansively, "Tomorrow morning, at the very latest, without ever showing your face again."

"Go *where*, ma'am?" says Jolie-Gray. She feels as if she has just been bodily picked up and thrown onto a boat going over the edge of the world.

"Anywhere," Lucette says, vinegary as her cousin Bertille, moving into the room and standing between Jolie-Gray and the dresser. She seems far too close. "Anywhere but here. Anywhere but within a several-mile circle of Esplanade Avenue." She pauses a moment. "*And* a several-mile circle of Maison Blanche Optical."

Jolie-Gray considers the map in her mind. Lucette would seem to be including all of New Orleans in these two interlocked circles.

Lucette goes on. "Furthermore, I must have your absolute promise that you *will* not go back to Grand Isle. I want no cock-and-bull stories about Dr. Marsh circulating, and *certainly* not in Grand Isle."

"Oh," says Jolie-Gray. "I have no stories about Dr. Marsh. There is nothing to tell." Again, Jolie-Gray's tongue flicks out to lick the little rivulet of salty, ferrous blood Lucette's slap has drawn. She wishes for invisibility so that Lucette will not interpret her tongue's poking at the split in her lip as criticism, chiding Lucette for her lack of control. It is just that the blood feels so messy. She thinks: *There is nowhere to go in Grand Isle anyway.*

Lucette observes to herself that the girl looks like a snake when she does this, and that it is well enough this happened early on.

Jolie-Gray sees herself in the triptych mirror behind Lucette. She notes with some surprise the incredulous lift of her forehead. She sees something like terror, or death. The idea that she might resemble a snake to Lucette—poisonous, powerful—does not occur to her.

The sound of the door shutting behind Lucette is heavy and hollow. The rest of the house seems so silent. An hour or so later, a small envelope slides under Jolie-Gray's door. There are no sounds of footsteps, no floor-creakings, before or after this. The envelope is face-up and has, in Lucette's prim, cursive hand, Jolie-Gray's name written on it, so strangely: *Miss Boisseneau,* as if no distance from Jolie-Gray could possibly be enough. But then why should that surprise her? Lucette has just told her plainly.

Jolie-Gray lies atop her coverlet all night and does not sleep. When the sky begins to lighten, to a periwinkle hue and then to lavender, she rises and packs her Gladstone bag. She strips the bed and folds the spread, neatly. She turns to look at the room and make sure she has changed the position of nothing; she will leave everything as she found it, as if she had not ever been here. She closes her eyes for a moment and feels her lids cool over eyes that are heated by sleeplessness. She drops the sheets into the laundry bin on the back porch as she passes, and she tiptoes down the back stairs.

It is pleasant and cool, walking out in the morning, but she has no idea where she is going. She has Lucette's envelope, and she has opened it and seen that indeed there is a substantial amount of money there. The feeling that seems to radiate from the soft bills is peculiar: It is as if no amount of money is too great for Lucette to pay, with joy, to get rid of her, just as no distance from her is sufficient.

She walks for miles as the sky brightens. She stops at the Café Du Monde. She has been here before, with the Marshes, on a Sunday morning after church. She orders a cup of the chicory coffee, by reputation so strong that it could dissolve her spoon. She scoops several mounds of white sugar into the dark drink, and somehow is surprised when she pulls the spoon out still intact.

The place's theatrical feel is romantic to her in the desolation of the moment. She imagines herself as an actress, and the lights around the mirrors that line the walls as bulbs in this actress's dressing room. Then she thinks: *I suppose I* am *embarking on a new role.*

Then she thinks: *I cannot be doing this.*

And she thinks: *But I am doing this.*

Once again she thinks: *Saint Jude, patron of all things impossible, be with me.* She says it again, out loud, whispering: "Be with me."

She looks at the other patrons of the café. There is a saggy-faced overly made-up older woman with brilliant red hair who has clearly been up all night. The smile on her lips is defiantly cheerful, but her eyes are the saddest Jolie-Gray has ever seen. *A whore,* she thinks. She is surprised at her own thoughts. The woman looks as if she ought to have been—perhaps was—painted by a French artist visiting New Orleans several decades earlier.

Something impels her to go over and sit by the woman. The woman turns squeakily in her stool and scowls at her as if she is an irritant. Jolie-Gray has anticipated this. She smiles at the woman, says nothing. No rejection by anyone else today has the power to hurt her. She is past that.

Jolie-Gray swivels to look out at the morning. She breathes it in: pink light, the air of the café heady with chicory-coffee aroma, an aura of promise. The sun is now fully up, and the sky is already starting to bleach out with its brilliant light. She knows she must move along but feels she should say something to this woman. She doesn't know what. "You know, it will be fine," Jolie-Gray says, smiling.

The woman breaks down into sudden dry, racking sobs.

Jolie-Gray thinks, *What now?* She gives the woman a capacious white paper napkin, and the woman puts her face into it. "Nothing is impossible," Jolie-Gray says. She thinks, *Why did I say that?*

The red-haired woman clears her throat. "Honey," she says in a gravelly, throaty voice, world-weary, smoke-worn. The tone is unreadable, but Jolie-Gray braces to be told to go to Hell. "Oh, honey, thank you," the woman says. Jolie-Gray can see into her eyes, see back fifty years to a girl her own age wearing a white batiste dress and three petticoats, twirling a parasol in Jackson Square, all the azaleas in bloom. The girl's hair is a delicate red, and the broad moiré sash of her dress a bright pink. This surprises and unnerves her.

"Have a really nice day," Jolie-Gray says as she leaves, and the woman waves with the big napkin.

As she walks, she prays the memorized prayers to Saint Jude, and then adds her own free-form petitions, which swirl in the air like the trail of a biplane she once saw at Pontchartrain Beach, doing tricks high above the sand. All she really has wanted, has typically asked of Saint Jude, is her mother's love, to please her mother—this would fill some gaping hole in her heart—but today she needs an answer regarding what she must do next. Apparently she is truly as odious as Bertille had thought early on. She has failed at the Marshes', too. But she has just told the old whore there is nothing impossible. Does she believe it?

She walks all the way to Canal Street, then past it. She finds herself in front of the Roosevelt Hotel, its grand brass-bedecked canopy hanging over the sidewalk. She stands gawking at it. Though she has been up for hours, her face still in some way feels unopened, a morning face. The wiry uniformed doorman looks askance at her. She continues to stare. The doorman comes down the steps, slowly, one at a time, as if to give her time to run away. He looks at her up close, as if she could not see him.

"What are you lookin' for, girl?" says the doorman. And then answers himself. "Work? Girl, you lookin' for work? Mr. Conigliari, he's looking for housekeepers."

Jolie-Gray blinks at him. She looks at the gold epaulets on his jacket. She looks at his fingernails, neat-clipped but deep-ridged and stained with tobacco. "Work," she repeats flatly. "Yes. Work."

He points her into the red-carpeted lobby. Then he half-apologizes, "Ain't nobody much workin' here this morning. Maybe you should come back. . . .Oh-oh! There! Yoo-hoo, Miz Vida-Jeanne. This young lady here might be just what you need."

The older woman looks at Jolie-Gray in some disbelief. "Today?" she asks, and her tone is as if they were picking up a conversation suspended some time ago, as if Jolie-Gray had applied and been approved and shown up in the nick of time.

"I can do this," says Jolie-Gray. "Yes ma'am. I can."

So she sets her Gladstone bag at the back of a linen closet, beside piles of towels, and cleans rooms at the Roosevelt, in a time when it is so difficult to get work that people are sleeping in alleys.

She wears a black uniform with a neat waistband and a white cut-work apron. She wears a little lace cap. She rents a room on Carondelet Street, three stories up, so that the urine and garbage smells from the alley diffuse and diminish somewhat before they reach her window. She is within the radius that Lucette has proscribed—the Maison Blanche building is not eight blocks away, across Canal Street—but this is the best she can manage, and Saint Jude has set this gift down plop in her lap. She begs Saint Jude's understanding of her disobedience of Lucette's order. But then, she reasons, he does not reciprocally expect the impossible from *her*.

She works for three years at the Roosevelt, stopping each day at the Jesuit church with its soaring Gothic-arch ceilings and fragrant banks of beeswax candles, unfolding her handkerchief on her head, praying to Saint Jude. She tries not to worry. She prays for her mother. She prays for her father. She prays for Lucette and Dr. Marsh and for their children. She sends money home to Grand Isle each month, with no return address on the envelope.

She wonders about Vincent and Cara Nell. She wishes she could send them something, a nice toy, a letter, but is pained thinking that Lucette would be outraged even at that gesture. She wonders what Dr. Marsh meant by that look he wore when he tried to catch her eye. She does not know that her father is very ill, soon to die, and grieves for her. She does not know that her mother is angry and envious that Gray cares for his daughter so much, even if he does not mention it often.

She never crosses paths with Dr. Marsh, despite the proximity of their workplaces. She credits Saint Jude with this favor. Once she sees a man who holds his shoulders like Dr. Marsh, from a distance, and she steps into a jewelry store till the man is safely past. The salesclerk smiles indulgently at her. Clearly she is not shopping for diamonds, wearing a Roosevelt Hotel maid's uniform.

She makes the hotel's beds tightly—no one can fold a sheet-corner as neatly as she can—and she polishes mirrors and marble dresser-tops and bathroom fixtures and tile till they shine.

One day a businessman visiting from the North tells her with a grandfatherly smile that she is a lovely girl. She blushes. She has forgotten that she is a lovely girl, if she ever knew it. She encounters him at midday three times during the week when she is airing his room and dusting the glass on the dresser.

She takes his suits to be cleaned, as she is supposed to, and runs the sweeper in his room, as she is supposed to. She writes directions to the Cabildo and Jean Lafitte's Blacksmith Shop so the man can go see them. She tells him where he can buy fine, comfortable Florsheim walking shoes, and which vendors have the best selection of postcards, and the name of a little store where he can find teacups and saucers that picture St. Louis Cathedral to bring home to his wife, and dancing donkey toys on plastic stands that say "Souvenir of the Vieux Carré" to bring home to his grandchildren, and boxes of creamy pecan pralines for his associates and neighbors.

When he checks out of the hotel, the man leaves her a tip in an envelope at the front desk. The tip is the equivalent of a week's wages. Miss Vida-Jeanne insists upon opening the envelope in front of Jolie-Gray before she gives it to her. Jolie-Gray does not object, but she does not understand the asymmetrical swoop of concern on Miss Vida-Jeanne's brow. "Thank you for your services," says the note. "You are a lovely girl." Miss Vida-Jeanne reads it aloud in a terrible voice. She scowls at Jolie-Gray.

"I told him where he could get a tea set that has the cathedral on it," Jolie-Gray says. "You know, that little shop the Italian lady runs? The teapot has all of Jackson Square painted on its side, and gold all around the rims." She pauses. "They're fluted," she adds, with her eyebrows raised in delight, thinking how much the gentleman's wife will be pleased by the gift.

Miss Vida-Jeanne frowns at her, furious. Jolie-Gray has seen this scowl before, in both Bertille and Lucette. Three years has done nothing to dim the look's menace.

She has been mortifying her flesh, fasting, as she has learned the saints did. She has read in a pamphlet at church that there is a woman far across the ocean in a small peasant village in Schleswig-Holstein who lives—today! in the modern world!—on the Eucharist alone. The front of the pamphlet, an artist's sketch, shows the young woman aglow with holiness. Jolie-Gray does not want to be foolish, or self-important, so she tries only for moderate self-abnegation.

She tries to eat as little as possible. Every morning she has coffee and dry Falkenstine's French bread. Every afternoon, on her break, she gets a dish of stewed okra from the hotel kitchen. It is overcooked and viscous, and she seasons it with salt and vinegar. On Sunday afternoons, when she can get a single alligator pear from the produce stand of the one-armed Italian at the French Market, she cuts it in half ceremonially and removes the smooth globe of a pit, pours in oil and vinegar—the single spoon of oil each week to keep her skin healthy, as Miss Vida-Jeanne instructs—and eats that instead, scooping a tiny saltcellar spoon with delight into the delicate flesh.

Every evening, in her room, she drinks a cut-glass tumbler of fig wine that she buys, a few bottles every once in a while, from a lady on Marigny Street. Then she drinks another glass, says her rosary, and goes to sleep. The next day she has coffee and bread in the morning, eats her bowl of okra in the afternoon, and at night drinks two, sometimes three, glasses of fig wine. It becomes a routine, maybe even a ritual. Sunday afternoons, the alligator pear.

One morning—it is Sunday, and a summer morning hot as the one on the day Lucette ejected her—she wakes early and goes walking. It is not long after Miss Vida-Jeanne has given her the warning look. A bit later she will go to church, then she will work in the afternoon, so she wears her uniform, her little white apron folded into her pocketbook.

She walks without aim, but she finds herself once again at the Café Du Monde. She enters and orders a heavy white mug of coffee and a basket of powdery-sweet, feather-light beignets, an exception, a Sabbath extravagance. She sits down and picks up a beignet and involuntarily sneezes, scattering powdered confectioner's sugar all over her fresh black skirt. She exclaims in dismay.

"Oh, honey, it will be fine," says a gravelly voice beside her. She turns to look. Though the woman is no longer dyeing her hair,

Jolie-Gray recognizes her as the old whore. Her white hair is tied back into a modest chignon in a net, as if she has finally acknowledged her own age, her mortality. Jolie-Gray wants to ask her something.

Instead the woman leans to her and says, as if in answer to something unasked, "Honey." She stops dead on that, like a heavy horse stopping. "Honey," she says again. "It would be nice if you could have your mother's love, but you can live without it."

Jolie-Gray blinks and says, "Well." She wants to say *Thank you,* but she cannot. She is thinking of Saint Jude: *Is something impossible, then?*

The woman nods her head yes. Jolie-Gray wants to believe she is responding not to the unasked question but to something inside her own head.

"I would like you to meet my friend Lalo," the woman suddenly says brightly, cocking her head. "Lalo owns a ship."

Jolie-Gray looks across the woman. Beyond her sits a young man with the look of a sailor about him. He is sinewy, jaunty, dark.

"How do you do?" Lalo says, leaning across the old whore. Then he says his name: "Lalo DiBello Merleau. Of DiBello Merleau, DBM Transport and Shipping."

He hands her a business card. The ink is a midnight blue. The card pictures a grand stylized ship cutting through midnight-blue waves.

Jolie-Gray wonders whether the elderly bawd is still practicing her trade, and whether this young man is a customer.

"No, she's retired," says Lalo, as if in response. Jolie-Gray has said nothing. "A couple of years now." Jolie-Gray wonders if her head has become like glass. "Would you like to see my ship?" he says.

Jolie-Gray says, politely, "I really had better eat my beignets before they cool. They're so nice when they're warm."

"I can wait." Lalo says. He sits on his stool with his arms crossed. He is the epitome of patience. The sleeves of his striped, sailorly-looking T-shirt are rolled, and his sun-browned arms seem to remind Jolie-Gray of someone else's. His white pants are spotless.

"I can vouch for him," says the old whore. "He's a good boy." She turns to pat him on the shoulder with an arthritic hand, its nails polished circus-wagon red.

Jolie-Gray eats her beignets. Then she drinks down her coffee and watches the sky growing pinker, then bluer. The coffee seems not to be cooling, and so she must drink in small sips.

Lalo sits with his arms crossed, smiling out into the day. Then he turns to her, "It's time," he says.

She has a strange moment. Who is this fellow: Death? The grim reaper in sailor garb? This is far too theatrical, but then she has not lived long enough to know that life out-theaters theater, that the stage can only aspire to the drama of daily life. Her eyes run up and down the backstage-style lightbulbs that line the café's myriad mirrors. So is this a play she has been cast in, then?

"No," he says. "I'm here to take you to see my ship."

"So you really . . ."

"I really," he says. And he really does. The ship is docked at a wharf not half a mile away. They walk together to it. Jolie-Gray feels light. She is carrying only her purse, a small linen bag with eighty cents in it— seven dimes, two nickels— and her ruffled white maid's apron. She swings it slightly as they walk. She does not understand this airiness. It is as if eating the beignets has lightened her.

The ship is a freighter. It carries bananas. They have been unloaded now, but the smell of banana oil is heavy, pervasive, palpable, filling the air all around the ship, hovering over the wharf. Lalo takes her arm and helps her to mount the gangplank, then steps up behind her.

"We sail at eleven," he says. "I expect you will want to come."

"What?" she says, not understanding.

"No time for a layover," he says. "We are heading for Guayaquil."

"I have mass at eleven," she says, "And I work at one."

"Not today," Lalo DiBello Merleau says, with assurance. There is nothing sinister in him.

"That's true?" Jolie-Gray asks. "And you do own this ship?"

"Own this ship and five more," Lalo says. "And I know how to run them. My father owned them, quite a number of years, and he died, and now they are mine. Would you be so gracious as to be my guest? You will have your own stateroom. If you should find Guayaquil not to your liking, you may certainly return right away."

"Oh," Jolie-Gray says. She trusts him. She suspects this is Saint Jude's answer to a question she didn't ask. "Then perhaps I will. Well. I will."

The ship dawdles in its channel, idled again and again by river traffic, until it is night; and then they are fully underway. As the pilot in the wheelhouse glides the big white ship past Grand Isle in the dark, heading to the Gulf, Jolie-Gray stands at the prow. Overhead there are minuscule, myriad stars, but the sky is as black as it ever might be.

Looking across the water, above the levee, toward the little town, Jolie-Gray cannot see the pink light of the neon-script sign on Dubois Aucoin's bar, though it is early enough that the neon is still lit. She cannot see the raw light of the swinging bare bulb in Leona-Rae Comeaux's kitchen. She cannot see the flickering red-glassed candle next to the tabernacle as Saint Clothilde's.

In the silence, as the giant ship noiselessly cuts through the water, she does not hear a pearl pop from the monstrance and roll down the aisle, or the tiny feet of the mouse that might be chasing it.

She takes it all in—the silence, the darkness—and she thinks: *This is impossible.* She thinks of Saint Jude and his tiny fire topknot. She laughs quietly to herself, there at the prow of the ship.

And suddenly she feels a flush of warmth, as when she has had two glasses of fig wine from the lady who makes it in her kitchen on Marigny Street. The flush rises from her chest to her throat, to her brain, to her hair, and she hears a small whoosh, an igniting, as when a gas burner is lit. Something in her senses that this has to do with the cumulative effect of all that fig wine, those hundreds of nights of it, as if she were a sponge cake soaked through with it.

She lifts her hands to her hair, and indeed, she is on fire. She knows as well that the flame itself is, on the one hand, all that envy—Bertille's, Lucette's, Miss Vida-Jeanne's—stored up in her tissues and still growing, now independent of her, in her absence; on the other hand, it is the source of her life.

The warmth is quite pleasant. It spreads to her shoulders. They flame up, like epaulets. She straightens herself, as if she were on display, though no one sees her. The effulgence of all this cool flame—for it is cool, though it feels like a flushing warmth to her, inside of it—lights the whole foredeck. She stands straight. She feels the breeze pouring over her. Should anyone see her, the sight would befuddle, astonish: a woman, entirely on fire.

Should Bertille see her daughter this way, she would once again click her tongue in disgust, make a ragged dry gag in her throat, at the showing-off.

Should Lucette or Miss Vida-Jeanne witness this, they would cluck undiluted repugnance. They would be certain, as well, that Lalo DiBello Merleau was extracting his pound of flesh payment for the voyage to the equator—*which* pound, they would know very well. Yes, they would be certain.

Should Gray, whose heart is filling up like a little pink vat with Bertille's sausage grease and spite, see his strawberry-blond daughter, once more before he dies, *en flambée* this way, like dessert at the Roosevelt, he would applaud.

The ship glides on, silently, through the dark channel. In his cabin, arms folded, Lalo DiBello Merleau, having finished his day's log, sits with his feet up, his bare sun-brown feet out of his rubber-soled deck shoes, wiggling his toes in delight, proud and happy to be of use.

The mouse in the darkened Grand Isle church rolls the pearl toward its hole, or does not.

Jolie-Gray wonders momentarily whether this is an example of what Saint Augustine meant by his definition of miracles: *If sponge cake on a silver tray carried by waiters at the Roosevelt* (she thinks, remembering that sight, observed from a corner of the dimly lit dining room) *can burn this way and not be consumed, might it not be that I can too?* She is asking Saint Jude for impossible answers.

On the prow of the ship, like a torch, Jolie-Gray lights the night. She goes on burning, cool as a memory, smelling the dark rich banana oil that suffuses every inch of the deck. She wiggles her fingers, from whose tips shoot blue flames. Out of her eye-corners she watches the fire flickering, dancing. She cranes her neck like a scout, like a swan, like a ship's figurehead carved by a sculptor commissioned by queens or the Vatican, out toward Ecuador.

Ingrid Hill has published stories in the *Southern Review,* **the** *Michigan Quarterly Review, Shenandoah,* **the** *North American Review, Louisiana Literature,* **and** *Story* **and a collection of fiction,** *Dixie Collection Interstate Blues.* **She has held fellowships from Yaddo and the MacDowell Colony and is a National Endowment for the Arts grant recipient. She grew up in New Orleans and is the mother of twelve children, including two sets of twins. She lives in Iowa City.**

JAMES HILL

I *was sipping a hazelnut latte one day with the ghost of Gustave Flaubert. He asked me the roots of this story. Flamboyantly, if unoriginally, I replied, "Jolie-Gray, c'est moi." Still, he was flattered. I was careful to qualify that. I'm neither nubile nor strawberry-blonde. I am, however, naïve and trusting and a fine gumbo chef. As a former Girl Scout, I'm clean, brave, reverent, thrifty, etc. Thus I tend to get under crabby folks' skin. The old trollop was born of a painting of Manet's. My Cajun grandma urged on me the devotion to Saint Jude, though her own favorite was Saint Dymphna, Patroness of Nervous Breakdowns. My father, a Swedish ship's captain, sailed for years back and forth to Ecuador with gargantuan loads of green bananas. On my bookshelf I have a book about prayer titled* Why Not Become Totally Fire? *I looked up at that book spine while musing on the trajectory this story might take, and there it went. Surely everyone knows firsthand someone who went up in flames from too much fig wine, or from excess of passion? Myself, I've been teased about drinking gin and tonics while reading the Bible. I have not yet spontaneously combusted. As for the mouse and the seventeenth pearl from the Sea of Japan, I just channeled them.* Eh voila, Monsieur Flaubert.

Linda Wendling

INAPPROPRIATE BABIES

(from *River Styx*)

That year, 1904, all the rice growers in Louisiana came down with the sickness, called *maladie des jambes*. I demanded French soap against it, and even though I was only eight, my mother made the nanny buy the soap for me. Still, not content with a mere bath that night, after my parents and my nanny were asleep, I took the new French soaps out of their brown wrappers and stood up on my bed naked, the wrappers all around me on the white coverlet, the moonlight blue on my small limbs. I vigorously rubbed the French soap, dry, all over my skin, scratched it under my fingernails, and put my nightie back on. Then I stuffed the soaps and their wrappers into my pillowcase to keep them near my face. As I lay back, relieved, I saw that the window was open a little, and the earthy mud smell of the rice fields drifted in over the sill with the gauzy, white curtains. I held my breath against the fresh air, warding off disease. With each mild, earthy current, I held my breath and buried my face in the bumpy soap pillow, their wrappers crackling when I moved. I did not so much fall asleep as faint, from holding my breath.

I was used to this habit, and it satisfied me.

Father had high praise for the rice disease. He predicted it would be a good sell. I got to help him haul his photographic equipment

into Mother's parlor. She fussed about the little tins of flash powder and the troops of puffy victims on her red Persian rug, but she
let him do it, so I knew it must be a promising disease. Father
offered our poorer, rice-growing neighbors one dollar to step into
our parlor and show him their strangely marked, edematous limbs.
And, of course, I was allowed to stay in the parlor and help, as
Father's only daughter, eight years the pride of his life. I wore
Mother's perfume for an antibiotic. I smoothed father's canvas
backdrop, hung now in the parlor. He painted them himself, precise, an artist. Painted, potted palms offered perfection over the
real.

Monsieur Thibideau came with his children. They all stood stiff
and obedient in their faded farm clothes. This was a family I knew.
For the way their swollen, blackened legs made me feel, I slowly,
secretly pushed all the air out of my lungs and held my breath. I
lay down immediately on Mother's red Persian carpet to remind
myself I was immune. How could a girl like me, whose mother
had such a rug, be like the Thibideaux? I was someone's special
girl.

But this strategy of lying on Mother's rug did not work. From
that angle, I could see thin half-moons of dirt in the Thibideau
nails where their hands hung limp at their sides. I curled my fingers
into the red plush rug and scratched back and forth till the fibers
slid under my nails and cleaned them. Rolling onto my back, I
saw Father over me dropping one silver dollar into Monsieur
Thibideau's hand. Monsieur Thibideau turned red. "It was my
understanding," he said, " that the one dollar was per person. Otherwise, why drag my children out of the rice fields now, when
there is so much work to be done?"

My father won through composure more than rightness. It was
his way. To win by virtue of his patience, his inability to fuss. "I am
interested," he said, "not in dissecting you all and your malady. I
am interested in the peculiarities of the Thibideau manifestation
of this disease, the Thibideau strain, if you are interested in being

paid to display it for me. However, how can I exhibit it as a unique strain if you are not in the photograph together? No, no, for science the Thibideau strain must remain together."

"This is not fair!" Monsieur Thibideau argued, but no matter how long he shouted at him about the bargain of sixteen limbs of maladie des jambes for the price of four, my father could not be made to understand.

"I am sorry," he shrugged. "*Je ne comprends pas.*"

Until finally, Monsieur Thibideau submitted out of tired disgust, posing, stern-faced, with his children. I lay on the rug watching, light-headed from holding my breath. One little boy had a large wart on his puffed-up thumb. His foot—thick with disease inside the boot, the skin on his leg ballooning and purple above it—touched the rug. I rolled and stood up very fast, head spinning now, and rubbed very hard at my fingers. He had a pretty little face. I had the peculiar distasteful feeling of tears. Stealing off to my room, I leaned against the door and held my breath to work up a good lack of air and fell into a satisfying faint. I dreamt in flat, clean sepias, where the bad things were turned into art. The germ-free dream of the photograph. When I woke up, a few minutes later, the Thibideaux were gone.

This was 1904, the year the St. Louis World's Fair was preparing to host the greatest collection of medical science exhibits and photographic exhibits the world had ever seen. Science and art amuck had doubled my father's already considerable fortune. He traveled all over the country, photographing every scientific phenomenon—and at a time when scientific breakthroughs were falling on the wake of the ones before them, like shuffled cards. His secret? He made two sets of prints—one for the scientific journals, one for the traveling freak shows. My father, always a shrewd businessman, cleaned up at both ends. The rice disease was predicted to be quite a success at the World's Fair, and it was in our own neighbors' limbs—a windfall right in my father's lap.

• • •

Around this time, a Frenchman in New Orleans wrote to my father asking him to come take a photograph of his three daughters. But my father was an artist and frowned on something so average as a normal portrait and tucked the letter into the top pocket of his coat, intending to decline. However, we knew the family would hear nothing since my father also frowned on writing tiresome or unpleasant letters. Instead, the letter would rest in his top coat pocket, along with several other yellowed pieces of similar mundaneness, constant reminders of things that he must not bother with. Carrying these reminders, he thought, took care of any other, grosser obligation to respond. When the letters were sufficiently crumbled, he would throw them away. So he put the letter there, and the family with three daughters in New Orleans was forgotten.

I was disappointed, of course. A tiresome, normal portrait in New Orleans sounded quite nice. I pictured the three pretty, French daughters, sitting solemn with their hair ribbons. After the photo, we might have had a hot chocolate with too much sugar.

Within that same week, a woman doctor also wrote to my father, explaining that she was very interested in gathering a population of premature infants for the same World's Fair the Thibideau photos were now headed for. The doctor and her colleague had invented a warming box meant to keep premature infants alive longer. She was gathering letters of application from doctors treating pregnant women whose babies did not stand much chance of survival. There were plenty of such subjects, mostly on missions and reservations, but there appeared to be people of money with troubling pregnancies as well. Unfortunately, family doctors, especially small-town doctors, sometimes neglected to keep in mind the discriminating, artistic eye needed to gather the right sort of babies for a World's Fair exhibit. They tended, instead, to recommend sick babies, willy-nilly.

Her letter drew to its climax at this point, a real economic coup: she asked my father if he would be interested in photographing the applicants to make intriguing posters and to also ensure that these infants—or their mothers, if the babies were not yet born—were of "appropriate quality to be in a World's Fair." My father said this meant "no Negro babies."

When I said, "What about the reservation babies? Are they all right?" he rubbed his chin and said, "I will have to check." He patted my head then, pronouncing me an interesting girl with a keen business eye, regarding the Indian baby question.

Well, this was, of course, the kind of letter important enough for my father to respond to. He did, saying he would photograph the applicants and weed out "inappropriate ones" from the beginning, making it clear that an additional fee for each rejection would be necessary, of course, since this would be unpleasant—you recall that my father abhorred unpleasant communications. And people who expected to have a dying child on their hands could be unpleasant if they could not have a space in the World's Fair. In this same letter, he sent not only a direct query regarding the Indian Baby Question, but also a photo of the *Thibideau Manifestation of Maladie des Jambes*. I think he wanted to impress the new client. I stood behind him as he sat in his chair, rubbing his clean, white fingers over the brown and white limbs of the Thibideaux, studying their faces for the most "compelling pathos." I held my breath as I looked at them and began to think perhaps I should have the price of a new ruler and perhaps a pencil as well for my important contribution of the Indian Baby Question. I filed this away for future usefulness.

We waited for the first bundle of letters from the incubator doctor. The day it came, Mother sent us off with a pie and sandwiches, and we headed for the destinations given us in the country doctors' letters, zigzagging efficiently from our estate to New Orleans, stopping at designated small towns along the way. I secretly packed one of Mother's handkerchiefs, sprinkled with her perfume. I could breathe into this to avoid disease and sad things. This eliminated much of the breath holding, which was beginning to give me headaches.

Twice on the way to New Orleans, Father borrowed a hotel's cellar or basement for a dark room. For a look at the photos, most proprietors lent the impromptu dark rooms for free.

Father kept his word. He earned the extra money he had demanded in that he did indeed weed out inappropriate babies. He stepped skillfully around direct questions of acceptance into the incubator exhibit. If the families were not French, his usual, mild Cajun accent became thick. I noticed that all of the parents were much too frantic about being in a silly fair.

Father would pretend to take photos for the purpose of both beauty and medical measurement, but really it was to measure the relative shade of a woman's skin, setting me next to her for comparison, posing me under the pretense of holding a tape measure near her belly, something that, of course, the woman could have done herself. If the babies had already been born, he would set them next to some object to measure them by, my little pale hand, of course, in the photo, holding the object of measure: an empty milk bottle, perhaps, or sometimes a large feather, or, if the family had one, a ruler. Of course, if we could see before we got there that the family was the wrong kind—if they tended more toward sepia than cream—we would turn around and not go at all.

If the family pushed to be accepted, to know that their child would get to be in one of the warming boxes—and especially, when they began to cry, Father would fall back on his best defense. *"Je ne comprends pas,"* he would say, shrugging, smiling kindly. Just like for Monsieur Thibideau, but more gently.

When we arrived in New Orleans, the first batch of photographs complete, we met the woman doctor in an open-air café with excellent beignets. I was allowed chicory coffee whenever Mother could not see, and this day was no exception. Other than to request a linen napkin to help with all the powdered sugar, I was polite and did not speak. The woman pored over Father's photographs, very pleased. "Oh, look how pitiful you've made this one look. You've brought out the shadows under her eyes. Your effects with light are impressive!"

Father shrugged, distracted. He smiled at me, wiped the sugar from my cheek with his thumb.

The doctor reached below the table and brought out a deep, narrow wooden box, the size of a baby. She set it on the table between us. "Here is the incubator," she said proudly. "We call it the Box. Easier for American fair-goers to comprehend." She smirked.

Father, who never paid consistent attention to anyone except me and Mother, nodded and tapped his coffee spoon on the edge of the Box. She pretended not to notice, though I could see she didn't like it.

"Now," she said. "Take this with you and at the next few homes, put the baby in the Box and get some pictures interesting enough for fair posters. You know what I mean by interesting? Don't make any promises, though, remember?"

He nodded, looking out at the Square. She shifted impatiently. Many important people were put off by Father's aloofness. She readjusted herself, lifted her chin, and shifted her attention to me. "So! Young lady! What are you going to see in New Orleans?"

"Father!" I said. "Can we go see Marie LeVeau, the Voodoo Queen?"

"Well!" she smiled, raising her eyebrows and leaning forward. She spoke to us with animation. "If you really want to see something, there's a little French girl right near here, just on the edge of the Quarter, in fact, who has recently had her arm cut off. She had an infection, you see, and it has become gangrenous."

This woke my father. "Say there!" he said. "This is someone's little girl!"

"Well, that's true, of course," the doctor said, "but without her arm, she becomes an excellent candidate for one of your wonderful and, I must say, expensive photographs."

"No," he said, touching my shoulder, but calmer now. "I meant this is someone's little girl."

"Oh," she said. "I have been indelicate." She sat back and smiled at us, but I did not like her face. "I understand. You fathers with your little girls—you are wise to be careful. You must watch them every minute. Especially in New Orleans." I wondered what she meant by that. How was this place more dangerous? Was this about the little French girl?

"Still," she continued, "it is a good photograph for someone in your profession. Nothing so different from what your little assistant has seen already and interesting fodder for a postcard, I imagine." (An ingratiating smile was directed at me.) "You ought to think about it."

In the end, of course, economics won out. We did go to see the little French girl. Father said I could give her one of my excellent German licorices, since I was so insistent. I was anxious to meet her, too, because I had become a little lonely for other children on this trip. But when we got there, everything changed.

The girl's father opened the door. He was a tall, very thin man, with a very red face. When my father announced who he was, the man shook Father's hand with both of his own, stooping a little. "Oh forgive us!" he said. "We had forgotten we ever wrote to you! How good of you to come now, but how sad. Still, how could we have known? And where could we have found you to let you know, once you had left?" His mouth shook a little, and my father's eyes looked to one side. I knew this protective strategy well.

"You see," the man said, sitting us down in his small, peculiar parlor. "After we sent for you, one of our little daughters became ill in her arm. It had to be removed, but—well—it was too late . . ." Again the mouth quivered.

Again my father looked to the side. I marveled that this man could be so indelicate. Didn't he know this was an unpleasant conversation? I looked around the house. He was somewhat poor. I forgave him his bad manners.

"Well," the man finished, his voice barely more than a whisper. "We are preparing her now."

I did not understand, but took this to mean that she needed a bath or a hair combing before posing for Father.

"Still," the man said, "now that you're here, if it doesn't offend you, I wonder—"

We waited. He rubbed both hands over his face and when they came down, I saw that he had smeared tears down his cheeks. "Still," he tried again. "Still, if it doesn't offend you, I wonder if, perhaps, we could do the photograph of the girls anyway? Prop her somehow between them?" Then he rushed to explain, afraid of offending: "Then, you see, her mother and I could still see our little Marie-Claire down through the years. We will miss her so."

Father set me in a worn green velvet chair that smelled of fried oyster sandwiches and said, "Don't leave this. You stay right here."

"Am I not to help with this one?" I complained.

"You stay right here. Don't get up."

"Am I not to help?" I whined.

"No."

I waited in the green chair, smelling the not unpleasant smell of the oysters. I remembered what the woman doctor had said: *your little girls—you must watch them every minute.* I frowned. How could he leave me alone? I would scold him for this later, perhaps when we were near a confectionery.

Before we left New Orleans, Father was allowed to make a quick darkroom at the Bourbon Orléans Hotel. He added three New Orleans babies and the one-armed Marie-Claire and her sisters to the big black book, the portfolio where he kept all his favorite or newest photographs.

We did try to find Marie LeVeau, but outside a voodoo shop, a strange, dark woman in too many skirts and no shoes tried to sell me a bag of *gris-gris*. My father slapped it gently from my hands, scowling fiercely at the woman. I saw her nails, on my sleeve, were very long and one was torn. He bought me a molasses stick instead, as we were leaving the Quarter, but gave it to me only after he washed and powdered my hands back at the hotel.

• • •

Our first stop outside of New Orleans was on a bayou. The house was far away from the road, and we had to walk on a wobbly, rotten-looking, wooden bridge over swamp land to get to the porch from the road. Spanish moss brushed my face as I passed beneath the trees. I was enjoying myself immensely. I looked for alligators but was disappointed in this. On the porch a tiny cloth bag the size and shape of a frog's underbelly—perhaps it was a frog's underbelly—hung from the split porch roof. The bag was glossy and where it stretched thin, I saw beneath its surface the edges of the tiny stones which filled it. The bag looked slick and wet. My heart began to pound in my ears.

Father saw this and squeezed my hand. "Just silly voodoo medicine," he whispered. "It can't hurt you."

Of course it was not our fault.

Because of the remoteness of the house, we were unable to tell until face to face with the father of this tiny home that the family was not suitable—he was Mexican. Very dark. What could we do? Father and I knew, of course, that a Mexican baby was inappropriate; the ink would come out too dark—but there was the father, grasping Father's hands.

He was much younger than Father, with thick black hair, very clean and soft-looking. He would have been handsome except that he was a laborer and he was Mexican, and his face carried too much emotion. His beautiful eyebrows formed an anxious peak at their center that was disagreeable. He shook both our hands, and when he looked into my face, his eyes were full. "I see you have a precious little girl of your own," he said.

I fingered Mother's handkerchief in my pocket and readied it. Could he really compare me to some daughter of his own? I was not, was not, was not like the children Father photographed, except, perhaps, the little French girl.

He pulled us into the house and showed us a tiny parlor with the kitchen right there in the middle of it. At the back was a tiny room, no larger than the pantry at home, but it had a bed in it and at the foot of that a cradle. The man bent and placed the backs of his fingers softly against the tiny form within. I peeked and saw a very small, dark baby forehead peering above the blanket, damp soft black hair sticking to its skin. This baby didn't move, though, or open its eyes, so I studied the room. There was not even room for a straight-back chair or wash stand.

"It just happened," the Mexican man said.

I sensed something important and paid attention.

"My wife, she died in childbirth. This morning—"

"Sh. Sh. Sh," Father said. Such talk about childbirth in front of his little girl. I raised my chin. *You must watch them every minute.*

"A neighbor has been trying to nurse my baby girl."

"Sh. Sh. Sh." Father frowned gently. Such talk, with me there, about nursing babies. "Shh."

The man nodded, distracted. He kept wringing his hands.

"Well," Father said. "We are very sorry. We just came here to tell you, though, that the Exhibition is full . . ."

The man's mouth fell open.

Father closed his eyes. ". . . that the Exhibition is full and we cannot . . ."

"No!"

Father cleared his throat. His eyes were still closed. "You must understand. There were too many babies, sir, and—"

"My name is Emmanuel!"

". . . Emmanuel. Too many babies, you see, and not enough . . ."

"No!" Emmanuel said. He gripped my father's arm, knocking me back a step, and Father stopped talking. I expected Father to do something about this, to say I was somebody's little girl, to call attention to what had been done to me, but instead he only swallowed, his arm looking thin as a boy's in Emmanuel's grip. I began the funny breathing, but Father did not hear that either, so I stopped.

That's when Emmanuel saw the Box.

"Is that it?" he whispered.

"Yes," Father said.

"Put her in it."

"Now really, there is no sense . . ."

"Put her in it!"

Father set down the Box on the kitchen table, and Emmanuel brought the tiny baby out from the cradle. It was so quiet. It moved to cry when he set it down in the Box, but it was too weak to make the sounds, so it just made a little grimace, gaping its mouth noiselessly. It did not open its eyes. I looked up into Emmanuel's face.

Emmanuel said, "She needs this Box."

Father said nothing.

"Take her picture."

Father sighed. He looked at the floor for a moment and then at the ceiling. He turned abruptly to leave, but Emmanuel stepped between us and the door. I sighed out loud, but Father did not look at me. He set me on a high, bare wooden stool near the front door. His forehead was damp, and his hands were clammy and cold. There were two thin carrots, partially cut, on the cracked wooden counter behind me. Someone had stopped their cooking abruptly, perhaps last night. The carrots were dried and beginning to pucker on the stump ends. I thought of the one-armed Marie-Claire and moved my elbow away from them. I saw that the lace on my sleeve was all dirty.

"Father," I said, "I've been dirtied—"

Father gave me his black portfolio book to occupy me. "We'll be leaving soon, Sweet," he said, but looking sternly at Emmanuel, who still blocked the door. Father looked small and timid. I looked at the portfolio in my hands.

"Am I not to assist this time either?" I complained.

"No."

I opened the book, feeling dangerous because he usually protected me from certain of the "maladie" photographs. Why was it allowed now? I knew I should be excited, but it felt wrong, and as

I turned the pages, I let my attention wander between Emmanuel's baby and Father's photographs. Emmanuel stood watching Father set up the camera, talking almost constantly, trying to win.

"Look," Father said. "I will take the photograph. Perhaps you are right. Perhaps when they see your little girl, they may change their minds. But I must tell you, truly, the exhibit is full. You can understand it would be immoral for them to remove some other baby so that your child . . ."

"Esmerelda."

". . . so that Esmerelda could take its place."

"What about this Box?" Emmanuel said. "There is no other baby in this Box."

"Well, yes, but you see, commitments have been made, papers signed—"

"Would it not be immoral to remove Esmerelda, now that she is in the Box?"

This bored me. I turned a page and there she was! The pretty little French girl with one arm! I remembered then that an injustice had been done. I had not been allowed to see her.

"Father!" I said. "Is this Marie-Claire? I didn't get to share my licorice!"

Father looked at me. He had forgotten for a minute that I was there. And now I was seeing the girl he had forbidden me to see in the oyster-smelling house.

"Yes, I know, Darling," he said. "Maybe you should put the book down now."

"No, I want to look."

Father retreated behind the camera lens. This was not the effect I had hoped for.

"I will take the photographs," he said. "But then we must go."

"You can't take her out of the Box. Not now that she is in there!"

"Father," I said, studying Marie-Claire's odd, white face. "Did it hurt her? When you took her picture? And did you have to set the arm somewhere?"

"What?" He looked at me. "No. Giselle, be quiet now."

"You know what will happen," Emmanuel said, "if you take her out of the Box." I could not tell whether Emmanuel was talking about what would happen to the baby or what would happen to us or both.

I looked back down. "Father, why is her face so white? Did you take the photograph properly?"

"Look at her," Emmanuel said. I kept glancing between Esmerelda and the strange, slumbering Marie-Claire. (Who sleeps, hunched and gray like that, for an expensive portrait? Was she a spoiled child? Or did the lost arm hurt too much?)

"Father, why can't she stand up?"

"See how beautiful she is?" Emmanuel still argued.

"Father, why is she so white?"

"*Je ne*—" Father said. "Oh, please—" He looked ill. He was white as Marie-Claire, with water on his upper lip. "Would you both please stop talking?" He bent again to his camera. He was paying no attention to me.

"You know what will happen," Emmanuel said.

"Father, *what* will happen?"

"You cannot remove her now she is in it."

"Did it hurt her, the picture-taking? *Answer* me. Why is she so white . . ."

And then something bad and cold gripped me in my chest. I knew what was wrong with Marie-Claire. I thought back to the smell of the oyster sandwich chair. I knew now why Marie-Claire was so white, and now my black velvet coat smelled dirty, smelled of her mother's fried oysters. I watched my father, his face wet and gray now, and me, here, alone on this stool, where Emmanuel's young wife had sliced the carrots to dead stumps but now was dead herself. *Your little girls—you must watch them every minute*. The dizziness I'd had with the Thibideaux was coming back.

I looked for Mother's handkerchief in my dirtied sleeve, but it was gone. I saw it on the floor, far below me. It touched a dirty dead carrot stump. I sniffed at my wrist, but there was no trace of perfume, no trace of soap. So I held my breath, my only choice left, and looked at the back of Father's wet shirt. *Your little girls— you must watch them . . .*

"You know what will happen if you take her out of that Box, don't you? You know what will happen!"

"What does he mean, Father?" It came out in a whisper.

"You know what will happen."

"Father," I puffed, "what does he mean? What will happen?" But Father didn't answer me. I took another gulp of air and tried a more important question. "Should he talk like that in front of me?" I shifted my glare to Emmanuel and said "*This* is someone's little girl!" since Father didn't say it. But Emmanuel only nodded solemnly. He thought I meant *the baby! The baby!*

I pushed through my dizziness and wobbled off the stool. Father stared only through the lens at Esmerelda, sweat in his eye. I snatched an empty milk bottle off the table and thrust it roughly into the Box, startling both men. I clenched the bottle tight and pushed my pretty pale forearm up against the side of Esmerelda's wrinkly brown form so that Father would have to look at me.

"This is someone's—" I wheezed, then caught the sound of Father's gasp as I thrust myself into the photograph. *Your little girls—you have to watch them every minute,* I was saying, though it didn't sound like me. My wheezing sounded scary and sad and far away, and I couldn't have Mother's handkerchief, and I was dirtied with Emmanuel's skin and Marie-Claire's oysters and the carrot stumps of the dead woman, and Father wasn't . . . *Watch them every minute . . .* and I saw suddenly how my pretty, white, white arm in Esmerelda's box must look through Father's lens—like the disembodied arm of Marie-Claire. And so it felt like all three of us little girls were there in the Box as it tipped with my leaning, the world went to sepia, and the cries of the fathers behind us sounded far, far away.

Linda Wendling is a James Jones First Novelist
Fellowship finalist and an Associated Writing
Programs Award 2000 nominee. She is the
winner of the 1999 Heartland Fiction Prize *(New
Letters)* and was a 1998 finalist for *Scribner's Best
of the Fiction Workshops* anthology. She has been a
recipient of the World's Best Short Short Story
Award (Florida State University Press) and the
Margery McKinney Short Story Award. She has
also received honors in the Carson McCullers
Prize for the Short Story (*STORY* magazine), the *Writer's Digest* Literary
Fiction Prize, and the *Alaska Quarterly Review* International Short Story
Award. Her stories have been published in a number of literary
magazines, including *River Styx, Sundog: The Southeast Review,* and *New
Letters;* one was anthologized in W.W. Norton's *Micro Fiction: An
Anthology of Really Short Stories.* She has taught writing for ten years at
the University of Missouri and also teaches at the St. Louis Writer's
Workshop.

"*Inappropriate Babies*" *began pushing its way into being while I was edit-
ing exhibit labels for the Missouri Historical Society and came across a
labeled photograph of a nurse at the 1904 St. Louis World's Fair. In the
photograph with the nurse were some smiling fairgoers, beaming at the
impossibly fragile infant in the nurse's arms. I am now at work on a novel by
the same name.*

Jane R. Shippen

I AM NOT LIKE NUÑEZ

(from *Meridian*)

I am not like my brother Nuñez. His father was a Honduran businessman, and the first time he heard our mama having sex he thought it was a cry for help. We lived behind the sewage treatment plant, in a trailer in a neighborhood of Atlanta called The Stink. Most of the old houses along Bolton Road had been torn down. And the streets by this time — I was in tenth grade and Nuñez was in ninth — were lined with new stucco houses with garages facing the road. School had let out early that day, because of tornadoes likely. And I waited at the corner for him to show up and then we started home. We walked together. We would sing songs. The kids in the new houses didn't go to our school. Sometimes they would be getting in and out of cars in their uniforms, but that day it was only noon and there were gusts of wind, and we didn't see anyone, except ladies here and there inside the big houses, straightening things from room to room.

Nuñez was the same height as me, but skinnier. The line of his mouth turned down at the corners, and he had the kind of knotty muscles that come not from working out but from being tense. We walked quickly together in long matched strides. On Bolton on the block before the Chevron there was only one old house left. When we got to it, I said, "That's my house." He said he wanted the big pink one farther down with the wall around it.

The one I liked was a gray house, clapboard, tilted on a hill. It was ugly and I loved it. It had a door off-center and only two upstairs windows set wide apart. It looked half-stoned and it leered at you like a man who won't ever amount to anything, like the kind of man our mom would choose.

Nuñez said it was called an American Four-Square, and he kept walking. I'm different from Nuñez. When I go in the grocery store I read *Time*. I do not look at *Dixie Living* or *Home Decour*. I don't know about houses, but I know what I like. The house—the American Four-Square—had stood empty for some time, being remodeled, and I did not tell my brother that it was my secret place. I just told him I liked it, and we walked quickly because the wind was picking up.

We cut behind the Chevron and lowered ourselves over the retaining wall and climbed down the Wadda Burger dumpster. It was raining, now and then, one big drop, by the time we got to the trailers. We usually sing:

> *All night all day, (oh lordy), angels watchin' over me, my lord.*
> *All night all day, (oh lordy), angels watchin' over me*

and when we get to our yard, and Mama answers, (*Oh lordy*) *Aaaangels*. But she didn't answer that day because we didn't sing.

The door of our house was wide open and there was a big rust-colored van parked behind Mama's Chevette. It had tinted windows, the kind of car that kidnappers drive. We heard a lady moan. Then she moaned again. Nuñez's eyes got big and mine did too, I'm sure. He whispered, "That's Mama."

She screamed louder. "What should we do?" he asked. "Should we run?"

I said, "No."

Then there was a lull in the screaming. He picked up a hammer from under the trailer, and tiptoed up the stairs and into the house, at which point the call started up again, this time wailing like an ambulance in traffic at five P.M. I climbed the steps. Inside, Nuñez was standing with his back to me, facing Mama's door at the end of the hall. His whole body was flexed, cupped around the hammer. I whispered, "They're making love." But he didn't move. Then the bedroom door slid back. There was a man there with short bleached-out hair and a red face. He was one of the younger ones. He giggled and wrested the hammer from Noonie, then turned, one hand on top of the doorframe to let him pass.

Nuñez went in Mama's room. They could sit on the bed and talk for hours. I went out to the kitchen, the tall stranger slapping his bare feet at my heels. "Geez, what time is it?" he said, giving the hammer a reckless swing. He was chitchatting me, but I wasn't in a casual mood.

He had on loose painter's pants and that's all. The tattoo on his chest was of a lady's face, drawn to look like it was a picture on a long, spiral-sliced piece of paper. I recognized it from a poster store. There were dishes and beer cans all over the kitchen, and burned pots of old food. The stranger drank from one of the beers and opened the fridge. My dad has a bull's skull tattooed on his lower back, so the horns rock just at the top of his jeans. But the stranger's body was blank on the other side. He started eating a cold salmon patty from a frisbee with his fingers. He sang, "Let me reach out and grab ya, Abra-abra—" with his mouth full. I could hear Mama laugh and then begin soft-talk with my little brother in the other room.

"You go by Sharky, right?" He said, "Your mom calls you Sharky. That's kind of a cute name. I go by Freak, short for Frequent Stops."

I moved so I could see the lady's face again, on the left side of his chest.

"Want to watch TV, Sharky? With a name like Sharky it's gotta be good." He talked like that, jumping around like a car radio set on scan. He clicked on the TV. He was built like my daddy, and even their hands were alike, long square-nosed fingers that kept moving. He sat right on top of the magazines and the blankets on the sofa. I sat on an end table. I could see the soft pine limbs sweep the window slats above his head.

"Your mom's a chatterbox but not you, huh? She said y'all was nothing alike. But I think y'all favor. People say y'all favor? It ain't going to storm. Serious now, lady. I think there's something of her in you." Then he lowered his voice and he leaned toward me, and he asked me, "What color is your mama's hair when she don't dye it?"

I was hungry, I wanted something to eat. I watched him bend over and put his work boots on and tie them. He had his belt in his hand and he stood up, took a step closer, "Did she marry your daddy? I know she didn't marry the boy's daddy 'cause he went back to Mexico, I heard."

I picked a scab on my knee. I said, "Mama's hair is just like mine, just hair color." And I cursed myself. Damn, I thought, Damn, I had not meant to say one word to him.

"Well you got real pretty hair and I mean that." And he turned to the TV and popped his belt at it and said, "Fuck you, Phil Donahue. Excuse my French."

The bottom of the screen said tornadoes were no longer in effect. I wondered, What kind of name is Frequent Stops, where did it come from? He turned the TV off and put his belt on, and in the quiet we could hear traffic off the interstate and also Nuñez talking in a soft voice to Mama.

"She loves that little mixed boy, don't she?" He said it in a gravely jealous tone. "God knows she can't get enough of him." And I kicked the table as a way to say Amen.

He grinned at me, and he went into the kitchen and got down a box of Lucky Charms. "I love y'all's house, man," he said, "I love it. All trailers are the same. It's like I know where everything's at." Then he walked down the hall to Mama's room.

There was nothing wrong with our house. We had a sofa and two chairs. Some of the cranks were broken off the windows and there was hole in the bathroom door I used to put raisins in. It was not the same as everyone's.

While Frequent Stops was in with Mama I poked around his coat. It was a leather jacket the same as the ones my daddy wore, and it had that same sweet dirt smell, and I thought, This is a smell I will be always going back to. I reached in the pocket and it had a bag of marijuana in it and I tucked that down inside my shirt. I did not even think about it. I thought, If I don't see him again I will have this. This smell, this little bit of drugs I stole, and I will put it in my sock drawer how a lady will do a rose or lavender.

He came back while I was still staring at his coat, moving away from it like it was the skin of some bad dream. "She's worried about *him,* says he's getting too big to manage. Well, she holds him like he was a five year old." He reached for his coat. "She says she got a headache coming on 'cause of the storm. Doesn't that stink? I told her there ain't going to be no storm."

Then he stepped toward me, and I didn't move, for fear the bag of marijuana would jog loose. He stood close, moving to reach up and touch my hair, but then Nuñez passed through the kitchen toward his room, and the stranger took it as his cue to go.

Frequent Stops stood on the top step, the overcast city-brown sky above him, his shirt and jacket under his arm. He put his hand across his chest's tattoo. "She's still some tender," he said to me, a sorry look in his eyes. The lights blinked on and off as he strode toward his car and he waved his coat at me and called after me, "Bye now, Sharky," and in my breath I said, "Don't go."

When Nuñez is lonely he closes himself in his room. He likes to draw facades of beautiful houses. I do not have that gift. After the stranger left, I went outside. Mama, I knew, had taken something so she could sleep and the storm wasn't coming after all.

> *And as I lay me down to sleep, (oh lordy) angels watchin' over*
> *me, my lord,*
> *I pray the lord my soul to keep, (oh lordy) angels watchin' over*
> *me.*

I sang that from the yard. And from the top of the steps my brother sang, *(She likes to sing about the) Aaaangels.* He came down to where I was and stood beside me. He had acne cream dotted on his face.

He said, "What was his name?" talking about Frequent Stops. I told him it didn't matter; we would not see him again.

"So was he nice?" he asked.

I reached in my shirt and held up the quarter bag of marijuana.

"Oh my god, did he give you this?" Nuñez cupped it in his hands like he was touching for the first time something private.

"No," I said, "I stole it."

Then he snatched it from my hand and ran inside. I could've gone after him, tickled and teased him until he gave it back. But I did not want to smoke it anyway. And I liked that now Noonie had something I had won for him. I didn't want to go inside.

I cut through thin woods the long way to Bolton Road. I was not like Nuñez, I roamed. And never once those nights did I step back from myself to see myself as a girl walking alone. I wasn't naive, I just didn't care enough to be afraid. As a little kid Nuñez had been afraid of the dark and nightmares, but I wasn't. I would just close my eyes. Just close my eyes and dare bad dreams to come.

Those nights when I was fifteen I would go inside the gray house, the American Four-Square—to check how she was coming along. She was left open all winter, but by spring I had to break in through the basement. Then I would stand in the front hall and look out at the street for a while, then leave. I didn't inspect or steal anything, I just stood there alone, owning its inside, walls holding in both the old and the unfinished space.

It would make me think about my daddy. His hair must be short now, he was out on parole. When he won his appeal he'd called me, he'd said, "Baby I won my case. I got that other life lifted up off me!" I was proud of him, he had gone prose. That's what set me up as not like Nuñez. He had not known his daddy. He did not even speak his native tongue, but I had a daddy I talked to. He always left some promise when he said good-bye and I did not know yet not to plan ahead. I was not like Nuñez. I had been to California. It was one of my getaways. Like the gray house. It was a finger pointing out into the future, like the first bus a lost person boards.

I walked home on the edge of the woods, where they met the high grass on the back side of the treatment plant. It was April and I took a minute to poise within life's pleasures, the breath of the world whole and warm against my T-shirt. Atlanta stretches on forever; it knows no full-on dark. I could see sessile and shepherd's purse buckle in gusts of wind. And walking up by the fence I saw two boys, one of them my brother. I did not know Noonie to leave the house at night. I did not know he had friends. But he was there, standing with his bony shoulders bent toward a boy his size. They were smoking it, the pot I'd stole. And I thought about Freak and that dark dirt smell, like radishes and sugar burning. And I thought, My brother—my half-brother—is going to sleep tonight with that smell on him, that sweet-complected smell.

I did not hear Nuñez come in that night, and the next morning, as usual Mama didn't rise to see us off, and I had to shake Nuñez and drag him from the bed to get us ready.

On our way to school he did not talk about the houses. He loped side to side, his every movement boasting the partyer's fatigue. Behind the Wadda Burger he said, "Oh my aching head."

I told him, "Pot doesn't make you hungover."

We scaled the dumpster and the wall, and we were in the Chevron parking lot. And he said, "Maybe that's not all I did."

"Where'd you go last night?" I asked him.

And he answered, "Honduras." Honduras was a word he used to mean: No Place, it's none of your biz.

"Did you have a good time?" I asked.

And he said, "Like singing."

And I was happy for him, honest, that he was finally getting a life. When we got to the gray house he said, "You're right, it's beautiful." And I smiled and busted out, burlesqueing mama:

And if I die before I wake, (oh lordy) angels watchin' over me, my lord, I pray the lord my soul to take, angels watchin' over me.

And Nuñez answered in his gunmetal-high harmonic *(She likes to sing about them) Aaangels.*

And all day at school that day I sang all the old songs to myself, the ones our mama sang to us on Sunday when we were small. Our mama was a stripper and we didn't go to church because she didn't like to see her customers in the pews on Sunday beside their wives.

At three P.M. I waited at the corner for Noonie, as was my custom, and that day I saw him coming from school with a friend for the first time, the boy from the night before. He was a light-skinned black boy with a smooth buzz and nice clothes. He had a soft stomach on him and his feet turned in. He didn't look like a bad kid, and they touched hands when they said good-bye. I thought, Well, one bag of marijuana and he goes and buys him a friend, and my stomach swung empty inside with that fifteen-year-old's *everybody-got-somebody-but-I-ain't-got-nobody* blues. I was afraid now Noonie wouldn't walk with me, and I would have to pass the new houses alone.

But he did walk with me, I was surprised to find, like nothing had changed. He said, "Sharky," and it felt like days since anyone had said my name. I liked having him with me, him swinging his black hair like Dorothy Hamill. I thought, What a fine figure we must cut.

When we got to the Four-Square, there were no workmen around it, and there were new kitchen cabinets waiting in the yard, white-enameled metal, made to look old.

Nuñez said, "Just look at this," and he touched a chrome handle. His eyes got shiny. "This is custom, Sharky. All this is custom."

He was fun to impress, so I gave up to him my secret: I told him the house was my special place. I told him how to get inside. He liked that, and we were happy and talking the whole way home, until we got to the Chevron. We were in our neighborhood then, and coming toward us we saw the slow moving van of Frequent

Stops. It pulled into the station and rolled up right beside us, and the window came down.

"Where's your mama at?" Freak leered at us, "'Cause that whore's got my bag of dope."

My throat closed. There was hot action in my head.

"I been through your whole damn house and it ain't in there and I ain't going to leave til I get it back." He got out of his car and got up in Nuñez's face and whispered, "Tell me where your mama's at."

A nice-looking lady came around the back where we were with the bathroom key in her hand and Freak put his hand on my shoulder, so the lady might think we were his. "The club don't open till six P.M. Tell me where your mama's at. Tell me where she's at and I'll let you alone."

I said, "Sometimes she goes in early."

"Well her car's there," and he jogged his head toward our road.

Not knowing any better, Noonie told him, "She's got some guy who takes her."

Freak was bad messed up; he was splashed with liquor and he growled at Nuñez: "You know where she's at. You know who she's off with, don't you?"

Nuñez's face was breaking.

I said, "She ain't got your marijuana."

"Then who does? Who does?" And he got back into the van, gunned it, and was gone.

Then the nice lady came out of the bathroom and got in her husband's Ford, and they drove close by us, slowly staring, like Americans on a safari.

When we got home there was a book and a beer on the steps where Frequent Stops had laid in wait. It was Mama's copy of *100 Ways to Meet Rich Men*. The door was open and, inside, the house was bad tore up. There was cereal tracked across the floor and clothes strewn everywhere. Our drawers were emptied on the beds. I thought about the stories you hear, how the wind comes and lifts up the mobile home you're in like a box kite. Or you would think, This is what the dream looks like afterwards. I went in my mama's room and put her things away.

When I was finished in there, Nuñez had done no work at all. He had just cleared the table and laid a dogwood branch on it and a drugstore candle. Everything could be a shambles. All he cared was that Mama would come home and praise him, say, "Oh sweet lamb, you've really got an eye." My brother only saw the easiest ways out.

I'm not like him, I have follow-through. After the kitchen looked okay, I went in my room. Frequent had pulled my winter clothes out from under the bottom bunk, and dumped my shoe-box full of make-up and awards on top of that. Frequent Stops had even opened up all my daddy's prison letters and I had to match each one to its envelope. Why would he care what's mine? I thought, flattered and amazed. But then the blues came back to me, from staring at the backward slant of my father's hand. He had made all this mess not to show me, but to show my mama. I wanted to think he had made this mess for me. I lay on my bed full of fear and shame, imagining. I thought I wanted the kind of man my mama would choose. I saw him kicking in the door for me. It never occurred to me this was not love, this, breaking and entering.

It was dark by the time I got the house picked up. Nuñez was on the sofa holding a radio, fooling with the knobs how a starved dog worries a naked bone. Nothing was coming in.

I put my shoes on and he asked me, "Where you off to?"

I said, "Honduras," and he scowled, "that's my word."

I left the house, and, on me, the world had a terrible grip, every-thing the same old same old. In the road, I picked up a handful of rocks. Nuñez was selfish. *Honduras* wasn't all his to claim. It was a country he had never been to. Just a word, a place men with jobs could come and leave from. I could use it also, whenever I liked, and I did not know then that it means *the depths*.

Like always, I called my daddy from the pay phone, but no one answered at his girlfriend's house. Then I stood in the Wadda Burger parking lot and threw rocks at the bats that flew up high around the lights. They were feeding on insects. And it was fun to confuse them; I could make them dive for the rocks. I liked to feel the eyes of the customers on me, and that night I made my tosses lower and lower. It was an experiment, and yes, the bats came down.

I fought all fear, until I was throwing no higher than my head. And all the bats were swooping close circles—I controlled them. Everyone around me knew I was worth watching. Then a tiny baby bat fell, and the other bats were gone. I bent down and nudged it with a stick. It was both pink and black with no fur yet. Then someone came up behind me and I screamed. The boys in their cars started laughing. It was Frequent Stops. He reached down for the baby bat, and I said, "Don't touch it or the mama won't come back."

"It's dead," he slurred. "Kill it."

He was god awful drunk and he bumped me as we stepped back to lean against his car. "See," I said, "It chirps like a smoke alarm and the mama hears it."

He was agitated, he was sweating and tense from fighting or crying. His eyes wove. He would not see it if the mama bat did come down.

I got in the van, to get the boys' eyes off me, and Frequent came back with a vanilla shake. He took the lid off and poured liquor in it and stirred it with his dirty finger. He said, "I'm real sorry. What's wrong with me, Sharky?"

I said, "For what? For wrecking our house?"

He kept saying, "I'm just real sorry."

The drink he gave me was cold and burned my nose with peppermint. He tore out of the parking lot before I could say No, and he took us onto 285. We flew till we hit traffic. He was grinding his teeth, "I just need somebody to talk to, Sharky."

And I kept drinking the sweet drink. We got stuck behind a rattle-trap El Camino. In the truckbed were a mattress and a Pac Man machine and three scrawny goats. He said, "Trash or Nigger."

It's a traveling game where you guess a person by their car. You can call it Ebony or Ivory, Black or White. But Frequent called it what my daddy called it. "Trash or Nigger," he asked again, "Let's play."

I said, "I don't want to."

The mattress had brown flowers and was leaning against some plywood, everything poorly arranged.

He said, "Well, I'll tell you: Driving that truck, that's a hippy vegetarian lady with great big tits."

Then he sped around it. There was an old black man driving. He had a creased face, a white church shirt on, and his eyes looked down at me, runny and yellow as a three-minute egg.

"Sometimes you win. Sometimes you lose," said Frequent. And he did not see that the man in the truck had judged us also. But I had seen how the old man had seen me. I saw myself in the game also, some piece of trash on the highway, not well-tied down.

I had been excited by the prospect of that trip, but then we circled back toward home on 41, and I saw that Freak was going nowhere. He had no plan. When we got back into The Stink, he pulled into the empty lot of the sewage treatment plant. He rolled the window down and sang: *Eew-eew, that smell.* We both got out of the car and I was drunk by this time, the sugar a big tangle in my mouth.

"You got real pretty hair. Honey color," he told me, and I saw I'd let it fall loose across my shoulders. I shook my head and it fell further and farther. His face was mapped with shadows from the chain-link fence around the lagoons. This wasn't bad air to me. It's a smell you can't smell anyway until once you've been outside it and come back.

"You're tall," he said, moving away, "I think you went and grew on me overnight." He hung his fingers in the fence and stared out.

The anger was dying inside him, and so I poked at it. I said, "Maybe Mama's home now." I said, "It wasn't her, anyway who stole your pot."

He turned around, smiling, "Well who did then?" He came toward me, "Huh? Who stole it, then?"

I was sleepy and he opened the side door of the van and pushed me down. Underneath his shirt I knew there would be that torn-up lady's face. He took my neck and was kissing me, pushing himself against me, kissing me. It was not going to be my first time. He pressed his jeans into me. I had had sex before. But I had never screamed like Mama. No one would ever think I cried for help.

He said, "Is your brother older or younger? My mom and dad just moved to Canada. Hey little girl, I got a joke for ya." He was on top of me, almost laughing. He cupped my breast with his left hand and he moved with his right to touch my chin.

I looked down. His knuckle was cut, like he'd put his fist through a door. I took him by the wrist and I saw the cut was new, a gray dent of skin pulled back and bruising. And I thought about the damage at my house he had done. I held his fist right up to him, "Where'd that come from?"

He broke my hold, and I tried to sit up, but he was kneading my hip bone with the butt of his left hand. I prayed for a flashlight, some guard to come. I said, "Where'd that cut come from? What did you bust? What did you go off and hit?"

He said, "Nobody."

Then a dim picture came to me of somebody at my house bleeding. I was drunk still, there were bats circling inside my head. I said, "Who'd you hit?"

"It was a freak thing." He said, "They ran off right after. I had a right to, anyway. He deserved it."

I said "Nuñez?"

My belly felt cold when he took his hand away. He got off me. He said, "Get up. You ain't worth the time. Maybe later," he said, and I got out of the back and slammed the side door, and when he saw me standing there in the parking lot shooting him a bird for beating up my little brother, he backed out and screeched away.

I wished afterwards I'd gone all the way with him, so I could go home self-satisfied, that I had something to use on my mama at my will when she deserved it. But when I got home, her car was there and she was asleep in her room. I stood over her, and my tongue moved in my mouth like a dancer in a cage. I did not even think of looking for a sign of blood or a fight. Mama was laying there exhausted from the day and night. Did she dream of dancing? Reenact moves without music? Like an animal, did she pace?

When she was young, she'd danced suspended above the other dancers. She'd worked at the Limelight, rolling with silver coins and housecats under its glass floor. I wondered, Did she dream the usual dreams, like falling, losing things? The hate emptied out of me—stepped to the side for other feelings, but I would not let guilt come. If she loved Frequent Stops it was hard to tell. I felt sorry for her, that she didn't think herself worth loving or hating. And Frequent would move on also, he would move sideways on to someone else, the way I meant to.

I said, "Mama?" and she didn't answer. I could've shaken her, but she was knocked out on pills. And I went back to wanting to steal her dirty boyfriend. She had never been there for me. I did not love her like Nuñez. I did not love anyone, just ideas, and now and then my daddy.

I had put the whole house back together. Mama did not know the mess she'd caused. I cussed her in my head for looking out for just herself. In the bathroom there was bloody toilet tissue in the trash. The sink was wiped clean and there was a tooth on it. A bottom one. Raw and red at the root. My brother had laid it there neatly to save it forever, memento of bad times. I thought in negative toward the gap that would be there now, public knowledge when he smiled. Mama had told us there was a Jesus-shaped hole in everyone's heart until the Lord finds you and fills it, just another of her lies. I always felt the hole in me but it wasn't Jesus-shaped; it kept changing. I knew we didn't have the money to fix a broken mouth. Nuñez was vain. This will tear him up, I thought, and I went looking for Nuñez.

I walked the long way through the woods and up by the rail-road. And I did not find him. Then I thought about it, us walking together, him from whom I had no secrets now. I had told Nuñez, and I went to the gray house full of tears. I thought we would walk our route home together, that I would comfort him, maybe singing.

The Four-Square was dark. I went in through the basement way, and when I climbed the stairs I could hear him talking and laugh-ing. It was hard to believe he was happy after getting his tooth knocked out. But that was him laughing. I sang, *And If I live another day, (oh lordy) angels watchin' over me, my lord . . .*

And I heard a splash and someone say, "Oh, shit." Then Nuñez said, "Oh, shit," also and when I got to the doorway of the big bathroom—I saw the boy—Nuñez's friend standing like a wet rat, just pulling up his pants. Nuñez was naked in the sunken tub, air jets roaring. He was grinning, very messed up. He said, "Don't leave me." But his friend looked nervous, and he shut the jets off, and took his shoes and shirt, stepping carefully across wine cooler bottles and a row of squat candles burning on the floor. The friend nodded and left.

"Put your clothes on, loser," I told Noonie and turned away. In the mirror he splashed and struggled to get out of the tub. He was drunk and stoned. His lip was swollen. I started feeling like we should get out. I said, "This place belongs to someone, Noonie."

His head bobbed, "God, it's beautiful."

The house was so well built, no sounds from the street got in and I felt trapped. He rambled, "I love you, Sharky. You're great," and he hung his arms around my neck. "This is funny."

I said, "What is?"

"Honduras," he said, "nothing, everything."

. . .

When we got home, he began to spew his heart again, "I'm not gay. Don't tell nobody." And I told him, "Of course, I won't," and I meant it, because, all and all, I want people to be happy.

When we got inside Mama had roused and was up waiting. Her voice cracked, "Where've you been? I've been worried sick."

Nuñez started crying and whining, "Look what he done, Mama," and he pulled down his bottom lip. There was the hole, a ragged trapdoor of bare gum. He sucked, and blood began to fill his mouth.

Mama held him by the elbows, "Oh sweet, sweet precious lamb, who done this to you?"

And he said, "That awful man."

I glared at him, "It was Frequent Stops."

Mama just kept looking at her son, "Oh baby, I'm so sorry. Why did he go and do that?" And the heat rose in my face because she wasn't angry. "It's all my fault," she went on, "'cause I run with such sorry guys. I'm sorry. Why'd he have to go and do that?"

Nuñez whined, "'Cause he thought I stole his pot, but I didn't steal his pot. I didn't."

Mama touched his cheek, "I know you didn't honey. I wish we knew who did."

And Nuñez whispered, "It was Sharky."

"Is that true Charlotte Kay?" she asked me, her red hair askew. "I should've known."

Nuñez pried loose from Mama and went into his room.

"Your brother doesn't have the wherewithal to steal his own crap out of the bowl. I should've known it was you. Sharky, why'd you go and do that?"

And I said, "I didn't have it in my hand but one minute, one minute. It was Nuñez stole it from me. I was gonna give it back."

"You think tattling is going to get you out of this stink? I can't take it anymore, Sharky, you've got to grow up, stop causing me this pain. It ain't easy taking care of you." She had thrown herself down on the counter. She told me I'd have to pay Freak back.

I thought to myself, And who's going to pay for that tooth? His broken face? It was Frequent she should be mad at and all the dirty other ones she'd let into our house.

She shook me by the shoulders, "Do you think it's easy what I do?"

I would go all the way with her next boyfriend or Frequent if I chose to. And I would let Mama find out. I would get pregnant by Frequent Stops and then she'd know what kind of deep shit I could get in. I said, "Let me go." And Mama did.

Nuñez had locked himself in the bathroom. I beat on the door and I yelled at him, "Brother, I got secrets on you too. I got bad secrets on you, you tattling faggot." And he started screaming. He started banging things around. And Mama came and stood beside me and she said to him, "Baby come out of there. It's going to be all right."

He stayed in there a long time. I sat on the sofa, sullen. Mama wasn't concerned with me anymore, only my brother. "I'm so worried about him," she kept saying, her head on the arm of the couch. Then we heard the bathroom door open and he left the house. He ran away. Mama ran and stood in the door, shouting after him, "Come back here, baby!"

Then she came inside and she went in the bathroom to wash her face, and she came back out: "My pills are gone. I had quaaludes and Xanax and Zoloft in there, Sharky, and they're all gone. We got to find him. Before he does something crazy."

"I know where he's at," I said. And Mama and I drove over to the gray house. She was hysterical crying. And I felt sick, a million bats swooping circles in my head. This was just like my brother, always looking for the easiest ways out. I said, "We'll find him, Mama."

We went in through the basement and Mama hit a light switch and the whole house flooded with light. She went through the downstairs rooms screaming his name. I thought I heard a noise as I climbed the stairs, but when I got to the big bathroom, the door was locked and it was dead quiet on the other side. I beat on the door and I screamed also, I screamed for help for the first time in my life, and Mama found me. She put her arm around me and she said, "You won't get in that way, Sharky," and after a few minutes she'd jimmied the lock with an emery board.

Nuñez was lying face down on the floor and there were empty pill bottles all around him. Mama didn't say anything. She was calm about it, like she knew he was going to be dead. She did not touch him. I think she thought he was beautiful, the way he was sleeping. Everything was done, in my mind. I had no anger for anyone, no fear. We would have to find a phone, call 911, we would have to try and save him, and there was going to be a lot of mutual tears, but for this moment we let him lie. We gave ourselves that one simple quietest time.

I looked at him, I thought I saw him breathing, and I began to lecture him in my mind: Taking pills, Nuñez? That's just aping Mama. Taking pills. Oh, I am not like you, brother. Taking pills is something easy and selfish. Well, I am not like you, Nuñez. I will not take the easy ways out. I'm not going to sleep with anyone just to hurt Mama. I am not like you. I will not ruin my whole life just to mess with hers.

I looked out the window. I stared into the commode. There were pills floating in it. Lots of them. I flushed it and the water level started rising; it was clogged with pills. Mama saw what I saw and she narrowed her brow.

I said, "He didn't take nothing."

She gave Nuñez a swift kick in the side.

"Ow," he yelped, curling up on the floor.

Mama said, "Son, what did you swallow?"

He said, "Nothing."

"You didn't take one pill?"

And he said, "No ma'am."

She collapsed like an empty sack against the wall.

"I was going to take some, but y'all didn't give me time," he whined, trying to defend himself, but it was no good. Mama had stopped coddling him.

"Do you know how much those pills cost? Do you know how hard they were to get?"

And he said, "No ma'am."

"Well you better find a way to make this up to me, son. This ain't funny. You think it's funny?"

He said "No ma'am."

The whole way home, Mama scolded and lectured Nuñez. She told him he was grounded for the next two months. That kind of discipline was new to us. She had to explain the very concept to him. She said she was going to stick to her word.

And the next day he stayed in his room, sucking on his broken tooth, ashamed. I felt sorry for him. I went in and I said, "Why don't you draw a picture or something?" I told him everything was going to be all right. He just mumbled, "Go away."

So I did. I went to the Four-Square one last time. It was raining and the workmen were gone. No one had touched the bathroom since we had left the night before. I unclogged the toilet and I cleaned up the candles, the wine cooler bottles, and the pill bottles, and I drained the stagnant water from the tub. I found the bag of marijuana under the sink and I tucked it in my shirt. I sat down on the tiles and scraped up the spilled wax with my thumb. When I was done, I lit one of the candles and I lay there on my back, imagining what it would be like to die. I pictured my brother lying there, on that floor, dead. How different my life could be. It was strange to me, that this place wasn't mine, that the beautiful couple who owned this house would move in to it, never knowing one bit about its story. I dribbled wax onto the floor, I was making lazy letters with the wax. I thought about Frequent Stops and where that old man might have been going with the mattress and the goats. Nuñez's whole name is Simon Paradiso Igriega y Nuñez. But my name isn't so pretty. I go by Sharky, Sharky Harmon, and I wrote that and I left it there.

*And if I live another day, (oh lordy) angels watchin' over me, my lord
I pray the lord to guide my way, (there must be) angels watchin'
over me.*

I sang that as I got to the door of our house when I got home,
so that Nuñez would know it was only me. And after a minute he
sang back: *(I think there must be) aaaangels watchin' over me.*

It was the year his voice was changing.

Jane R. Shippen grew up in Atlanta, Georgia.
She attended the University of North Carolina at
Chapel Hill and the University of Virginia, where
she was the recipient of two Academy of American
Poets prizes and the Henry Hoyns Fellowship.
She has read her poems at the Geraldine R.
Dodge Poetry Festival in Waterloo, New Jersey,
and the National Gallery of Art. Her work has

appeared in the *Carolina Quarterly, Arts & Letters, Meridian,* and the
Buenos Aires Herald Magazine. She spent 2000 in Argentina as a
Fulbright Fellow in Creative Writing. She lives in Charlottesville,
Virginia.

*F*or about two weeks this story was called "Had I Been Nuñez," and I
couldn't get the tenses right. It was too pluperfect, once-was, had-been,
like an old newspaper not worth bringing in from the rain. So, finally, I gave
up and I wrote "I Am Not Like Nuñez" on the top of a fresh sheet of paper,
and for the next ten hours I had Sharky cruising through my head.

   I grew up a few miles from this story, in a neck of city-woods that smelled
less like sewage, more like car exhaust and English ivy, but I went to school
with girls like Sharky. Our hearts are not that different.

   The lesson I learned by writing this is that teenage girls are not like bats:
they tend to survive, whether or not their mothers come when they cry.
Adolescence can be a terrible time because you start to see the rotten
framework of your life that, all through childhood, had been invisible. But

you have to go through that to find the joy that comes when you see the shambles all around you and realize you're going to make your own way in this world, regardless. Then you can wink back at your house and say, Well, at least it was not like everyone's. You're grown when you have found that grace.

George Singleton

PUBLIC RELATIONS

(from *The Georgia Review*)

I hadn't even ordered from the bar yet when, out of nowhere, I said this: "The women's movement of the late 1960's ruined our educational system." I sat with my wife Ardis, my boss and his wife, and a woman who wanted to hire me out to revive her company. This was an overpriced restaurant in downtown Greenville where BMW executives brought visiting Germans, where Michelin people brought their French. The place could've been called Casablanca's. The woman needing a consultant owned a slight chain of health food/karaoke joints in the Carolinas and needed someone like me to leak out fake news that everybody else's alfalfa sprouts contained hepatitis B. My résumé ran ten pages long in nine-point type with such ruses. I'm the guy behind brush-rinse-repeat at the toothpaste company; the water company hired me to come up with that "eight glasses a day" rule. I'm the anti-PR man responsible for claiming grits as the cure-all for fire ant mounds, thus disabling the insecticide industry while causing the demand for instant grits to double.

Ardis kicked me. You'd've thought I got a bullhorn and started listing off statistics about World War II right there in the restaurant. My boss—a peckerhead named Jacob who insisted on a ladder motif in both home and office—forced a laugh. What didn't bother me whatsoever about sounding harsh, and even irrational, concerns the owner of the health food stores, a woman who saw herself above everyone else just because she could pronounce a slew of herbs in Latin and list their supposed remedies. She had "found herself one with the Native Americans" and legally changed her name to Naomi Locust Wind. That bugged me.

"You must be joking," Naomi Locust Wind said. Listen, she was whiter than a loaf of Sunbeam bread. I had more reason to change my name to that of an Algonquin chief: I'd done some pro bono work on the Cherokee reservation's conversion from bingo outlet to full-fledged land of casinos, and even got to smoke a peace pipe with some kid back behind one of those rubber-tomahawk stores.

The waiter came up and asked if I'd like the usual. I said, "Yes, a carafe of Manhattans," because that's what I drank. It had nothing to do with a $24 sale of land. My boss ordered a vodka tonic, like a pussy. His wife ordered white wine. Ardis said she'd have a carafe of martinis and the telephone number of a cab company. Naomi Locust Wind said this day was her day to go without liquid, which would've pissed off my water company account.

I said, "When we had good teachers it was because there was nothing else for smart women to look forward to doing. Hell, they became housewives, secretaries, or teachers."

"I have to disagree with you, V.O.," Jacob's wife said. She never liked me in the first place. Her name was Mimi, no lie.

I said, "Listen. When I was in fourth grade I had a fifty-year-old woman named Mrs. Flowers for a teacher. She'd graduated from goddamn Vassar. In the fifth grade I had a woman named Mrs. Breland. She went to Columbia or someplace like that."

"Weren't you lucky," Naomi said. "I went to Smith."

I said, "See? Before the women's movement you couldn't have gone on to run your own business. You'd've taught kids at best, and those kids would've gone on to know the English language because of you."

My wife said to Naomi, "Do you know Laurel Hyman-Jones? I took a workshop with her one time up in Raleigh. She was teaching at Smith at the time." Ardis could paint a realistic portrait if she wanted, but did her best to make everything look primitive. She spent a lot of time perfecting the value of flat. I loved my wife, and respected her tenacity.

The waiter brought our drinks. I didn't light a cigarette when Naomi Locust Wind shook her head.

"Here's what I'm saying," I said. "In the old days, women with IQ's of 120 and above could only become teachers. After about 1970 all the smart women went on to become lawyers, doctors, and businesswomen. That left the teaching profession with a shelf of nonspectacular scholars to lead our kids. Plus, with more women in the workforce outside of teaching, stupid men went into teaching seeing as their spots in banking and insurance got taken up. I'm not laying the blame on anyone, ma'am."

Does this sound like a faulty cause and effect argument? Does this sound like the words of a misogynist? Hotdamn, I put stupid men into my little theory, and maybe even put them behind smart women teachers and second-level women teachers. I poured half a Manhattan into my martini-style glass. I was prepared to go into some kind of *reductio ad absurdum* argument about how, with the advent of computers, only ditch diggers, asphalt workers, roofers, television talk show hosts, and evangelists will be around to call roll each morning in the elementary schools of America.

Mimi said, "I always thought I'd be a teacher until I spent a semester practice teaching my senior year. Luckily I met Jacob."

Ardis shoved her heel into my left toe so I wouldn't make a point. Later on—and this is a totally different story—she took to wearing golf spikes when we went out to dinner, or had people over.

Naomi unfolded her menu. I didn't say anything about the steak, pork, lamb, pheasant, alligator tail, or rabbit. Then the goof-ball waiter came up, looked me straight in the face, and asked, "Do you know the perfect way to prepare quail?"

When I said, "How," even I understood that it sounded like I'd made fun of those extras in any cowboy movie.

• • •

After we had ordered and the waiter departed, Jacob said to me, "V.O., I wanted you to meet Naomi because I thought you'd be perfect for finding her a way to separate her chain of health food and karaoke stores from the thousand others that have sprouted up in the Southeast." He raised his eyebrows, which wrinkled his massive forehead. His upper visage looked like a topographical map of the changing Sahara.

"'Sprouted up.' That's precious," Mimi said.

Ardis kept looking at her menu. She had asked the waiter if she could keep hers to look over. I think she was probably looking for a personal sign pointing out whether she should get up and leave or not. My wife liked those search-a-word games, too.

"Lure's an interesting last name," Naomi said to me. "What does the V.O. stand for?"

Jacob sat forward to say what he always said. The table behind us was filled with six men talking in three different languages about grand prix racing, something no one in South Carolina understood. "It stands for Vice Operator. V.O. can find ways to ruin Fortune 500 businesses in one working day."

My wife touched Naomi's hand. "It doesn't stand for anything. His parents didn't have imagination. They couldn't have worked in the business world *or* taught school." Her carafe of martinis was dry, dry.

I said, "It stands for V.O., truly. V.O. Lure. Velour. It sounds like *velour*. My daddy worked in the textile mill."

"Naomi's father was a farmer," my boss said. "That's where she got her basic understanding of pollination. And cross-pollination."

Mimi said, "I never understood biology. Osmosis—that's part of biology, isn't it?" Mimi had ordered spaghetti.

Without a twitch of smirk on her face, Naomi Locust Wind said to Ardis, "How did you meet up with this Neanderthal?" I ordered my wife another carafe. Although I didn't know it at the beginning of the evening, evidently I wanted to get fired. And I kind of wanted to see a big catfight.

"We met right after V.O. invented the White Trash Monopoly

game. You probably don't sell it at your stores. I'd just gotten out of graduate school and had a part-time job working for a patent lawyer. V.O. came in. Love at first sight."

In any movie Ardis would've leaned over and kissed me, would've said, "Ain't that so, honey?" in any Hollywood production. She didn't give me a glance.

"Ginkgo biloba's supposed to help people see clearer in more ways than one," Naomi Locust Wind said. "You might want to take a good ten or twenty drops in a glass of filtered spring water every day."

Okay, so I might go on about doing pro bono work for the Cherokee nation, but I've also turned against clients when they treated me like a rambling dolt in out-of-style glasses. I'm the consultant responsible for putting beanie babies where they got to, then back to where they belonged. I don't want to brag, but between slugs of my Manhattan—before I could even distinguish whether the bartender put one or two cherries in the carafe— I knew that it would only take me one call to NewsChannel 4 and thirty seconds on the Internet to ruin Naomi Locust Wind's Ginseng-Along cafés with news of chemically enhanced paba or whatever. Man, I had the means to hire outright hoodlums who'd infiltrate each store and leave trace evidence of things odd people don't want on their fucking maize.

Jacob sat back against his chair and said, "Now, now."

"We should play Twenty Questions," Mimi said. "Let's play I Spy with My Little Eye." She didn't look unlike a woman who worked as a flapper in a previous life.

I'll give Ardis this: she would've stood by me if I'd caught the pope's robe on fire. She said, "I take that St. John's wort stuff that's supposed to cure minor depression. It worked until tonight."

I *could've* faded away until my dinner showed up. I said, "Everything didn't come out the way I meant for it to come out. Listen. In the old days, we all got taught by women teachers. They were all right. We trusted them. Nowadays we don't trust teachers, and we shouldn't. Something happened. It happened after Nixon. It happened somewhere along the line. I dare anyone at this table to go look up SAT scores, dropout rate, violence in the schools, and PTA attendance. Fuck, I remember during science fair week there were kids who built rockets. I saw on the news the other day where a little boy won regionals with a misspelled posterboard explaining cocoons and butterflies. That's too easy."

The waiter brought salads. We all got regular salads—spinach and endive—with the house dressing. There were no choices, like ranch or Thousand Island. It was some kind of raspberry vinaigrette shit I didn't like, and I had it in my mind that if the chef was over fifteen years old he or she would've known that there was more than one way to do anything. Unfortunately I said, "I wish the chef wasn't so sure of himself."

"How do you know the chef's a man?" Naomi said. "After everything else you've said, maybe it's a woman, seeing as we've infiltrated every aspect of the workforce that seems to threaten you."

I held a piece of red cabbage on my fork and said, "You know, with a name like Locust Wind, shouldn't you be wearing some fucking beads or something? Give me a break, Pocahontas. At least go get yourself some moccasins, or a feather to put in the back of your hair."

Even the French, Dutch, and German people seated around us shut up on this one. My boss said how I could clean out my desk and computer in the morning, right after I told him how to fix the Ginseng-Alongs. Ardis began humming; she picked up her menu and didn't return my look. Jacob's wife Mimi craned her neck backwards towards the bartender for another glass of wine. Naomi slipped off her shoe and touched my leg—accidentally, I'm sure. The band in the corner played a polka.

When the food came Naomi Locust Wind didn't waste time. I'm not sure what she ordered, but it involved shellfish and angel hair pasta. I'd never seen anyone take care of a plate like she did. Me, I couldn't even figure out what direction to cut my mackerel without it falling apart altogether. By the time I decided what to do with the skin and eyeballs, Naomi was sitting there as if she wanted to order cordials.

"I've been intentionally hard on you people," she said. "I'll be the first to admit that I don't trust anyone, and it causes me to be hard on everyone with whom I have to deal."

I said, "Perfect English."

My ex-boss said, "Don't think we don't know what you do and don't really want," which I couldn't follow. Jacob held a fork to his mouth and kept his eyebrows raised. He'd ordered a shrimp quesadilla and wore guacamole on the tip of his nose.

Ardis said to him, "We should start all over. Still, promise me you'll fire V.O. because of this." To me she said, "What in the world made you say that thing about the feminist movement and the education system?"

"Sometimes I just make connections," I said. "Excuse me for thinking. If I'd've been taught in the 1980s we wouldn't have to worry about thinking. We'd all be sitting around talking about how to carry a hollow egg around for a month, pretending it was a baby."

Naomi Locust Wind said, "I have a niece in third grade. She knows how to put a condom on her finger. Next thing you know, some parent presses charges against her teacher for molestation."

I didn't say, "That's what I'm talking about." I didn't say, "She can put a rubber on her finger, but she doesn't know the capital of her home state." I let it go.

We sat there behind our used plates and silverware. The foreign diners lit cigars and laughed as if someone was doing pull-my-finger routines. I poured my drink to the brim, then poured for Ardis. My wife said, "I've heard of people fasting for one day out of the week, but not not drinking liquids. Tell me again what that does for you?"

Naomi Locust Wind accidentally ran her stockinged foot halfway up my thigh. She said, "I don't know." She paused and then said, "Oh, what the hell," taking my glass and slugging down half of it. "I have this theory that the body fills with toxins, and that toxins even come from plain water. I also believe that it's good to shock the system so it becomes adjusted to harsher situations. It's kind of like how plants become frost hardened. But it's a personal theory. There's no medical proof."

The waiter came up and handed us dessert menus. I didn't open mine. Mimi, of all people, said, "It seems to me you should be doing the opposite. If you want your body to adjust to harsh conditions —like maybe you want it to be ready for post-nuclear-holocaust life—then you should guzzle down a quart of vodka per day."

I handed the waiter a five-dollar bill and told him to ask the band to play something by Merle Haggard or George Jones.

Naomi Locust Wind stared at my ex-boss's wife for a ten count, turned to me, and said, "What do stupid women do now, in your opinion? There's always been stupid women who couldn't teach, or become secretaries. Do you think that all a stupid woman could do after the women's movement is become a housewife?"

I said, "Women who can't make it in the business world and who can't make it teaching do the same thing that men do who can't handle either job. They sit out front of abortion clinics with vulgar signs. Or they back their stupid husbands, who believe that the Confederate flag needs to fly over the state capitol so everyone can remember his heritage. Listen, I'm Irish, but I don't have to drink whiskey, eat potatoes, and kill Englishmen every day to remember what I come from."

I'd been contacted by the anti-abortion front in the past. They wanted me to invent the perfect ad campaign so all young women kept their babies. I told those numbnuts that I'd get right back to them as soon as I completed a twelve-step lobotomy program. In the past I'd given other smartass answers to PR queries, and that's why Jacob and I worked out of a Butler building in the middle of Pickens County, far from where extremists would be willing to travel in order to shoot ammunition towards us. We thrived on word-of-mouth. Hotdamn, we got hired out by big, big companies and by people far, far away from South Carolina. And all of this worked, especially after what we did for and against the powdered aspirin industry. Even one of those mercenary magazines did a spread on us.

Mimi folded and refolded her used napkin. Ardis tried to turn the conversation towards humid weather conditions. My ex-boss clenched a butter knife, and Naomi Locust Wind said, "Very Obnoxious. Vainglory Ontologist. Vortical Operative."

"It's plain V.O., I swear," I said. "You'd think that I'd drink that drink—VO—but it would be too obvious." I'm not exaggerating when I say that Naomi Locust Wind kept staring at me.

Jacob said, "I heard a funny joke today. It's one of those Little Johnny jokes, but I can't remember it. Have y'all heard a new Little Johnny joke?"

Mimi leaned over and said something to her husband. I said I hadn't heard a new Little Johnny joke. Jacob handed me a credit card. He said, "You people can figure out how to smash the competition. Forge my signature. Let's you and me talk at nine o'clock sharp tomorrow." He and his wife left at the end of the house band playing "White Lightning," and right before "Mama Tried."

Naomi Locust Wind ordered a margarita, even though I told her how the French and Germans knew nothing about tequila. She said, "My real name's Naomi Ridgeway. I don't know anything about tequila, either. Maybe I've forgotten my own heritage."

Ardis said, "Another carafe of martinis, with extra olives!" like that, even though the waiter stood at our table. He looked at us for a three count, then said, "I don't want to cast any aspersions or make any assumptions, but in these litigious days I am required to mention how driving under the influence is against the law, that some fifteen thousand people are killed in accidents per year involving drunks, et cetera, et cetera. The average lifespan of an umbrella is two years. I like to throw that in, too, whenever I make this speech. I used to work in the resource center of the library." He could've worked for me.

Naomi Locust Wind said, "I could use a man like you managing one of my stores. Hey, what kind of money are you making here? How many Bob Dylan songs do you know? I can give you about twenty-five grand a year plus free insurance and a 401(k) plan. Do you know anything about health food?"

"I know that the scallops you just ate were really whitefish."

The waiter's name was Glenn. He had introduced himself like this: "My name's G-l-e-n-n Glenn." He now quit his job, evidently, and sat down at the table with us—with me, my wife Ardis who tried to make her work look like an idiot painted it, and the woman who changed her name so it sounded more earthy. I'm not saying that I would've fallen for Naomi Locust Wind, but I knew that no foot would linger on my inseam again once the waiter sat down.

"Are y'all having a good night?" Glenn asked.

"I've probably lost a job. Your future boss has a chain of health food stores that won't do as well as they could, and Ardis here," I pointed a thumb at my wife, "probably wants to leave me. Who's our waiter now? I want another round of drinks."

Naomi Locust Wind said, "Maybe you can settle a bet for us, Glenn. How old are you?"

"I'm twenty-two."

"So you came up through the educational system after 1970, right?"

He sat for a minute trying to do math in his head—which proves my point right there, by the way—before saying, "I graduated from high school in 1996."

I said, "What's the capital of North Dakota? Name as many presidents as you can. What were the dates of World War I, World War II, and Vietnam? Name pi."

Ardis said, "Give it a break, V.O."

Glenn said, "I don't have to be a prawn in your little game." I swear to God. He might've known the difference between whitefish and scallops, but put him at a chessboard and shrimp get taken.

Naomi Locust Wind held up one palm. She said, "He's being an asshole. He's an asshole."

Another waiter showed up with a portable telephone. He handed it to me and said, "It's for you."

I said, "What?"

My ex-boss was on the other end. He said, "Little Johnny goes off to Catholic camp and finds a nun half naked. She's putting on a new habit and stands next to her old habit on the floor. Little Johnny points to it and says, 'What's that?' The nun says, 'Oh, that old thing—it's my bad habit.' Johnny says, 'Nuns don't keep any of their bad habits?' The nun shakes her head and says, 'No, but the priest still likes altar boys.'"

I said, "That ain't funny."

Jacob said, "It's funny if you're not Catholic. It's funny if you're employed. Listen, V.O., did I miss something tonight? Were we acting out some kind of good-PR-man/bad-PR-man roles that I wasn't in on? I know you think you're being funny and/or shocking, but it doesn't work that way. That's how we lost the NRA account. It's how we lost the tobacco board account. I think you know that I think it's best if we part ways."

Naomi Locust Wind pulled on her margarita with a straw, leaned over to Glenn, stuck the other end in his mouth, and served him some new kind of shooter. Ardis looked over her menu again. I said loudly, "Well, if you're really bent on leaving Mimi, I'll ask Naomi if she's interested," and hung up.

"What?" Ardis said.

"He remembered that Little Johnny joke." Naomi and Glenn turned my way. "He said he didn't want to tell it at the table for fear of a fork in his leg. It was about Little Johnny going out West, finding a naked Indian maiden in her teepee, pointing at her crotch, and asking her what it was. The Indian princess said . . ."

"Maiden," my wife said. It didn't bother me that she interrupted, seeing as I was having to make up the joke as I went.

"The Indian maiden said, 'This is Little Beaver.' Little Johnny stared at it a minute and said, 'Now it makes sense. My mom's got one that must be Big Beaver, which explains how my daddy's dick got whittled down to nothing.'"

No one said anything. For the first time, I could feel bourbon high in my alimentary canal. Glenn laughed, which automatically lost him his new job. Naomi Locust Wind said, "I don't know how you people stay in business." She didn't throw out any money on the table. Before she left she said, "I don't need you two palefaces trying to develop Ginseng-Alongs. I can get a number of well-known folk singers to endorse what I have to offer." Palefaces! Our ex-waiter followed her out. I yelled out something about John Denver.

My wife stirred her drink. "You didn't say anything about the thousand other minorities, V.O. Why didn't you say something bad about the Maori?"

"Listen. What I said about women and the educational system was meant to be a compliment towards the entire gender known as female. This all got started because none of us can look past what we're expecting."

Ardis laughed for the first time that evening. She said, "I see myself single, on the beach, surrounded by men offering to buy me drinks with little umbrellas. It'll be Tahiti. They'll call me the female Gauguin."

When Ardis left the table I thought she'd gone out to hail a cab. I sat there thinking how easy it was to lie about a company's product in order to nudge buyers that way, and how much easier it was to ruin somebody's competition so that consumers had no other choice but to choose what's left. Two words: Exxon Valdez.

About thirty minutes after I paid the check with Jacob's credit card—then burned the thing in the ashtray—I realized that Ardis didn't go to look for a cab. She'd either gotten one for herself or driven home drunk. I thought this: it seems like I could figure out the right thing to say in every situation so as not to fuck up continually, seeing that I had worked with some of President Clinton's advisors, that I had worked with the agents of NFL players who needed to explain their recent arrests, et cetera.

A new waiter came up and handed me a phone. He said nothing. I expected my student loan cops for some reason, but Ardis said, "I'm at the Hyatt. I'm around the block at the Hyatt, room 222. Just like that old TV show. Room 222."

I said, "I remember that show. What're you doing?"

"I have the car keys, so you can't drive home. And no matter how cosmopolitan Greenville tries to get, it's still a cotton-mill town with only a half-dozen taxis. I paid my driver twenty bucks to tell his colleagues over the radio not to pick you up."

I said, "Good trick. Maybe when I have to hang my own shingle you can be my partner. I've been looking for someone as debonair and conniving as me. As I."

Ardis said, "I've ordered a bottle of champagne from room service. I want to see how long I can keep you drunk. I don't want you sobering up and going back to work for Jacob. He's not a good person. He's not a good person for you. And the fake Native American's bad for everybody, by the way."

I thought about saying that judge-not-lest-you-be-judged thing from the Bible, but knew it sounded judgmental. I said, "God-damn, I just burned Jacob's credit card. We could've used it."

My wife—who would later change her mind about me altogether—said, "I paid for the room. Don't worry. This is my way of telling you how much I love you, even though you're an asshole. This is my way of saying that I think PR work has turned you into something that, deep down, you're not. Outside of my art, my main project is to change you back into the man I knew who invented White Trash Monopoly."

Listen, I'd wanted to quit my job for ten years. I promised myself that I'd quit once I came up with another game or gag gift that could be sold at every Stuckey's up and down I-95. I said, "Room 222."

"It was a good, moral TV show about human beings getting along, V.O."

I placed the telephone down. I asked for a to-go cup, didn't stumble around, and left with that high-step walk of drunks worried about level floors growing shin-high barriers. I turned right out of the restaurant-not-called-Casablanca's, and walked uphill towards Main Street. At the first alley I heard near-ululating sobs, and then I saw Naomi Locust Wind on her haunches. G-l-e-n-n stroked her head as if shining a bowling ball.

I almost said, "Man, no wonder you don't drink. It must be true what they say about Native Americans' capacity to handle alcohol." I almost said, "Boy, it doesn't matter how much you shake that eight ball, the answer's going to be 'Definitely No.'"

I high-stepped onward, though. I passed an obvious group of magnet high school students playing Go on the steps of the Atlanta Bread Company. I passed a homeless man curled inside a Subway restaurant doorway. I didn't stop until I got to the Hyatt, all the while repeating the room number. Inside the eight-floors-high atrium, a middle-aged bellhop asked me if I had luggage. We stared at each other until the middle elevator door opened. He didn't take from my drink when I offered it.

"Maybe you can settle this," I said. "Were you in elementary school before the women's movement? I've been in an argument all night long. I just need to figure some things out."

He sniffed hard twice. "I graduated from Sterling High School, right here in Greenville. 1968. This was before integration, sir. I had other things to think about besides the women's movement."

I said, "Man. I agree." He didn't ask what floor I was going to. Neither of us moved to push a button.

"If you're asking me if I can read and write, then I'll tell you that, yes, I can. I know the capitals. I know my continents and most of their countries. I can tell you every Greyhound stop between here and New York, here and New Orleans, and here and Miami. Ask me anything about biology, math, or the poets of the Harlem Renaissance. Don't judge me 'cause I'm standing here with a drunk man inside an elevator. On Sundays I talk truth to the people of Mount Zion AME church. Ask me about the Bible, New or Old Testament. Ask me about how people treat each other these days."

I said, "No. No, I wasn't judging. Believe me, I wasn't saying anything about your intelligence."

He hit the 2 without me saying anything. When the elevator door opened, my wife stood there wearing a hotel sheet over her head. Later on she told me she was pretending to be a ghost, nothing else. I believed her. But at the time I could only say, "Wrong floor. Take me back down."

George Singleton's first collection, *These People Are Us,* was published in March of 2001. His stories have appeared in *Harper's Magazine, Playboy,* the *Georgia Review,* the *Southern Review,* the *North American Review,* and elsewhere. This is his fourth appearance in *New Stories from the South.* He teaches fiction writing at the South Carolina Governor's School for the Arts and Humanities.

GLENDA GUION

I wrote one story about this character, V.O., and then I wanted to write another. I wasn't working on a novel. Let me make it clear that these were just two stories, written back to back. In the first story—which was called "Crawl Space"—V.O. dealt with a little person who came to work on the ducts beneath V.O.'s house. Then, more than likely, I wanted to see how much I could push the boundaries of political correctness. I've actually heard of people changing their names to Native American, Indian-sounding names because they "felt their pain," so to speak. That rubs me the wrong way, as I'm sure it does any valid Cherokee, Lakota, Hopi, Cheyenne, et al., human being. My second V.O. story became "Public Relations."

William Gay

THE PAPERHANGER

(from *Harper's*)

The vanishing of the doctor's wife's child in broad daylight was an event so cataclysmic that it forever divided time into the then and the now, the before and the after. In later years, fortified with a pitcher of silica-dry vodka martinis, she had cause to replay the events preceding the disappearance. They were tawdry and banal but in retrospect freighted with menace, a foreshadowing of what was to come, like a footman or a fool preceding a king into a room.

She had been quarreling with the paperhanger. Her four-year-old daughter, Zeineb, was standing directly behind the paperhanger where he knelt smoothing air bubbles out with a wide plastic trowel. Zeineb had her fingers in the paperhanger's hair. The paperhanger's hair was shoulder length and the color of flax and the child was delighted with it. The paperhanger was accustomed to her doing this and he did not even turn around. He just went on with his work. His arms were smooth and brown and corded with muscle and in the light that fell upon the paperhanger through stained-glass panels the doctor's wife could see that they were lightly downed with fine golden hair. She studied these arms bemusedly while she formulated her thoughts.

You tell me so much a roll, she said. The doctor's wife was from Pakistan and her speech was still heavily accented. I do not know single-bolt rolls and double-bolt rolls. You tell me double-bolt price but you are installing single-bolt rolls. My friend has told me. It is cost me perhaps twice as much.

The paperhanger, still on his knees, turned. He smiled up at her. He had pale blue eyes. I did tell you so much a roll, he said. You bought the rolls.

The child, not yet vanished, was watching the paperhanger's eyes. She was a scaled-down clone of the mother, the mother viewed through the wrong end of a telescope, and the paperhanger suspected that as she grew neither her features nor her expression would alter, she would just grow larger, like something being aired up with a hand pump.

And you are leave lumps, the doctor's wife said, gesturing at the wall.

I do not leave lumps, the paperhanger said. You've seen my work before. These are not lumps. The paper is wet. The paste is wet. Everything will shrink down and flatten out. He smiled again. He had clean even teeth. And besides, he said, I gave you my special cockteaser rate. I don't know what you're complaining about.

Her mouth worked convulsively. She looked for a moment as if he'd slapped her. When words did come they came in a fine spray of spit. You are trash, she said. You are scum.

Hands on knees, he was pushing erect, the girl's dark fingers trailing out of his hair. Don't call me trash, he said, as if it were perfectly all right to call him scum, but he was already talking to her back. She had whirled on her heels and went twisting her hips through an arched doorway into the cathedraled living room. The paperhanger looked down at the child. Her face glowed with a strange constrained glee, as if she and the paperhanger shared some secret the rest of the world hadn't caught on to yet.

In the living room the builder was supervising the installation of a chandelier that depended from the vaulted ceiling by a long golden chain. The builder was a short bearded man dancing about, showing her the features of the chandelier, smiling obsequiously.

She gave him a flat angry look. She waved a dismissive hand toward the ceiling. Whatever, she said.

She went out the front door onto the porch and down a makeshift walkway of two-by-tens into the front yard where her car was parked. The car was a silver-gray Mercedes her husband had given her for their anniversary. When she cranked the engine its idle was scarcely perceptible.

She powered down the window. Zeineb, she called. Across the razed earth of the unlandscaped yard a man in a grease-stained T-shirt was booming down the chains securing a backhoe to a low-boy hooked to a gravel truck. The sun was low in the west and bloodred behind this tableau and man and tractor looked flat and dimensionless as something decorative stamped from tin. She blew the horn. The man turned, raised an arm as if she'd signaled him.

Zeineb, she called again.

She got out of the car and started impatiently up the walkway. Behind her the gravel truck started, and truck and backhoe pulled out of the drive and down toward the road.

The paperhanger was stowing away his T square and trowels in his wooden toolbox. Where is Zeineb? the doctor's wife asked. She followed you out, the paperhanger told her. He glanced about, as if the girl might be hiding somewhere. There was nowhere to hide.

Where is my child? she asked the builder. The electrician climbed down from the ladder. The paperhanger came out of the bathroom with his tools. The builder was looking all around. His elfin features were touched with chagrin, as if this missing child were just something else he was going to be held accountable for.

Likely she's hiding in a closet, the paperhanger said. Playing a trick on you.

Zeineb does not play tricks, the doctor's wife said. Her eyes kept darting about the huge room, the shadows that lurked in the corners. There was already an undercurrent of panic in her voice and all her poise and self-confidence seemed to have vanished with the child.

The paperhanger set down his toolbox and went through the

house, opening and closing doors. It was a huge house and there were a lot of closets. There was no child in any of them.

The electrician was searching upstairs. The builder had gone through the French doors that opened onto the unfinished veranda and was peering into the back yard. The back yard was a maze of convoluted ditch excavated for the septic tank field line and beyond that there was just woods. She's playing in that ditch, the builder said, going down the flagstone steps.

She wasn't, though. She wasn't anywhere. They searched the house and grounds. They moved with jerky haste. They kept glancing toward the woods where the day was waning first. The builder kept shaking his head. She's got to be *somewhere,* he said.

Call someone, the doctor's wife said. Call the police.

It's a little early for the police, the builder said. She's got to be here.

You call them anyway. I have a phone in my car. I will call my husband.

While she called, the paperhanger and the electrician continued to search. They had looked everywhere and were forced to search places they'd already looked. If this ain't the goddamnedest thing I ever saw, the electrician said.

The doctor's wife got out of the Mercedes and slammed the door. Suddenly she stopped and clasped a hand to her forehead. She screamed. The man with the tractor, she cried. Somehow my child is gone with the tractor man.

Oh Jesus, the builder said. What have we got ourselves into here?

The high sheriff that year was a ruminative man named Bellwether. He stood beside the county cruiser talking to the paperhanger while deputies ranged the grounds. Other men were inside looking in places that had already been searched numberless times. Bellwether had been in the woods and he was picking cockleburs off his khakis and out of his socks. He was watching the woods, where dark was gathering and seeping across the field like a stain.

I've got to get men out here, Bellwether said. A lot of men and a lot of lights. We're going to have to search every inch of these woods.

You'll play hell doing it, the paperhanger said. These woods stretch all the way to Lawrence County. This is the edge of the Harrikan. Down in there's where all those old mines used to be. Allens Creek.

I don't give a shit if they stretch all the way to Fairbanks, Alaska, Bellwether said. They've got to be searched. It'll just take a lot of men.

The raw earth yard was full of cars. Doctor Jamahl had come in a sleek black Lexus. He berated his wife. Why weren't you watching her? he asked. Unlike his wife's, the doctor's speech was impeccable. She covered her face with her palms and wept. The doctor still wore his green surgeon's smock and it was flecked with bright dots of blood as a butcher's smock might be.

I need to feed a few cows, the paperhanger said. I'll feed my stock pretty quick and come back and help hunt.

You don't mind if I look in your truck, do you?

Do what?

I've got to cover my ass. If that little girl don't turn up damn quick this is going to be over my head. TBI, FBI, network news. I've got to eliminate everything.

Eliminate away, the paperhanger said.

The sheriff searched the floorboard of the paperhanger's pickup truck. He shined his huge flashlight under the seat and felt behind it with his hands.

I had to look, he said apologetically.

Of course you did, the paperhanger said.

Full dark had fallen before he returned. He had fed his cattle and stowed away his tools and picked up a six-pack of San Miguel beer and he sat in the back of the pickup truck drinking it. The paperhanger had been in the Navy and stationed in the Philippines and San Miguel was the only beer he could drink. He had to go out of town to buy it, but he figured it was worth it. He liked the exotic labels, the dark bitter taste on the back of his tongue, the way the chilled bottles felt held against his forehead.

A motley crowd of curiosity seekers and searchers thronged the yard. There was a vaguely festive air. He watched all this with a dispassionate eye, as if he were charged with grading the participants, comparing this with other spectacles he'd seen. Coffee urns had been brought in and set up on tables, sandwiches prepared and handed out to the weary searchers. A crane had been hauled in and the septic tank reclaimed from the ground. It swayed from a taut cable while men with lights searched the impacted earth beneath it for a child, for the very trace of a child. Through the far dark woods lights crossed and recrossed, darted to and fro like fireflies. The doctor and the doctor's wife sat in folding camp chairs looking drained, stunned, waiting for their child to be delivered into their arms.

The doctor was a short portly man with a benevolent expression. He had a moon-shaped face, with light and dark areas of skin that looked swirled, as if the pigment coloring him had not been properly mixed. He had been educated at Princeton. When he had established his practice he had returned to Pakistan to find a wife befitting his station. The woman he had selected had been chosen on the basis of her beauty. In retrospect, perhaps more consideration should have been given to other qualities. She was still beautiful but he was thinking that certain faults might outweigh this. She seemed to have trouble keeping up with her children. She could lose a four-year-old child in a room no larger than six hundred square feet and she could not find it again.

The paperhanger drained his bottle and set it by his foot in the bed of the truck. He studied the doctor's wife's ravaged face through the deep blue light. The first time he had seen her she had hired him to paint a bedroom in the house they were living in while the doctor's mansion was being built. There was an arrogance about her that cried out to be taken down a notch or two. She flirted with him, backed away, flirted again. She would treat him as if he were a stain on the bathroom rug and then stand close by him while he worked until he was dizzy with the smell of her, with the heat that seemed to radiate off her body. She stood by him while he knelt painting baseboards and after an infinite moment leaned carefully the weight of a thigh against his shoulder. You'd better move it, he thought. She didn't. He laughed and turned his face into her groin. She gave a strangled cry and slapped him hard. The paintbrush flew away and speckled the dark rose walls with antique white. You filthy beast, she said. You are some kind of monster. She stormed out of the room and he could hear her slamming doors behind her.

Well, I was looking for a job when I found this one. He smiled philosophically to himself.

But he had not been fired. In fact now he had been hired again. Perhaps there was something here to ponder.

At midnight he gave up his vigil. Some souls more hardy than his kept up the watch. The earth here was worn smooth by the useless traffic of the searchers. Driving out, he met a line of pickup trucks with civil-defense tags. Grimfaced men sat aligned in their beds. Some clutched rifles loosely by their barrels, as if they would lay to waste whatever monster, man or beast, would snatch up a child in its slaverous jaws and vanish, prey and predator, in the space between two heartbeats.

Even more dubious reminders of civilization as these fell away. He drove into the Harrikan, where he lived. A world so dark and forlorn light itself seemed at a premium. Whippoorwills swept red-eyed up from the roadside. Old abandoned foundries and furnaces rolled past, grim and dark as forsaken prisons. Down a ridge here was an abandoned graveyard, if you knew where to look. The paperhanger did. He had dug up a few of the graves, examined with curiosity what remained, buttons, belt buckles, a cameo brooch. The bones he laid out like a child with a Tinkertoy, arranging them the way they went in juryrigged resurrection.

He braked hard on a curve, the truck slewing in the gravel. A bobcat had crossed the road, graceful as a wraith, fierce and lanterneyed in the headlights, gone so swiftly it might have been a stage prop swung across the road on wires.

Bellwether and a deputy drove to the backhoe operator's house. He lived up a gravel road that wound through a great stand of cedars. He lived in a board-and-batten house with a tin roof rusted to a warm umber. They parked before it and got out, adjusting their gunbelts.

Bellwether had a search warrant with the ink scarcely dry. The operator was outraged.

Look at it this way, Bellwether explained patiently. I've got to cover my ass. Everything has got to be considered. You know how kids are. Never thinking. What if she run under the wheels of your truck when you was backing out? What if quicklike you put the body in your truck to get rid of somewhere?

What if quicklike you get the hell off my property, the operator said.

Everything has to be considered, the sheriff said again. Nobody's accusing anybody of anything just yet.

The operator's wife stood glowering at them. To have something to do with his hands, the operator began to construct a cigarette. He had huge red hands thickly sown with brown freckles. They trembled. I ain't got a thing in this round world to hide, he said.

Bellwether and his men searched everywhere they could think of to look. Finally they stood uncertainly in the operator's yard, out of place in their neat khakis, their polished leather.

Now get the hell off my land, the operator said. If all you think of me is that I could run over a little kid and then throw it off in the bushes like a dead cat or something then I don't even want to see your goddamn face. I want you gone and I want you by God gone now.

Everything had to be considered, the sheriff said.

Then maybe you need to consider that paperhanger.

What about him?

That paperhanger is one sick puppy.

He was still there when I got there, the sheriff said. Three witnesses swore nobody ever left, not even for a minute, and one of them was the child's mother. I searched his truck myself.

Then he's a sick puppy with a damn good alibi, the operator said.

That was all. There was no ransom note, no child that turned up two counties over with amnesia. She was a page turned, a door closed, a lost ball in the high weeds. She was a child no larger than a doll, but the void she left behind her was unreckonable. Yet there was no end to it. No finality. There was no moment when someone could say, turning from a mounded grave, Well, this has been unbearable, but you've got to go on with your life. Life did not go on.

At the doctor's wife's insistence an intensive investigation was focused on the backhoe operator. Forensic experts from the FBI examined every millimeter of the gravel truck, paying special attention to the wheels. They were examined with every modern crime-fighting device the government possessed, and there was not a microscopic particle of tissue or blood, no telltale chip of fingernail, no hair ribbon.

Work ceased on the mansion. Some subcontractors were discharged outright, while others simply drifted away. There was no one to care if the work was done, no one to pay them. The half-finished veranda's raw wood grayed in the fall, then winter, rains. The ditches were left fallow and uncovered and half-filled with water. Kudzu crept from the woods. The hollyhocks and oleanders the doctor's wife had planted grew entangled and rampant. The imported windows were stoned by double-dared boys who whirled and fled. Already this house where a child had vanished was acquiring an unhealthy, diseased reputation.

The doctor and his wife sat entombed in separate prisons replaying real and imagined grievances. The doctor felt that his wife's neglect had sent his child into the abstract. The doctor's wife drank vodka martinis and watched talk shows where passed an endless procession of vengeful people who had not had children vanish, and felt, perhaps rightly, that the fates had dealt her from the bottom of the deck, and she prayed with intensity for a miracle.

Then one day she was just gone. The Mercedes and part of her clothing and personal possessions were gone too. He idly wondered where she was, but he did not search for her.

Sitting in his armchair cradling a great marmalade cat and a bottle of J&B and observing with bemused detachment the gradations of light at the window, the doctor remembered studying literature at Princeton. He had particular cause to reconsider the poetry of William Butler Yeats. For how surely things fell apart, how surely the center did not hold.

His practice fell into a ruin. His colleagues made sympathetic allowances for him at first, but there are limits to these things. He made erroneous diagnoses, prescribed the wrong medicines not once or twice but as a matter of course.

Just as there is a deepening progression to misfortune, so too there is a point beyond which things can only get worse. They did. A middle-aged woman he was operating on died.

He had made an incision to remove a ruptured appendix and the incised flesh was clamped aside while he made ready to slice it out. It was not there. He stared in drunken disbelief. He began to search under things, organs, intestines, a rising tide of blood. The appendix was not there. It had gone into the abstract, atrophied, been removed twenty-five years before, he had sliced through the selfsame scar. He was rummaging through her abdominal cavity like an irritated man fumbling through a drawer for a clean pair of socks, finally bellowing in rage and wringing his hands in bloody vexation while nurses began to cry out, another surgeon was brought on the run as a closer, and he was carried from the operating room.

Came then days of sitting in the armchair while he was besieged by contingency lawyers, action news teams, a long line of process servers. There was nothing he could do. It was out of his hands and into the hands of the people who are paid to do these things. He sat cradling the bottle of J&B with the marmalade cat snuggled against his portly midriff. He would study the window, where the light drained away in a process he no longer had an understanding of, and sip the scotch and every now and then stroke the cat's head gently. The cat purred against his breast as reassuringly as the hum of an air conditioner.

He left in the middle of the night. He began to load his possessions into the Lexus. At first he chose items with a great degree of consideration. The first thing he loaded was a set of custom-made monogrammed golf clubs. Then his stereo receiver, Denon AC3, $1,750. A copy of *This Side of Paradise* autographed by Fitzgerald that he had bought as an investment. By the time the Lexus was half full he was just grabbing things at random and stuffing them into the back seat, a half-eaten pizza, half a case of cat food, a single brocade house shoe.

He drove west past the hospital, the country club, the city-limit sign. He was thinking no thoughts at all, and all the destination he had was the amount of highway the headlights showed him.

In the slow rains of late fall the doctor's wife returned to the unfinished mansion. She used to sit in a camp chair on the ruined veranda and drink chilled martinis she poured from the pitcher she carried in a foam ice chest. Dark fell early these November days. Raincrows husbanding some far cornfield called through the smoky autumn air. The sound was fiercely evocative, reminding her of something but she could not have said what.

She went into the room where she had lost the child. The light was failing. The high corners of the room were in deepening shadow but she could not see the nests of dirt daubers clustered on the rich flocked wallpaper, a spider swing from a chandelier on a strand of spun glass. Some animal's dried blackened stool curled like a slug against the baseboards. The silence in the room was enormous.

One day she arrived and was surprised to find the paperhanger there. He was sitting on a yellow four-wheeler drinking a bottle of beer. He made to go when he saw her but she waved him back. Stay and talk with me, she said.

The paperhanger was much changed. His pale locks had been shorn away in a makeshift haircut as if scissored in the dark or by a blind barber and his cheeks were covered with a soft curly beard.

You have grow a beard.

Yes.

You are strange with it.

The paperhanger sipped from his San Miguel. He smiled. I was strange without it, he said. He arose from the four-wheeler and came over and sat on the flagstone steps. He stared across the mutilated yard toward the treeline. The yard was like a funhouse maze seen from above, its twistings and turnings bereft of mystery.

You are working somewhere now?

No. I don't take so many jobs anymore. There's only me, and I don't need much. What has become of the doctor?

She shrugged. Many things have change, she said. He has gone. The banks have foreclose. What is that you ride?

An ATV. A four-wheeler.

It goes well in the woods?

It was made for that.

You could take me in the woods. How much would you charge me?

For what?

To go in the woods. You could drive me. I will pay you.

Why?

To search for my child's body.

I wouldn't charge anybody anything to search for a child's body, the paperhanger said. But she's not in these woods. Nothing could have stayed hidden, the way these woods were searched.

Sometimes I think she just kept walking. Perhaps just walking away from the men looking. Far into the woods.

Into the woods, the paperhanger thought. If she had just kept walking in a straight line with no time out for eating or sleeping, where would she be? Kentucky, Algiers, who knew.

I'll take you when the rains stop, he said. But we won't find a child.

The doctor's wife shook her head. It is a mystery, she said. She drank from her cocktail glass. Where could she have gone? How could she have gone?

There was a man named David Lang, the paperhanger said. Up in Galletin, back in the late 1800s. He was crossing a barn lot in full view of his wife and two children and he just vanished. Went into thin air. There was a judge in a wagon turning into the yard and he saw it too. It was just like he took a step in this world and his foot came down in another one. He was never seen again.

She gave him a sad smile, bitter and one-cornered. You make fun with me.

No. It's true. I have it in a book. I'll show you.

I have a book with dragons, fairies. A book where hobbits live in the middle earth. They are lies. I think most books are lies. Perhaps all books. I have prayed for a miracle but I am not worthy of one. I have prayed for her to come from the dead, then just to find her body. That would be a miracle to me. There are no miracles.

She rose unsteadily, swayed slightly, leaning to take up the cooler. The paperhanger watched her. I have to go now, she said. When the rains stop we will search.

Can you drive?

Of course I can drive. I have drive out here.

I mean are you capable of driving now. You seem a little drunk.

I drink to forget but it is not enough, she said. I can drive.

After a while he heard her leave in the Mercedes, the tires spinning in the gravel drive. He lit a cigarette. He sat smoking it, watching the rain string off the roof. He seemed to be waiting for something. Dusk was falling like a shroud, the world going dark and formless the way it had begun. He drank the last of the beer, sat holding the bottle, the foam bitter in the back of his mouth. A chill touched him. He felt something watching him. He turned. From the corner of the ruined veranda a child was watching him. He stood up. He heard the beer bottle break on the flagstones. The child went sprinting past the hollyhocks toward the brush at the edge of the yard, tiny sepia child with an intent sloe-eyed face, real as she had ever been, translucent as winter light through dirty glass.

The doctor's wife's hands were laced loosely about his waist as they came down through a thin stand of sassafras, edging over the ridge where the ghost of a road was, a road more sensed than seen that faced into a half acre of tilting stones and fading granite tablets. Other graves marked only by their declivities in the earth, folk so far beyond the pale even the legibility of their identities had been leached away by the weathers.

Leaves drifted, huge poplar leaves veined with amber so golden they might have been coin of the realm for a finer world than this one. He cut the ignition of the four-wheeler and got off. Past the lowering trees the sky was a blue of an improbable intensity, a fierce cobalt blue shot through with dense golden light.

She slid off the rear and steadied herself a moment with a hand on his arm. Where are we? she asked. Why are we here?

The paperhanger had disengaged his arm and was strolling among the gravestones reading such inscriptions as were legible, as if he might find forebear or antecedent in this moldering earth. The doctor's wife was retrieving her martinis from the luggage carrier of the ATV. She stood looking about uncertainly. A graven angel with broken wings crouched on a truncated marble column like a gargoyle. Its stone eyes regarded her with a blind benignity. Some of these graves have been rob, she said.

You can't rob the dead, he said. They have nothing left to steal.

It is a sacrilege, she said. It is forbidden to disturb the dead. You have done this.

The paperhanger took a cigarette pack from his pocket and felt it, but it was empty, and he balled it up and threw it away. The line between graverobbing and archaeology has always looked a little blurry to me, he said. I was studying their culture, trying to get a fix on what their lives were like.

She was watching him with a kind of benumbed horror. Standing hip-slung and lost like a parody of her former self. Strange and anomalous in her fashionable but mismatched clothing, as if she'd put on the first garment that fell to hand. Someday, he thought, she might rise and wander out into the daylight world wearing nothing at all, the way she had come into it. With her diamond watch and the cocktail glass she carried like a used-up talisman.

You have break the law, she told him.

I got a government grant, the paperhanger said contemptuously.

Why are we here? We are supposed to be searching for my child.

If you're looking for a body the first place to look is the graveyard, he said. If you want a book don't you go to the library?

I am paying you, she said. You are in my employ. I do not want to be here. I want you to do as I say or carry me to my car if you will not.

Actually, the paperhanger said, I had a story to tell you. About my wife.

He paused, as if leaving a space for her comment, but when she made none he went on. I had a wife. My childhood sweetheart. She became a nurse, went to work in one of these drug rehab places. After she was there a while she got a faraway look in her eyes. Look at me without seeing me. She got in tight with her supervisor. They started having meetings to go to. Conferences. Sometimes just the two of them would confer, generally in a motel. The night I watched them walk into the Holiday Inn in Franklin I decided to kill her. No impetuous spur-of-the-moment thing. I thought it all out and it would be the perfect crime.

The doctor's wife didn't say anything. She just watched him.

A grave is the best place to dispose of a body, the paperhanger said. The grave is its normal destination anyway. I could dig up a grave and then just keep on digging. Save everything carefully. Put

my body there and fill in part of the earth, and then restore everything the way it was. The coffin, if any of it was left. The bones and
such. A good settling rain and the fall leaves and you're home free.
Now that's eternity for you.

Did you kill someone, she breathed. Her voice was barely audible.

Did I or did I not, he said. You decide. You have the powers of
a god. You can make me a murderer or just a heartbroke guy
whose wife quit him. What do you think? Anyway, I don't have a
wife. I expect she just walked off into the abstract like that Lang
guy I told you about.

I want to go, she said. I want to go where my car is.

He was sitting on a gravestone watching her out of his pale eyes.
He might not have heard.

I will walk.

Just whatever suits you, the paperhanger said. Abruptly, he was
standing in front of her. She had not seen him arise from the headstone or stride across the graves, but like a jerky splice in a film he
was before her, a hand cupping each of her breasts, staring down
into her face.

Under the merciless weight of the sun her face was stunned and
vacuous. He studied it intently, missing no detail. Fine wrinkles
crept from the corners of her eyes and mouth like hairline cracks
in porcelain. Grime was impacted in her pores, in the crepe flesh
of her throat. How surely everything had fallen from her: beauty,
wealth, social position, arrogance. Humanity itself, for by now she
seemed scarcely human, beleaguered so by the fates that she suffered his hands on her breasts as just one more cross to bear, one
more indignity to endure.

How far you've come, the paperhanger said in wonder. I believe
you're about down to my level now, don't you?

It does not matter, the doctor's wife said. There is no longer one
thing that matters.

Slowly and with enormous lassitude her body slumped toward
him, and in his exultance it seemed not a motion in itself but simply the completion of one begun long ago with the fateful weight

of a thigh, a motion that began in one world and completed itself in another one.

From what seemed a great distance he watched her fall toward him like an angel descending, wings spread, from an infinite height, striking the earth gently, tilting, then righting itself.

The weight of moonlight tracking across the paperhanger's face awoke him from where he took his rest. Filigrees of light through the gauzy curtains swept across him in stately silence like the translucent ghosts of insects. He stirred, lay still then for a moment getting his bearings, a fix on where he was.

He was in his bed, lying on his back. He could see a huge orange moon poised beyond the bedroom window, inksketch tree branches that raked its face like claws. He could see his feet bookending the San Miguel bottle that his hands clasped erect on his abdomen, the amber bottle hard-edged and defined against the pale window, dark atavistic monolith reared against a harvest moon.

He could smell her. A musk compounded of stale sweat and alcohol, the rank smell of her sex. Dissolution, ruin, loss. He turned to study her where she lay asleep, her open mouth a dark cavity in her face. She was naked, legs outflung, pale breasts pooled like cooling wax. She stirred restively, groaned in her sleep. He could hear the rasp of her breathing. Her breath was fetid on his face, corrupt, a graveyard smell. He watched her in disgust, in a dull self-loathing.

He drank from the bottle, lowered it. Sometimes, he told her sleeping face, you do things you can't undo. You break things you just can't fix. Before you mean to, before you know you've done it. And you were right, there are things only a miracle can set to rights.

He sat clasping the bottle. He touched his miscut hair, the soft down of his beard. He had forgotten what he looked like, he hadn't seen his reflection in a mirror for so long. Unbidden, Zeineb's face swam into his memory. He remembered the look on the child's face when the doctor's wife had spun on her heel: spite had crossed it like a flicker of heat lightning. She stuck her tongue out at him. His hand snaked out like a serpent and closed on her throat and snapped her neck before he could call it back, sloe eyes wild and wide, pink tongue caught between tiny seed-pearl teeth like a bitten-off rosebud. Her hair swung sidewise, her head lolled onto his clasped hand. The tray of the toolbox was out before he knew it, he was stuffing her into the toolbox like a ragdoll. So small, so small, hardly there at all.

He arose. Silhouetted naked against the moon-drenched window, he drained the bottle. He looked about for a place to set it, leaned and wedged it between the heavy flesh of her upper thighs. He stood in silence, watching her. He seemed philosophical, possessed of some hard-won wisdom. The paperhanger knew so well that while few are deserving of a miracle, fewer still can make one come to pass.

He went out of the room. Doors opened, doors closed. Footsteps softly climbing a staircase, descending. She dreamed on. When he came back into the room he was cradling a plastic-wrapped bundle stiffly in his arms. He placed it gently beside the drunk woman. He folded the plastic sheeting back like a caul.

What had been a child. What the graveyard earth had spared the freezer had preserved. Ice crystals snared in the hair like windy snowflakes whirled there, in the lashes. A doll from a madhouse assembly line.

He took her arm, laid it across the child. She pulled away from the cold. He firmly brought the arm back, arranging them like mannequins, madonna and child. He studied this tableau, then went out of his house for the last time. The door closed gently behind him on its keeperspring.

The paperhanger left in the Mercedes, heading west into the open country, tracking into wide-open territories he could infect like a malignant spore. Without knowing it, he followed the selfsame route the doctor had taken some eight months earlier, and in a world of infinite possibilities where all journeys share a common end, perhaps they are together, taking the evening air on a ruined veranda among the hollyhocks and oleanders, the doctor sipping his scotch and the paperhanger his San Miguel, gentlemen of leisure discussing the vagaries of life and pondering deep into the night not just the possibility but the inevitability of miracles.

William Gay is the author of two novels, *The Long Home* and *Provinces of Night*. His stories have appeared in *Oxford American, Harper's Magazine*, and other magazines, as well as in *New Stories from the South 1999* and *2000*.

MAUDE SCHUYLER CLAY

I always saw "The Paperhanger" as a sort of dark fairy tale that takes place in a geography of the imagination where nothing is quite what it seems and normal rules and order no longer apply. The first thing I had was the last paragraph, so I essentially had to write the story to get there.

Robert Love Taylor

PINK MIRACLE IN EAST TENNESSEE

(from *The Ohio Review*)

I.

By the time Pink Miracle found Uncle Laclede, his uncle had forgotten how to play the fiddle, had forgotten, in fact, that he had a nephew named Pink or a brother named Blue living in Oklahoma. Blue? he said. I don't rightly recall.

Blue or maybe you remember him as Bluford, Pink said. Bluford Miracle from Freedom, Oklahoma. I'm Blue's boy Pink. Gideon Pinkney Miracle.

Oklahoma?

It was July of 1908. Pink was twenty-one years old in February. The year before, Oklahoma Territory had been joined to Indian Territory and made into the State of Oklahoma. He had left Freedom, O.T., when he was fourteen years old and not once gone back nor had the desire to. His mother was dead, and his father would've worked him to death on land that wouldn't produce anything but potatoes hardly the size of beans. Once he left something behind, it was left for good. That was the way he was, he guessed — at this time of his life, anyway. But when he saw on the front page of the *Memphis Commercial Appeal* a cartoon drawing of an Indian maiden marrying a white man, he looked at it with interest and began to think in earnest that he might one day go back there.

Look here, he said to Sonny Boy, the blues man who had become his friend and teacher. Look here, Sonny Boy, what do you make of this picture?

Sonny Boy took off his dark glasses. The two of them were sitting at the bar in Pee Wee's, in dim light, but Sonny Boy always kept those dark glasses on his face.

I don't think much, he said, squinting, putting the glasses back on.

It's where I came from, Pink said. Oklahoma.

You don't say. I thought you from the Delta.

This was a high compliment and in fact a misconception Pink had slyly encouraged, though never outright telling anybody on Beale he was from the Delta.

I used to think you were blind, too, he told Sonny Boy.

I ain't never been blind a day of my life.

I ain't never been from the Delta.

You play blues on that fiddle like you from the Delta. If I was blind, hearing you play, I'd say you a black boy from the Delta.

You look like a blind man, wearing them dark glasses all the time.

Can't stand the light. Too much light in the world for a old man like Sonny Boy Jimson. They's worse things than being blind.

Well, Pink said. I wish I might have come from the Delta instead of from Oklahoma.

Black man from the Delta wish he be white, use that Golden Peacock skin bleach by the tub's full, slick-straightening his kinked hair with a hot comb and grease. You wish you was a black man, boy?

Pink, remembering with some amusement how he'd tried rubbing his face black with charcoal when he'd first come to Memphis, reckoned he didn't have any choice in the matter.

Naw, he said. I wish I could get my fiddle to sounding like your guitar, though.

It ain't no guitar, son. It's a fiddle. Can't make a fiddle sound like a guitar. Too bad it is a fiddle, maybe, but it ain't going to be no guitar. White man ain't gone be black, neither, nor black man white. Mostly, it's the black want to be white. You in the minority if you want to be black. Don't know many black folks want to be black. Shee-it. Black folks with religion, they want to be like Jesus. Everybody know Jesus, He white. And God, His Daddy, why ain't He gone be white, too? So most folks, they want to be like they father in heaven. Me, why, I wish I was a Arab riding high up on a camel. Out on some big old desert, long way from Beale, honey, coming up to a oasis, the palm trees waving, them harem girls singing and dancing, black as night, willowy, I tell you they is willowy, son, they seeing me on that camel in my dark glasses, my guitar on my back, a-waving and a-calling to me. Come on here, now, Sonny Boy, them willowy harem girls calling. Whooee— that's what I wish. Now, listen here. You got to hear what that fiddle can speak. Let it talk in its own words. You understand what I'm saying?

He did not, but he knew enough to know he'd better be figuring out what Sonny Boy meant.

The Indian maiden in the cartoon wore a dress with beads and long fringe all over it. She had a feather in her hair and on her headband was inscribed "I.T." She wore beaded moccasins. The white man wore a broad-brimmed cowboy hat and a dark coat with tails. He had on cowboy boots and his hatband had the letters "O.T." written on it. The minister wore thick-lensed glasses and his broad toothy smile was like the president's. The caption read, I pronounce you Oklahoma.

It wasn't much, surely not enough in itself to make him consider returning to the state of his birth. He had never seen an Indian maiden in such fringe and with a feather in her hair. In fact, he had never seen an Indian maiden to his knowledge until he had left Freedom and was adrifting down in eastern Oklahoma, in those days still Indian Territory. There were some right nice-looking young ladies that he caught glimpses of from time to time, and some not so nice-looking, gone to fat early. All of them dressed pretty much like the women in O.T., all homespun and plain, in bonnets with nary a feather, though occasionally a ribbon or two, and instead of beaded moccasins they wore old high-top button shoes, dusty.

As for cowboys, he would guess he'd seen some of them, all right, for the Strip was cattle country when opened and, going by his daddy's luck, should have stayed that, ill-suited to farming. Pink had seen cowboys in the Freedom store and heard their talk about the long drives up the Chisholm Trail. They were rough-looking fellows to a man that you could not imagine donning a tail-coat or even a frayed Jim-swinger such as the Baptist preacher, Reverend Smallwood, wore when preaching. Their hats, though set at rakish angles, looked like a horse had stepped all over them.

So it couldn't have been that the picture reminded him of Freedom. Maybe it was just the idea of seeing Oklahoma mentioned so prominently in this Memphis newspaper, which he would not even have bothered to buy if he hadn't seen the picture right there on the front page, staring up at him from the newsstand like it meant for him to see it. It was as if he had figured Oklahoma existed only in his mind, and now he was made to see that it was an actual place out there to the west of Arkansas that he had left behind. It put a different light on things. The place kept on going, it appeared, in his absence, and changed. Why, his daddy might be driving cattle now, wearing a Stetson, married to an Indian maiden, for all he knew.

He wished his daddy well. Maybe if things had gone better, Daddy would be a better person, the soddy long gone or else Daddy long gone from it. If Mama still lived, sure Pink would want to go back and would have been back many times. But his mama was long dead and he couldn't muster up any affection for that man who had worked him like a mule and tried to keep his fiddle from him, calling it the devil's box. He thought it likely that Daddy would not have changed much, unless for the worse, becoming more and more righteous even if he had prospered. Nor did the thought of his brothers Junior and Ollard or his sisters Josephine and Ellen stir up much longing or affection in his heart.

They never did do their share. Anyway, they would be all grown up and he would not know them, nor they him. Likely they had moved on and had families of their own, eking out a living on a hardscrabble quarter-section that some earlier settler had already worked to death and failed at.

It was the wonder of himself, it may be, that was drawing him back: the wonder, in good part, that he felt so little desire to go back. Who was he to judge Oklahoma, the place of his birth, his daddy, brothers, sisters. And what would they make of him, if they knew him now? He imagined that he might return himself to that soddy now, safe, aloof, beyond whatever malice might still be festering beneath his father's dirt roof. Playing the Delta blues had done that for him, he believed. The strength of people like Sonny Boy Jimson had come to him through the blues.

Maybe his daddy was strong, too, but not that strong. He looked at the picture in the paper again, the white man taking an Indian bride. Well, couldn't hurt nothing. The artist hadn't made her so dark that you would mistake her for African. Couldn't have put such a picture on the front page of the *Commercial Appeal*. No, sir. Still, plenty of white men came down to Beale and found themselves black women to make love to. These white men might have been married or might not. They did not wed the black women they loved, though, nor even propose to them, and this, to Pink, was downright folly. After falling out with Dinah, he had fallen in love with a black woman. Her name was Mariah England. Was a singer, a cousin of Sonny Boy Jimson's. He asked her to marry him and she turned him down. She was nice about it, but she turned him down flat, boy.

This place here, Pink said to Sonny Boy, pointing to the cartoon. This place is where I come from.

Is they camels in that place, Pink?

Cattle. It's all cattle, mainly.

I never liked a cow. Never did me no harm, but I never liked 'em all the same. You can't trust a cow, my opinion.

I'm not aiming to go back there just yet.

What is it you aiming to do then, showing me that picture.

It's just a picture. It's not Oklahoma.

That Teddy Roosevelt there, dress up like a preacher, ain't it, marrying them two folks. I think he ack lack a preacher. More preacher than president, my opinion. Lotta words, lotta struttin. What is he, do you reckon, preacher or president? Was a soldier-boy, once 'pon a time, climbing old San Juan Hill and ashooting the Spaniards right and left to kingdom come. What you reckon he is, preacher or soldier or president? Why he always got that big smile on his face? You think he know something we don't know? I think he just wishing hisself along, making hisself up as he goes. My opinion. That's why he so happy, grinning all the time. He ain't nobody different than you and me, boy, forgetting where he come from and going where he is headed.

Pink allowed as to how that might be so.

The question is this, Sonny Boy said. Where is it you headed?

I'm not going back to Oklahoma.

That tell me where you not going. But where you headed, Delta boy?

Nowhere, Pink said. Right here where I am is where I want to be.

This wasn't true, though. He did like Memphis—hadn't he stayed here going-on seven years now? Dinah had played out soon enough, sure, but while she lasted she was what he needed and he considered her the best of all the women he had loved ever since, even the kindly Mariah England. He still saw Dinah now and then on Beale, though she had moved away from the neighborhood. Some said she was holed up in a shack over in the Greasy Plank, near where W. C. Handy lived. Some said she was actually living with W. C. Handy, his white concubine. Some said she didn't live anywhere at all, just made her way up and down the river, New Orleans to Memphis and back, living off of whoever was convenient and foolish enough. Last time Pink had seen her was a year ago in Hammitt Ashford's saloon, across the street and down the block from Pee Wee's. She came up behind him, always mischievous, touching his bowing arm while he was playing, and, seeing her, he didn't mind missing the beat, caught it soon enough, nobody the wiser except for Sonny Boy, playing by his side. They had been playing "Stagolee."

Memphis, in the persons of Dinah and Sonny Boy and Mariah England and Hammitt Ashford and Sweet Cindy Lewis and Fireball Jimmy Franklin and Little Willie Jackson and Joey "the Duke" Dumas and plenty of other old-timers, some of them on Beale since the typhoid epidemic of 1878, living to tell about it, this was the Memphis that, after he proved himself worthy, had taken him in. He no longer had to go down to the docks and wait to be chosen for work in the cotton fields. He didn't have to report to no mill or factory at the break of day, answer to a hard-hearted boss, and work his ass off until dusk. Instead, he could play his fiddle at Pee Wee's or Ashford's or the Panama or even the Palace (not just on amateur nights either), all on Beale Street, and be treated like a king. Even better, feel like a king, because of the music, the musicians playing with him, leading him into the music, making him play his way into and then out of feelings he didn't ever know he had. Rotgut flowed, cocaine was plentiful and cheap, and the saloons fed you, even if they didn't pay much more than it cost to rent a room. Just a few months ago, he believed he might could live this way forever.

Still, he would have to go, would have to move on. It was time. He could feel it, he could even see himself leaving Memphis, waving good-bye to Sonny Boy from the window of the train. For he knew this was not after all where he had been headed when he left Freedom, O.T., in nineteen aught-one, aged fourteen years. It was close, but it wasn't the place. That cowboy in the cartoon might have been the image of his daddy. It wasn't enough to send him packing back to Oklahoma, no, but it shook him up, and then the music lost something, as if the thought of Daddy had been enough to jinx his bow arm, hoodoo his fiddle.

You ain't who you think you are, boy, was what he heard his fiddle telling him.

Well, who am I, then? he asked as he drew the bow across the strings. Tell me who I am.

Sweet Cindy Lewis sang, her voice as full of longing and sadness as his mama's ever had been. The duke's trombone wailed and moaned through its mute, as angry as it was sad. And his fiddle, all it could do was scoff at him, taunt him. You ain't who you think you are.

It's all right, honey, Sweet Cindy said.

You gone come back, the duke said.

But where was he going?

Not long after the new year, 1908, he saw, while walking past the Gayoso Hotel, a man in a broad-brim cowboy hat step out of a Hansom cab. The man paused at the curb, reaching in his pocket, and looked Pink in the eye. He wasn't the man from the cartoon, no, he couldn't be, but he looked enough like that man to give Pink the shivers, and it all came back, the death of his mama, his visit to her grave, the warm Oklahoma sun shining down, her telling him he had to get right with himself, and he seemed to hear her again, just as certainly her voice as that time, only not so understandable, as if she spoke from a great distance, had gotten farther and farther away from him. He stopped dead still, right there at the entrance to the fine Gayoso Hotel, a black man in a gold-buttoned uniform looking him up and down, the man in the white cowboy hat stepping briskly past him, the Hansom cab clattering away, the big dappled horse dropping a steaming column of shit onto the cobblestone street. What he felt was cold, dead, and the last thing he remembered before falling was his mama's voice, distant but now clear, shrill: Laclede, the voice said. La-Clede Miracle.

He woke in his own room. Sonny Boy sat beside the bed, shoulders slumped, head bowed, eyes closed. Pink watched him—it seemed for a long time, the light, dim though it was, shifting, now reflecting from Sonny Boy's cheekbones, now from his long sloping nose, his flaring nostrils. Sonny Boy wasn't a big man, but when he played, he made Pink think of a machine, efficient and powerful. Sitting in this small room, he looked like the old man he was, fading fast, his flesh losing out, skin drawing into his bones. His breath came in great sucking gasps, followed by such long silences before the next that Pink kept imagining there would be no other.

Pink felt wide-awake himself. The words he had heard before he lost consciousness still rang in his ears. It was the force of the revelation that had felled him, he was certain, the power of his mother's voice. He trembled even now, in its wake.

II.

Uncle Laclede had apparently not heard the news of Oklahoma's statehood or had forgotten it, as he seemed to have forgotten so much else, including his brother Blue. Maybe news from outside did not ever reach these mountains at all. They seemed so far off and beautiful and wild and terrible they might have been another world. Everything grew here, it seemed, such greenery as Pink had never seen, and where it was not a green tangle of leaves and vines it was rocky cliffs, boulders, fast-flowing rivers, winding creeks. Not much in the way of crops, true. You saw little patches back behind some of the cabins, but they had to run up the hillsides, mostly steep ascents and rocky. It was wild things that wanted to grow here, grow with such a dizzy beauty that it made your heart beat faster just to look upon it. For a fellow such as Pink, growing up in a country where shrubs had a hard time of it, let alone a tree, and what they called a hill was sometimes not easy to tell from the flatness surrounding it, a mountain rising out of all manner of tall thick trees was truly an unusual thing, and here you saw one mountain after another, each with its own edges and curves, soft or hard, its dark groves and thickets, sudden clifftops and caves, even the rocks something to give you pause. And when you thought you were getting used to one mountain, it changed on you as you approached it from a different angle. You could never take it all in.

He tried to imagine his daddy leaving this place, the long western trip that ended in Oklahoma, the reverse of his own journey. Well, he figured, that flattened land might have looked good if all you'd seen before in your life was mountains, mountains that kept you from planting all the crops you wanted, mountains that wasn't of much use at all save to look at and, he guessed, hunt squirrels and rabbits in and cut trees off of and sell for lumber. There was whiskey made in the hidden places — he'd known about moonshine and blockaders in the Ozarks, heard how the custom started in the Appalachian Mountains — but his daddy would've had no truck with that livelihood. Now there were mines, coal mines. He'd heard the coal camps spoke of with some enthusiasm as he made his way across the ridges of Middle Tennessee, but that was mainly to the north, up in the Kentucky and Virginia and West Virginia mountains.

He wasn't interested in going down inside a mountain. No, sir, that didn't interest him at all. It might have tempted his daddy, though, if there had been a coal camp available when he set out for Kansas in order to get to Oklahoma. If his daddy would set up housekeeping in a sod house made upon a dry plain for the promise of profit, he'd think nothing of digging into the depths of the earth if the pay was good.

It sure had not been easy getting up to where Uncle Laclede lived, and it occurred to Pink that maybe Uncle Laclede didn't want to be found. He was far up on a mountain, amongst no neighbors that you could see, in a house made of logs crisscrossed all over with shiny leafy vines.

Cosby was the name of the place Pink remembered his daddy mentioning in connection with Uncle Laclede. It was near Knoxville, he thought Daddy had said, but the ticket agent at the L & N Depot in Knoxville had never heard of it, and neither had the first dozen or more people on Gay Street that Pink stopped to ask. Then it was a dozen more before a fellow could tell him, in a general sense, how to get there. It was for sure out of the way, not far from Knoxville, maybe, as the crow flies, but a good two days' journey on winding mountain roads, hitching rides on rickety wagons drawn by mules that to a man looked like they might give out at any moment, wagon-wheels squeaking and wobbling, the mountains lifting up higher and higher, blue and pointy in the distance, the roads narrower and narrower, ever rocky and dusty and deep-rutted, lined by thorny and twisted shrubs such as Pink had never seen the likes of, some of them as tall as Oklahoma trees.

And then Cosby wasn't hardly nothing at all, a general store, a schoolhouse, a graveyard, a few ramshackle houses here and there, spaced far apart. A post office was in the general store, and here Pink learned that Laclede Miracle lived beyond the graveyard, up high, back deeper, past where the logging roads ended, up on Snake Den Mountain, near the bald. The man at the general store, a plump fellow with a mustache so thick it covered up his lips, said a man might walk the distance if he had tolerable shoe-leather and didn't mind a rocky path, but he'd be a far sight better off on horseback. He then offered to sell Pink a horse, but the price was high and the horse, with its buckteeth, sharp jawbone, and long ears, looked as ancient and temperamental as the mules that hauled him this far. Calculating that he had a good six hours of daylight left in this fine cloudless midsummer day, he reckoned he'd climb the mountain afoot, and after the man pointed him toward the creek, where the trail began, he set out at a brisk pace, his fiddle case swinging from one arm, his satchel from the other.

Up he went, soon out of breath, working up a sweat, much set upon by all manner of swarming insects—they whined in his ears and swooped into his nostrils and bit at his neck and arms and he couldn't swat at them without stopping and putting down his fiddle case and satchel. Itching all over, sweat-soaked, he stopped to stretch out on a sunny rock ledge that looked safe from chiggers, but, hearing the whir of a rattler and concluding that what he really wanted was shade, chiggers or not, he quickly moved on. The trail kept disappearing, leading him into thickets of the twisted shrubs such as had lined the road to Cosby, some of these thickets so dense that, except for the thorns, it was like walking through a cave. He was frequently thirsty, grateful when the creek reappeared and he could dip his hands into the clear, swift-flowing stream and drink to his heart's content and then splash the cool water over his head and soak his swollen, aching feet.

He was about to keel over, his legs weak and shaky, back giving out, bitten all over by big black flies, spooked by snakes, and it was almost dark, the air starting to cool, when at last he saw, set deep in a hollow in a little clearing alongside the creek, the shadowy outline of the log house. Uncle Laclede, he hollered, walking quickly up to its low-slung front porch. When he stepped up onto that porch, a plank snapped, gave way, and his foot went right through. He was stuck like that, trying to pull his foot loose, when a man in a white gown stepped out from the dark doorway, followed by a woman dressed in the same fashion. They had already gone to bed, Pink realized, the gowns were nightshirts.

Uncle Laclede, Pink said.

What is your business, the man said. His voice was gravelly, low. He was a small man, much smaller than he had been in Pink's mind. His shoulders sloped, his back was humped, his head tiny— must have been larger at one time—and his neck scrawny and stringy as an old rooster's. He appeared to have about three teeth, small and brown and spaced far apart. The resemblance to his father was not obvious, and at first Pink thought he might after all have the wrong man. But the man answered to Laclede Miracle, and when he trained his eyes on Pink it felt like his daddy had caught him at last.

You're my daddy's brother, he said. Pulling his foot loose from the porch, catching his pants-leg on a nail, ripping them, he backed off out of the shadows so that the man could see him in what daylight was left.

Watch your step, the woman said, her voice as gravelly as the man's. She was right tall for a woman, a good head taller than Uncle Laclede, about Pink's height, he'd say, maybe even a little taller, which would make her almost six foot. Her gray hair billowed out all over her head, wavy and thick, falling below her waist.

Thank you, ma'am.

I've told him fix that. Might as well talk to a nail on the wall.

What's your business, the man said.

I'm your brother Blue's boy, Pink said, and he mentioned Oklahoma, still getting no sign of recognition.

It's Miracle, isn't it? he asked the man. You're a Miracle?

Maybe, the man said. Maybe not.

You play the fiddle, don't you.

One time I did, yes. How'd you know that.

You give me this fiddle, Pink said, holding up the black case.

That ain't no fiddle, Uncle Laclede said.

The fiddle's inside it, Pink said. Here, I'll show you.

Uncle Laclede backed away, as if Pink was trying to hand him a rattler or spider or some such poisonous varmint. The woman stepped to one side, her thick hair swinging as she walked, which she now did, walking quickly around Uncle Laclede and putting herself between him and Pink as if to prevent a fight. She had broad, sharp-boned shoulders, and long hands extended from the sleeves of the nightshirt, which was, Pink now saw, decorated with what seemed to be tiny red butterflies all over the top. Her face was thin and sharp-edged and shiny like his mama's, and when, after a slight pause to look him up and down, she was upon him, hugging him tight, saying, I know who you are, son, I know you, sure I know you, boy—he felt like he had come home.

He don't recollect much at all no more, Ida Miracle told Pink. They's good days and bad, of course. Mostly bad, though, seems like. Some days he looks at me like I'm a rank stranger. We all have a cross to bear. God don't pile on no more than a body can stand to carry. Lord knows, I'm a stranger to myself, some days. Mercy.

Pink had been at his uncle's cabin three days. The cabin had a big room with a sleeping loft and a lean-to added on to the back for the kitchen, with a big wood stove and a safe and shelves for canned goods. Uncle Laclede and Aunt Ida slept in the loft, Pink on a pallet in the corner of the big room downstairs. The floor was splintery and a little soft in places, with considerable gaps between some of the boards for the convenience of spiders and daddy long-legs and June bugs and other crawling critters. In the mornings Uncle Laclede went off into the woods without saying where he was going, carrying a dinner pail and a shotgun. He was back for supper, which he seemed able to consume rapidly in spite of his few teeth, and then not long after, he and Aunt Ida excused themselves, climbed up to the loft, and went to bed.

At first, seeing that Uncle Laclede didn't know him, Pink thought he'd just move on, he'd found out all he was going to find out, but Ida told him he might ought to wait a spell and see what transpired. It might be that Uncle Laclede would suddenly remember everything, and then he would certainly be happy to reminisce with his nephew and hear the news about his brother out in Oklahoma. He might even play his fiddle again, you never knew. There was a fiddle hung up on the wall by its neck from a leather thong looped over a nail. He used to play that thing all the time, Ida said. Every time there was a square dance in this country, they'd call on Laclede Miracle to play for it, and he never said no. I know he enjoyed it, I just know he did.

Ida was so friendly toward Pink, hugging him and all the time touching and patting him and feeding him, that he wondered if her mind, too, had gone a little astray and she might be confusing him with someone else. But soon enough he saw that it was just her nature to be that way. She knew him, all right, had once, long ago, been out to Oklahoma Territory with Laclede. She remembered Pink's mama well, could see her as plain as day standing over the stove in that dark soddy. You was knee-high to a grasshopper, she told Pink, and there was a baby crawling on the floor, a little girl, I believe, and two little boys chasing around, and your mama big with another tyke. Your daddy Blue tried to talk Laclede into coming out there. There was going to be other land openings, he said, and he wanted Laclede and him to go after some of it together, but Laclede, he said he had to have him a mountain in sight, he couldn't live in such a flattened-out place as that Oklahoma. This would have been in '94, I believe.

That would make me seven years old, Pink said. All of us was borned except Josephine. That would've been Josephine in the oven, borned in eighteen hunnert and ninety-four.

Yes, we was sent word of the birth after we come back. A right pretty woman, your mama, and strong, so I thought. And gone now—how long did you say?

It was aught-zero. Eight years next month.

My. We was never told. Not one word did we hear about your mama's passing.

August, aught-zero. It was God-awful hot.

We haven't heard a word from your daddy for the longest time. And you say you don't even know where he is now?

He don't know where I am and I don't know where he is. That suits us both, I imagine. Likely he is at the same place I left him in.

I admired your mama.

Yes, ma'am.

Your papa worked hard. I reckon he was too busy to write letters. It was your mama sent us word of the babies. And then we heard nothing.

Folks have to get on.

Yes, they surely do. I'll tell you, though, a family's not much count if it's no forgiveness. It's mighty lonely, mighty mean for a fellow that's put out and has to go it alone.

I never wanted no one to go with me when I went. It's just the way I like it.

All them Miracles, I just don't know. Seems like something went wrong somewhere.

I didn't do wrong. Mama sent me a sign. It was nothing needing forgiving that I did when I went away.

We never had no children live long enough to need forgiving. Two dead in the breach, another in the crib. It was a judgment, Laclede said. A mercy, I sometimes think. Laclede thought the world of your daddy. Bluford, he said to me, Bluford, says he, is the only one of my brothers and sisters worth a tinker's damn. And he was the one left this country altogether. Never looked back, I guess.

I never knew any other of Daddy's kin.

No. It's a hardness between them. They look to their own, I guess.

Mama's sister came once that I recall. Her people was Spiveys. From Kentucky. Mama was borned in Jasper County, Missouri, but she always said her people was from Kentucky. Once she took us back to Missouri. I don't recollect much of that trip, though. Must have met her folks, but I was too young to remember them. They didn't come to the burying. I wonder if Daddy told them she was dead. Likely they are dead now, too.

They talked like that, Pink and Ida, while Uncle Laclede was away off in the woods somewhere—making moonshine, Pink figured—and it was passing strange at first for Pink, but he came to like this woman and how she would talk of many things it had never occurred to him to think about. He began to believe that his thinking, up until this point, had not amounted to much. He looked at Uncle Laclede, sitting across from him at the supper table, saying nothing, looking at nothing except what lay before him—beans and cornbread and salet greens—and he thought about his daddy, saw him as if in the dark cool of the soddy. What did his daddy know, out in that flat country, what did his daddy think when he walked out into his parched fields, breathing dust. He did not imagine that Blue Miracle would forget him the way Uncle Laclede had forgotten most everything. If Daddy forgot, it would be his intention to forget. It would be to say that this son of mine who run off in the dead of night no longer exists, is dead in my heart.

He has been dead in my heart, too, Pink thought. But can I make him alive there? Is that what I ought to be trying to do?

A week had passed and still Uncle Laclede had not remembered, each night looking at Pink as if he was a suspicious character, a stranger who ought long ago to have gone away. Pink decided that he should go away, he was a stranger and Laclede was a stranger to him and was determined to stay that way. What had he expected from this visit. It was folly, that's all. His mama's words had been nothing, some other sound from the street, a squeaking wagon wheel, the whinny of a horse at the moment when his dizziness struck. As for the dizziness, well, a man could drink himself into such a state. He had seen it happen. It was in fact what Sonny Boy told him happened. Bad whiskey.

I'll go back to Knoxville for a spell, he announced at the supper table. It was a town he had taken a liking to while asking directions to Cosby, he informed Ida (Laclede's attention focused, apparently, on his plate). People in Knoxville didn't know much, he told her, most of them being unaware of the existence of a place in their own state called Cosby, but they was friendly.

It was then that Uncle Laclede suddenly had something to say.

God holp a man with friends such as them, Uncle Laclede said.

Why, Laclede, honey, Aunt Ida said.

Before Pink could ask him for more information, Uncle Laclede looked him in the eye and said:

You're Blue's boy, ain't you.

Ida grinned, as if to say, see, didn't I tell you he'd remember, and she handed Pink a hunk of cornbread, hot from the skillet.

Yes, sir, Pink said.

Tell him I remember, Laclede said.

Yes, sir. Remember what, sir.

Son, that stradavary was made by Samuel Dewberry of Chattanooga in eighteen and sixty-seven. He was Ma's cousin, was Samuel Dewberry. Son of old Uncle Zeke Dewberry that was Grandma Dewberry's baby brother, killed at Lookout Mountain. I was a lad back then. Lord, a lad. Ma took me with her to Chattanooga. I aver I never saw a place like that. I couldn't stop looking at all the people. But most of all, do you know what I remember? I remember Samuel Dewberry's hands. He had such long old fingers, longest I ever did see, the veins thick and purple and twisted every which way. Right scary they was. I remember them well to this day. Yes, sir, I surely do.

He stopped, shivered, and Pink had the idea that Uncle Laclede was back there in Chattanooga, seeing those hands of cousin Samuel Dewberry's again. Aunt Ida passed Uncle Laclede the cornbread. He looked at it, and he had tears in his eyes, but he broke off a small portion of the cornbread and set it carefully on his plate.

I could hardly carry that fiddle, he said, sniffing. I was just a lad.

He broke off a chunk of cornbread, put it in his mouth, and swallowed it almost without chewing.

But you learned to play it, honey, Aunt Ida said. You know you did.

Yes, I did. Snuck off Saturday nights to the dances at McKinley's barn and watched them fiddlers. That's how I learned myself the fiddle, by watching how them old fiddlers did it and then going back and doing it. I taught myself, I tell you. Ain't a soul showed me a damn thing. I saw it all myself, and done it.

Ida stood behind Laclede, her hand on his shoulder. She leaned down and softly said to him:

Don't you imagine you could still play, honey?

I mought could play, yes.

Well, then—

The tears were flowing freely now.

I reckon they're all dead, all them old fiddlers.

You ain't, though.

No, I ain't.

This young man come a long ways to hear you play the fiddle.

I know who he is.

Of course you do.

I would hear him play, would he favor me with a tune.

Pink, not wasting a minute, took out the stradavary and played "Soldier's Joy." He played it with energy and care, he believed, the way he remembered learning it from his uncle, leaving out the slides and twists he'd picked up on Beale Street. But when he was

finished, Uncle Laclede's eyes were dry and he said, In a hunnert
more years, you mought get the hang of that tune, boy.

Yes, sir, he said. I mean to work at it.

Fetch me that fiddle, son.

Pink handed him the fiddle, and Uncle Laclede played something Pink had never heard before. His tone might have been a little scratchy, his hold on the bow surely weaker than in former
years, but the tune had a slippery, eerie sweetness to it, moving in
strange ways, one part giving way to the other before you knew it,
with sudden shifts of chord, and the strings resounding like so
many tongues.

What was that called, Pink asked.

Soldier's Joy, Uncle Laclede said.

Lord have mercy. I'd have never known it.

That's right. A hunnert years from now, maybe you'll know it.

And I thought I'd learned that one from you. First tune I ever
did learn.

Must've forgot it.

I reckon I've heard dozens of fiddlers play that tune, and not one
played it that way.

Learned that one from old man Linton Givens from over to
Sugar Cove.

I thought I learned it from the way you played it.

Old man Givens was eighty years old if he was a day. His daddy
fought at King's Mountain.

Did he make it up?

Make up what.

That tune. "Soldier's Joy."

Old man Givens? No, sir. Said he had it from his daddy. I expect
his daddy mought've made it up. They was heroes in them days.
They did the deeds of heroes and made up songs to match. Yes, sir.

It was the one tune I thought I had from you. I kept playing it
the way I remembered you playing it. It meant something to me
for that reason.

It appears you got it wrong. Try it now.

Pink tried, but it wasn't any use and he knew it. His bow jerked up when it should have come down, and his fingers lit on notes that didn't belong in any version of that tune. He'd have to hear it again, work it out, slow, one phrase at a time. Better, he would play it along with Uncle Laclede, get the feel of the rugged bowing and listen for the cunning notes that had come to Uncle Laclede from old man Linton Givens. But Uncle Laclede would play no more that evening, and Pink had the idea Uncle Laclede didn't want him to learn his version of this tune.

It's time a man got some rest, he said, pushing his plate away.

Pink lay awake for a long time on his pallet that night. Outside, crickets rubbed their wings like mad. He kept thinking of that tune, trying to hear it again in his mind the way Uncle Laclede played it. How could he ever remember it, such twists and turns, the crazy songs of the crickets on top of it? Did he ever play it right, then forget, or else change it without knowing? And then in the dark of the room he heard clearly. It wasn't a sound at all. He wasn't meant to go back, nor make things again the way they were, make them right. He had come back as far as he could. He was here, in the country that his daddy and his daddy's people had come from, and from here on out, saving the music, it was anybody's guess.

Robert Love Taylor was born in Oklahoma City and grew up there. He teaches at Bucknell, where for many years he was coeditor of *West Branch*. His fiction has appeared in the *Southern Review*, the *Ohio Review*, the *Hudson Review*, *Shenandoah*, the *Georgia Review*, and many others, as well as in *Best American Short Stories*, *Prize Stories: The O. Henry Awards*, *The Pushcart Prize*, and *New Stories from the South*. His novel *The Lost Sister* won the Oklahoma Book Award.

JULIA TAYLOR

Pink Miracle put in a brief appearance in my novel The Lost Sister *and ever since then I've had him in the back of my mind as a character who deserves his own story. He's a fiddler, after all, and since I too play the fiddle, it seemed natural that I'd want to use him in order to explore feelings and ideas that connect me to the southern Appalachian fiddle music of the early twentieth century. I had to wait until he was ready to come forward, though. I've traveled from Oklahoma to East Tennessee many times, and likely it was on one of those passages through Memphis, stalled in traffic on I-40, listening to blues playing on the radio, that I imagined the young Pink Miracle, an Okie fiddler among the blues musicians of Beale Street in the first decade of the century. From there it was just a matter of conceiving the circumstances that would propel him onward to East Tennessee in search of his fiddling ancestor, the uncle who gave him his Chattanooga Strad.*

Jim Grimsley

JESUS IS SENDING YOU THIS MESSAGE

(from *Ontario Review*)

No telling how many times I had ridden home beside her on the train before she gave the message and I noticed. Sitting sleek and composed with her hands clamped firmly on her purse, she was, that day, dressed primly in a pleated skirt and sensible shoes of navy blue, with a bright, fluffy tie at her throat. An older woman, of the generation in which proper ladies wore gloves, like those she carried, folded in her hands, she was blessed with smooth, supple skin the color of dark roast coffee beans; it would have been a flawless skin except for the tiny moles growing out of some of her pores. Her nose was broad and rounded at the end. Her silver-blue hair, streaked, straightened, and shaped into sweeping curves, encased her skull like a helmet, and when she moved the whole stiff mass moved with her, protecting the delicate workings inside, the receiver into which Jesus beamed the message.

She wore a hat that first day I heard her speak, of navy blue felt, with a round brim nicely upturned, and a satin ribbon around the crown, resting gently on the waves and spikes of her hairdo. She rocked forward in her seat, hands clasped around her purse, and glanced at everyone around her. Her eyes brushed mine with the slightest hesitation and moved on. Moments later, she said, in a loud, firm voice, "Good evening, everybody. How is everybody doing?"

She waited, with a fresh, open look, perfectly unafraid. I felt a moment of discomfort, standing so close to her, thinking she was just another crazy person talking on the train while the rest of us made our way home from a day's work in downtown Atlanta. Quiet grew around her and she allowed it to reach its maximum radius, then continued. "Jesus told me to give this message to the people. The Lord is coming back soon, the wait is nearly over. You need to be getting right with God, you don't have much time. Woeful days are coming, when he will bring a destruction on all wickedness of all peoples. Fire will burn in the cities and hellfire and damnation will come to them that have earned it. Then Jesus will come like the light of all things, amen. So you need to hear the message this time, because the Bible says it will come a destruction on the cities, even on this city, too, and it will be too late for you once Jesus gets here. That's what Jesus told me to tell the people. Thanks for listening."

Sitting back with a sense of gliding, at the end she gave a nervous look in various directions, including a glance into my face, the only glimmer of fear she showed, or so I fancied; and she showed that same moment of fear and hesitation every time I saw her, or else I imagined it each time.

The moment passed and I was left with a vague irritation, that first day, but nothing more. But the next morning I boarded the train and found her waiting again, in the exact same seat but this time wearing one of those cotton dresses made of hunter-green fabric covered with white polka dots, a white collar, big white buttons down the front, a white belt and a full skirt. Her bosom swelled ample and high over the cinched belt. A white hat rode the whorls of her hair. She had the same look on her face, as if an invisible page hung before her eyes, words only she could see. Moments after the train left King Memorial Station, she shifted forward, rolling on those ample hips, and glanced at me and opened her mouth and spoke.

I felt, then and later, that she aimed her message at me, though this must have been my imagination, since outwardly she gave no sign of noticing me in any particular way, other than to glance at me with all the rest. But even as early as that second hearing she made me angry with this message, spoken that time so early in the morning. The train arrived at the Georgia State Station and I burst out the door, hurtling toward the escalator. On the short, humid walk to my job at a nearby hospital, I seethed with thoughts of the message-giver which only subsided when I reached my office and found the classical music station playing Bach's Goldberg Variations, soothing piano by Konstantin Lifschitz, enabling me to breathe again.

She became a fixture in my life, after that. She gave the message mornings and afternoons, though most often in the afternoons, always from a seated position, always on the tracks between the Georgia State Station and the Martin Luther King, Jr., Memorial Station. I heard her give the speech going in both directions, and the message never varied, even by one word. She had clearly rehearsed these sentences, and the thought of this added to my resentment of her. She spoke calmly, not with the fervor of a prophet but rather with the grace of a Sunday School teacher. Completing the message as the train pulled into one station or the other, she composed herself and settled back against her seat. By the time the doors opened and new passengers boarded, no one would ever have known that she had, only moments before, shared with us her certainties about the end of time.

Each day, each instance of the message, filled me with contempt for this need she had to put herself forward, to flaunt her Christianity in that manner. Each moment when she shifted forward in her seat to commence her little sermon, I glared at her with narrow eyes as if I could silence her with the completeness of my disapproval.

I am an educated man, a cultivated man. I am not the type of person who would ever speak aloud on a train, unless there were some purpose to it, as saying to the person next to me, "Excuse me, you are standing on my foot" or "Please take your elbow out of my lungs." I am the type of person who believes other people should obey the same rules I do, among them, namely, that no one should presume to deliver Golgothan messages on a commuter train when people are tired and simply want to get home as peaceably as possible. It seemed clear to me that this message could not come from Jesus because He would be too polite to send it. So I listened to her words every day, during a period of peak ridership, in transit from Georgia State to King Memorial or vice versa; and I disliked her every day as well, increasingly.

I see that I have claimed this happened every day. But when I examine my memories, I understand that, while frequently we did ride in the same car on the same train, just as frequently we did not. In the afternoon, I most often caught the 4:36 P.M. eastbound on my way home. Being a creature who takes comfort in habits, I always entered the Georgia State Station from the same direction, crossed the vaulted lobby at the same angle, climbed the same four flights of granite steps to the platform, and waited there next to the same wooden bench. Never sitting on the bench, for fear of dirtying my trousers. But I waited precisely in that spot for the train, because I had calculated from experience that most of the time the lead car pulled up to that point and I had only to step forward to be aboard.

In the mornings I followed a similarly exact routine riding from Inman Park to King Memorial and then on to Georgia State.

On some afternoons I reached the platform only to find the train waiting, and in that case I stepped into the nearest door; or I reached the platform as the door chimes rang and the doors slid closed in my face and then I had to wait for the 4:43 P.M. train; or someone was standing in my waiting place and I had to wait somewhere else and board the wrong car; or someone from work offered me a ride; or I was sick or on vacation or holiday; on many days I never saw her, never heard her give the message. But most afternoons my precise timing and luck brought me to the same place, to the space in the alcove, studying the faded roses on the message woman's cloth bag.

She was a creature of habit like me and liked to sit in one of those seats next to my support pole, or the ones across from me and my pole, so that she was always riding sideways on the train. When I had heard the message often enough to expect her, even to presume she would be sitting there, I began to dread her as well, as soon as I climbed to my waiting place on the platform; though I refused to vary my own routine. I listened for the sounds of the approaching train, watched for the splash of light along the tunnel wall. By the time the train pulled to a stop in front of me and I stepped forward to be the first in line, to board the train first, I had already begun to hate her, as though I knew she were there, as though I could see her sitting with that air of purpose in her usual seat. When I stepped onto the train, when I saw her sitting with that purse raised up like the defensive wall of a highly rounded city, my contempt boiled to loathing and I stood in my usual place fuming that she was certain to speak again, that she would say those words from Jesus that were so intrusive, words that should not be spoken in a public place where people are trapped and have no choice but to listen.

She did, without fail, speak that message each time I saw her. Moving forward in her seat and glancing at her audience, in spite of my longing for her silence, she spoke.

I began to feel, during her soliloquy, the impulse to answer her back, to say, Jesus did not send any message through you for me. The idea of talking back to her, once formed, became part of the whole routine. In my head I framed messages that I would like to give her, brief scenes in which I triumphed over her there on the train; in which I, in fact, transformed her, causing her to understand that there are people in this world who do not need revealed truth on commuter trains or, indeed, in any other setting, excepting perhaps that of the church. There are decent, Christian folk who do not care to live with visions of burning destruction, who are content whether Jesus should come back or not; who are, in fact, happy to wait for him as long as He chooses to tarry. In my fantasy she was overcome with shame at her own effrontery and slid, chagrined, flat against her seat back, never again uttering even a sigh.

My fantasies entirely convinced me of my own way of thinking, so that, when she slipped slightly forward in her seat and gave that sweeping glance to those standing closest, for a long time I thought my silent fury rose up because of the rudeness of her remarks, because her words were not wanted by anybody. I was a Christian myself, a churchgoer, and I did not wish to hear them.

But then one day, at the close of the message, when the woman was easing back into her seat, another black woman seated near her said, "Amen, sister," in a loud clear voice, and an elderly white man nodded his head serenely, as if Jesus had told him the same thing; and I became more angry than ever.

The next day, trembling in my waiting place, the certainty that she would be present delivered me a shivering rage. I heard the familiar drawn-out hoot of the train in the tunnel and witnessed its glide into the station, and I stepped across the platform in the usual way and suddenly realized the train had pulled up too far, that my special door was not where it was supposed to be, and I was actually forced to push and shove my way onto the train with the rest. The train filled to overflowing, I suppose because the train before it had been delayed, and when the doors closed I could not see whether the message woman was there or not. I remained ignorant, my heart fluttering, until, a few dozen yards down the track, her familiar voice rang out, "Good evening everybody. How is everybody doing?"

I ground my back teeth together and pursed my lips and frowned to get the hard line between my eyebrows. I am a tooth grinder, as my dentist will tell you, and I flex my jaw almost constantly, and waken some mornings with tension headaches and the fear that I will soon have facial cancer. But at especial times I grind my teeth in anger, and I did so that afternoon on the train.

I began to study the other people. At first I detected only those who agreed with her, the other older black woman, dressed as she was dressed, with what one might describe as a churchwoman's flare for the benign; and, sometimes, older, white women dressed in a similar vein who signaled their approval demurely with their eyes; or else women of a lower class who nodded, their faces elastic with expanding wrinkles, and said, "You're speaking for the Lord now," and raised their hands for a little of that invisible holy ghost that is always present in the air.

My only allies were, in fact, silent men and groups of teenagers, who were always guaranteed to burst into gales of laughter when she finished speaking the message. Once a loud and sassy girl with huge round thighs and buttocks waited till the end of the message and said, in a crisp, loud voice, "Old grammaw," and her friends hooted and ducked their heads slapping each other this way and that. The message woman simply blinked and watched the space on the wall directly across from her head, as if nothing penetrated the world in which she sat.

A moment later, with breathtaking grace, she leaned forward without looking down and pulled, from the cloth bag, a Bible so worn and thumbed it could only be called formidable, covered in black leather, with patches of bright gold on the edges. She opened the book and started to read silently from the New Testament, one of the gospels where all Jesus's speeches flared up from the page in red ink. The teenagers watched her and fell mostly silent, though one of them would snicker now and then.

One night I dreamed of her lips as she shaped the word "woeful," the fact that the shape of her lips scarcely resembled the sound; her need to replenish her lipstick became very clear to me. She favored a strong red, though not too much of it. Her lips were dark brown at the edges, tapering to pink on the inside. In the dream I saw all this very clearly. Then I awoke with the sheets damp at my neck and a drop of sweat on my meager chest hairs and I became terrified.

I attended St. Luke's Episcopal Church on Peachtree Street, a fine old liberal church with a respectful pastor who occasionally challenged his congregation to greater sacrifice but certainly never threatened us with fiery destruction. While our congregation offered less prestige than a Buckhead church, I felt it was the next best thing. During services, I found myself watching my neighbors on the pews, the young professionals side by side with the old professionals, the gays, the blacks, the well-dressed and the gauchely dressed, the matrons, the widowers, the boys, the girls, the children, the teenagers, the wild bunch, the quiet ones: I studied them, the mostly white faces, and wondered what touch of God would be required to get any of them to speak on a train? Or to hear a message from God at all?

I have heard of white people attending church services in black congregations, like the African Methodist Episcopal Church, or, more often, the Ebenezer Baptist Church in Sweet Auburn, the historic district of downtown Atlanta where Martin Luther King was a preacher and Martin Luther King, Jr., came into the world. But now, when I rode through the shadows of those black churches, I wondered what sort of religion could be practiced there, to arouse in such an ordinary woman the need to predict the end of time to perfect strangers. To speak on a train, actually to do so, to move forward in her seat and open her mouth, how long did she feel the need to take this action before the first time she delivered the message? And the words that she spoke, where did they come from? Did Jesus speak to her in a way He never employed with me?

Seated in the wooden pew of the St. Luke's Episcopal sanctuary, listening to the swell of the organ playing one more verse of "Just As I Am Without One Plea," I listened for the voice of God, even for the echo of the voice of God as He spoke to someone else, and I heard only our thin, reedy voices risen somewhat in song. Then it occurred to me, the question that finally drove me to take action: Was the Christ in her church, who filled her mouth with speech, more real than the Christ in mine?

One day she wore a gold brooch with a silver enamel center and I stood so close to her I could see myself reflected in its surface, a helpless, ridiculous expression on my tiny, pinched face. She had yet to give the message that day, the train having only begun to slide out of Georgia State Station along the curve of track beyond, and I had been forced to stand far closer to her than ever before; added to that, the brooch offended me deeply, being so large and rounded, jutting out from her white rayon blouse with its fussy ruffled collar. But even more offensive was the presence of my own reflection in the milky surface of the brooch, nested near the center of her cleavage. Impossible that I should be so reflected, that my image should seem so tiny and insignificant. The volcano of anger at last boiled over as she rolled those large hips forward and smiled and said those words of preamble, "Good evening, everybody. How is everybody doing?"

"Everybody is doing fine without your message," I said. "Why don't you, for once, sit there and shut your mouth."

As if she had foreseen just such a moment, she hesitated in her forward motion and raised her eyes to mine. In the eyes I saw neither mildness nor serenity but a sharp pinpoint of fury. People around us were tittering and whispering and pointing as the ripple of my words spread out across our pond. "Who does he think he is, what's wrong with him?" I heard, but she kept her eyes glued to mine through that instant, and spoke without hesitation back to me. "I believe I am welcome to speak Jesus's words on this train," she said, "and God bless you in your heart." Then, smiling again, she leaned forward and began, as always, as if I had said nothing, as if I were not present at all. "Good evening, everybody. How is everybody doing? Jesus told me to give this message to the people."

Those around us listened raptly, and I stood there, unable to recede. She spoke with the calm that had been absent from her eyes when she turned her face up to mine, and she delivered the message with the same precision, even the same pauses, as on every other occasion. Her hands she folded over her purse, her white gloves folded in her hands, the small bit of veil from her hat arranged attractively over her forehead. She spoke, "Woeful times are coming," with that movement of lips of which I had dreamed, in need of a touch of lipstick, I noted, even in my distraction and mortification. I had dreamed this actual moment, I too had foreseen everything.

She completed the message and returned to her resting position. She never so much as glanced at me. Those around her approved of every word, a few "Amens" were whispered, and many faces, black and white, glared at me disapprovingly for my rudeness.

Why had I spoken? Was it simply my reflection in the awful brooch? Had my workday at the hospital piqued my temper to that point? Or was it worse than that? Had I felt so free to speak to this woman for reasons I hardly cared to imagine?

At Inman Park Station I stumbled from the open door and felt the relief of all those who remained behind me. I wondered what they said to one another after I fled. In my mind, like an endless reel of film, the whole sequence of moments replayed itself again and again: my anger, my reflection in the brooch, my sudden, unthinking need to spit words at her, and all that followed, the whole moment of her triumph and my humiliation.

Afterward, I could no longer follow the course of my old habits. I changed everything to avoid her, taking an earlier train from Inman Park and heading home on, as a rule, the 4:50 P.M. train from Georgia State Station. I abandoned my old standing-and-waiting place for a location far down the platform, on the bridge that crosses over Piedmont Avenue below the State Capitol Building where I could see the gleaming dome of real gold leaf. But, as happens, one afternoon when hurrying to the train, I found it had already arrived at the station and I darted heedlessly into the first open door. She was sitting in her usual place and saw me at once, she lifted her face and knew me, I am certain of it, but she said nothing at all. My heart pounded and I nearly fled to the other end of the car; but then I got my breath and held my ground and waited. This time I will listen, I thought. This time I will hear her message as if it really comes to me from Jesus, and I will receive these words into my heart, and I will change, I will never be angry again.

But she merely sat there and never moved forward, never spoke. Her worn Bible showed itself in the faded flowered bag but she never lifted it out, never opened it or read it. The train reached King Memorial Station and still she had not spoken, nor would she meet my eye again. She simply gazed, placid and withdrawn, at the advertisement for Bronner Brothers hair care products behind my head, and at the passing landscape through the windows, the cemetery where Margaret Mitchell was buried, the old cotton sack factory and the chic renovated cottages of Cabbagetown. We rode to Inman Park and I left the train, feeling hollow and even bereft.

At home I bagged the garbage and walked and fed Herman, my aging schnauzer. The life of a bachelor has always suited me, I have never wanted much company, but that evening I called a friend from church and asked her out to dinner. She made some excuse, clearly embarrassed by the invitation, and I hung up the phone feeling even more lonely than before. I felt as if I had been drifting out to sea for a very long time without noticing, and that today I had lost sight of land forever, my continent disappearing over the horizon, while I drifted on and on. I felt the urge to cry and wish, now, I could report that I actually had.

I have seen the message woman since, on occasion. She rides the train as I do, every day, though where she boards and where she departs I have never learned. I picture her as a schoolteacher or teacher's aide, or as a librarian, perhaps employed in Midtown or in West End near the Joel Chandler Harris house. I picture her surrounded by children to whom she tells stories, and sometimes I try to imagine the stories she might tell, rolling words pouring out of her in that voice that had become, at one time, so very familiar to me. Most often I picture her in the front pew of a church, enraptured by the power of some thunderous sermon descending over her from the mouth of a faceless preacher, surrounding her with the voice of God.

When I am present with her, I know she recognizes me and always will, as the white man who told her to shut up, who tried to stifle Jesus's message. She sits neatly and silently folded in the seat, and I stand in my narrow space with my arms glued to my side, my breath coming a bit labored. She waits, and I wait, but no message comes. I slide out of the train at my appointed place and picture her then, moving forward in the seat as the train accelerates toward the next station up the line; she glances around at everybody and begins again, wetting her lips and speaking those words that I hear, these days, all the more clearly in her silence.

Jim Grimsley is a playwright and novelist who lives in Atlanta. He's published five novels (including a fantasy novel, *Kirith Kirin*), and has won a number of prizes for his fiction, including the Sue Kaufman Prize from the American Academy and Institute of Arts and Letters. He is playwright in residence at 7Stages Theatre and About Face Theatre in Chicago and, in 1987, received the George Oppenheimer/*Newsday* Award for best new American playwright for *Mr. Universe.* His collection, *Mr. Universe and Other Plays,* was a 1998 Lambda finalist for drama. He received the Lila Wallace–*Reader's Digest* Writer's Award in 1997 and teaches writing at Emory University in Atlanta, Georgia.

For twenty years I worked at a public hospital in downtown Atlanta, and during many of those years I rode to work every morning on the train. During a certain period when I had become particularly settled into this routine, a woman put herself forward on the train, much as I describe in this story, with much the same message. As months passed, I frequently heard her deliver her message in this way, and, as far as I could tell, the speech never varied by a single word.

Marshall Boswell

IN BETWEEN THINGS

(from *The Missouri Review*)

In between things, Parker slept with Rachel. He kept telling himself he wouldn't do it, even insisted, sometimes out loud, that the mere thought of doing it was completely out of the question. Yet for one reason or another, reasons he did not always care to examine, he just kept doing it. Over and over again. Even after he'd said he wouldn't. And he said it all the time. He said it when she called, he said it while he was saying yes it would be all right if she came over, and he said it—sometimes out loud—as he waited for her to come over. At least part of him said it. One part of him said he shouldn't do it, and the other part went ahead and did it anyway.

Even while he did it he said he shouldn't do it, so clearly there were two Parkers at work here: the one who said and the one who did; the word versus the deed. But in this battle between pen and sword, the sword was mightier by a pretty large margin.

He referred to this state of affairs as the Rachel Situation. The reference was mostly private, since not many of his friends even knew there was a Rachel Situation, though most of them knew Rachel. They knew Rachel and they knew Parker used to date Rachel and they knew that Parker no longer dated Rachel; they just didn't know there was a Rachel Situation. For the Rachel Situation was further complicated by the fact that Rachel was one of

the "things" he was "in between." He was in between Rachel and
someone else who hadn't shown up yet, some spectacular woman
who would represent, in full, the last person on earth he would
ever desire. More than the girl of his dreams, she was the future
incarnate. He knew that when she finally arrived in his life in all
her perfection, he'd be a whole person at last, fully integrated, all
problems solved. And in the meantime, he was sustaining intimate,
sexually charged break-up proceedings with his past.

When he wasn't busy with the Rachel Situation, Parker pursued
his new life—not really the future incarnate so much as the interim
existence he began when he inaugurated break-up proceedings
proper. This new life, in which he sold telephone services to small
businesses, took place in the real world. The real world was that
vast, frightening expanse of metropolitan Atlanta that stretched
with teeming busyness and activity beyond the walls of the graduate school where he and Rachel were once mutually enrolled.
Back then, Parker and his graduate student colleagues liked to the-
orize about the real world. Many of them wrote papers about the
real world. Some of them taught entry-level freshman courses that
prepared young people to flourish in the real world. A few of his
more flippant colleagues taught their students to interpret adver-
tisements and television talk shows in the manner of literary works,
all in order to demonstrate the relative importance of the real
world over that of the purely textual and idealistic. Still and all, few
of these people had ever actually gone to the real world. Some had
visited, some had fled, but no one in Parker's immediate set had
ever really lived in the real world itself. It was just this abstract
place *out there,* this throbbing, clashing, quaking world of the
ineluctably real. And now Parker lived there himself. Nowadays,
as he fought his way through rush-hour traffic, or picked up his
dry cleaning, or stood in line at the supermarket in his suit and tie
with a little tote basket piled high with frozen pasta entrées, he
would say to himself, I'm finally here, I'm finally *a real person.*

Rachel, on the other hand, was still in graduate school. A petite,
elfish sprite of a girl with enormous clear green eyes and a tangle

of ginger-colored hair usually bundled into a roll at the back of her head, she eschewed Parker's real world for the world of the mind, of student loans and poor health insurance, of identity politics and bad haircuts and perpetual unemployment. Although nearly a year had passed since she had filed her dissertation—"Clitoral Envy and Masculine Anxiety in the Works of John Webster"— she was still trying desperately to locate that most elusive treasure in all of modern academia, a job. In the meantime she picked up section after section of Freshman Composition. On those mornings when Parker slept at her place, he would lie back on her mattress and watch her as she bustled about the apartment before class, her tube socks sliding along the hardwood floors and her cat, a mangy mutt named Margerey Kempe, crawling underfoot. For class preparation she would often jump onto the bed and march around in her underwear intoning her lecture to the bedroom walls, a coffee cup in one hand and a rhetoric and comp reader flapping in the other, while Parker, still in the bed, avoided her marching feet ("Geez, Rachel, the *coffee*"). At eight-fifteen he would gather his things and walk out the door, Rachel running out behind him with a sheaf of freshman essays fluttering under her arm and a bagel clamped between her teeth, and he would continue watching her as she climbed into her old Volkswagen Rabbit and peeled out of her gravel driveway to meet her morning section. Some days she wore billowy peasant dresses. Other days she left the house in low-slung boys' corduroys, thrift-store bowling shirts, and untied Keds sneakers. A dedicated and passionate teacher, she always included her home phone number on her course syllabi, and on rainy evenings when Parker was staying over at her place, her male students, perhaps responding to the melancholy weather, would often call for help. Parker relished answering these phone calls. "Um, gosh, I'm sorry," the students would say upon hearing his voice, "I thought, I, um . . . Listen, is Professor Moore there?" Handing her the phone, Parker would say, "One of your students, Professor, looking for an *extension*," drawing out that last word. Rachel would scrunch her nose and take the receiver. "Oh, *hi*, Josh," she'd say,

turning her back to Parker and making her voice soft and consol-
ing. "Is there a problem, is everything okay?"

Despite the fact that they were officially broken up, Parker spent
lots of time at her apartment. He preferred her place, actually, to
his own. A spacious, musty-smelling ground-floor duplex, Rachel's
pad was a funhouse of clutter and chaos with miles of hardwood
floors, a kitchen full of dilapidated makeshift computer equipment,
tapestries on the walls, chenille-covered couches and chairs, an
antique wooden dining table buried in mail and shopping bags,
three lava lamps and five beanbag chairs, a completely outfitted
and mint-condition Barbie Dream House, and, in the cavernous,
echoing bathroom, an above-ground lion-clawed bathtub surrounded by mounds and mounds of thick, waterlogged fashion
magazines and literary quarterlies. After lovemaking, as Rachel
cleaned up in this same bathroom, Parker would thumb through
her books, most of which fell under the general rubric of contemporary gender theory. The book jackets featured bawdy woodcut
illustrations from the Middle Ages and elegantly written critical
hosannas, while inside lay the densest, most impenetrable prose he
had ever read in his life, formatted in sleek Minion font and
printed on sturdy, acid-free paper by some craft-conscious university press in the Midwest. He wasn't interested in the prose, however. He wanted to read Rachel's annotations. They spoke to him,
seemed to possess for him a strange, almost cabalistic significance.
Opening the volume on the bedside table, for instance, he might
encounter the following random passage underlined in Rachel's
neat, scholarly hand; in the margin he might detect a mysterious
"P" followed by a question mark:

> Although the phe-no(mono)logical "Self," which is, undoubt-
> edly, a Cartesian, i.e., patriarchal, fiction, can only be (re)con-
> stituted in relation to an equally fictional "Other," this unstable
> relation of *différance* is always already thwarted by a de(sire)ing
> of the totalized Ego, site of masculine "certainty," of longed-for
> stability. For Ego itself is inevitably "predator of the Other," and

hence we see that the fantasy of masculine hegemony exists in a vacuum defined wholly by, and inscribed entirely within, its relationship to this Other, which is itself not only unstable, necessarily and unavoidably unstable, but also, by a similar species of (male) hegemonic logic, undermined by the very same metaphysical "*un*-cert(aint)y" posited by . . .

In a panic he would snap the book shut and put it back where he found it, his hands shaking with paranoia and dread.

Back in bed, Rachel would narrate for him the most recent Grad Bash. Having once been a graduate student himself in the same department, Parker more or less knew all the principal characters.

"First of all," Rachel would begin, supine in bed beside him with her leg hoisted into the candlelight so as to cast a lurid shadow on the wall opposite her bureau, "Carey brought his new flame, a forty-eight-year-old Hispanic woman who works for Morgan Stanley, worth several mil, easy. She was a trip, man, Esmerelda was her name, very touchy-feely. Anyway, and then Ethan corners me for like an hour to tell me all about his latest crisis, which basically boils down to, Should I come out before or after my oral exams? Honestly, he was reduced to framing the question in precisely those terms. Christ. Oh, and I forgot to tell you, guess which faculty member was getting stoned in Jennifer's bedroom . . . ?"

These accounts would course through him like an Alka-Seltzer. What was he doing? What had he been doing for the last fifteen (twenty? twenty-five?) minutes? What was he doing with his *life*?

"Sounds positively dreadful," he'd say.

"*You'd* think so," shrinking away from him.

No, they were not going out—not anymore, anyway. Their breakup had been final, way back when. And they certainly weren't seeing each other. Rather, they were seeing other people. That was the important thing: to see other people. And they both planned to start seeing other people, just as soon as they quit not seeing one another. Nevertheless, there had been sightings. One Friday night he and Rachel took in a movie, for instance, and they were sighted. They were sighted at a taco joint. There were the occasional street sightings: a lot of their arguments took place out of doors. But, so far, they had avoided being the subject of a Rumor. So they were okay. They were just two lonely people trying to sustain an intimate breakup. And sustain it indefinitely.

About two months into the Rachel Situation, Parker and Rachel began devising a set of rules.

Rule 1. *Each partner is free to date without consulting the other.* This was the single most important rule of all. So far, Parker had yet to invoke it, though he planned to do so any day now. More to the point, Rachel, so far as he knew, had not invoked it either, though he had no way of knowing this for sure, since the rule, by its very wording, ruled out all possible knowledge of its being invoked— which was the whole point, as Parker very well knew.

Rule 2. *Neither partner is allowed to feel guilty.* Rachel, not Parker, devised this one, astounding as that may sound. She devised it for Parker, though she also claimed to be bound by it. How this rule was supposed to work out in practice Parker never figured out. Of all the rules they devised for one another, this was the most difficult one of all. For Parker, anyway.

Rule 3. A *partner can spend the night at another partner's apartment but only when said partner is too intoxicated to drive.* They both broke this one pretty freely.

Rule 4. *Neither partner is permitted to leave a trace of his/her presence at the other partner's apartment.* By way of minor exceptions, Rachel left two changes of underwear, her Wellesley sweatshirt, her warm-up pants, her hair dryer, her toothbrush, her Hillary Clinton coffee mug, and a box of tampons at Parker's apartment; Parker left a pair of army fatigues, several pairs of boxers, his toothbrush, and his electric razor at Rachel's apartment.

Rule 5. *If either partner sleeps with anyone else, all contact ceases immediately.* Both were adamant about this one. *Immediately,* they liked to remind one another. *No exceptions.* It was implicitly understood, moreover, that this rule canceled out Rule Number One, while Rule Number One did not in any way cancel out Rule

Number Five. In other words, Rule Number One prevailed insofar as all activity remained within its purview, yet the moment Rule Number One turned into Rule Number Five, the earlier rule was to be instantly revoked in favor of the newer, more inclusive and urgent rule. Paper covers rock, rock covers scissors, scissors cut paper.

In the wake of particularly larky bouts of sex, Rachel would sometimes declare, "You think this isn't a relationship, but it is."

"This? A relationship?"

"Yes: this."

"Was our other relationship this good?"

"Sometimes. A lot more often than you're ready to admit."

She was right, of course, which was why he continued sleeping with her long after he had gone through the hassle of breaking up with her—unexpectedly and without much warning, Rachel was always quick to add. Yet if it was so good, why did he break up with her in the first place? And why did he continue doing this?

Parker had his reasons, which he explained to Rachel more than once. For breaking up, he liked to cite the fact that he was not prepared for that most terrifying plunge of all, the Long-Term Commitment. Rachel, on the other hand, had wanted an LTC, which was a perfectly laudable thing for her to want, he was always quick to tell her. But since he didn't want one, what other choice did they have but to break up?

"Um," Rachel would say, her index finger fully extended, "let's see: for one thing, we could have—"

And there was also the matter of condomless sex, he said. That was a real selling point. Two weeks after they first started going out, he and Rachel got tested for HIV, and the day they returned home with their negative test results was also the first day they permitted themselves the luxury of condomless sex. Rachel was on the pill, neither partner was diseased in any way, monogamy seemed the next step, so why not? Now, nearly two years after that fateful day, both Parker and Rachel were operating under the exact same conditions. Since their breakup, for instance, neither partner had slept with anyone new. "No reason to feel flattered," Rachel always added. "No flattery taken," he would reply. So each time they swore off one another, each time they insisted they were going to leave each other alone, each time they agreed it would be best if they didn't do this kind of thing anymore, they always did so under the remarkable dispensation of a monogamous HIV-negative couple.

"Fair enough. I'll give you that one. What else?"

Well, and there was the whole exciting process of giving in to one another over and over again. That might have been the biggest selling point of all. Parker's wise and knowing friends, none of whom would have approved of the Rachel Situation had they known it existed, weren't around when she stopped at the front door of his downstairs apartment and looked down at her feet, hovering between resolution and surrender, while he waited only three feet away and told himself that tonight he would let her walk away and end it for good. They weren't there to see the look on her face as she took her hand from the doorknob and met his eyes. They weren't there during that unbearably thrilling moment when he locked his fingers behind his neck and she shook her head and said, "Shit." And they were nowhere in sight when he and Rachel removed the Tristan-and-Iseult sword lodged between them and rolled hungrily into all that glorious, forbidden space.

"Oh God," she said, dropping back onto the pillow, her hands in her hair, "now we sound like Cheever characters."

What he didn't explain to Rachel was how much he loved the way things stood between them right now, the delicate balance they were sustaining, this tension-filled battleground between full commitment and wide-open singlehood, between past and future. It was the best of both worlds. After lovemaking, they would lie in bed and talk about themselves, she relating selected details of her daily existence, and he doing the same. On those languid evenings her life appeared to him like a winding hallway lined with a bewildering procession of closed doors she led him past on her way to the porch out back. Similarly, he handed his life to her in little incomplete bundles. Like many of their old lovers' spats, these furtive, guarded bull sessions kept the two of them together and sustained their distance, all at the same time. Drifting off to sleep with the first twinge of regret tickling his stomach, he would nevertheless say to himself that his life right now was just about perfect, a golden mean between two alternatives he found too frightening to contemplate. He was like Goldilocks in the baby bear's bed: not too hard, not too soft, but somewhere comfortably, safely, in between.

Three months and two weeks into the Rachel Situation, Parker finally invoked Rule Number One.

Her name was Kimberly Willis, from Marketing. She wasn't really the girl of the future; she was more like Miss Right Now. All sharp angles and protruding elbows, with a pointed chin and a thick sheath of permed hair that looked a bit like dried ramen noodles, she was attractive enough in her own way, a source of both desire and paranoia. Though they were in different departments, he ran into her every day in the break room, and every time he saw her she was hunkered down in the corner with a girlfriend or two, the group of them whispering, conspiring, giggling, and after a month or two he discerned that Kimberly Willis was the leader of the pack. He soon grew convinced she was giggling about him. That's why he asked her out in the first place: to assuage his fear. And the minute she tilted her head and said, "Um, sure, why not," he realized he'd made a serious mistake.

"Oh my God," she gushed at dinner that night, "you've seriously never heard the story about her and him? I totally can't believe it: I thought *everyone* knew this story."

"I guess I'm out of the loop."

"*Totally*. Okay, now you have to promise you won't tell anyone I told you this."

"I thought everyone already knew it."

"Well, everyone but her. Promise? Solemnly swear? Good. Now, to understand this story, you have to know about Jeff. You *do* know about Jeff, don't you?"

He smiled. "Am I supposed to know about him?"

"Oh my *God!* You are totally going to flip out when I tell you this. Okay, so Jeff, who used to date this other girl who isn't there anymore—whole *nother* story right there—well, he asked this *unnamed person* to join him in Chicago. Follow me?"

He followed her. Before he quit graduate school he used to complain to Rachel that the only people they ever saw were the other people from the department. "Real people don't live this way," he complained. "Real people go to work and come home and *then* live their lives. We never leave work. We see the same people all day, every night, every weekend. Work follows us everywhere we go. And that's why everyone we know is so neurotic and screwed up." Now that Parker was officially in the real world, he was surprised to learn that no one there ever left work either. In real life, people went to work and came home and then went back out to spend more time with the other people from work. Where, apparently, they talked about people from work.

"Really?" he said, in response to a dramatic pause in Kimberly's story. "Isn't that something. So what happened next?"

Right about this time he spotted Rachel. She was sitting in a booth on the other side of the restaurant, scribbling in a spiral notebook and nursing a beer. Uncharacteristically, she had her hair down, and through the drapery of her bangs he could detect the wiry glint of her glasses. She was wearing the denim vest he had given her on her birthday several years ago, as well as the peach, ankle-length skirt he always loved, the one that outlined so perfectly the articulate slope of her hips. This was how she looked when he wasn't around, it suddenly dawned on him. Then he realized that if he didn't already know her, if he hadn't already dated and broken up with her, he would have wanted to meet her. He could even imagine himself not speaking to her tonight—he was, after all, on a date—and then spending the rest of the week mooning about his apartment in a lovesick fog, excoriating himself for not mustering up the courage to approach her out of the blue and ask her out on a date. So at least he was spared all that.

". . . and so when Jeff comes to work on Monday, this Person Who Will Go Nameless goes up to him and she's like . . ."

Earlier that day Rachel had called him at work to ask him if he was coming over that night, and when he told her no, he wasn't, she said nothing for what seemed like a very long time. Then she coughed and told him Fine and hung up.

". . . so then Jeff was all like—"

"Could you hold that thought for a minute?"

Kimberly Willis jerked her head once, as if she had just been electrocuted. Her eyelashes beat like bumblebee wings. "Gosh, I'm sorry. I didn't mean to—"

"No, no, it's not . . . I just have to—" With what he hoped was an embarrassed look on his face—not too difficult to conjure, actually, given the situation—he jerked his thumb over his shoulder and arched his eyebrows.

"Oh, *right*." Kimberly gave him a sage nod, leaned forward, scowled. "I think it's called a *bathroom*."

As he approached Rachel's table, he kept his eyes on her cheek, a sliver of which poked through the cascade of her bangs. From past experience he knew she was one of the world's most inept liars, a woman woefully ill equipped for subterfuge. If Rachel had seen him earlier, her cheek would betray her.

It did.

"You shouldn't write in the dark like that," he said when he got to her table. "You'll ruin your eyes."

For a confused moment or two she acted surprised to see him. Then she sat back and sighed. The spiral notebook lay open on the table. The right-hand page was smooth and flat while the left-hand page bowed slightly, the underside tinted blue with aggressive penmanship. Beside the spiral lay a greeting card, also face down. She stroked her pen. "For the last ten minutes I've been sitting here trying to figure out how to leave."

"You could try the door."

"You and that girl are sitting beside it."

Parker looked for himself. His and Kimberly's table leaned flush against the front window, two tables away from the entrance. His seat, empty at the moment, faced the door, while Kimberly's faced the passageway leading to the restaurant's bar area. Kimberly stared at him from her seat. Without altering her expression by the merest twitch, she waved. Inanely, he waved back.

"So," Rachel was saying, "I thought I'd sit here and doodle in my notebook and then leave when you two finished your meal, if that's okay with you."

"Rachel, listen—"

"That *is* a home perm I'm seeing, isn't it?"

"When you called at work today, I—"

"She must be an old student of yours. Or a *young* student, I should say."

"She's not a student. She's in Marketing. Look, if you want us to—"

"Marketing? Isn't that where they create all these false expectations and phony desires to make people want things they don't really need? Or am I getting that confused with pornography?"

"Tell you what," Parker said evenly, "we'll leave. How's that sound? We haven't even ordered yet, so no one should mind."

"Oh, no you don't." Rachel seized a big burlap backpack off her seat and began shoveling in her wallet, her spiral notebook, her glasses, muttering, "You just stay here and eat your little dinner and discuss your little marketing strategies with your cute little friend over there, all right? In the meantime I have *tons* of reading to do, excuse me, whole libraries of it, shelves and shelves of reading, so actually this is *just* the break I've been waiting for, all I needed was an excuse to get out that front door and home to my cozy little bed and my cozy kitty cat and my, my, *shit,* where is that waitress, I need to pay for this thing." She was standing beside him now, her full backpack slung across one shoulder and the check fluttering between her fingers. Her scent cut through the smoke and steam of the restaurant and tickled the back of his throat.

"I think you pay up front."

"Don't we always." Waving the check in his face, she turned on her boot heels and stepped away.

"Rachel, wait."

Her shoulders drooped. The backpack swung once along the curve of her spine; his stomach swung with it. He knew he had to say something; he just couldn't decide what it should be. There was no rule for where they were now. There was the rule about dating, there was the rule about guilt, there was the rule about sleeping with someone else. Rules 1, 2, and 5, respectively. But there was no rule for this.

"I'm waiting," she said, without turning around.

"This is awkward, that's all. We didn't anticipate this."

"*Who* didn't anticipate it?" Now she faced him. "What is it we didn't anticipate, Parker?"

"This," he gestured. "Bumping into one another. Seeing the other person. What*ever*."

"Fine." She patted him lightly on the chest. "Then here's a new addendum to Rule Number One. Each partner must warn the other where *not* to go when said partner is out on a date. How's that?"

"Rachel, please, this is stupid."

"What part of the addendum did you not understand?"

"No, I got it, that sounds fine. It's a good addendum."

"So you're square on this?"

"Yes, I'm square. I—"

"Good. Then tomorrow night you are forbidden to go anywhere *near* the Rusty Spoon. Do we understand each other? Excellent. Now, if you'll excuse me, I'm going to pay my bill."

She marched off, her skirt swaying one way and her backpack swaying the other. Before she exited earshot, he asked, "Can I call you tonight?"

And Rachel, still moving toward the cash register, waved the bill in the air and replied, "Parker, go Five yourself."

• • •

The next evening he sat crouched and uncomfortable behind a mound of bushes bordering Rachel's duplex. He was staring at a car. For the last hour and a half he had been hiding here in silence and apprehension watching car after car drift mysteriously along Rachel's quaint, deeply wooded street, only to pass her place and penetrate deeper into the humid night. But now a car had finally stopped. He stood up and squinted. Accord? Acura? Something fairly nondescript in any case, flat and squat with rounded edges and a low-lying hood. His heart pounded in his ears.

Presently the passenger door opened. A female foot emerged from the open door, followed by a small, feminine form dressed in a dark charcoal skirt and white blouse. She clutched a spiral notebook to her chest. Before turning around, she bent over and said something to the driver and then laughed, a tiny sound that barely penetrated the roaring in Parker's head. Then she shoved the door closed with her hip and, with a wave to the retreating car, walked slowly toward the door, the notebook still cradled against her chest.

"Hey," he whispered from the bushes.

Rachel stopped and stared blankly into the night.

He stood and cleared his throat.

"There are laws against stalking, you know."

"I'll risk it," he replied, and stepped away from his hiding place.

As if this sort of thing were perfectly normal, she proceeded down the walkway, Parker following along behind, and then she sat down on the porch steps, facing the street. He sat next to her, his arms crossed along his knees.

"You're barefoot," she pointed out.

"I left in a hurry." He wiggled his toes. "It was a boring night anyway. A shoeless kind of night, you might say. How about you? How was your night?"

"Life altering."

"Interesting you should say that, because that's exactly what I came here to tell you. I'm also altering my life."

"Parker, look: I'm tired, I'm cranky, and I really need to—"

"Wait, hear me out, Rachel. Just listen to me for a second. This is important. I was home tonight cleaning my toilet, right? And I'm crawling around there on my hands and knees, scrubbing the porcelain and drinking beer, and I'm thinking to myself, What's wrong with this picture? Have I been keeping myself free so I can stay home on Friday night and clean my toilet? Because that's basically what I do on nights I'm not with you. I clean my toilet, I rearrange my CDs, I, you know, I surf the Net or whatever."

"So it's me or the toilet is what you're telling me here."

"I'm not finished. So there I am, on my hands and knees, like I said, and I'm also thinking to myself, You hate this. You hate the thought of her being out with someone else. Admit it, Parker, you're jealous. It was just like you last night, Rachel, when you saw me and Kimberly."

"Wrong. It was *nothing* like you and Kimberly."

"No, I didn't mean that. Wait—"

"Just say what you're trying to tell me, Parker, and make it quick because I've got things to do."

"All I'm saying is, I can't stand it any longer. This whole thing is stupid, the whole setup, this in-between thing we're sustaining right now. It's gotta stop. You know what I mean?"

"Yep." The answer came so fast it sounded as if she'd dropped the "e." Yp.

"Well, okay then; we agree. So I was thinking—"

"It's over."

"No, no, that's not it. Rachel, listen. I just think we've got to go one way or the other. No more sitting on the fence."

"And which way do you think we should go, Parker?" She leaned back against the porch column, softening her presence somehow. A raindrop hit his face, followed by another.

"I'm not sure." He hugged his knees. "I just know I want things to change."

More rain fell. Already the patio emitted a light, humid scent of damp wood. "Actually," she whispered, "I've got a confession to make."

His heart lurched. A new twist. He had no idea if this was good news or bad news, if it would elate him or crush him. In either case, he was being saved from making a decision he feared he wouldn't be able to make, and he took comfort from this knowledge. Rachel was saving him. As usual. "Yes?"

"Well, for starters, I didn't have a date tonight."

He let a moment pass before he said, "I see."

"No, I'm pretty sure you don't, Parker. I'm telling you I had dinner with my dissertation advisor."

He nodded without much conviction.

"Parker, look at me." He obeyed. Tears rimmed her eyes, those big, brilliant green eyes. *Surrender,* said a voice in his head. *Let go.* "I got a job offer this week."

Not the twist he had in mind. Not even the *bend* he had in mind. "Say again?"

"A job, Parker. As in, you know, a paycheck and all that."

"Oh, but Rachel," he smiled and reached out to take her hand, "that's terrific news. I mean, *isn't* it? Isn't this what you've been working for?"

"More or less." She jerked her hand away.

"More or less? What kind of job is it?"

"A teaching job. Small state college with good reputation. Manageable course load. Private office."

He laughed. "Sounds great."

"One-year contract, but they tell me it turns into a tenure-track next year."

He raised his hands as if speechless with admiration. "Even better."

"It's in Massachusetts, Parker." She was looking at him again. Her expression, which she now presented for examination, offered no clue as to what she might be thinking.

"That's quite a hike."

"And here's the best part." She turned away. "They have a couple of extra sections I can take on this summer if I want them."

The rain now dripped off the roof and sprayed the tops of his bare feet. "And do you?"

"My advisor says it'd be a good idea. He says it could help me a lot next year when they decide whether or not to keep me on for the duration. I think the term for it is 'departmental service,' which is just an academic euphemism for kissing ass."

He listened to the soft spring rain, to the sound it made as it pattered across the leaves and rattled the gutters. "Wow," he whispered.

"How's that for a confession? Didn't see that one coming, did you?"

"Yeah, that's pretty left field." He felt her slump away from him. Cars passed by slowly, their tires licking the road. "So I guess you're gonna take it."

"More than likely."

"And when do you leave?"

"In a couple of weeks. Early June." She faced him now. "Actually, I'm lying."

He felt himself blink once, very slowly. "About what, exactly?"

"The date. New faculty orientation starts this Monday. That means I'm leaving tomorrow." Now she watched his face for a reaction, though Parker had no idea what she was seeing for the simple reason that he had no idea what he was thinking. Both Parkers were at work now, the one Rachel was looking at and the one wondering what Rachel was looking at. At this very moment one of them was undergoing a very intense set of emotions, while the other was wondering what those emotions could possibly be. So which was which? That really was the question, wasn't it? In a weird sort of way, it had *always* been the question. "So," she sighed, "finish telling me how you were going to alter your life."

He rallied enough to answer, "You just did it for me."

"Hoo, don't I wish." She exhaled dramatically, then shook her head. "Wouldn't that have been something? Me altering your life?"

"You did alter it, Rachel. You know that."

"Oh, Parker. I was a very small part of your life." She lifted her pinched fingers to her squinting right eye. "A teensy little part.

The, I don't know, the sex part or something. Hah, that's exactly what I was: a Sex Part. It's almost like being Sex Partner, but not *quite*."

"You were much more than that."

"I was?"

"Yes, you were."

"Why are you using the past tense?"

"I didn't realize I was."

"Well, you are." With a dramatic sigh she stretched her legs out into the rain and leaned back onto her hands. "Do you know when I decided to take this job?"

"No." At some point his hands had begun shaking. He had no idea which part of him was responsible, nor did he have any idea what was happening to him right now. He just knew that it was important, whatever it was. He was living through one of those moments that would stay with him for a very long time.

"About two seconds ago."

"You're lying."

"Isn't it pretty to think so?" She looked down at his feet and laughed. "And look at you: barefoot and repentant. It almost makes a girl think." She stood up now. When he turned to her at last he found himself staring at her skirt, then at her hip. He had to look way up to locate her face, but it lay in shadows, her hair hanging down like a lampshade. She towered over him with her notepad, huge and terrifying and mysteriously no longer his. She was already receding. She was already gone.

From her lofty perch she opened the spiral. He now stared at the cardboard underside with all the detachment of a drugged patient in a dentist's chair. When her knee grazed his back he was so startled he looked away, embarrassed, and only gradually did he register that a square pink envelope, stiff and heavy, had dropped into his lap. "You might as well have that," she said. "For what it's worth." He then heard her shuffle across her porch and rattle, perhaps more aggressively than usual, her monstrous clump of keys.

The deadbolt sounded with a distant hollow thump; Margerey Kempe squealed a worried hello. One final creak of the door and she was really gone. He held his breath. The moment hung, and for a thrilling, unbearable instant it seemed as if she was going to come back. But then the creak came, followed quickly by the rattle of the door and the sad slide and drop of the deadbolt.

The envelope lay like a hatchet blade between his thighs. He took it gingerly between his trembling fingers and ran his thumb along the seal. But the flap was free: she hadn't sealed the envelope yet. Nor, he noticed when he turned it around, had she addressed it. He tugged loose a thick, glossy greeting card. The front featured a print reproduction of Van Gogh's *The Starry Night*. He opened the card. Yesterday's date was written, in Rachel's careful hand, along the upper right-hand corner. Otherwise the card was blank, save for the following inscription, also in Rachel's hand:

> *Parker,*
> *By the time you read this I will have*

Nothing more. That was all she had written. He stared and stared at this sentence for a good two, maybe three minutes. A thick raindrop fell from overhead and splattered on the card, causing the word "read" to spider outward and sink deeper into the thick paper, so that it looked like a small aquatic creature sealed in a microscope slide. Another drop fell, then another. He did not move until the entire sentence, salutation and all, was completely illegible, the ink running like cheap mascara into all that clean, unsullied white space, and when the card was no longer legible he dropped it onto the porch step and stood up. The girl of the past had become the girl of the future—perfect, unattainable, celestially remote—and now he was a single Parker at last, lonely and clear-eyed and hopelessly, helplessly in love.

Marshall Boswell teaches fiction writing and American literature at Rhodes College in Memphis, Tennessee. Previously his stories have appeared in *New England Review, Shenandoah,* the *Missouri Review, Playboy,* and elsewhere. Earlier this year he published a critical study of John Updike's Rabbit novels entitled *John Updike's Rabbit Tetralogy: Mastered Irony in Motion.* He has completed a new novel entitled *Alternative Atlanta.*

COURTESY OF RHODES COLLEGE

"*In Between Things*" *began as a paragraph without a story. Whereas the opening sentences arrived intact, from nowhere, they bluntly refused to yield up a workable piece of fiction. Version begat version. All over my hard drive I found cryptically numbered files named "between.doc." Then somewhere around my sixth or seventh stab at the thing I began to see all that rejected material as the beginning of a new novel. Only then was I able to start the story afresh and finally finish it.*

During all these changes and transformations, that opening paragraph remained untouched, down to the last comma. I now realize those seven or eight sentences were a breakthrough of sorts. Perhaps this is what they mean by "finding your voice"—I don't know. In any case, a novel emerged from this story, so I remain deeply attached to it. I'm glad other people liked it as well.

Readers always like to know if stories are autobiographical. I'll simply say that I, too, was once involved in an in-between thing, much like Parker. I got out of mine by marrying my Rachel.

Nicola Mason

THE WHIMSIED WORLD

(from *Epoch*)

LIFE WITH HAM

If heartbreaks were hams, a delivery boy would ring the bell the morning after the breakup, his arms full of smokehouse sorrow, spiral cut. In the weeks to come, you use the ham in sandwiches and casseroles. Soups and quiches. Omelets. Tacos and pastas and pies. But no matter how much you consume, the ham never gets any smaller. Instead, it grows pinker, occasionally bleeds when you bite into it, and the scent of hickory permeates the house, puffing from the windows so your neighbors lift their heads to sniff the air.

Just when you think you've gotten used to this state of affairs (used to the flensing light of morning, used to the stickpin days, used to your car grinding, your pencils snapping, your head threatening to split like a melon in your hands), the ham begins to cry at night in the fridge—long ululations so mournful that the dog hides under the bed. The ham is lonely with your lettuce; the lettuce never listens. Lonely ten times over with your cheese. Your olives are clubby and disdain it. It is friendless among the jams, repulsed by the propositions of your Dijonnaise. At three A.M. you stagger from the bed, torn from the comforts of dream. The ham cowers under your glare, huddles behind the bulwark of the milk,

226

then, in a show of hope, peeks out. Henceforth the dog snores at your feet, and the ham, hiccuping softly, nestles against your ribs.

Now when you walk the dog, the ham comes too, and it seems happy to tumble briskly along at your side. In the park, you see other people with hams. One woman has dressed hers in a bonnet and is wheeling it around in a stroller. Near the water, a jogger scolds his ham and kicks it if it gets in his way. Another woman reclines on a bench, reading, occasionally reaching over to pat the ham sitting next to her.

You walk, and the sun makes claims on your senses, chasing the chill from your skin. The lake ripples and shines, a blue elucidation, like a bell that melted while sounding its clearest note. The grass is springy underfoot. Soon the wind kicks up, and the dog lunges after minicyclones of leaves, dragging you with him, nearly ripping off your arm, and you are laughing.

At home your ham seems less juicy, tinged with gray. Sticks and grass are stuck to its honeyed glaze. You mean to clean it, to sigh and weep the way it likes, but you forget, then stumble over it on the way to the john. That night, in sleep, you push the ham from the bed, and it rolls down the hall and out the dog-door. Tumbling along the street, it careens off the curb, then bounces down the steps at Haskell High. The ham is ragged by Third Street. By Tenth, it's a muddy pulp. As it splashes through puddles and weaves through traffic and trundles over gravel and braves the tires of the crosstown bus, your ham is shredding, leaving slices of itself along the road, under bushes and cars, dropping pink portions at intersections, and by the time it arrives at the house of your former love and bumps its way onto the porch—past the dim flare of the geranium and the rusting ten-speed and his favorite worn brogans left out of habit by the door—by the time the ham rocks to rest on his mat, there is nothing left but bone.

THE DREAM OF EMERALDS

If emeralds were animals, they would grow greener in winter; the wind would whine like a dog at the door as it moves across their flat, refractive sides. They would feed on the palest lichens so as not to pollute themselves, and search under leaves for bits of mica, which would glow in the hard cruets of their bellies like coals from a fire that makes night colder, glassier, air more apt to be shattered. In sleep their dreams would be of the world gone crystal. Trees sparkling. Water frozen mid-flow. Clouds glinting, trapped in the solid sky. The emeralds stir as dreams overtake them. They tumble against one another in earthen burrows, clacking like billiard balls, and in the forest someone is walking toward the sound, to find on the ground above the burrow a lozenge of freshly formed ice.

In the wild the emeralds fatten and grow clumsy, over the course of a year sometimes quadrupling in size. Hunters find them easy prey, luminous bird's eggs that call your eyes to their cores as though something will be revealed there, small but shudderingly pure. They are heaped high at markets, sorted and sold by the dozen in cheap cardboard cartons, duller in captivity but still lustrous enough to drip from a chandelier or, hollowed, to form a chalice that chills drinks without refrigeration. Whoever sips from this cup will tremble with sudden envy, and sometime later—a week, a month—bite out brittle accusations.

With the onset of fall the chandelier starts to rustle and turn. The temperature of the room drops two degrees. The emeralds are remembering their freedom, sensing the oncoming cold. They are also listening to the calls of their brethren, who are now beginning their exodus. The emeralds are abandoning the forests and dells, their burrows and fields, their native waters and lands. They are fleeing their predators, moving north, always north, and at night to hide their numbers. The ones left behind hear them but dimly. The emeralds' cry is nothing more than a vibration, the highest timbre of a tuning fork. The chandeliers spin in the darkness of dining rooms and entrance halls, slowly at first, then faster. The cry is borne on the wind, carrying into cupboards so that the hollowed chalice cracks. The emeralds are on the move, seeking climes that others have forsaken, places that glitter with cutting clarity and thrust into the sky jagged ramparts of broken bone. The dream is in the night air. The air becomes it, holds it, fixes it like a blind man's last spark of sight:

Emeralds and ice. Green suns in snow.

HOUSE HUNTED

If hunters were housesitters, yours would stand in the doorway and wave his blaze-orange cap as you back out of the driveway. Noticing your wife's uncertain frown behind the glass, he would pat his pistol and call, *Don't worry 'bout a thing,* then give the thumbs-up to your son, bored in the backseat and swimming a shark toward your throat. Later, in your living room, the hunter whistles old standards as he unpacks his duffel, methodically lifting out guns and boxes of shells, a mess kit, canned goods, a flaying knife, and hand-carved animal calls. Making the rounds, he examines window latches for signs of entry and, sweeping his eyes across the yard, notes the trees that might prevent a clean shot, the garden bench (good cover), the tined thrust of your pitchfork— primitive but useful in a pinch.

The hunter cocks his head: sound from above. In the attic something is rustling, scuttling, and in a lightning move he unloads his shotgun into the ceiling. Flakes of plaster flutter down, coating the furniture with ash. Pellets make a stippled sunburst on the ceiling. For a moment the hunter worries he's been impulsive, rash, but there it is: silence like a blow to the head, the kind that shows you sapphires. Gray squirrel stiffening in a pink bed of insulation. The home secure. The day's killing done, as a favor to you. He pokes a finger in your potted plant to see if it's too dry.

In the bathroom he touches up the bootblack on his face, neatens his camouflage collar, then washes his hands, working not to grimace at the lilac-scented soap. Soon he's got a good campfire going on the oriental, feeding legs from your dining-room chairs into the blaze. The baked beans have begun to bubble, giving off gases the way that corpses give off souls. The smoke detectors dangle viscera, each battery boasting a neat bullethole through its gut.

In the gray haze your home has become, the hunter relaxes,

crossing his legs at the ankle, mopping his brow with your silk power-tie. He lifts an animal call and blows a sharp note, then again, the sound shrill and throaty at once, part warning, part sob. Your possessions ghost in and out as the smoke curls toward an open window—the sofa blackening like a mushroom, the recliner fainted away, the china cabinet floating through a fog, clutching tureens to its breast. The hunter whittles a toothpick from the coffee table, settling down for a splintery chew. His cap falls over his forehead, his eyelids sag. But in the woods his summons has been heeded, and now the leaves of your barberry stir. A hoofprint among your foxgloves—cloven signature. The hunter slumbers before the fire, his lashes twitching as he follows the flurry of doves in his dream. And there, beyond the bedroom, it emerges. Flanks quivering. Eyes fevered in the flames. This astonishing creature. This wildest of guests.

THE OPEN ROAD

If rattlesnakes were roadsters, you would drive yours day and night just to hear the dry menace of maracas when you signal or hit the brakes. Saturday afternoons would be spent in the driveway, rubbing expensive oils onto scales, buffing the diamondback to a shine so liquid, so slitheringly sleek, you swallow hard, then, when that doesn't help, duck into the garage for a cry.

From the house your family watches your ministrations. They think you obsessed. As you run your hand along your snake's reticulations, polish its gleaming eyes, you understand this may be true but think *What of it?* At work you follow the rules and bite your tongue. Rumors of cutbacks have slunk through every cubicle. When you've had all you can take and speak sharply into the phone, you worry for hours that the line was monitored, that the caller was a plant. Now your wife stares from the kitchen window with a pucker of distress. Resentment bleeds into your mouth.

On the road, the snake responds like a dream. You can feel its coiled power beneath your feet, its desire to lash and dart. It is summer and all about you is mayhem: kids dashing at the sprinkler in that tight young ache to be wet, dogs cocking their legs at every post, martins slicing the sky with razor wings. The trees are flagging you down, all fluttery, like slender women with handkerchiefs. You don't stop; nothing can persuade you to slow. Not lights, not cops, not cliffs. Nothing can temper the feeling of never that is clawing its way up your throat.

The road has opened before you and now holds up its heart like a thing exposed during surgery, a ruptured passage pieced together with yellow stitching. Beneath you the snake seems to lunge, and you realize you've come full circle. This is your street.

Ahead your house sits bleakly with its dull brick brethren. The driveway lolls like a tongue gone white in sleep. Your wife's dumpling face rises, a moon in your mind, one that holds you weakly in its light. When you approach, you rev the engine, knowing this will draw her to the door, and the snake, as though sensing your thoughts, sounds its warning rattle. You have waited what seems your whole life to show her the fangs.

SOUL MUSIC

If monks were punks, they'd get out more. You'd see them on skateboards over by the university, passing out flyers that say *Love Thy Brother OR ELSE,* their robes flipping up to show some calf when they jump the curbs. They would loiter around the mall, stalking shoppers who hurry toward shiny sport utility vehicles, cars that have never seen anything one could call *terrain.* "Hey," a monk would shout. "Yeah, I'm talkin' to you. You got a prob with the Big Guy?" He runs his hand over a fender. "Nice wheels. Looks like He's been good to you." The monk leans close, grins, his tonsure slick with sunscreen. "I got a message, right? Tithe or you're going *down*." Across the parking lot, another monk jumps a jowly fellow trying to sneak out the Sears service entrance. "Nice move, bro. You think He don't know? Now fork over the bustier." Inside, monks lean against a wall near the food court. One lights up a Marlboro and hunkers into his cowl. The other keeps watch, eyes flicking over storefronts—American Outfitter, The Body

Shop, Vitamin Planet, Knives 'R' Us. He murmurs, "They all got to come here sometime."

Back at the monastery, a monk with a spray can is hard at work on sacred graffiti. One wall reads FASTING ROCKS! in five-foot bubble letters. The hall leading to the sacristy blooms with the dripping directive FALSE PROPHETS, BITE ME. Back in the kitchen, monks on bread-making duty play hacky-sack with balls of dough, and in the courtyard a monk sights down a scepter at squirrels digging up his narcissus. "Dudda-dat," he says, jerking in time with his make-do machine gun. "Dudda-dudda-dut-dut-dudda-dudda-dat!" A line has formed outside the holy tattooing parlor, which is running a Father's Day special—two pectorals for the price of one—your choice: the burning bush (extra bushy), Magdalene showing some thigh, Abraham's blade (red with sacrifice), or a buxom pillar of salt.

But the greatest excitement is here, in the sanctuary, where the monks are gathering for tonight's big concert. The altar has been dismantled. The pews are packed sandal to sandal. Monks shove one another to get closer to the stage, setting off a rippling reaction, a brown eddy in a lake of monks, a sea of monks, their pates shining through an acrid nimbus of smoke. The performers have arrived in a bus out back, and the hall grows hushed as they take the stage. Quietly they file onto risers. No drum set in sight. No bass. No keyboard or screaming axe. Only monks, who now begin to chant in their hallmark sonority. Their voices swell—louder, louder still—until the stained-glass windows start to buzz in their ogival frames. The crowd goes wild. Monks crying and clawing their faces. Monks surging forward, straining to touch the hems of the chanters' robes. The first flame appears, a monk thrusting his lighter high in the air. Then another, and another. Monks sweating and swaying and flicking Bic after Bic until the sanctuary is full of tiny lights, radiant with them—each man a votive, each pew a shrine.

Nicola Mason is an editor at Louisiana State University Press. Her fiction has been published in the *Oxford American,* the *Missouri Review, New England Review, Shenandoah, Chelsea, Southern Exposure,* and *64,* among others. In 1998 she received an individual artist fellowship from the Louisiana Council for the Arts, and in 2000 she was awarded a fellowship from the National Endowment for the Arts. She is currently at work on a novel.

ANN LANG

I had wanted to write miniatures for some time. I love the form. It's extreme in a way—so compact—and that's freeing in that it discourages you from doing the usual things. I liked the idea of warping "story" to suit the form.

The short-shorts I had seen were discrete units, each unto itself. My hope was to write something that would work that way but would also become more elaborate piece by piece and work as a whole. Eventually I came up with a linking concept I thought I could have some fun with. My husband and I tossed things around until we had a lot of goofy possibilities—if rubies were radishes, if slinkys were suspicions, if wishes were hearses.

When I sat down at the computer, some of these ideas seemed to suggest situations or emotional contexts. Little narratives emerged—and they turned the world into a very curious place.

TWO LIVES

(from *Meridian*)

There was a man, his name was John. John Cantrell. He was driving northeast on an interstate highway, fifty-some miles south of Roanoke, Virginia. A ten-mile stretch of the road was incomplete in this area and Cantrell negotiated the construction zone with some impatience. Parts of it were like driving down a creek bed. He had been in the car for a long time, all the way over from Nashville, and he was slightly nauseous from drinking whisky half the night before and coffee all through the day.

When the bad stretch finally fell behind him he emerged on a strip of virgin highway, six lanes of it with an eight-foot concrete divider down the middle. Farmland rolled up the hills to his right, where the road was bordered with a shiny new fence the highway department must have had to pay for. On his left, the concrete barrier completely blocked his view. He flicked his thumb against the button on the wheel to restart the cruise control, then twisted up the knob of the tape machine. It was beginning to get dark, but he had not put on the headlamps, and for some reason he was all alone on the road.

The car was a lightweight foreign sedan, faintly silvery like the highway itself in the evening dim, and still new enough to be fun to drive. In the trunk were two suitcases, some boxes of stereo equipment, and an electronic keyboard—all that John Cantrell had troubled to extract. Along with the car itself, that was. His lawyer had let him know he was "stoopit" for taking so little. In Charleston, the week previous, Cantrell, his wife, and the two lawyers had gathered around a sheaf of paperwork and consummated the conspiracy to assassinate their marriage. The conspiracy was amicably organized, calm and smooth and with its every hair in place. The fees were paid, the property divided, the children neatly sawed in half. Everything was beyond the thought of an improvement. Cantrell's lawyer was not from Charleston, but had moved there from somewhere in Massachusetts, which was where he'd learned to talk. Then again, no one stayed put any more. Not John Cantrell, who didn't even know where he was going now, maybe to New York, where he had once lived for a time. He was driving fifteen miles over the speed limit, drilling down the center lane, screaming tunelessly along with the tape in the deck.

"*Truth or consequences . . .*" he howled. "*Which one will it be . . .*" The deck was turned up past the point of distortion. The car came down a gentle slope into a long straightaway. Adjusting to the change of grade, it gave itself some gas. On that same surge of energy the doe came floating over the concrete barrier with an Olympian grace and landed in the far left lane with her legs bunched up beneath her.

The doe was very large, and in the twilight she looked silver-grey as the highway or Cantrell's car. She was scarcely visible, scarcely seemed real. Cantrell was not a brilliant driver, but for once he reacted smoothly, perhaps because he was not at first impressed with any real sense of danger. He tapped the brake to release the cruise control and pulled the car to the right lane, meaning to pass the doe with maximum clearance. It was the doe who got it wrong. Cantrell didn't see her again until she materialized, straining all out like a cheetah, stretched point-blank across the frame of his windshield; she must have decided to go for it. Still he didn't panic. There was a second, enough for him to swing the car back to the center lane. He almost missed her.

The right fender of the car smashed into the doe's hindquarter.

Cantrell saw this very plainly; he even thought the doe turned her head and looked at him for an instant. The shock of impact was enough to throw him back in the seat. His skull slapped on the molded headrest and a burst of white light covered some unknown passage of time. When he recovered, he was coasting to a shaky stop on the road's shoulder.

The tape still bellowed at him, the overdriven speakers buzzing. He turned it off, noticing as he moved his hand that his fingers were trembling slightly. A line of the song rang on in his ears: *someone said that time would ease the pain* . . . Each syllable drew itself out agonizingly. He shook his head and got out of the car.

The cruise control had been set for seventy. The car was aluminum, light as foil, so he knew the whole front end would be mangled. It was not. He couldn't even find a dent. It was as if nothing had happened at all. Stiff-legged, he walked around to the rear of the car and unlocked the trunk. Everything was packed as it had been. When he opened the case of the keyboard, there was no sign it had suffered any insult. He closed the trunk and looked back down the highway.

The grade lowered steeply from the shoulder to a ditch and beyond it rose onto a cleared hillside full of yellowed grass. On this knoll there was a single oak tree with a few brown leaves clinging to the branches, beside a paintless barn whose siding had been partly stripped. The peeling tin on the barn roof groaned in the chill autumn wind that also lifted Cantrell's hair. Beyond the knoll the land rose again more sharply to a ridge all lined with cedar trees; a couple of crows were flying up above them. The new fence stretched away down the road as far as he could see. There was no sign of the deer at all.

He got back into the car, the door clapping hollowly to close the metal cabin. His ears still rang with engine noise and loud music as he crept cautiously up the right-hand lane. There was an exit within sight of where he had pulled over, and he parked in front of a gas station with a small convenience store. Inside, he stood agape at the counter, then asked for a pack of cigarettes. The cashier looked at him strangely. Cantrell hadn't smoked in so long he didn't remember what kind he liked. But he selected a brand and paid for it and went to the car, the square package feeling oddly light and flimsy in his hand.

He was wondering if after all there was an afterlife, if perhaps he had been killed when he hit the deer. Events were not corresponding to his notion of ordinary reality. But when he approached the car this time he saw a sort of smudge on the front fender. He stopped to examine the bumper, a fancy, rubberized, springloaded gadget. The right corner of it was coated with stiff brown and white bristles from the doe, but there was no blood or any other sign. Cantrell went back into the store.

"I hit a deer," he said. "Back yonder . . ."

The cashier told him he could find a highway patrol station about a mile back down from where he'd come. Cantrell bought himself a Coke and drank half of it, leaning on his car and smoking a cigarette. The tobacco gave him an unfamiliar giddy rush. By the time he got into the car again the trembling in his hands had stopped.

The highway patrol station was a box of pebbled concrete sitting in a pool of empty parking lot; it looked more like a travel information center than anything to do with the police. A burly woman in a brown uniform tended the counter. Her hair was short and curly, dyed an unlikely shade of yellow.

"I hit a doe," Cantrell said, "a big one. I was headed north, just over there. I know I hit her pretty hard but I couldn't find her afterwards."

"Are you all right?" the patrolwoman said. She sounded like she really cared to know.

"I'm fine," Cantrell said. "My car's all right. I wonder about that deer, though. She's bound to be hurt, I was going . . . I was going pretty fast. I don't see how she was good to get out of sight, really."

The patrolwoman nodded. "Sometimes they'll do that way," she said.

Do what? Cantrell thought. He didn't say it.

"We'll keep an eye out," the patrolwoman said, and reached behind her for a phone.

Cantrell drove slowly north again, along the same stretch of road. He thought he could mark the place on the divider where the doe had first come over. It was getting darker but there was still light enough for him to find her if she'd been there. He realized she would have had to jump the new fence to get clear out of sight, and it was five or six feet high. She wasn't there, she was nowhere. As he passed the exit where he'd stopped, he turned the tape back on and picked up speed with that same song singing at him once again. He turned on the headlights, had a tepid sip of Coke and lit another cigarette.

Full darkness sealed him into the car, into his head. The mountains began spinning back, invisible in the dark behind him. He felt vestiges of his hangover returning. All the last night he'd spent drinking with a college friend in Nashville, where they'd been to Vanderbilt together. Richard had stayed on for law school and joined a firm in the town. He was urbane and charming, his outer surface betraying little of the boa constrictor's toughness that lay thinly under his skin. Richard was divorced also, and on his second marriage. John Cantrell remembered boozily declaring that he would never remarry himself, although in the back of his mind he knew it was as likely as not that he would.

They had spun through a couple of undergraduate hangouts, and ended up among swarms of other drunken businessmen in Printer's Alley. Here strippers, at a strategically safe distance from him, unveiled their skin to Cantrell's sight. One had a head of impossible yellow hair, like that patrolwoman, though done in a French twist instead of curls. He couldn't remember anything else about her, except the strange dead vacancy of her stare; her face must have been rather close to his, for him to notice that. He couldn't recall if Richard had still been with him at that point. But he was free now, to do what he liked. It didn't really matter.

North of Roanoke he pulled off the highway and stopped at the first motel back down the state road toward town. It was a place he'd stayed before, though there was nothing special to recommend it. Since the last time it had been taken over by a family of Indians. Cantrell smelled curry spices rolling from the rear when the small tired man came from behind the curtain to check him in.

He put the key in its pocket and drove further toward town, to a liquor store where he bought a pint of bourbon. There was a grocery next to it and although he wasn't hungry in the least, he went in and bought a package of baloney and a sack of soft bread. Then he drove back to the motel.

His room was second to last on a long single-story building that looked a little like a brick chickenhouse. Only one other car was parked in the lot, a mini pickup, ten doors down. There was a concrete slab for a porch in front and to the right of each room door was a metal spring rocker, painted bright red. The room's interior smelled strongly of deodorant chemicals. Cantrell unwound the crank window in the bathroom, picked up the ice bucket, and went out, leaving the door ajar so the room would air.

The ice machine was at the opposite end of the building, on a corner overlooking the motel pool. Of course it was too cold for swimming, but the gate to the storm fence surrounding it dangled open, and Cantrell stepped through it onto the fan of pink concrete surrounding the rim. The pool was a long rectangle, its neglected water gone swamp black. He walked to the deep end and paused by the posts of the diving board, dismounted for the winter. The rooms and the pool were on a rise above the state road and the cubicle of the office, where the manager's family lived. On the far side of the road, the hills lifted up again toward the Blue Ridge; Cantrell knew the mountains were there although in the dark he could not see them.

The damp ice bucket was chilling the crook of his arm where he held it. He went back to the room and poured himself a drink. The dull colors of the enclosure depressed him a little. He turned on the television and sat on the end of the bed clicking the channel dial, but he couldn't watch it. He took his glass and the bottle still in the bag and went outside, leaving the door open and the TV on for the companionship of the sound of it.

A man was toiling up the crumbling pavement from the road, on foot. Cantrell sat in the red rocker, watching him come. When the man had climbed the steps at the end of the slab, Cantrell raised a hand to him, and got the same flat gesture in return, palm out. The man sat on the slab and took off his worn brogans and entered the end room, leaving the shoes outside the door.

The bottle was lightening in the sack. Cantrell sipped and smoked his cigarettes. There were a few house lights low on the slopes across the road, and occasionally a car droned by in the yellow cone of its headlights. It was entertaining to smoke, though he couldn't recapture the narcotic high of the first one that afternoon. Still, he was free to pursue it now, if he wanted to. It was getting colder, but he liked sitting out better than the closeness of the room. Inside, the television chattered and sang, and from the open doorway a bar of light fell out and stained the shoes of the man who'd come to the motel without a car. Cantrell himself sat in darkness on the other side of the door, the rocker creaking under a slight movement he kept going with his heels. His mind kept trying to erase itself over and over like a tape. There had been no conventional difficulties in his marriage, no infidelity or problematic in-laws or trouble over money. It had just stopped. John Cantrell had spent a year and a half constructing noisy, complicated arguments, some intended for Melissa and others for himself. His head was always whining with them. . . . Then they collapsed into a state of wordless misery. Then nothing, or not much, a stump severed just above the problem's root.

He got up finally, went into the room and shut the door. Mechanically, he folded bread around some pieces of baloney and forced himself to eat it, enough to ward off the whirlies, he thought. He took some precautionary aspirins and got into the bed. A movie played: Suzanne Somers on a beach. After this the television's image broke into bands of colored light. Cantrell still had to keep one eye on the set, to stop the room from spinning.

Now he wished he had done his drinking in some bar, among other people. Flashes from the night before kept surfacing and sinking in his head. Of course he couldn't have made it back to the hotel in the condition he was in now. But he had the idea of finding a woman somewhere, bringing her back here and using her sordidly, underneath this grubby coverlet. The room was right for such a scene. But this was an abstract notion, completely disconnected from his body. Under the whir of static, his face went slack.

The doe was coming down the hill, her step limber and light as if she walked on cushions of air above the ground. There were trees to cover her, maples and oaks and a sweetgum tree. Under a carpet of dry leaves, the sweetgum balls turned queerly when her hooves landed on them. Every few paces she stopped to look and listen, revolving her long mule ears and turning her muzzle into the wind. She was alone, this side of the road; the others in the herd had crossed a few minutes earlier.

All day the road had rushed and roared like a steel waterfall but now it was empty, nothing moving either way. The doe came up to the shoulder, picking her hooves up high. She was on an invisible trail that deer had followed for ages before any road interrupted it, and though she had some experience of the road she was not afraid of it now. And the rest of the herd was on the other side. Her tail shot up, she darted across the first three lanes and lifted easily in the air to clear the divider.

When she landed she was poised to continue, but she saw something coming at her out of the silvery pools of twilight on the road's grey back. It hummed and shivered toward her, insectlike; she didn't know what it might do. But she had not really stopped herself, the movement carried her on. Just ahead she could see the fence, the wire squares blurring slightly. In two more steps she would make the jump. It struck her high on her back leg, spinning her out of kilter, whipsawing her head around so that for a moment she saw the face of the man swimming uncertainly under glass like a fish in an aquarium.

She was still moving, she had not been knocked right down, though there was one step missing from her gait. Something snagged as she went over the fence, and she did fall on the other side, sliding down the embankment and kicking and struggling to rise and go on. Then she was up, loping over the knoll and past the barn. She couldn't feel the pain yet, but a numbness as if something had been removed from her. She carried this dead sensation into the screen of cedar trees. Above her the two crows called to one another in their black voices.

John Cantrell sat up sharply in the motel bed, turning his hands over and over sweatily, they seemed to be bleeding from the lurid radiance the TV spilled on them. His chest was blazing with heartburn. He turned off the television and felt his way to the bathroom in the dark and found the switch inside the doorframe there. The tiles on the wall were minty green, the grout between them blackened with some fungus that also spotted across the floor. In the mirror, his eye resembled an animal's eye; he turned his face away from it. Alka Seltzer sizzled in the motel's plastic cup. He went into the bedroom, sipping the medicine, and slipped the bourbon from its sack, as though the measure of it might give a clue to his condition.

There was about a quarter of the bottle left, maybe a third. He set it down. Beside it, the red and black target on the cigarette pack seemed to aim itself at him. He had bought Lucky Strikes. Although his mouth was papery and sore, he sat on the bed's edge and smoked in the dark, finishing the Alka Seltzer too. In the mirror above the television, he saw the head of the cigarette dipping and glowing, illuminating his nose and mouth and leaving his eyes in skull-like hollows. He scrubbed the butt out on the ashtray and drew his legs up onto the bed. In the next room, the other man was talking in a low monotone, repeating the same words over and over, Cantrell thought, though he could not distinguish them. The man might have been talking to himself, on the phone, or indeed there could have been someone with him in the room, yet Cantrell felt certain he was entirely alone.

In his dream his little daughter was walking on a curbstone, hands out like a tightrope walker or a gymnast, looking back over her shoulder to harvest his admiration of this feat. The dream did not change, there was no twist of the danger it could easily have supplied, only Cantrell was suddenly swamped with dread. He called for the child to come to him but she would not listen. Somehow he could not reach her with his hand. Panic swelled into his throat; he could not quite awaken but he managed to leave this dream for another. His wife, Melissa, was telling him a thing of great import, which she held cupped in her hands like a small flame. He knew she meant to tell him that he was leaving her but at the same time she seemed to say that she was pregnant with their first child. He was looking not into both her eyes but only one of them; it was longlashed, black and liquid, like the eye of the doe.

Frost grew like lichen over the windowpane, a first tinge of daylight behind it. Cantrell flushed with relief to see that the night was coming to an end. He had awakened gasping and sweating but when he got up he didn't feel half as bad as he'd expected. He put on his clothes and shoes, boiled water in a hotpot he had with him, and stirred in instant coffee. With the cup steaming in his hands, he stepped out onto the porch.

Frost was crawling over the other man's shoes, still lined up outside the last door. Frost sealed the windshield of Cantrell's car, and shimmered on the patchy grass of the motel lawn. A fine mist was lifting from the road as it might have from a river. Beyond and above it, the mountain peaks were as blue as their name.

Cantrell reentered the room, made himself a baloney sandwich, and ate it with fair appetite. He noticed the package of cigarettes and dropped it into the wastebasket without much thinking about what he was doing. The wind blew into the half-open doorway; his eyes stung a little. He picked up the pint of whisky, meaning to spike his coffee, but after a moment put it down again without unscrewing the top. In the mirror, his eyes were bloodshot. He would have to get better at being alone.

With a second cup of coffee he went outside again, walking up and down the parking lot to shake out his stiffness. Under the pretty sunrise, the frost was melting speedily; after all it wouldn't be so much colder than the day before. Cantrell set his mug on the car's roof and groped for his key to check the trunk. Everything was in good order. He closed it and came back to the front of the car and squatted down to examine the front bumper. The deer bristles had mostly blown free of the black rubber; only a few still clung there, few enough to count. He wiped them away, then rubbed his palm on his pants leg as he stood up. A shock of dizziness staggered him as he rose, but in an instant it passed and he was unchanged. In spite of everything that had happened, he still did not believe that anything could ever really hurt him.

Madison Smartt Bell is the author of ten novels and two collections of short stories. His eighth novel, *All Soul's Rising,* was a finalist for the 1995 National Book Award and the 1996 PEN/Faulkner Award. His tenth, *Master of the Crossroads,* was published in October 2000.

Born and raised in Tennessee, he has lived in New York and in London and now lives in Baltimore, Maryland. A graduate of Princeton University and Hollins College, he has taught in various creative writing programs, including the Iowa Writers' Workshop and the Johns Hopkins University Writing Seminars. Since 1984 he has taught at Goucher College, along with his wife, the poet Elizabeth Spires. He is currently director of the Kratz Center for Creative Writing at Goucher College.

The Hollins Motel, not far off I-83 and the Hollins campus, is where I stayed for a week or so at the start of my M.A. year at Hollins. And I usually stop there when I pass through Roanoke, still. I am usually the only guest and sometimes wonder if the place really exists on days when I'm not staying there. Maybe it just swirls up out of the mist when I need it. But a number of ideas have had their start there, including my first novel, and a much later one, Ten Indians, *and this little story too. I hit the deer on my way there that year, pretty much in the manner here described, but I think it was maybe a year or so later that the story came together in my mind.*

Carrie Brown

FATHER JUDGE RUN

(from *The Oxford American*)

Someone was shouting, one of the young lady guests at the Inn, from the top of the stairs. "Water!" she cried, and he knew if he went into the front hall full of the early hour's light, he would see one of the girls leaning over the banister, her wrapper closed over her collarbones, the pitcher dangling from her hand, her hair in two long dark ropes down her back, like his mother's. They were all Bradshaw cousins, come for the town's August picnic, but there were so many of them they could not all be put up at the Bradshaws' farm below the Peaks of Otter.

He looked out the kitchen window. The sun was up, white and round and hot, clearing the oak trees at the end of the Inn's long garden with its parallel rows of boxwood and its sundial standing alone at the end on its bed of flagstones. He tried to imagine his mother, all the way on the other side of the mountains in West Virginia, sitting up in her high white bed in the sanatorium at White Hall.

"My room here is bright as heaven, Lucullus," she had written him. "The sunshine makes me better every day."

The voice called again. "Lu-*suh*-lus! The pitchers are empty! We need to wash!"

In the dining room, the iridescent parrot swayed on its perch in the black iron cage suspended over the sideboard. "Water, water, water!" it shrieked in a high, effeminate voice. "Fishers of men!"

Lucullus hardly ever recognized the source of the parrot's utterances, but Signora Adelphi, the black cook who'd raised Miss Massie Rivers and now ran the kitchen at the Inn, could almost always place the fragment correctly in the Book of Leviticus or in Proverbs or Revelation. He knew this one, though—*I will make you fishers of men.* He leaned into the dining room from his place at the table, where he had been sitting and polishing the copper, and watched the bird pick up a piece of apple in its claw and look at it sideways. Lucullus put down the polishing rag. Were the parrot's odd coincidences of language deliberate? He could never be sure. It made him wary to contemplate the possible depths of the parrot's intelligence.

The parrot had belonged to Miss Massie Rivers's brother, Henry, who had been a missionary in Darkest Africa. He had died, Lucullus had heard, of a disease that ate up his skin in great mouthfuls. When word came of his death, Miss Massie Rivers had left the Inn in Signora Adelphi's hands and gone all the way over to the continent to fetch her dead brother's body and his possessions, though there couldn't have been much left of either, people said. She had come back a month later with nothing but trunks of books and the parrot. The books she put in the Inn's shadowy library, where the men guests sat after dinner, smoking in cane chairs.

She had arrived home on the train, on a hot, overcast afternoon, clouds of gnats hovering in the trees. Lucullus had been dispatched to meet her train by Signora, who told him he could help carry things along with Marcus, the narrow-shouldered, quiet man who was cousin to Signora and worked sometimes at the Inn.

He had worried at the time that he might be asked to carry Henry the Missionary Brother, or what was left of him; he supposed Miss Massie Rivers would have had him burned to ash and bone, reduced to a manageable size. But when she descended to the platform under the depot's green tin roof, in a long black skirt and a black and white striped blouse that made her look like a pirate, Miss Massie Rivers had handed Lucullus a parrot's cage instead, draped with an odd, fringed cloth the color of verdigris. There were dark pouches beneath her eyes.

"Careful, Lucullus," she'd whispered, as if she'd lost her voice. She had not asked him how he'd been.

She must have stayed awake all night that first day back, unpacking the books, for she was still there when Lucullus had come to work the next morning. She was sitting on the floor surrounded by books, still in the same dress, her black hair in two wild wings. The room smelled of mildew and cold ash. She had not looked up from her book when Lucullus opened the door to the library.

She had been crying, though; he could see that. It made her uglier than usual. Behind her back, some of the boys in town called her F.O.P., for Face of a Pig. She had no husband. They said it was because she was too wretchedly ugly, with a pasty face the shape of a turnip. Her cheeks looked as though she held something there inside them, a nugget of gold or a bone; a man would have a heart attack waking up beside her, the boys said. Lucullus thought she wasn't at all pretty, not anything like his own delicate and beautiful mother, who sewed such lovely clothes and now was "wasting away," people said quietly, in the sanatorium at White Hall. But after Miss Massie Rivers's missionary brother died and she had come back from Africa, Lucullus had been struck less by her blank, heavy face than by the great difficulty she appeared to have in accomplishing things, as if she could not remember how to lay the table or beat the carpets or twist a chicken's neck.

He'd watched her standing in the yard, leaning on the axe as if she were out of breath, chickens fussing around her feet.

"What's she doing?" Signora Adelphi would say from the stove.

He'd wanted to go outside and put the axe into Miss Massie Rivers's hand. Something about her immobility, her vagueness, made him feel frightened. It was as if the whole world—first his mother, now Miss Massie Rivers—was succumbing to an indefinite and invisible enemy. She should get on with things, he'd thought anxiously, watching her through the window. But he could not voice such thoughts to Signora, much less to Miss

ivory dominoes. The fragile pink teacups had shivered in their saucers on the table. Feet pounded overhead; there were eight people at the Inn that day, on their way to Richmond. He'd brought them chipped ice and mint the night before, and one of the ladies had pinched his cheek and asked if he were Miss Massie Rivers's son.

Lucullus had looked up at her, startled. "No, ma'am," he'd said, and had gone away downstairs on watery legs. His own mother, he'd wanted to say, was a beauty. His own mother drank a cup of milk with a raw egg in it, every day, and lounged in fields of daisies. His own mother was over where the air was better. "There is a fine class of people here, Lucullus," she'd written. "And many priests and sisters."

His own mother, he'd wanted to shout, was with the best people.

He hadn't known enough at first to be frightened of the parrot. "Hello. What's your name?" he'd tried over and over again that first morning, waiting stubbornly by the cage. He touched his finger to the bars.

"Pluck it out! Pluck it out! Pluck it out!" the bird had screeched, following up with a high forlorn noise ending on a trembling waver that made the hair on Lucullus's arms stand up. He had jumped away from the cage as the parrot leaned toward him. This was a terrifying creature, with its voice of judgment, and echoes of the jungle, and menacing eye. In the kitchen, Signora screamed with laughter over her pots.

"Watch your eyes, young Lucullus!" she called.

He'd gone away fast over the floors that shined like ice. There were potatoes to peel, and he wanted to do his job well. He would write his mother in a letter that he had earned enough to come and visit her in White Hall, see how she was getting along. No one will need to worry anymore, Mother, he would write, I'm making money. And his mother would read his words, sitting up in the bright light in her high bed in the sanatorium, sunlight and fine air all around her like in heaven, and be happy.

"Ask and it shall be given," said the parrot in a sad voice, as Lucullus went away.

The table in the dining room had been laid with place settings for the twelve jurors who would be sequestered there for lunch that day, each plate rimmed with crimson, a cluster of dark grapes painted in the center. A black man was on trial for stealing apples and pigs. The jury would convict him unanimously later that afternoon, after a heavy dinner of mutton and gravy, stewed okra with pimentos like bits of red flesh that Lucullus was afraid to touch with his bare hands when he scraped the plates, roast potatoes, and quince pie.

"Pluck it out, pluck it out!" the bird sang. But no one was listening.

There was the voice again. "Lu-*suh*-lus! Can't you hear? Water! We need to get ready!"

He put down the rag with which he'd been polishing the copper and hurried now to fill the bucket from the well at the end of the stone path between the banks of daisies. He pumped the rusty arm; did all girls want to wash so often? Did they all need such prodigious amounts of water? He peered over the edge of the well, down into the mossy murkiness. There was nothing to be seen there, no end in sight, but the water in his bucket was black and bright and swayed against the sides.

Going through the dining room on his way to fill the girls' pitchers so they could wash and make themselves pretty for the picnic, Lucullus glanced at the parrot. It was murmuring something to itself in a tender voice, fishing in its rainbow of feathers for lice. Lucullus had come to feel that the parrot's presence was like having a ghost in the house. He was eleven and did not think he believed in ghosts, but Miss Massie Rivers frightened him now that she had come back from Darkest Africa with her silent ways and distracted manner, and the parrot frightened him when it screamed, "Cloud of the Lord, cloud of the Lord!" as if the cloud that had lain upon the tabernacle were hovering overhead now, tangling in the branches of the oak trees that grew close around the Inn. And when he had to go home in the dark now, down the alley and then along the edge of the tobacco field, splashing through the cold waters of Father Judge Run, he was frightened and thought of his mother. *Help me, save me,* he prayed incoherently, tripping over stones, his heart pounding.

Sometimes it seemed to him that Miss Massie Rivers's dead brother was actually inside the parrot, had somehow inhabited its muscular body. He thought Miss Massie Rivers believed so, too, for sometimes he'd find her standing in the dining room, staring in at the bird, and one afternoon he'd come through with a load of polished brass for the fireplace to find her poised, very still, by the window under the Boston fern, the parrot sitting calmly on her shoulder.

"I've made a friend, Lucullus," she said, smiling for the first time since she'd come home. "What do you think?" But he didn't like the bird. Its head swiveled round to catch you at something. And if Henry the Missionary Brother *was* there, what kind of man had he been?

"Behold," the parrot would command from the dining room. "Behold, behold, behold." And Lucullus heard the missionary's weary voice as he bent over a guttering candle in a tent, the yellow eyes of lions burning through the bush.

But Henry couldn't have been all Holiness, for the parrot had a repertoire of disgusting noises to go with its Bible verses—belches and burps and other indiscretions. It made Signora Adelphi clutch her sides with stifled laughter to hear the parrot silence conversation in the dining room with a series of escalating explosions.

Lucullus, plucking chickens or splitting wood at the back step, would hear the parrot's ugly noises and see Signora's shaking back, and an unpleasant, giddy feeling would come over him. He wanted to stop it, or else give up somehow—though what was there to relinquish?—and let things take their inevitable course; he had a sense that terrible forces were gathering around them, a feeling the parrot's insane exorcisms exacerbated. *Why doesn't somebody shut it up?* he wondered fiercely. But he would laugh meanwhile, and the two feelings—of horror and helplessness—would grow unbearable, as though he had swallowed something solid, a rock, or a spoon, its handle tickling his throat. He would throw down the little hatchet, hard, into the sparkling dust, tears in his eyes.

"Shepherd of Is-ra-el," the parrot would say complacently, after a satisfying belch, and sometimes then the guests would finally explode into laughter after the awful, embarrassed silence.

"She wants a change," Signora said when he came back from delivering the pitchers to the girls upstairs. She was splitting lemons for the lemonade jugs for the picnic, spooning in glistening hills of sugar. It was a month after Miss Massie Rivers's return from Africa. "Mark me, Lucullus," Signora said. "She's going to shut down this old inn and go away. You and me and Marcus going to have to find a different place."

Lucullus stopped up short at the table.

Signora tossed the lemon rinds in a bucket. "Get me that ham."

He fetched it for her, the dead weight of it in his arms, and heaved it onto the table.

"She's just weary," Signora went on. "She's had a long life of weariness. Even as a little baby she was weary already. She said she might go back where Henry was, but I don't think she'll do that." Pink slices of ham fell away from the knife. "I could go cook for Mrs. Fletcher," Signora said after a moment, plucking up a little shaving of meat and tasting it. "She's only asked me a hundred times." She sighed. "One time ending, another beginning."

Lucullus blinked. "What will I do?" His thoughts came slowly, but they were immense and without dimension, too big, as if he were coming up into the air at the top of a mountain after being in the clouds, and was seeing at last the terrifying slide away down into nothingness below him. This was what had been in store, the bad thing he'd felt, listening to the parrot. He'd never make his money now. He'd never get to White Hall.

"Be a little man," his mother had written. "Help your father in every way."

Six months before, on a bright March morning, she'd been carried away in a chair to the wagon that would take her to the train and then to the sanatorium. He had not been allowed to go; his father had hardly even seemed to notice him that morning, and his mother opened her eyes only once, when the chair was tilted into the wagon, a look of despair on her face. Lucullus had waited awhile, and then had walked down the road where the wagon had disappeared. In the place where the tracks ran among willow trees, after crossing the pebbled, shallow bottom of Father Judge Run, he had seen a short trail of blood and had followed it a few feet, trying to decipher its sudden turns, until it gave out. The blood, dark and barely wet to the touch, had filled him with dread. He'd knelt in the cold water of the stream and scrubbed at his hands until they were raw.

Signora glanced over at him now. She held a splinter of ham toward him, speared with a knife. "Plenty of jobs for boys like you," she said, wagging the knife at him until he took the ham. "You'll be back to school in September, anyway."

"There's not jobs!" he protested. "Not good ones, anyway. No other boy has a job earns him so much money as this one! They're all jealous of me!" But he did not know if this was true. He'd started at the Inn that June when school had let out, a job arranged for him by his father, who helped Miss Massie Rivers with the Inn's business affairs from time to time, and since then he had hardly seen any of his friends. He had not really wanted to play with them. Whenever he saw them, he could not stop thinking of their mothers.

He worked seven days a week instead. He wanted to have lots of money by the end of the summer, enough to go alone to White Hall and climb the long hill to the hospital where his mother rested, and then enough to help his father, a lawyer with a sad manner and reluctant voice who never seemed to get paid in anything but fish on a string or a hog or jars of honey. They would not take good care of his mother if they were not paid at the sanatorium, Lucullus sensed. They might even send her home, not yet well, if the bills were not settled. Out you go! they would say, pushing her in her chair to the gates.

And now he would have nothing, or not enough. And it was all because of Miss Massie Rivers and her—what was it? Her *unwillingness*. She had no right! She was ugly and no one liked her, except Signora, who had taken care of her when she was a little girl.

"She should do what she pleases," Signora said then, scooping up the stack of ham slices and putting them on a plate. "She's never hurt anybody. Ugly people like her should get to do what they like at the end."

At the end? The end of what?

The parrot was exhorting them from the other room. The girls were calling for more water. Doors were slamming overhead. Lucullus saw his mother, her dress plucked up by crows, lifted into the ether over the mountains. In the kitchen, the room darkened as a flock of birds sank into the magnolia tree by the window.

The young ladies, the Bradshaw cousins, came downstairs finally about ten, after hours of washing. They formed a flotilla of flounces and whispery hats, laughing, and smelling of soap. Signora and Marcus and Lucullus loaded the hampers into the creaking wagon when it stopped on the ring of grass between the oak trees in front of the Inn. Carter Lovingston's two gray mares stamped in the harness. Boys in white shirts, and women in broad, shallow hats, little girls in sausage curls, and young men with pink cheeks leaned out over the sides and cried to the girl cousins. "Come on! Hurry, hurry!"

In the kitchen, Signora sat down in a chair. "Enough," she said aloud, and began snoring quick as a wink.

The parrot called out, "Deliver thyself!" in a cheerful tone, and then cackled like a lunatic. It flung heaps of seed on the floor, using its beak like a shovel. Lucullus edged past the bird and sidled into the kitchen, softly chinking pennies in his pocket.

Signora opened her eyes. "What are you doing?"

Lucullus stopped by her knee and shrugged. "Working."

"Go on," she said. "Go catch up with them. A picnic is for young folk. I can't sleep with you working around me all the time. Don't you know when to rest?"

"Give me a job, Signora," he pleaded. "I don't want to go to any picnic. Want me to wash out these bowls?"

"Take off my shoes for me," she said instead.

Lucullus knelt at her feet to unlace her shoes. Her legs grew out of her brown shoes like two tree trunks. Her toes were little brown burls, curled over atop one another. Lucullus thought suddenly of Finn the mortician, who laid out people's naked bodies on a stone, and he felt strange. Signora's feet were so hard-worked and sad.

Signora leaned back in the chair and closed her eyes. "Away now." She waved at him.

Lucullus lingered. "Somebody spilled the pot of violets in the hall," he said, standing up. "There's dirt all over. One of them did it with her umbrella."

Signora waved at him again, her eyes still closed. She had made six coconut cakes for the picnic. Lucullus walked over to the stove and looked at the coconut shavings left in the bowl.

"Where's *her*?" he asked after a minute.

"Sent her down to see about some ducks," Signora said, still with her eyes closed. "Give her something to do, get her some air. She can pick out some ducks."

Lucullus tried to pull out a chair quietly so he could sit down. He was suddenly afraid to leave the room, leave Signora.

But she opened her eyes and glared at him. "I don't like being watched while I sleep," she said. "Bad things can happen."

Lucullus stood up.

"There's a piece of cake for you in the dining room," she said, leaning back again and closing her eyes one last time. "On a nice plate. You go eat and let me rest."

Lucullus ate his cake, sitting alone at the end of the big table that shone darkly like a pool of water. Then he went and stood in front of the parrot's cage. The bird tiptoed over on its perch to look at him, and then hurried away to the far side of the cage, as if it didn't like what it saw.

"Pretty bird," Lucullus said, in a whisper.

"Shhhh." The parrot edged away.

Lucullus picked up a chair and brought it over to the sideboard and then climbed on top of it. When he tried to lift the parrot's cage, it was too heavy for him, heavy as a safe. Trembling under its weight, he managed to replace it on its hook, and then climbed down from the chair and stood by the sideboard. Sweat had broken out along his hairline.

In the hall, the crystal pendants on the candelabra tinkled suddenly. Lucullus froze. Sunbeams advanced along the floor. But no shape of Miss Massie Rivers darkened the door. The sunlight lay there, quivering.

"Shhhh," said the parrot again, warning.

But Lucullus reached up and opened the trap door on the cage. When he extended his hand, the parrot looked at it disdainfully, as though the thing proceeding slowly toward its perch were something inferior. Lucullus rested his hand on the perch, hovering just beside the parrot's two mighty feet. Finally, the parrot bent down and pried at Lucullus's thumbnail with its hooked beak. It looked up at Lucullus and cocked its head.

Lucullus held his breath.

The bird looked away when it stepped at last onto Lucullus's hand, as if disguising its capitulation with nonchalance. It would stand on Lucullus's hand, because that was what a hand was for, but it would not acknowledge its captor. Lucullus was astonished at the creature's puny weight; somehow, the cage's heavy black bars had suggested that the bird might be capable of terrifying feats of strength. But it weighed nothing at all, not even as much as a cup of water. *Faker!* he thought. *Pretender!*

Perhaps it would fly away now. The air would be cleared. The Inn would be full of comforting silence, a promise of rest. It would have been an accident.

But the bird didn't move. It even bowed its head when he slipped the sack over it, as if it were used to clandestine journeys into a dark estate, as if it knew what waited there at the end and was not afraid.

It was not until he was almost home, the parrot stunned into silence, the sack held gently under his shirt, that he realized the other purpose of the heavy bars on the bird's cage, the iron cage that looked as if it could withstand fire and flood. The bars were not just for keeping the bird a prisoner, he thought, and felt ashamed.

In the jungle, there must have been many enemies.

They had no animals, but his mother kept two peacocks who roamed the lawn in her absence like disappointed lovers. Lucullus chased the peacocks away, and now the parrot sat quietly in a squirrel trap in the gloomy shadows of an empty stall. Lucullus knelt before it, his fingers at the wire mesh. "Pretty bird," he said. "Pretty bird." The parrot had said nothing at all since they'd arrived at the barn an hour ago.

"Hello," Lucullus tried again. "Hello, bird." He wanted the bird to speak to him now, to tell him what to do. He realized that he had been counting on that in some way. He had not thought about what he would do.

And then he heard the clanging of fire bells.

The parrot screamed violently. Lucullus jumped up. "Don't," he said, frightened. "Don't make that noise." He knelt down again before it. "Pretty bird, pretty bird," he said desperately. "Nice bird." And then the parrot began to make a whimpering noise, the sound of a man weeping quietly, Henry the Missionary Brother alone in his mud hut at night, when he knew he was dying. Lucullus put his hands over his ears. But he could still hear the fire bells.

He peered in at the bird. It jerked its head in and out of its collar of emerald feathers as if it were strangling and struggling to breathe.

His fingers shook as he fumbled with the old latch. At last it gave way and opened. "Quick," Lucullus said. "Fly away. You're free." For if the bird flew away, everything would be as it had been. Miss Massie Rivers would not go away and close the Inn. He would have his job. His mother would come home. The air would be clear, bright as the stream bed of Father Judge Run. The cloud of the tabernacle would remove itself from the trees.

But the bird didn't budge. Lucullus inched his hand into the cage. The parrot came out of its neck-twisting trance and bit him, quick, on the knuckle.

Lucullus sat down, sucking his sore finger. He was so tired. He put his head down into a pillow of straw. Far away, the sound of the fire bells drained into the sky. The parrot made little clucking noises, fussing with itself, picking up its feet and nibbling at them. Overhead, sunlight shone like stars through the chinks in the barn roof.

When Lucullus woke up, the parrot was gone. He jumped up, dazed, but it was almost dark in the barn; he must have slept away the whole afternoon.

"Bird? Bird?" He searched the rafters, but there was nothing. No cry of lamentation, no word of accusation.

The picnic would be over. The girls would be back at the Inn, soiled and tired, wanting ice or coffee. Everyone would be looking for him.

And for the parrot.

Why had he done this? He felt his stomach curdle. His skin prickled, as if tiny, uncomfortable quills were sprouting from his chest and loins. Who had he wanted to hurt most? His father? His mother? No, certainly not his mother—though she had not even touched his hand when she left. Was it Miss Massie Rivers, for forgetting she owed him money? For being so unaware of them all? The air had grown thick and sour around them since she'd come back from Africa, the days full of the parrot's spells and portents. At night, Miss Massie Rivers would drape the cloth over the parrot's cage and whisper to it through the bars. Sitting in the kitchen, watching this ritual through the open door, Lucullus had thought of the icy healing wind that blew along the halls of the sanatorium, of his mother standing at the open window, her nightdress billowing.

"Bird?" he called out again now. "Please."

But there was no answer.

By the time he got to the edge of the tobacco field, he could smell the fire. The twilit air was full of dark bits of bitter-tasting ash that stuck to his lips. He came up into town; a crowd of noisy boys were up in the full, dark velvet of the oak trees by the post office, talking and leaning out along the branches, trying to get a better look.

Hurrying past the post office window, Lucullus thought of the posters of wanted men hanging inside on the white walls; he was always afraid to look at them.

"Young Lucullus!" It was Marcus, standing in the shadows of W. Ward Hill's Real Estate, resting, thin and old, like a dark grasshopper against the tall letters painted on the side of the building advertising Buggies, Harnesses, and Wagons. He waved Lucullus over.

"Oh, it's terrible," Marcus said when Lucullus stood before him. Marcus nodded as if Lucullus had said so himself and Marcus was only agreeing with him. "Terrible."

Lucullus stared up at him. Marcus stepped away out of the shadows and came close to him. He looked down into Lucullus's face. "Oh," he said at last. "You ain't seen it yet." There was a little hesitation. Marcus stared at him. "Where you been?"

Lucullus glanced behind him at the boys massed in the tree; their shapes seemed grotesque and threatening among the shiny leaves, their flapping white shirts ghostly like loose bandages. "I heard the fire bells," he whispered. "I fell asleep."

Marcus watched him. "It's all gone," he said slowly. "And everything in it."

Lucullus felt himself begin to pant, as if he had run a long distance. He heard men shouting two streets away where the Inn was. Had been.

"Hold on," said Marcus kindly, seeing Lucullus's panic. "Signora's safe. The Missus is safe. She wasn't home, and Signora got out. But I'll tell what I heard," he said. "People don't waste time, do they?" He leaned toward Lucullus. "They say she done it herself." He nodded sadly and then closed his eyes as if in prayer. When he opened them, Lucullus could see how the old man's eyes were reddened. "I'm going on now," Marcus said, "see about Signora."

Lucullus watched him go. He stood under the oak tree. Some of the boys called to him to come up, but he shook his head. After a time, he went away down the alley toward the Inn.

Miss Massie Rivers was standing alone near the old well in a patch of trampled and blackened phlox and mignonette. Men milled around her in the early dark of evening, filling buckets and tossing them onto the heaving pile of ash and bright embers that groaned and creaked like something at sea. The Inn's chimneys stood up, blackened, against a sky that had gone from dusk to night, but was filled with an odd light, as though the floating ash in the air glowed with bright life. Sloping parts of the Inn's shingled roof sagged from the brick.

Miss Massie Rivers did not seem to notice the people around her but stood quietly, her face expressionless.

Lucullus slid toward her and the remains of the fire like a ghost among the oak trees; their wide trunks were warm against his hands. Soon he was near enough to touch her if he'd wanted, and now he could see she was trembling. Someone came and tried to lead her away, but she shook her head, and he saw her lips move, saying something to the people. Then she stood alone again. She had wanted to go away, he thought. That's what Signora had said. But would she have set her own place on fire? What was the need for it? he thought helplessly. What if the world turned out to be a place where you had to reduce what you once loved to ash before you could change? He stood behind her, trying to listen.

Something had been happening to Miss Massie Rivers. He thought if he could get close enough now, he would know what it was that happened to people when they were disappointed, when they were in grief.

She turned around quickly, as if she had known he was there.

"Oh, Lucullus," she said, and he saw that her face was composed. "Your father's worried. You should go and find him."

But he didn't move; he wanted her to stop shaking. She seemed to understand that there was more to be said, that he was waiting. She turned away again to look at the ruins of the Inn. A smear of dark ash was laid down over her bare arm as though she had been scored. Her dress smelled of smoke. She gave a long sigh, and her body quieted.

"I'm sorry about your job, Lucullus," she said quietly. "I know how you worked so hard. I'll speak to someone on your behalf." She paused. Flames climbed the brick walls, fell away. "Don't believe what you hear, Lucullus," she said then. "I would never have laid such a fine old place to waste. They only say such things because—" she stopped. "Why do they say such things?" She looked at him, as if genuinely puzzled. "Because I have no husband?" She licked her lips. "Well," she said, as if he had confirmed it, "that's a lesson."

She turned away, but he could see a strange, sad joy in her face. "Isn't it funny?" she said. "Do you know what I am sorriest for?" She went on, she didn't wait for him to answer. "I am sorry about Henry's parrot. He made me laugh." She smiled at Lucullus, and he thought then that she had a kind of bravery to her face, like a head on a coin. The fire behind her seemed like something that had burned everything but her.

"He made us all laugh, didn't he? Henry had him for years and years. Listening to that funny bird, it was almost as if I had Henry back again." She sighed. "I might have moved on, you know, sold the Inn or just closed it up for a time and traveled. But I would have taken that bird with me."

She looked down on Lucullus, and then she put a cold, dirty

hand briefly on his head. "I owe you money, I think," she said. "Don't worry. I have money." She smiled at him. "Go and see your father. He's worried to death."

He ran through the field and down the lane where the wagon had driven away his mother. He ran over Father Judge Run, the stream full of the rippling sound of conversation, the voices of his childhood murmuring in the dark, and across the still-warm grass of his lawn. The barn door was open. He slipped inside and stood in the darkness, breathing hard. *I am only eleven,* he thought, *but I have already committed a sin. Will my mother die now?*

He dropped to his knees and clasped his hands together. He looked up into the rafters. *Forgive me,* he prayed. *Come back.*

But there was no sound other than his own frantic whispering.

Behind him, the open barn door glowed with a wet gray light. He glanced over his shoulder. Did he see a shape move there against the light? He stood up, for now he needed to be prepared.

The sound of his own voice fell away, a rock rolling downhill. "Hello!" he screamed. "Hello, hello, hello!"

But no one was there.

When he quieted at last, when he stopped crying, he sat stiffly, like someone who is on the other side of the mountain now, some-one who has crossed the river and passed through the darkest night and is now in a foreign place where nothing seems familiar. He stared around him at the bales of hay, the wagon removed from its axles and laid to rest. Swallows gusted in and out of the barn door, their wings forked. And then, as if the barn had no roof, as if the sound were traveling from the stars, he heard the voice.

"Pretty bird," it called from the rafters, out of the gloom. "Hello."

Lucullus leapt to his feet, trying to see in the darkness, his legs trembling beneath him.

"Hello!" he called back. "Oh, hello!"

And when the parrot flew down to land on his arm, it seemed to Lucullus like an angel of the tropics, a flash of emerald and sapphire and ruby, swooping through the soft, warm night air of his father's empty barn.

"Let's have a picture, Son," his father said, when Lucullus and Miss Massie Rivers were settled on a bench at the depot, waiting for the train that would take Lucullus to White Hall. His father liked to take pictures; he was the only father Lucullus knew who had a camera. He set up the tripod some distance away from them down the platform, and then ducked under the cloth. "Hold still," he called out, muffled. "Hold still."

Miss Massie Rivers had come to see Lucullus off; she herself would be going over to Europe and would be gone when he got back from his visit to White Hall. She was to sail on a big ship, she had told him, where she would sit on deck with the parrot and watch for whales.

Lucullus felt her beside him, her skirt brushing his thigh. "Miss Massie Rivers," he said urgently, quietly, so his father might not hear. He knew now, waiting for the train that would take him to the sanatorium, where he would see his mother at last, that he could not leave without telling the truth.

"You have your ticket?" she asked him. "Your father gave you the money?"

"Oh, yes," he said quickly. "Thank you."

She nodded. "It's your reward, Lucullus. I told your father so. Don't think of it as charity." She reached up a finger to the parrot, who sat hunched over her shoulder. It swiped amiably at her hand with its beak. She inclined her heavy cheek toward it.

Lucullus looked away. His father was still under the black cloth, his shoulders moving like thunderclouds massing on the horizon. Behind him ran the shining tracks, away, away, away into the future. The train would come soon. He stood up.

"Miss Massie—" he began. "The truth—"

But her body beside him shifted, grown alert. This stopped him. He realized that the truth might not always have been a kind thing for Miss Massie Rivers to have heard in her lifetime. But she reached up to put her arm over his shoulder where he stood now beside her. "Lucullus," she whispered, looking toward Lucullus's father. "Do you know what I found? In the ashes of the fire? I found the parrot's cage."

Lucullus held his breath.

"The door was open, you see," she said quietly. "Someone had carelessly left open the door on the cage. A small mistake, to be sure, but in fact a fortunate one, as we have now seen. I have come to think of that person, that person who left the door open, as my—friend."

"Just another minute," his father called to them.

Miss Massie Rivers squared her shoulders to face the camera. Her fingers felt light on his shoulder, and warm. "So it was a blessing." She shrugged. "He could just fly away."

Lucullus looked up. They could hear the train's whistle, though they could not see it yet, not for another minute. *I just found him,* he'd told her the night of the fire, coming back to the Inn with the parrot under his shirt. *He was just up in an old tree around here.*

But what was she doing now? She was forgiving him. But she didn't understand. He hadn't just opened the cage and forgotten to close it. He had taken her bird, stolen it. He had wanted it to fly away.

"What if the bird didn't just—fly away?" he asked the air over their heads, the air now ticking with electricity, something approaching.

The train's whistle sounded again, nearer now. "What if someone—stole it?" he said.

Miss Massie Rivers was silent beside him, and in the silence Lucullus felt his soul leave his body for an instant, a sensation of utter weightlessness like a bird in flight, as if he had risen above the place he knew and could now see beyond it, over the charred remains of the Inn, over the town, the fields, his house, all the way to the bright, silver vein of Father Judge Run that divided what he had known with all that would come next. What was it? Oh, what was it? What could he see?

"Ah," she said after a long moment.

The shape of Lucullus's father at the end of the platform surged once more under the black drape. One white arm emerged, a finger raised.

"Stolen it. I see." She paused. "And you are wondering—if that makes a difference."

He turned to look at her.

She squinted at the train, which had appeared now, a black thumb nosing around the corner of the hill. "No, Lucullus," she said then. "I think it makes no difference, in the end." She looked at him from where she sat. Her face was grave at first, and then it gave way into gentleness. Nothing could make her pretty, he thought. But a person could like her, very much.

"You have an absolutely clean heart now," she said. "Perfectly clean. You may go and see your mother with a clean heart."

She turned away from Lucullus, to face the oncoming train and his father's shape, still bent over and struggling beneath the drape. She patted his shoulder. "Smile for your father, Lucullus," she said. "We'll always remember this day."

Carrie Brown is the author of the novels *Rose's Garden,* which won the 1998 Barnes & Noble Discover Award for best first novel of the year, *Lamb in Love,* and most recently, *The Hatbox Baby.* A graduate of Brown University, Carrie also holds an M.F.A. from the University of Virginia, where she was a Henry Hoyns Fellow. She lives with her husband, the novelist John Gregory Brown, and their three children in Virginia.

JERRY BAUER

"*F*ather Judge Run" was originally a commission from the Chicago Museum of Contemporary Photography for a show of pictures by Southern photographers called "Some Southern Stories." The criteria was that *the pictures were to have been inspired by something from literature. In an interesting reversal, the exhibition's curators also wanted to create a booklet, to be distributed at the opening, of stories inspired by photographs. I went down to the local historical society in the town where I live and spent a day looking through the collections there. I came home with about ten photographs and stuck them up on the wall. This is the story that resulted, inspired by one particular picture. One day I hope to write the others.*

Edith Pearlman

SKIN DEEP

(from *The Antioch Review*)

Tuesday, after work, Robert, a widower of fifty, slid the last remnants of his wife's wardrobe into the Saint Vincent de Paul collection bin near Miami City Hall. He kept her pearls, and he kept the lilac shrug she had worn every day toward the end, almost a year ago. That final week the little sweater had begun to unravel as if it, too, had an unstoppable disease. The rest of the clothing, even the cherished Armani suit, he surrendered to the box.

Tuesday, after work, Livia, an unmarried woman of thirty-five, stopped in at a dispirited beauty salon on the border of Boston and Godolphin.

Livia was tall, as tall as many men, and large, too; she hunched a little, out of habit. Today as always she wore a gray jumpsuit with the name of a Boston hospital embroidered on its pocket. Her soft skin was impressionable: it took brief markings from whatever it touched. From her own fingers, if she rested her face on them. From the bedspread in her parents' room — as a child she had lain for entire afternoons on that corrugated fabric, daydreaming of ships, or ships' engines, or nothing at all. Her cheek would remain furrowed all through dinner. These days, after eight hours in the ambulance, after cleaning the vehicle and completing the checklist and signing out, she would sometimes slump in momentary weariness on the bench outside the hospital where smokers gathered, and lean the side of her head against a cinderblock. When she stood up, curlicues were engraved in her skin.

Livia's brambly dark hair was scraped into bunches on either side of her head, like extra ears. Masha the hairdresser was too wise to suggest a different style. "Oh, ho, you should wear the clumps," she'd said at Livia's first visit. "When you bend over a damaged child, when the child opens his eyes, what does he want to see? Minnie Mouse!" Today, though, because Masha knew that the daughter of Livia's older sister was about to be married in a splendid ceremony down in Miami, Masha permitted herself a liberty. After the trim she demonstrated to Livia, using her own fingers as combs, how the dense hair could be considered as one thicket not two; how it could be brought gently back and held with a couple of modest barettes, these ones here and you can have them for nothing. Then she restored the bunches.

Livia said thank you and paid the fee and five dollars extra, though most people didn't tip Masha because she was the owner. Then Livia bought *Popular Mechanics* at the newsstand and picked up some takeout at the Golden Dragon and walked home.

Robert's housekeeper had left a casserole. Robert made the salad. His three children ate greens with some enthusiasm whenever he added a mystery ingredient—horseradish, say, or slivers of macadamia nuts. Once he had minced a twist of black licorice; it kept them guessing until dessert.

Livia's father was reading at the kitchen table, his white hair falling over his brow. Livia put the Golden Dragon cartons in the center of the table. She set out two plates and two forks and a waterglass for herself and a wineglass for her father. He was a courteous, after-hours lush; this would be his first drink of the day.

They always talked a little. Sometimes he invited Livia to describe the ambulance whipping through traffic, its siren making mortals turn their heads. Within the vehicle, Livia told him, the siren was faint. "I can't hear it, I can't hear it," one sick woman moaned. "You're not supposed to, it's to scare other drivers," said Livia, caressing the thin hand.

Livia described passengers, too, at her father's request. Decades earlier he had studied medicine for a couple of years before return-ing with relief to the lab; and his fine mind, undamaged by booze, retained the entire anatomy textbook. Livia didn't tell him certain things about her job, like the times the gloves split. Sometimes Universal Precautions had to be ignored—the man who stopped breathing last Wednesday in that wreck of a room; the plastic device protected her lips from his, but some saliva, who knew.

Her father mentioned his own work. Though his sentences began comprehensibly they soon lapsed into terms that were famil-iar but not understood. She listened anyway. Phosphorylation process: she liked those syllables.

He talked, and noticed Livia's gaze, and remembered her mother, who had listened attentively, too, until the day she left him. He missed her. The evenings Livia went out to play squash he missed her, too. But: "Are you happy this way?" he'd wondered, just last week. To him happiness was having something to do and someone to come home to, but to a girl like Livia . . . "I mean: is there anything you want?" he clarified. She was silent. "A circular saw," she'd said at last, and grinned.

Livia put the half-empty cartons into the refrigerator. She put tonight's plates and glasses into the dishwasher where last night's already reposed. She ran the dishwasher every few days and the clotheswasher once a week. When her sister came up to visit, all the appliances whirred every day, and the toaster got turned upside down and shaken: what a storm of crumbs.

Her sister was ten years older than Livia, her sister's daughter ten years younger. In families the hospital served, generations were more thoroughly tangled: nieces older than aunts, mothers and daughters pregnant in pairs. Last summer one of the toddlers who—how-could-it-happen-he-just-fell-out-of-the-window, How!

—one such toddler seemed to belong to a dozen mothers: teenagers twenties thirties a couple of ancients. Three of these progenitors had clambered aboard the ambulance with the little boy. He yelled throughout the ride—a good sign—and at the hospital was pronounced unhurt. "Lucky," Bud the driver muttered to Livia; in his opinion the kids were chucked. Other out-the-windows fared less well.

Wednesday, Robert bought three new novels at the Miami Mall. He bought ten storybooks, too. His eight-year-old demanded to be read to every night. The girl's eyes fastened on the far wall. Sometimes Robert doubted that she was listening, but later he heard her repeating the tales in bed, though with unchildish twists: the glass slipper didn't fit, the beast remained a beast.

Carrying the books in two paper sacks he boarded the water taxi. It sped across the glinting bay. Robert watched the bearded pilot flatter some tourists. Maybe he, too, should stop shaving—a beard might suit his bony jaw.

In the back room of his newest optical shop in South Beach he examined the gratifying receipts. He peeked into the front room and saw all three opticians occupied with customers. He slipped off to an oceanside café. Families walked by; honeymooners; gay couples. He removed his jacket, he stretched his long legs, he sipped his coffee, all without becoming comfortable. Behind his chair a caged parrot squawked.

Wednesday, Bud was driving like the devil. On their third case he outran the dispatcher; when Livia tried to reconnect she got only cackle. They smacked to a stop against the curb. Not a car accident; no one had fallen from a window; this was an asthma attack. The child, a black Cape Verdean, had turned gray. His mauve lips bared his teeth. Bud carried him to the ambulance and ran around to the driver's seat. Livia got in. The fat mother, silent in her panic, heaved herself on board. Livia shut the doors. Bud started the engine. Livia's stethoscope traveled the narrow chest, no, air wasn't moving, not enough of it. She unsheathed the needle and inserted it. The small body tensed further, seemed to hurl its muscles at the world in a renewed determination to go on living, and then the breathing grew easier, the mouth relaxed. Livia met the mother's gaze. "All right."

After dinner that night her father, two bottles of Merlot under his arm, paused before leaving the kitchen. "Saturday," he said. "As the grandfather I suppose I should make a toast."

"Sure."

"In German do you think?"

Livia said: "That whole crowd down in Miami, they're all fluent in Spanish. I don't think German's their thing."

"But I don't speak Spanish."

"English might be best."

"Oh yes."

*   *   *

Thursday, after school, Robert's older son indifferently lost a tennis match. Robert watched, sorrowful and annoyed.

He drove home with the kids. The telephone was ringing. The caller was a woman he had met a week earlier—one of those energetic insightful females who seemed to populate the whole of Dade County. "Oh, I would have loved to," he told her. "I admire that quartet—but I'm busy Saturday." Silence. "So sorry," he lied. He hung up, and saw that each of the three children was intently looking in some other direction.

Thursday, Bud and Livia were summoned to a little single-family stretch of the city, everything bright as paint, petunias in the borders. The house had yellow siding and a picture window with a toy parrot. A neighbor had made the call. How still this street was at three in the afternoon, all the children inside watching television. Bud and Livia ran up the path. They banged on the door. Nothing. Bud carded it open, didn't have to use his shoulder or cut a chain. They went in; and there was a blond woman in a soft print dress sitting on the floor with her back against a chair slip-covered in a different print. A boy of about five lay across her lap with his head thrown back as if his throat had been slit. A girl, seven years old maybe, lay on the floor beside the woman. There was a kitchen knife in the mother's hand. She looked up at the jumpsuited intruders. "He's stopped screaming," she said conversationally; and Bud walked toward her like a friend, arms at his side, palms forward; and Livia reached the kitchen with one giant step, she knew where it was, how many of these little places had she seen, heart attacks happened here, strokes, kids swallowed things, old folks broke hips. Snatching a dishtowel she ran into the dining room; she sidled under the arched door and right up beside the mother who was waving the knife vaguely and talking to Bud. Livia lifted the knife by its blade out of the mother's weakening fist. The woman kept gesturing as if she hadn't noticed she'd lost her sharp pal. The children lay silent in their sacrificial positions. Livia examined them as well as she could. The woman didn't try to stop Livia, even when Livia's head was practically in her lap. The children were unharmed.

The police came with a straightjacket. The jacket wasn't necessary. Livia easily dislodged the little boy and the woman scrambled to her feet and walked between her escorts, smiling, glancing at her own face in the hall mirror the way Masha sometimes did when she was cutting Livia's hair.

And now it was Livia who was sitting on the floor, and the boy's head was in her lap. The girl stayed where she was.

"There was a bird," Livia began.

The boy grimaced as if stifling a scream.

"Once upon a time," Livia corrected, "there was a bird. He was a plain bird, a gray bird, and his songs went up and down the scale, all scales. . . . He lived alone in a cave on the side of a hill."

"Birds live in nests," said the girl.

"Yes, they do. But this one didn't. He liked living alone in his cave. But he didn't like being just gray. One day a wizard came, a wizard with a sack. The wizard said in a growly voice: I will give you a bright feather for every note you give me."

"How could—" began the girl; and the boy drew a violent breath; and the girl said, "Oh, all right."

"So the bird gave a note and the wizard gave a feather and pretty soon the bird's songs were not as beautiful as they had been though still nice and his feathers were green and blue as well as gray; and the wizard's voice wasn't so growly and his sack was smaller. After another while the bird had only a few songs, and he had red feathers now too, and the wizard's voice was getting sweeter, and—"

The social worker arrived, the one with white hair in a tapering braid. The boy by this time had achieved a half-sitting position, his head on Livia's breast, his buzz-cut hair against her cheek; when she moved her head to answer the social worker's questions the social worker noticed her stippled skin. The social worker got down on the floor and spoke softly to the children. She said they'd be going to live for a while in another house. . . .

"Don't scream, Larry, I'll kill you," said the girl.

The social worker said she'd help them pack some clothes and their very favorite toys. She stood up and extended her hands, and first the girl and then the boy stood up also and each took a hand and they left the room. Only the girl looked back at Livia. "Your face is all dots."

"Dead meat, those kids," said Bud when the three had gone upstairs. "Would you finish that story, Livy?"

"Maybe later." She hauled herself up from the spotless rug.

*   *   *

Friday afternoon Robert trimmed his bougainvillea.

Friday afternoon Livia and her father flew to Miami. Livia's sister and niece were waiting at the airport, plump and dimpled.

"She's a bundle of nerves," said Livia's sister in the car.

"I'm a block of ice; *you're* hysterical," said the bride.

"Tonight is just a little party."

There turned out to be fifty people on the patio. Livia's brother-in-law was putting on weight. The bridegroom was pale.

*   *   *

Saturday, Robert took his children swimming. Then he and his daughter dropped the boys at a cookout and picked up the baby-sitter.

Saturday, Livia and her father hung around their motel pool until it was time to get dressed. At five-fifteen a hired car picked them up. Livia's father was wearing a pin-striped suit. He looked both sprucer than usual and less spruce, as if he had made an effort and it had undone him.

An usher seated them in the front row of a glass-and-gold hall. The procession began. The bride and groom took their vows. Afterwards Livia joined the receiving line for a while and accepted congratulations; then she stepped away and stood in an alcove until people started drifting into a glass-and-gold dining room. Livia's table number was different from her father's; he was at One, the head table, and she was at Three. Idly fingering her cheek she made her way from the double-digit tables near the entrance toward the lower numbers at the rear. The room was filling steadily.

Robert saw her. His heart unmistakeably lurched.

He saw a tall, sturdy woman with a quantity of dark curls restrained by two barettes. She wore an unbecoming aqua dress. He guessed that she was not dowdy but rather beyond the reach of fashion, like a ship's figurehead. Her face was unmade-up except for a bit of splotchy rouge. The eyebrows were shaggy, the eyes brown, the whole comforting visage topped and surrounded by that irrepressible hair. Forty? She looked as if she'd be indifferent to many of the things he liked—comfort, travel; and she probably had no taste for reading, either. She was not a woman novels were written for or about.

Livia, adjusting one of Masha's unfamiliar barettes, found table Three, and joined a pair of cousins she hadn't seen in twenty years. The other guests were neighbors, and the local pharmacist, and a Sunday School teacher.

Robert noticed Livia once again, later, from the dance floor, where he was more or less executing a tango. She was plowing toward table One after her father's toast, delivered in French. Then he lost sight of her. *His* table, Twenty-two, might have been labeled Singles Not in the First Youth. One of the women—the one he was dancing with—was a divorced lawyer, nervous and amusing.

It had not occurred to Livia's sister to put Livia at Twenty-two.

The prince doesn't always find his way to the sleeping beauty. Robert's daughter knew that, and she guessed that the sleeping beauty sometimes likes it that way. But suppose that Livia *had* been seated at Twenty-two—or that Robert, stirred, had sought her out at Three. Suppose he had discovered in her an impartial kindness uncomplicated by introspection, a kindness that made sympathy and even empathy seem like performance pieces. Suppose he paid court; suppose he invented business to take him north, his visits surprising but not perturbing her.

One day, venturing to touch her face, he would watch the imprint of his own forefinger fade, slowly, as if to mock his unsated longing.

———

Edith Pearlman's first collection of short stories, *Vaquita,* won the Drue Heinz Literature Prize in 1996. Recent work has appeared in national magazines, literary reviews, anthologies, and in *Best American Short Stories 1998, Best American Short Stories 2000,* and *The Pushcart Prize XXV.* She received the *Antioch Review*'s 1999 Award for Distinguished Prose.

JOSHUA DALSIMER

I am working on a new collection which will include "Skin Deep." That story and some of the others reflect my interest in people who are happily solitary, or contentedly asexual, or both. Livia—whom I think of as the New Woman—wandered around my mind for a long time as a character, as did the old-fashioned Robert; but not until an extended stay in hedonistic Miami did I find the place for them not to meet.

Kurt Rheinheimer

SHOES

(from *The Nebraska Review*)

Back to the north and west from the crowded South Carolina coast, the land runs hot and flat and sandy, with small pines clustering here and there along the Pee Dee River as it snakes its way—inky and thick-looking—toward the ocean. It's the trees and the sandy soil that make the river look black, that give it a feel of danger when you look down on it from a highway bridge. In the fields that roll away from the river, the flat land yields tobacco and cotton—crops from the last century, growing now in the same fields as a hundred years ago and waiting to be picked by smallish, scruffy people who look like they might be from the last century, too.

The county roads, most of them paved now, lead back through the fields and out to low-built, bad houses. Most of the houses from that last century—built poorly and of wood and ever-threatened by fire—have returned to the land, and so the oldest houses you see are the flat-roofed shanties built in the twenties or so, many of them abandoned and falling down. The ones that are lived in—mostly by older people—tend to have no car beside them, or maybe a GM monster from the seventies sinking slowly into the sand. Then there are houses built not long before those cars were, square one-stories, some with brick facades and all with not much room in them.

Then the trailers came, set down at any angle most anywhere back onto a field along these roads. The first generation of them—long and thin and white—must have seemed like salvation at the time. Here was cheap housing that looked like it had lots of room and all the conveniences till you moved in and things started falling off in your hands. Now most of those trailers, just a few decades old, are abandoned and decaying, their cheap siding tearing off in chunks and their doors hanging open like old men with missing teeth. Often not far from one of them is a newer trailer—maybe a doublewide, as if twice as much of bad materials set down on the hot sand will do better than the older trailers, which were probably better made.

People who don't live here—who travel through this part of South Carolina on their way to the beach—say you could put them on any one of these hot two-lanes and they'd have no idea at all where they were, because all the roads look the same. It's an endless reach of flat land, of low-growing crops begging for even more sun, of criss-crossed roadways leading past the bad housing set back against a sad little tree or two.

June Terry knows all these roads, and can tell you how each one is different from the others. She knows them because for sixteen years she has driven them twice a day for the 180 or so days a year that the schools are open. Her own run-down house back along one of them—it's one of the bigger ones, with a brick face on it—is different from all the others because except for the morning run and the evening run, it has a big, orange-yellow schoolbus sitting next to it. She parks it next to the dead '78 Camaro that broke down six years back, the same day that Eddie Terry decided he'd had enough of her. He walked away from the house one evening near dusk—away from his busted car and his angry wife, and never came back. He went to the ocean, she came to learn, and the most recent she's heard is that he has part ownership in one of the piers there along the Grand Strand. Taking tackle and bait money from families on vacation so they can stand out on the pier for an hour or two before they realize that nobody catches anything.

What occurs to her as being the same down here—more than the roads—are the kids who've gotten on her bus over the years. Whether they are white or black, they are always the same scraggly, undersized low-country kids every fall when school starts up. The only things that change some are what they carry and how they dress. The old brown paper sacks for lunches disappeared years ago, and then you had kiddie-movie characters on metal lunch boxes, and then space-movie characters on plastic lunch boxes. Now you see fewer and fewer boxes at all, what with the county lunch program. And the shirts. Used to be people just wore shirts—a blue shirt or a red shirt or a white shirt. Now every shirt has a message. A brand or a slogan or a big picture of a cartoon character. Still ratty and worn, the shirts, but all with something to say.

This is on an afternoon run a week and a half ago, with three weeks left in the school year. It is the junior high run, which comes after the elementary run. It is Friday, her last trip of the day, and she is looking forward to parking the big can and settling in. She has an invitation to go to the beach for the weekend with two of the girls from transportation in town, but hasn't decided if it'll be that or settling in with the offerings of her new dish—one of those little ones that can get you a billion channels without the dish being so big that people tell you how they see you joined up with the rest of those now growing the state flower out in their yards. It is hot, like it is almost all the school year. Her run goes deep into the county, where the roads get even narrower and the houses even smaller and more run-down. She has the last kid—Kinnie is the name printed on his little backpack—a kid who only comes about half the time, and lives out in the worst excuse for a house of any kid she's ever delivered. It's concrete, like an old military bunker or something, perfectly square as far as she can tell, and about as big as one room in a regular house. No windows. It looks like there never were any windows—just these up-and-down rectangular holes about as big as folded-up newspaper every few feet across the front.

About a mile down the two miles of road she has to drive to drop Kinnie off, she sees a young man at the side of the road ahead of her. Though she doesn't know how exactly, she recognizes almost immediately that it is Petie Carroll. Maybe it is the tilt of his head and the blondish, out-of-control hair that is the same as back in elementary school. She drove him all through elementary and into junior high until he quit, in the seventh grade, as well as she can remember. That was six or eight years ago, so as she heads toward him she calculates that he must be twenty by now. He's still smallish, still sort of hollow-eyed. He's waving her down. Kids over the years have tried from time to time to get a ride with her when it had nothing to do with school, and though it's against policy, there have been a half dozen times when she's done it. She doesn't know exactly why she let him in, especially without telling him to wait till she's dropped Kinnie and is on her way back, but she does.

"Junie," he says to her, and grins.

"Peter," she says. She knows he hates being called Petie—the name he started school with, because it was such an easy tease. "Petie went peepee in the Pee Dee," or something like that was a favorite taunt. As he got older, he worked hard at getting people to call him Carroll, but then that sounded too girly and the last she knew him he had gone back to Peter.

"Just Pete," he corrects.

"Where are you headed?"

"Back toward your area maybe," he says, and looks down. As he gets even with the seat where Kinnie is, he makes a fake punch at the little boy. Kinnie flinches and can't figure out whether to smile or not. Petie walks on to the back of the bus—the very last seat, where he always tried to sit.

"Haven't seen you," June says up into the mirror when he's seated.

"You, either," he says.

She lets them bounce along a ways and then tries again. "Where you been?"

"Everywhere, nowhere," he says in a sing-songy way, like she's a parent. She wonders why she let him in. In all her days driving, he was one of the three or four who gave her the most trouble. He started tiny—first grade, she thinks it was, when he got off the bus and wrote a crude-printing SHIT in the dust on the side. It got worse from there. He once climbed out one of those little half-window spaces you have on school buses and ran across a field away from her for some reason while she was letting another kid out. You don't like to see any kid drop out of school, but she can't say as she missed him too much after he left. Which makes it all the harder for her to decide what she was thinking to pick him up.

"You were up in Columbia for a while, weren't you?" she tries. She's heard that he lived with an aunt for a time until maybe a year ago, although she's not sure she's seen him in the time since either.

"Might of been," he says, and looks up at the ceiling, working on being bored.

"You ride the bus just like you used to," she says.

"You drive it even slower," he says.

They are almost at Kinnie's house, "You know Kinnie?" she asks. "Who?"

"Kinnie up here. The other passenger."

"Sure," he says, overdoing a sarcastic tone. "I know all the little weenie heads around here."

Kinnie almost smiles at June as he gets off. He can't bring himself to turn his head to look at you full face, or say anything, but sometimes he'll move his head half a turn that way, or maybe raise his hand up six inches as if to wave.

Kinnie gets off. He could be Petie ten years ago, except he's perhaps even smaller for his age. "See you Monday, Kinnie," she calls to him as he starts down the forlorn, grassed-over rock driveway toward the bunker. He moves his head again a little ways to one side.

"No, you won't," Petie says into her hair, and then there is something cold and metal being pushed into her neck. "It's loaded," he says. "It's not aimed at you, that's just the barrel across your neck so you know it's here, okay?"

She's not sure if she's supposed to answer. She feels halfway between laughing and crying. She doesn't answer.

"Okay?"

"Okay, okay," she tells him, with just a little impatience. "You want the bus, Pete, you can have it. Just let me out here and you'll be halfway out of the county before I could get to a phone."

He pulls the metal away from her neck. "Who'd want this piece of shit?" he says, looking around. He puts the metal back on her. "I think I'd rather have a chauffeur, you know?" As she wonders again if she's supposed to answer, she also has to overcome the temptation to taunt him that the reason he doesn't want the bus is that he doesn't know how to drive it. This is a kid she drove to school, who ran off the bus so he could pee in the bushes, who couldn't talk to a girl, who forgot his bookbag half the time. It's hard, despite the cold metal that she does believe to be a gun, to take him seriously. She asks him where they're going.

"No place," he says. "Who says we're going anywhere?"

She starts to ask him what he wants the bus for when her stomach sinks with the realization that maybe she's what he wants. She thinks to tell him she's twice as old as he is, but stops. What if that's *not* what he's thinking of?

"Not fucking Columbia," he says after a moment, and again pulls the metal away. She strains her eyes as far to the right as she can without turning her head to try to see what he has. She can't see it. She asks him why not Columbia.

"Who wants to know?" he says. He touches her quickly with the metal and pulls it away.

"Just wondering," she says, not venturing to remind him that he brought it up. They are still a mile from the closest thing to a main road in this part of the county, which is still a nothing two-lane where you see a car every five minutes.

They are quiet for a minute or so, the bus jostling like the old cans do. He sits in the seat immediately behind her. "Don't think it's not still right on you," he says.

"I don't," she tells him. While he's quiet, she tries to figure out how frightened she is. And then wonders why she is thinking about that instead of how to get this over with. She decides there's really nothing she can do right then and that she's not all that frightened because she doesn't think he'll shoot her. He's just a kid from the sand same as the rest of them, the same sand as she is. And maybe it's not a gun anyway.

At the intersection, they see their first cars. Two of them—one coming toward them to go down the road they've been and the other crossing in front of them in the direction she turns to go home. June pauses at the stop sign and watches them both go. She knows both drivers, and waves the same way she always does. She can't tell what Pete is doing, but there's nothing against her neck. When the cars are gone, she turns right same as always. Pete is quiet while she makes the turn.

"You wave like a weenie," he tells her.

"Practice," she says.

He snorts a small laugh at his nose.

"So you going on home?" he says. "Park the little bus beside the little house and eat some little dinner?"

She feels fear then. He does want her. "No," she tries, "the old can has to be serviced and they're waiting for me at transportation."

He snorts again. "That's good," he says. "That's good. On a Friday afternoon. I bet."

"Okay," she says, this time without thinking, "where *are* we going?"

"The beach!" he shouts, and laughs out loud.

"The beach? It's half an hour away."

"So?"

"Well, we'll have to get gas."

"So?"

"They'll know us."

"Big deal. Drive to where they don't and if they do, we'll say it's a field trip. You ever drive for field trips or are you too good for that?"

"One kid on a field trip?" she says. "One man?"

"Whatever," he says.

"The beach," she says after a few quiet moments.

"Damn straight," he says.

"When were you there last?" she asks.

"Who wants to know?"

The road is flat and open ahead of them, with the sun still high and the air hot. She is suddenly tired of this. Without thinking she slows the bus down.

"What are you doing?" he says. She feels the metal again.

"Take that away from my neck," she tells him.

He moves it a little, then puts it back. "I'm in charge here, remember?"

"I do remember Pete, and I don't need the metal reminder, okay? Let's just do this," she says, now speaking faster than she should, "let's just find out what the hell it is you want and then we'll see if I can really help, and if I can, I will and you don't need the gun there or whatever, okay? And if I can't help, then I won't, no matter how much you do that. Okay? So what is it you want?"

"I told you," he says.

"Tell me again."

"The beach."

"You want to go to the beach."

"Right."

"Myrtle?"

"Yeah, like down in there."

"But where exactly?"

"I don't know, just down there," he says with a hint of anger.

"Just down there," she repeats. "Okay, Pete, let's do that then. You take your big weapon away from my neck and go sit down in a seat, and if nobody stops us, I'll take you to the beach."

"The hell you will," he says. "It's a trick."

She puts the brake on and turns to him at the same time. His eyes pop open wide. There is a gun in his hand. "Look," she says, "it's not a trick—you don't hurt me and I'll take you where you want to go, okay?"

"Sure you will," he says. The gun is quiet in his lap.

She moves back to highway speed and they're on their way. He's quiet behind her. The air is hot but at least moving around. The bus bounces along, creaking louder than crickets, the way it does when it's empty. When they get near her house, he warns her not to make the turn.

"I told you I'll do what you want," she says impatiently. "But you never told me you're not going to hurt me."

"Probably I won't," he says. She can picture the little grin on his face, like the time he or one of his friends coated the steering wheel with motor oil.

"What about a car, Pete? We could take my car and be more comfortable?"

"This is a damn bus trip," he says immediately and forcefully. "The field trip to the beach."

She wants to tell him it can still be a field trip in a car, but she doesn't. "Well, how about this then—how about you move out from right behind me and sit over there on the other side in the front seat. You could still fill me full of holes from there if you had to."

He gets up. "This isn't like a joke, Junie," he says.

"You don't have to tell me," she says.

The gas is no big deal. They are out on the highway by then, and nobody knows them and nobody pays any attention. It's too early for the big crowds of cars that come down on the summer week-ends, but there's a steady flow of plates from North Carolina and Virginia mostly, and so a school bus—even with South Carolina plates—stopping in for gas is nothing to draw attention.

"Before long one of us is going to have to use the bathroom," June tells him when they're started again.

"Not me," he says, "I don't pee anymore at all."

As they move along the highway, he seems more and more interested in where they're going and less and less in her. "Where's that pottery place?" he asks. She tells him it's on a different highway. Then he asks if this is really the way to the beach or is she jerking him around again. She says it is the way and she never jerked him around in the first place.

"Yeah, right," he says. "You'd be the first." He has stayed in the seat she put him. He has spent most of the time at the window. They are up to nearly 55, and the bus is bouncing more than she's ever felt it. She realizes that when you go this fast in a school bus that there is basically no back end to it. It sits up high and over-reacts to every bump in the road.

As they come up on the bridge over the river, Pete tells her to slow down. "I mean it," he says, his tone reverting to the start of things.

"Take it easy," she tells him. "We'll do it, we'll slow down."

"Can you stop on the bridge?" he says.

She turns to look at him. "You don't have your driver's license, do you, Pete?" she says without thinking.

"Fuck you, too," he says without turning toward her, without reaching for the gun.

She feels a push of shame at shaming him and foolhardiness for offending him. "We can stop at the far side of the bridge and walk back up," she offers.

"Don't even try to trick me," he says.

They ride in silence for a while. The air is getting thicker. You can smell the ocean. When they are nearly upon the coast, she asks him quietly if he's got a place picked out yet.

"Place for what?" he says.

"To go," she says.

"Paint ball," he says.

"What?"

"Paint ball." He looks at her hard, as if to judge if he's made a mistake, or she has.

"What's paint ball?"

"You lie, Juniejune, you lie."

"I don't," she says, "I don't."

"Where you go in and put on these helmets and get these guns and shoot paint at guys. You run and shoot."

"Where is it?"

"Like Myrtle."

When he can't tell her where, she talks him into letting them stop and ask, and for her to use the bathroom. She finds out the place is right down in the middle of Myrtle, where she knows she'll have a hard time parking. She asks Pete what she's supposed to do while he goes in. He doesn't hesitate a second to tell her what she does is pay and then wait. They drive around for fifteen minutes and she finally finds a long enough spot—ten blocks from the paint ball place. They get out without incident, and there is no sign of the gun. He walks more slowly than she'd have thought, looking at everybody carefully. It is a Friday night in early summer and the streets are full of beach-dressed people. They wear T-shirts that say things she doesn't even think, much less say, even less show off to the world. Baseball hats on everybody. Big shoes, big shorts, big people. Peter is dressed in a pair of torn khaki shorts that hang way too low and a plain white T-shirt that is worn thin. A pair of old-time tennis shoes with no socks and holes worn through where the little toes are. You can almost feel him envying the things other people have on. "Some bumpin' shoes," is the only thing he says to her while they walk. When he gets a step ahead of her at one point, she catches his face as he watches everyone. It's opened up in the eyes and the mouth, almost like a much younger kid seeing things for the first time. Then, as if he feels her eyes, he spins all of a sudden and tells her to stay even with him.

The paint ball place feels creepy to June. You go in on the ground floor and take a dirty elevator up to a dark hallway with red velvet walls. Then you come out to a sort of open area with windows out over the main street. There's loud rock music and a kid in a tie-dye shirt to take your money. It's eight dollars. Unbelievable. She hasn't thought about the money to finance this kidnapping. There's nearly fifty dollars in her wallet. She pays, and sits on this little platform kind of thing with other adults and kids waiting. Peter walks around in a hurry, as if he can't wait. The other people waiting are much younger than he is, but he doesn't seem to notice. Then six or eight sweaty boys appear out of a curtain she hadn't seen. They are grinning and pushing at each other, talking about *blasting* that guy and *toasting* somebody else.

By the time Peter comes out and begs to do it again, she is pretty well convinced that it has been a long time since he's been to the beach. His bravado is lost while he asks her to pay again, with a boyish desperation. "Just once more?" he says. "Please?"

After the second time, he is sweaty and breathing hard, and says he wants a Coke.

"How about one of those fancy Sno-Cones?" she hears herself say, "with the shaved ice?"

"I want a Coke," he says.

She feeds quarters to the machine in the red hallway and they head out into the evening. There is more noise. More music, more color, and more smells. More people. Cars move slowly down the street in the middle of it all, honking and waving. She has never been to New Orleans, but on TV she has seen the people on that one street there, and wonders if this is sort of the poor-man's New Orleans. Peter is more wide-eyed than ever.

"Let's get a foot-long," he tells her.

"Oh, we're including me, too, now?" she says, risking sarcasm.

"Aren't you hungry?"

In the end he gets his foot-long and she gets a cheese steak sub. Way too much money and way too many calories, but hey, they are on vacation, Peter and Junie, right? She was supposed to be at the beach with a couple of friends and wasn't going to do it, and now she's here sort of playing mom to what seems more and more to be a boy—a slightly deranged boy, but probably harmless. When the food is gone—they walked the whole time they ate—he wants to see the water.

"See the water?" she asks him. He has, she decides then, never been to the ocean. He has lived the twenty years of his life thirty or so miles inland, or in the inner city in Columbia, and has never been here. Half the nation, it seems, will get into its cars in the next few weeks, and drive down here to waste money at the arcade—maybe the reason Peter hasn't asked for that is that he doesn't know it's there—and at the paint ball and the race cars and the water park and the piers, and even play in the surf . . . and here is a boy who is a South Carolina native from just up the road and he's never been. He has missed the field trips. His family has likely never been cohesive enough to get here, and so now he has kidnapped the school bus driver to make the trip. She wants to ask him about all that, to comfort him, but cannot.

At the water, he peels off his shirt, and the ratty shoes just sort of come off as he runs to the water. The surf is relatively calm, and she guesses the water is not cold enough to shock him, because he stays in. He looks up and down the beach at those in the water around him, but doesn't go as far out as most of them. He does awkward dives at the little waves and tries to ride a few in, with no success. He walks back out with a grin, picks up his shoes and his shirt and then tells her he needs shoes.

"Shoes?" she says. "Yeah, you do need shoes, but this is your field trip, right? Not a shopping trip. I only have about thirty dollars left, Pete."

"So?"

"So shoes cost lots more than that."

"Oh," he says. "Time for the plastic then, huh, Junie baby?"

"Peter, you need to get your family to buy you shoes."

"Yeah, right," he says. "Like some more of these from the Salvation Army store?" He holds up his shoes. "Besides," he says, "don't forget who's in charge here, right?"

"Yes, Peter, we know who's in charge, but now you're going to add robbery to the kidnapping charges."

"I can get you paid back," he says next. "The worker comes next week and you can tell her what you got me. She'll give it all back."

"Yeah, right," she says.

He looks at her with a quick smile, as if in recognition of her echo of his phrase.

On the way back to the bus to go to the mall, they see one of the shaved-ice places, and he agrees to try one. Once they're in the bus, and drive past the game arcade, he detours them there for an hour and for twenty-five dollars. It is nearly dark now, and June is tired. "So," she tells him, "once we do the shoes, then we're going home?"

"Could be," he says. "Could be."

At the shoe store, the sales people are dressed like referees. There are six or eight of them, probably all about Pete's age, but different looking. They have fuller faces and bodies, cleaner hair, a stronger look about them. They glance at Pete and June and move on to ask others if they can help them. The walls are filled with shoes. Pete's eyes are as wide as when they got to Myrtle Beach.

"What kind do you think I should get?" he says.

"Well," she says, "those there are women's, so let's move down to the men's."

"Oh," he says, without anger.

There are more shoes in more colors than she has ever seen. The kids who get on her bus have slowly moved toward these shoes, but are behind these models. The shoes on her passengers started out white and innocent-looking sixteen years ago—just little tennies so your feet didn't get sand on them while you were in the playground, or fried on the bottom when you walked out to the bus in the afternoon. Then maybe there was some blue color in there, or even black. All leading up to what you see here—shoes that look like a cross between an army tank and an automatic weapon. Big shoots of color going in all directions. Pieces of shoe tongue and shoe side and shoe sole zooming up and out all over other parts of the shoes.

One of the sales girls gives Pete a pair of socks and he tries on a pair. When he stands up in them, his raggy wet shorts and his scrawny size make him seem anchored down by the shoes, sort of held to the floor by shoes that seem way too big and way too colorful for his little body and Salvation Army clothes. It's as if he's all Pee Dee from the top of his head to his ankles, and then something completely different at the feet. He struts around the store once they're on, grinning more openly than he has the whole trip. The sales people seem to have lost some of their wariness, as if they sense a boy about to walk away in something he's never had before.

And what she's never had before is a Visa charge receipt for a pair of shoes that cost more than three times what she's ever paid for shoes for herself. Pete tells the girl in the referee shirt she can throw the old shoes away. She makes a face at the thought of having to handle them, and then tells them thanks very much.

"These are great," Pete says when they're outside. As they walk to the bus she talks to him about heading back. He says she could leave him here. She tells him she doesn't think that's too good because then she could get into even more trouble than she already will be in.

"I'm twenty-one," he tells her. "I can do what I want."

"Right, but when I get back and they want to know why I stole a school bus to go to Myrtle Beach on a Friday night, then I'll have to tell them, and then they'll be after you. If we go on back and I can tell them you'd never been to the beach before, but agreed to come on back, then I think they'll be a lot easier on the both of us."

He seems to be considering this as they get back on the bus. When they're started, he asks if they can go back the same way they came. "Across that bridge where we didn't stop," he says. She tells him they can.

"What about the gun?" she asks when they're back on the highway. "If you didn't have that and hadn't sort of threatened me with it, that might help, too."

"I might need it sometime," he says.

"What if they lock you up and you never get to need it?"

"Nobody's going to lock me up." There's an edge of temper in his voice.

She turns back toward him. "I hope not, Pete, I hope not."

"How far's the bridge?" he says.

"Just up here a little ways."

"So you'll stop and we'll walk up there and look down at it?"

"If that's what you want." The bridge they are approaching is not particularly long, but it is one of those they build now where there's a long grade up to it and then it arches way above the water-way, as if to prepare for the possibility of the hugest flood ever.

In the dark, with cars whizzing by next to them as they walk, the bridge seems even higher up. She thought as they got out of the bus that Pete might take the gun up there and throw it in, but she can't see for sure if he has it or not. For a long distance as they walk up the bridge, there is nothing to see below but the black where the little trees are. Then, as they near the top, she can see the darker black band of the water. It is water, it occurs to her, that has run from back where she and Pete are from, water that has carried the heat and sweat of the cotton and tobacco fields down here close to the ocean, water that the Pee Dee flowed into to help build this larger flow of water to the sea.

At the top of the bridge, Pete stands still, leaning on the railing and looking down for what seems like a long time, sometimes at his shoes and sometimes as if he's trying to see down into the dark water. "It's flat-out dark down there," he says. In something between slow motion and déjà vu, she knows what will happen before it does, or at least as it does. She is too instantly frozen with dread to react and too far away to reach for him even if she could. As she feels her breath leave her, he is over the little guardrail in one vault, on his way down through the night and into the deeper black.

Kurt Rheinheimer's fiction has appeared in many
magazines, ranging from *Redbook* to *Michigan
Quarterly Review*. "Shoes" marks his fourth
appearance in *New Stories from the South*. The
editor of *Blue Ridge Country* magazine, he lives in
Roanoke, Virginia, with his wife and their five
sons. He is a daily runner and a lifelong devotee
of the Baltimore Orioles. He is at work on two
collections of stories.

DOUG MILLER

*I feel fortunate when a story is suggested by geography, as those seem to
carry themselves best from start to finish. My hope at first sentence is to
stay with the land for long enough that I can feel myself there again and
then to trust that the feel of the place, once established, will yield not only
the characters but also what will happen to them. Such was the happy
circumstance here; the landscape of northeastern South Carolina, seen from
afar, gets all the credit.*

Stephen Coyne

HUNTING COUNTRY

(from *The Southern Review*)

She heard the old fool pull into the driveway. How could she miss him? A hundred times she had told him to get his truck fixed, but he never would do it. He couldn't hear was the problem, and he wouldn't admit that he couldn't hear, so what did he care if he drove something that sounded like a castrated pig?

His dogs were gone again. Edna could tell that just by the sound of things. Three thousand dollars' worth of bluetick mixes running loose in the woods somewhere. It wasn't such a big number anymore—three thousand dollars—unless you were a pulpwooder and didn't make but eight or nine thousand a year. Oh, a young man might make more than that, but then again, young men these days had better sense than to be pulpwooders.

But forty years ago, when she first met him, pulping was the thing to do. All you needed was a chain saw and enough courage to use it. Lots of men were afraid of such saws back then, and good reason, too. Many a one sawed through a boot top or cut a branch that sprung back and snapped him into the next world. But not Coy. He was strong. A chain saw was nothing more to him than a tamed scream at the end of his big arms. In five minutes he could bring down a tree it'd take two men with a crosscut an hour to fell. That was back before the big woods were cut over. Back when you could get three loads of pulpwood from the laps of a single tree.

It seemed to her that in those days everywhere Coy turned another tree was coming down, and there was Coy, standing over the carcass, cutting off the money and loading it onto his truck. Now, all these years later, his forearms were still bigger than most men's calves, but they were laced with varicose veins, and sometimes they hurt so bad that Coy couldn't cut. Even though it was only planted pine not much bigger around than her leg, he still couldn't cut. He never said anything. But he'd come home with half a load or less, and she'd know.

When they were young, though, their wood lot was always stacked high, and as far as they knew, they were rich. First thing Coy always wanted was good dogs. Bluetick and redbone—howlers and criers. On nights when the moon shone down on mist that filled the hollows, the two of them would load the dogs into the truck and drive into the country. They'd turn the dogs loose and sit in the truck, listening to the howls echo through the woods. It put the hair up on Edna's arms, it was so beautiful and eerie. Seemed like it was the sound of their two spirits spinning through those trees, chasing after what they knew they needed while their bodies stayed in the truck doing what bodies could think to do.

Then came kids, and he went without her after that, he and his buddies. They weren't content to sit in the truck and listen but had to get liquored up, put pistols in their pockets, and light out through the woods, chasing the sounds and sometimes finding the dogs around a tree. She never understood why they had to carry it that far, why they wanted to see the coon's eyes shine in their flashlight beams, why they'd shoot until it fell, or until it died in the arms of the tree. Sometimes Coy told her about coons that seemed to disappear, right out of the tree, somehow, so that the dogs had to be tied up and dragged back to the truck.

And sometimes, of course, they'd lose the dogs. There'd be a howling out there, but liquor and the hollows confused the sounds. The men would wander into briars or cripples until finally they'd quit. Coy'd come home alone, then, and she'd be able to tell whether he was mad from the way he closed the truck door and by the sound of his steps on the back porch. If the dogs had struck hard and tracked fast, they might have just left the men behind. He'd be excited then, and his steps would be quick and loud — what a coon, strong and smart. You could lose dogs over an animal like that and feel proud. But if the dogs had wandered and fretted and never struck hard but wouldn't come when they blew the horn, he'd be mad. His steps would be slower and quiet like he was trying to sneak up on something. He'd tell her he didn't care if he never found them dogs again. She'd remind him what they cost, but he'd swear and say it was a small amount to lose to be rid of something that couldn't do what it was put on Earth to do.

But anymore, it was hard to tell how he felt by the sound of his steps because he didn't step so much as shuffle. She heard him head toward the shed to put away his pistol and take off his boots. He ought not hunt was what she thought. For one thing there was nobody to go with him. His last friend, Mr. Logan, was in the White Oak Nursing Home now because it got to the point where he had forgotten how to get home from the store. And there was no way Edna would go with Coy into the woods. Not now, not at her age. No, she had long ago given up foolishness like that. So he went by himself, and it wasn't safe. Time was you had to worry about bears and even panthers. Thank goodness those times were gone, but it wasn't any safer now because the things that stalked old people were a whole lot fiercer than wild animals.

She knew all she needed to know about that. She was old when she had kids — thirty by the time the last was born. And each one brought more trouble — more falling down and foolishness, more sickness and fussing. Wasn't until the kids were grown and gone that she felt safe again. But by then her joints ached when the weather got bad, and one day she tripped over a rug and hit a chair before she wound up on the floor with a broken wrist. It never healed right, and so she was never again the woman she once had been.

No, it was plain as chestnuts—by a certain age a person ought to admit that he can't catch what runs in the woods anymore. He ought to stay home and be glad he's got a clean, warm place where he can sit in comfort and remember a time when he could catch most anything he wanted to. Stay home. Watch TV. Read the paper. Lock the door.

Coy stepped into the kitchen and stood there in his dirty socks, looking at her across the room.

"Well?" she said. He turned away and got a drink of water. "Where are they this time?"

"Ain't no woods no more," he said. "You can drive all the way to Polk County and not pass nothing but saplings no bigger 'round than a dog's waist, and the ground underneath choked with weeds and green briars. Take a weasel to find a coon in such a mess as that. I don't even know why I keep dogs no more."

"Well," she said, "sounds like you don't."

"Ain't even hardly a tree big enough to hold a good-sized coon."

"You ought to sell them dogs."

"Down to Polk County, right there by the Green River, there's still some woods, but they've cut over parts of it, so you walk a while and then you come to a thicket can't a gnat get through. And if they do strike in there, why you can't halfway hear because the sound don't carry through a mess like that."

No, she thought, the old fool's ears were twice as big as when he was young, but the bigger they got the worse they seemed to work.

"Better get some sleep," she said. "So you can hunt them tomorrow."

"I'm going to bed," he said, and she nodded.

But he didn't get up early the next morning and drive the dirt roads looking for the dogs. And he didn't go out in the evening either. All he did was mess around in his shed all day, filling boxes and trash bags. When he came in to wash his hands for supper, she stood right next to him and looked him in the eye. "It's good money," she said, "just starving to death out there."

He turned from the sink and said, "Huh?"

It was bad being deaf, but she had to admit it had its uses.

They sat in the living room all evening watching her shows. He stared at the TV, but she didn't think he was paying attention. He never once asked her to run the volume up, and he only seemed to come to himself when girls in bathing suits flashed across the screen.

"Get up," she wanted to tell him. "What sort of a man sits there and watches shows like this, like he's in a trance?"

In the middle of *Murder She Wrote,* he pushed himself out of his chair. "I'm going to bed," he said, like he had lost some sort of battle he had been fighting. She watched him slouch up the stairs, then turned back to her show. It was no use trusting an old man. Once they couldn't work, they weren't good for a single thing. She was half-tempted to go find those dogs herself—find them and sell them.

He didn't go out looking the next morning either. And at supper he wouldn't say anything to her but "Huh?" After dinner, he sat in the living room all evening while the room got dark. He didn't even hear the phone when it rang.

The young man on the other end said he had found some dogs at his place and the tags had this number on it.

"Yes," Edna said. "Let me let you talk to my husband."

She held the phone toward Coy, and he groaned coming out of the chair. "Where?" he said into the phone. "Wait a minute."

He gave the phone back to her. "I can't tell what he's saying."

She got the location and hung up. "Let's go," she said.

He filled two bowls with food and put them in the back of the truck next to the dog cages. "You drive," he told her.

She headed them down the Coxe Road, the truck screaming all the way. They turned onto the Watson Road, which was dirt, and then onto a farm road, which was just two ruts through the woods. The road climbed a hill and wound between white oaks into the driveway of an old log house.

"I know this place," Coy said. "There was a bear tore the convertible top off a man's car lived here. Must've been forty years ago. Fool left food in the backseat, and the bear went right through the top. Fellow run him off by throwing stones. Saved some of the food, but the roof of that car was ruint."

The first thing that came to greet them was a Labrador retriever. It looked like a shadow in their headlights. The dog lifted its leg and marked their tires.

"That dog ain't no kind of use around here," Coy said.

Next came three dogs, their tails between their legs. Edna recognized the bluetick markings, but the dogs seemed smaller, somehow, than their dogs. They bred them down, these days. Coy had explained it to her. They mixed in bird dog so they could hunt better in brush. He didn't like it. Little dogs for chasing little coons through little woods. Not a thing to be proud of, but it was all you could do anymore since the world had gotten so small and so filled up with children and pups and saplings that there was hardly anyplace for something full-grown. The Lab jumped back and forth, bowing to play. One of the mixes wrestled with it.

"Useless," Coy mumbled.

Next came a young man in short pants. He had a little goatee and a big smile.

Edna smiled back at the boy and glanced over at Coy. He didn't seem to notice the boy, though. He was looking straight ahead, and she followed his eyes. A girl, also in short pants and wearing the top to a bathing suit, was headed their way. She stopped to pet the dogs, which gathered around and followed her to the truck.

The boy was talking a streak about how they had seen the dogs yesterday at twilight but that they wouldn't come out of the woods. Then this evening they must have gotten the courage to come up and make friends with Jessie (Edna didn't know whether this was the black dog or the girl). The boy had managed to read the number on one of their collars, and so he had called, and goodness they really loved the sound coon dogs made in the woods at night, but Laura didn't like the idea of killing coons. (So Edna knew, then, that Laura most likely was the girl.) The boy had told

Laura that lots of times hunters didn't even bother to follow the dogs but just let them run to hear their music and then called them back and went home. Sometimes, though, the dogs wouldn't come, and so they left them, knowing they would go someplace or other when they got hungry enough. Just a good thing they found somebody honest this time, the boy said. Yes, Jessie and Laura both liked them just fine. Real nice coon dogs.

Edna had never heard the like. This boy was some sort of Yankee, or maybe he was just from Charlotte, but either way he was one of those people that comes at you talking and leaves you talking and never shuts up enough to let the world catch its breath. Nice coon dogs. What foolishness. The young could have it worse than the old. A good coon dog didn't care a thing about people except for food. No, all a coon dog cared about was the woods and what his nose could take him to.

"Well, they sure are friendly," the boy was saying, "and pretty—they sing fine at night. Why, with the moon full and . . ."

She turned to Coy. "You going to feed them?"

"Ain't mine," he said.

"What?" she said.

He looked her straight in the eye and said, "Huh?"

How long? she wondered. How long before Coy wouldn't be able to find his way home from the store either? She had fallen in love with this man. She had wanted to spend her life with him, and she had. She had lived with him until, now, it seemed like there was hardly anything left.

She got out of the truck and put the food bowls on the ground. The dogs didn't even bother to smell what was there.

"Oh," said the boy. "Laura made bacon and eggs for them a little while ago."

"They sure were hungry," said Laura, and she smiled sweetly at the dogs.

"Let's go," Coy said. "Get in the truck."

"I'll help you load them up," the boy said, and he bent down and picked up one of the dogs. It wasn't like Coy did it. Coy picked dogs up by the scruff of the neck and the skin of their rumps, and he pitched them like bales of hay. This boy put his arms underneath and held the dog the way Jesus holds the lamb in that picture. Edna didn't open the cage door. She just looked at the boy with his arms under the dog, and the dog looking surprised and yet somehow content, like it didn't care if it never ran in the woods again.

Coy leaned out the window. "That ain't mine," he said.

"But it's got your number right here on the collar," the boy said.

Coy squinted at the boy. "What do you reckon you'd do, short pants, if a bear come through the roof of *your* car?"

The boy cocked his head and smiled. "Huh?" he said.

Edna was about to argue with the old fool, right there in front of strangers. This was good money here, their money, but it'd do no good to argue with him now—she knew that—not with his foolish mind made up. She put the bowls back in the truck and got behind the wheel. They could come back another day, or she could. The truck screamed when she started it. Then she turned around and drove down the ruts, leaving the boy and girl standing there in a swirl of dogs and exhaust.

When they turned onto the Watson Road, Edna said, "Have you gone completely crazy, or are you only halfway there? That's three thousand dollars' worth of dogs."

"Ain't mine," he said.

They were a mile down the road, just crossing White Oak Creek, when he told her to pull over and shut the truck off. The trees were still big along the creek because the law wouldn't let loggers cut there. The darkness was deep, and it smelled cool and rich.

"Now," he said, and his head cocked like he heard something. "Them's my dogs."

She listened to the breeze high in the leaves and to the water hissing across rocks in the creek. If there had been some hounds sounding it would have been like the old days—back when she and Coy thought that the woods would go on forever and that they would go on forever, too, back when a whole forest of tall trees held the stars higher in the sky.

"Forty years," he said. "It ain't a long time to kill every bear and cut every tree."

She nodded. "It's enough," she said.

They stared through the windshield at the darkness. "I done my share of it," Coy said. "Must've cut a million trees, but I can't work no more, Edna. I can't hear the dogs no more. And there ain't no woods no more. Only little patches, like this, to make a man miserable."

Well, it was true. He couldn't work, and he knew he couldn't work. She started the truck and pulled onto the road. The woods glided past, and she could smell the soft, rich smells.

"Can you hear 'em?" Coy said.

She did not look at him. She didn't need to. He was familiar to her in every wrinkle and pain. He was hers to have and to hold, but it was as if her hand had closed on sand, and the harder she squeezed, the quicker it ran between her fingers.

The leaves were turning yellow already. Another winter would be on them soon. Well, so what if he didn't want his own dogs? That was fine with her, but to leave them at some stranger's house, well, it was foolish—a waste of money they didn't have. Just when she thought she knew the exact shape of the old fool's foolishness, here it had gone and taken on a new shape, and now she was going to have to figure him out all over again.

Tomorrow. She would come back tomorrow and gather them up and sell them.

"Do you hear?"

She stopped at the intersection with Coxe Road. The truck screamed, and the cicadas were working themselves up into crazy rhythms. No, she did not hear old hounds running through the woods of a deaf man's memory. She did not hear their mournful cries when they struck trail, did not hear how their music got sadder and more desperate the closer they got to what they wanted. What was it, she had always wondered, what was it that drove them to chase after things that made them seem so unhappy?

Coy was leaning his head out the window, listening. He was out there somewhere, spinning on ahead of her. She wanted to cry his name, wanted to say, "Coy, what's happening to you? Where is the man I used to know?" She wanted to bring him back to her, wanted to have him and to hold him, but getting what you wanted—holding it in your hand or in your heart—getting what you wanted only meant that it was going to be gone from your life forever.

She pulled onto the highway. Countless times she had driven this road, but all of a sudden she wasn't sure if it wound left or right. Left, she thought left, but she slowed down anyway, just in case there might be a surprise for her up ahead.

Stephen Coyne lives in Sioux City, Iowa, where he moved after a twenty-year sojourn in North Carolina. His stories and poems have appeared in the *Southern Review,* the *Georgia Review, American Short Fiction,* the *South Carolina Review, Prairie Schooner,* and elsewhere.

I lived for a time in a log cabin in Green Creek, North Carolina. Local lore had it that ten years before I arrived, a bear had ransacked the place. By my day, though, the bears were gone, and the area was a favorite spot for coon hunters. I was often chilled and thrilled by the hounds sounding in the hollows, and come day I would sometimes find lost dogs hanging around at the edge of the woods. If they were tame enough to approach, I'd get the owner's phone number from their collars and arrange to have the dogs picked up. The old deaf man who drove out one day was a poignant figure to me, and his disapproving wife was a ready-made character.

John Barth

THE REST OF YOUR LIFE

(from *TriQuarterly*)

"Sounds like the beginning of a story," in my busy wife's opinion, and I quite agreed, although just what story remained to be seen.

What had happened, I'd told her over breakfast, was that the calendar function on our home computer appeared to have died. When I called up the word-processor's stationery format, for example, the date automatically supplied under my "business" letterhead read *August 27, 1956*. Likewise on our other letterhead formats, our e-mail transmissions and receptions—anything on which the machine routinely noted month, day, and year. I had first noticed the error while catching up on personal and business correspondence the evening before this breakfast-time report (the date of which, by weak coincidence, happened to be *July 27, 1996*, just one month short of the fortieth anniversary of that letterhead date). Wondering mildly how many items I might have dispatched under that odd, out-of-date heading—for as my wife would now and then remind me, I had become less detail-attentive and generally more forgetful than I once was—I made the correction both on the correspondence in hand and on the computer's clock/calendar control . . . and then forgot to mention the matter when Julia came home from her Friday-night aerobics group. Up at first light next morning as usual in recent years, I let the "working girl" sleep on (her weekend pleasure) while I fetched in the morning newspaper, scanned its headlines over coffee—OLYMPIC BOMB INVESTIGATION CONTINUES, TWA 800 CRASH CAUSE STILL UNKNOWN—set out our daily vitamins and other pills and the fixings of the breakfast that we would presently make together, then holed up in my home office to check for e-mail and do a bit of deskwork until she was up and about. Again, I noticed, the date read August 27, 1956. I corrected it and experimentally restarted the machine.

August 27, 1956. Must be a dead battery, I opined over our Saturday-morning omelet.

Looking up from the paper's Business section: "Desktop computers have batteries?"

Some sort of little battery, I believed I remembered, to keep the clock going when the thing's shut down. Maybe to keep certain memory-functions intact between start-ups, although I hadn't noticed any other problems thus far. Not my line; I would check the user's manual.

"How come it doesn't default—Is that the right word?"

Default, yes. (Words *were* my line.)

"How come it doesn't default to the last date you set it to, or come up with a different wrong date each time? Why always August Whatever, Nineteen Whenever?"

Twenty-Seven, '56. Good question, but not one that I could answer.

Encouragingly: "Sounds like the beginning of a story."

Yes, well. We finished breakfast, did our daily stretchies together (hers more vigorous than mine, as she's the family jock), refilled our coffee mugs, and addressed our separate Saturday chores and amusements: for Julia, first her round-robin tennis group, then fresh-veggie shopping at the village farmers' market, then housework and gardening, interspersed with laps in our backyard pool; for yours truly, a bit of bookkeeping at the desk and then odd jobs about the house and grounds, maybe a bit of afternoon crabbing in the tidal cove that fronts our property. Then dinner *à deux* and our usual evening routine: a bit of reading, a bit of television, maybe an e-mail to one of our off-sprung offspring, maybe even a few recorder-piano duets, although we make music together less frequently than we used to. Then to bed, seldom later than half past ten.

Then the Sunday. Then a new week.

We had done all right, Julia and I; even rather well. Classmates and college sweethearts at the state university, we had married on our joint commencement day — shortly after World War II, when Americans wed younger than nowadays — and promptly thereafter did our bit for the postwar baby boom, turning out three healthy youngsters in four years. I had majored in journalism, Julia in education, and although she'd graduated summa cum laude while I had simply graduated, after the manner of the time she had set her professional credentials mostly aside to do the Mommy track while Daddy earned us all a living. I had duly done that, too: first at a little New England weekly, where I learned what college hadn't taught me about newspapering; then at an upstate New York daily; then at a major midwestern daily, where on the strength of a Nieman Fellowship year at Harvard (the young American journalist's next-best thing to a Pulitzer prize) I had switched from the Metro desk to Features; then at the Sunday magazine of Our Nation's Capital's leading rag — from which, as of my sixty-fifth birthday this time last year, I retired as associate editor to try my hand at free-lancing. Over those busy decades, as our nestlings fledged and one by one took wing, Julia had moved from subbing in their sundry schools to part-time academic counseling — whatever could be shifted with my "career moves" and expanded with the kids' independence — thence to supervisoring in the county school system and most recently, since our move from city to country, to fulltiming as Assistant Director of Development for a small local college. No journalist or educator expects to get rich, especially with three college tuitions to pay; but we had husbanded (and wifed) our resources, invested our savings prudently along with modest inheritances from our late parents, and watched those investments grow through the prosperous American decades that raised the Dow Jones from about 600 to nearly 6,000. Anon we had sold our suburban-D.C. house at a jim-dandy profit and more or less retired—half of us, anyhow—to five handsomely wooded acres on the high banks of a cove off the Potomac's Virginia shore, complete with swimming pool, goose-hunting blind, guest wing for the kids and grandkids, His and Hers in the two-car garage, and a brace of motorboats at the pier: one little, for crabbing and such, the other not so little, for serious fishing with old buddies from the *Post*. Enough pension, dividend, and Social Security income to keep the show going even without what I scored for the occasional column or magazine-piece, not to mention Julia's quite-good salary. Her own woman at last, as she liked to tease, *she* meant to keep on fulltiming until they threw her out: the Grandma Moses of development directors.

What's more, this prevailing good fortune, not entirely a matter of luck, applied to our physical and marital health as well. Both had survived their share of setbacks and even the odd knockdown, but in our mid-sixties we were still mentally, physically, and maritally intact, our midlife crises safely behind us and late-life ones yet to come, parents in the grave and grown-up children scattered about the republic with kids and midlife crises of their own. On balance, a much-blessed life indeed.

And by no means over! Quite apart from the famously increasing longevity of us First-Worlders, J and I had our parents' genes going for us, which had carried that foursome in not-bad health right up to bye-bye time in their late eighties and early nineties. Barring accident, we had an odds-on chance of twenty-plus years ahead: longer than our teen-age grandkids had walked the earth.

"Time enough to make a few more career moves of my own," Julia teased whenever I spoke of this.

August 27, 1956. I recorrected the date, went on with my work, with the weekend, with our life; took the Macintosh in on Monday for rebatterying or whatever and made shift meanwhile with

Julia's new laptop and my trusty old Hermes manual typewriter—
stored in our attic ever since personal computers came online
—until the patient was cured and discharged. The problem was,
in fact, a dead logic-board battery, the service person presently
informed me, and then tech-talked over my head for a bit about
CMOS and BIOS circuitry. He couldn't explain, however, why the
date-function defaulted consistently to August 27, 1956, rather than
to the date of the machine's assembly, say (no earlier than 1993),
or of the manufacture of its logic board. Did electronic data-
processors in any form, not to mention PCs and Macintoshes,
even exist on August 27, 1956?

Truth to tell, I don't have all that much to do at the desk these
days, and so "making shift" was no big deal. Indeed, while both
Julia and Mac were out of the house I turned my fascination with
that presumably arbitrary but spookily insistent date into a bit of
a project. We veteran journalists do not incline to superstition; a
healthy skepticism, to put it mildly, goes with the territory. But
why August? Why the 27th? Why 1956? Was something trying to
tell me something?

Out of professional habit I checked the nearest references to
hand, especially the historical-events chronology in my much-
thumbed *World Almanac*. In 1956, it reminded me, we were
halfway through what the almanac called "The American Decade."
Dwight Eisenhower was about to be landslided into his second
presidential term; Nikita Khrushchev was de-Stalinizing the USSR;
Israel, Britain, and France were about to snatch back the Suez
Canal from Egypt, which had nationalized it when we-all declined
to finance President Nasser's Aswan dam; the Soviet–U.S. space
race was up and running, but *Sputnik* hadn't yet galvanized the
competition; our Korean war was finished, our Vietnamese in-
volvement scarcely begun . . . et cetera.

What couldn't I have done back in my old office, with the *Post*'s
mighty databases and info-sniffing software! But to what end?
Since the computer-repair facility was associated with "Julia's college," I contented myself with a side-trip to the campus library

when I drove in to retrieve the machine. A modest facility ("But we're working on it," my wife liked to declare), its microfilm stacks didn't include back numbers of my former employer; they did file the *New York Times,* however, and from the reel *Jul. 21, 1956–Dec. 5, 1956* I photocopied the front page for Monday, August 27. SOVIET NUCLEAR TEST IN ASIA REPORTED BY WHITE HOUSE was the lead story, subheaded, U.S. Contrasts Moscow's Secrecy With Advance Washington Warnings. Among the other front-page news: BRITISH CHARGE MAKARIOS DIRECTED REBELS IN CYPRUS and EISENHOWER STAY IN WEST EXTENDED (the President was golfing in Pebble Beach, California, from where the nuclear-test story had also been filed). The lead photo was of the newly nominated Democratic Presidential and Vice-Presidential candidates, Adlai E. Stevenson and Estes Kefauver, leaving church together with members of their families on the previous day; the story below, however, was headlined TV SURVEY OF CONVENTIONS FINDS VIEWING OFF SHARPLY, and reported that neither the Republican nor the Democratic national conventions, recently concluded, had attracted as many viewers on any one evening as had Elvis Presley and Ed Sullivan.

So: It had been a Monday, that day forty Augusts past (its upcoming anniversary, I had already determined, would be a Tuesday). I showed the page to Julia over lunch, which we sometimes met for when I had errands near her campus.

"Still Eight Twenty-Seven Fifty-Sixing, are you?" She pretended concern at my "fixation" but scanned the photocopy with mild interest, sighing at the shot of Stevenson (whose lost cause we had ardently supported in the second presidential election of our voting life) and predicting that *this* year's upcoming political conventions, so carefully orchestrated for television, would lose far more viewers to the comedian Jerry Seinfeld than that year's had to Elvis Presley. And she pointed out to me—How hadn't I noticed it myself?—that the Soviet nuclear-test story had been filed "Special to the *New York Times*" by a sometime professional acquaintance of ours, currently a public-television celebrity and syndicated columnist, but back then already making his name as a young White House reporter for the Baltimore *Sun*.

While I, I reminded Julia, was still clawing my way up from the Boondock *Weekly Banner* to the Rochester *Democrat and Chronicle*. Don't rub it in.

"Who's rubbing?" She ordered the shrimp salad and checked her watch. "It was an okay paper already, and you made it a better one. Which reminds me . . ." And she changed the subject to the college's plan to install fiber-optic computer cables in every dormitory room during the upcoming academic year, in order to give the students faster access to the Internet. Her scheduled one o'clock meeting with a potential corporate sponsor of that improvement cut our lunch-date short; I wished her luck and watched her exit in her spiffy tailored suit while I (in my casual khakis, sportshirt, and Old Fart walking shoes) finished my sandwich and took care of the check.

Yes indeedy, I mused to myself, homeward bound then: the dear old *Democrap and Chronic Ill*—as we used to call it when things screwed up at the city desk. Heroic snow-belt winters; summers clouded by the "Great Lakes effect," though much pleasanter in August than our subtropical summertime Chesapeake, and blessedly hurricane-free. The inexhaustible energy of an ambitious twenty-six-year-old, chasing down story-leads at all hours, learning the ins and outs of our newly adopted city as perhaps only a Metro reporter can, yet at the same time helping Julia with our three preschoolers, maintaining and even remodeling our low-budget first house, and still finding time over and above for entertaining friends, for going to parties and concerts (a welcome change from Boondockville)—time for everything, back when there was never enough time for anything! Whereas nowadays it sometimes seemed to me that with ample leisure for everything, less and less got done; July's routine chores barely finished before August's were upon me.

Once Mac was back in place (and correctly reading, when I

booted him up, *August 6, 1996*) I did a bit more homework with the aid of some time-line software that I used occasionally when researching magazine pieces. By 1956, it reminded me, the world newly had or was on the cusp of having nuclear power plants, portable electric saws, Scrabble, electric typewriters and tooth-brushes and clothes dryers, oral polio vaccine, aerosol spray cans, home air conditioners, aluminum foil, lightweight bicycles with shiftable gears and caliper brakes, wash-and-wear fabrics, credit cards, garbage disposers, epoxy glue, Frisbees, milk cartons, panty-hose, ballpoint pens, FM radio, and stereophonic sound systems. Still waiting in the wings were antiperspirants, automobile air con-ditioning and cruise control, aluminum cans, birth control pills, bumper stickers, pocket calculators, decaf coffee, microwave ovens, felt-tip pens, photocopiers, home-delivery pizza, transistor radios, home computers (as I'd suspected), contact lenses, disposable dia-pers, running shoes, Teflon, scuba gear, skateboards, wraparound sunglasses, audiocassettes (not to mention VCRs), touchtone tele-phones (not to mention cordlesses, cellulars, and answering machines), color and cable television, Valium, Velcro, battery-powered wristwatches, digital anythings, and waterbeds.

"Disposable diapers," Julia sighed that evening when I spieled through this inventory: "Where were they when we needed them?"

Fifty-Six was the year Grace Kelly married Prince Rainier the Third, I told her, and Ringling Brothers folded their last canvas circus tent, and the *Andrea Doria* went down, and Chevrolet intro-duced fuel-injected engines. Harry Belafonte. The aforementioned Elvis. *I Love Lucy.* . . .

"I *did* love Lucy," my wife remembered. The early evening was airless, sultry; indeed, the whole week had been unnaturally calm, scarcely a ripple out on our cove, and this at the peak of the Atlantic hurricane season, with Arturo, Bertha, Carlos, and Danielle already safely behind us, and who knew whom to come. Back in '56, if I remembered correctly, the tropical storms all bore Anglo female names; I'd have to check.

We were sipping fresh-peach frozen daiquiris out on our pier while comparing His and Her day, our summer custom before prepping dinner. As Julia was now the nine-to-fiver, I routinely made the cocktails and hors d'oeuvres and barbecued the entree as often as possible, although it was still she who planned the menus and directed most of the preparation. She'd had a frustrating after-noon; hadn't hit it off with that potential co-sponsor of the col-lege's fiber-optic upgrade, an Old Boy type whose patronizing manner had strained her professional diplomacy to the limit. Excuse her, she warned me, if the male-chauvinist bastard had left her short of patience.

Enough about 1956, then, I suggested.

"No, go on. Obsessional or not, it soothes me."

Steak eighty-eight cents a pound, milk twenty-four cents a quart, bread eighteen cents a loaf. Average cost of a new car seventeen hundred bucks—remember our jim-dandy Chevy wagon?

"A Fifty-Five bought new in Fifty-Six, when the dealer was stuck with it." Our first new car, it had been: two-tone green and ivory. "Or was it a Fifty-Six bought late in the model year?"

A bargain, whichever. Median price of a new house—get this—eleven thousand seven hundred. I think we paid ten five for Mai-son Faute de Mieux.

"Dear Maison Faute de Mieux." Pet name for our first-ever house, afore-referred to. "But what was the median U.S. income back then?"

Just under two thousand per capita per annum. My fifty-six hun-dred from the *D and C* was princely for a new hand.

Julia winced her eyes shut in mid-sip. Headache? I wondered.

"Unfortunate choice of abbreviations." It had been in '56 or '57, she reminded me (as I had unwittingly just reminded her) that she'd found herself pregnant for the fourth time, accidentally in this instance, and we had decided not only to terminate the pregnancy by dilation and curettage—D & C, in ob/gyn lingo, and a code-term too for abortion in those pre-*Roe v. Wade* days—but to forestall fur-ther such accidents by vasectomy. "Shall we change the subject?"

Agreed—for a cluster of long- and well-buried memories was thereby evoked, of a less nostalgic character than our first house and new car. Duly shifting subjects, What's that floating white thing? I asked her, and pointed toward a something-or-other drifting usward on the ebbing tide.

"Don't see it." With her drink-free hand Julia shaded her eyes from the lowering sun. "Okay, I see it. Paper plate?"

It was an object indeed the diameter of a paper or plastic dinner plate, though several times thicker, floating edge-up and nine-tenths submerged in the flat calm creek. On its present leisurely course it would pass either just before or just under the cross-T where we sat, a not unwelcome diversion. Our sport-fishing boat, *Byline,* was tied up alongside; I stepped aboard, fetched back a crabber's dip-net, and retrieved the visitor when it drifted within reach.

"Well, now."

It was, of all unlikely flotsam, a *clock:* a plain white plastic wall clock, battery powered (didn't have those back in '56). Perhaps blown off some up-creek neighbor's boathouse? But there'd been no wind. Maybe negligently Frisbee'd into the cove after rain got to it? Anyhow quite drowned now, the space between its face and its plastic "crystal" half filled with tidewater (hence its slight remaining buoyancy), and stopped, mirabile dictu, at almost exactly 3:45, so that when I held it twelve o'clock high, the outstretched hands marked its internal waterline like a miniature horizon.

Time and tide, right? Then, before I'd even thought of the other obvious connection, Julia said, "Now we're in for it: not only August twenty-seventh, but *three forty-five* on August twenty-seventh. A.M. or P.M., I wonder?"

We tisked and chuckled; during our coveside residency a number of souvenirs had washed up on our reedy shoreline along with the usual litter of plastic bags and discarded drink-containers from the creek beyond—wildfowl decoys, life vests, fishermen's hats, crabtrap floats—but none so curious or portentous. In a novel or a movie, I supposed to Julia, the couple would begin to wonder whether some plot was thickening; whether something was trying to tell them something, and whether 3:45 A.M. or P.M. meant Eastern Daylight Time in 1956 or 1996.

"At three forty-five A.M. Eight Twenty-Seven '96," Julia declared, "your loving wife intends to be sound asleep. You can tell her the news over breakfast." And she wondered aloud, as we moved in from the pier to start dinner, what we had each been up to at 3:45 in the afternoon of August 27 forty years ago in Rochester, New York.

Another memory-buzz, and it was well that we were single-filing, for I felt my face burn. Would it not have been that very summer, if not necessarily that month . . . but yes, right around the time of "our" abortion. . . .

Without mentioning it to Julia, I resolved to check out discreetly, if I could, a certain little matter that I hadn't had occasion to remember for years, perhaps even for decades. My intention had been to drop the dripping clock *trouvée* into our trash bin, but as I passed through the garage en route to setting up the patio barbecue oven (didn't have those in '56, at least not with charcoal-lighting fluid and liquid propane igniters) I decided to hang it instead on a nearby tool-hook, to remind me to notice whether anything Significant would happen to happen at the indicated hour three weeks hence.

Not that I would likely need reminding. Unsuperstitious as I am and idle as was my interest in that approaching "anniversary," I was more curious than ever now about what—in Julia's and my joint timeline if not in America's and the world's—it might be the fortieth anniversary of. I was half tempted to ask the *Democrat and Chronicle*'s morgue-keepers to fax me a copy of the paper's Metro-section front page for August 27, 1956, to see what had been going on in town that day (but the reported news would be of the day before; perhaps I ought to check headlines for the 28th) and whether I myself had bylined any Rochester stories while my more successful friend was filing White House specials to the *Times*. But I resisted the temptation. Frame-by-framing through Julia's college's microfilm files had reminded me how each day's newspaper is indeed like a frame in time's ongoing movie. We retrospective viewers know, as the "actors" themselves did not, how at least some of those stories will end: that Stevenson and Kefauver will be overwhelmed in November by Eisenhower and Nixon; that the U.S.–Soviet arms race will effectively end with the collapse of the U.S.S.R. in 1989. Of others we may remember the "beginning" but not the "end," or vice versa; of others yet (e.g., in my case, Britain's troubles with Archbishop Makarios in Cyprus) neither the prologue nor the sequel. But who was to say that what would turn out to be the *really* significant event of any given day—even internationally, not to mention locally—would be front-page news? Next week's or month's lead story often begins as today's page-six squib or goes unreported altogether at the time: Einstein's formulation of relativity theory, the top-secret first successful test of a thermonuclear bomb. And unlike the President's golf games, what ordinary person's most life-affecting events—birth, marriage, career successes and failures, child-conceptions, infidelities and other betrayals, divorce, major accident, illness, death—make the headlines, or in most instances even the inside pages? I reminded myself, moreover, that such "frames" as hours, day-dates, year-numbers—all such convenient divisions of time—are more or less our human inventions, more or less relative to our personal or cultural-historical point of view: What would "August 27, 1956" mean to an Aztec or a classical Greek? Oblivious to time zones and calendars, though not to astronomical rhythms, the world rolls on; our life-processes likewise, oblivious to chronological age though not to aging.

8/27/56. No need to consult the *D and C:* prompted by some old résumés and certain other items in my home-office files, my ever-slipperier memory began to clarify the personal picture. In the late spring of that year, Julia and I and our three preschoolers had moved to our first real city—in our new Chevy wagon, it now came back to me, bought earlier in Boondockville on the strength of my Rochester job offer, and so it had been a leftover '55 after all. After checking neighborhoods and public-school districts against our freshly elevated budgetary ceiling, we had bought "Maison Faute de Mieux," its to-the-hilt mortgage to be amortized by the laughably distant year 1986. And on July 1 I had begun my first more or less big-time newspaper job, for which I'd been hired on the strength of a really rather impressive portfolio from what I'm calling the Boondock *Weekly Banner*. No *annus mirabilis,* maybe, 1956, but a major corner-turn in my/our life: formal education and professional apprenticeship finished; family established and now appropriately housed; children safely through babyhood and about to commence their own schooling; our six-year marriage well past the honeymoon stage but not yet seriously strained; and my first major success scored in what would turn out to be a quite creditable career (for if I could point to some, like that *Times*/PBS fellow, who had done better, I could point to ever so many more who'd done less well) in a field that by and large served the public interest, not just our personal welfare. Reviewed thus, in the story of both our married life and my professional life the summer of '56 could be said to have marked the end of the Beginning and the beginning of the Middle.

Over that evening's cocktail-on-the-pier, "You left something out," Julia said, and my face reflushed, for I had indeed skirted a thing or two that my day's digging had exhumed. But what she meant, to my relief, was that it had been that same summer—when George Jr. was five, Anne-Marie four, and Jeannette about to turn three—that their mother had felt free at last to begin her own "career," however tentatively and part-time, by working for "pay" (i.e., reduced kiddie-tuition) in our daughters' nursery school.

Right she was; sorry about that.

"It may seem nothing to you, George, but to me it mattered." Properly so.

She looked out across the cove, where the sun was lowering on another steamy August day. "I've often envied Anne-Marie and

Jeannette their *assumption* that their careers are as important as their husbands'."

I'm sure you have. By ear I couldn't tell whether "their husbands" ended with an apostrophe. The fact was, though, that if our elder daughter and her spouse, both academics, had managed some measure of professional parity in their university, our younger daughter's legal career had proved more important to her than marriage and motherhood; she'd left her CPA husband in Boston with custody of their ten-year-old to take a promotion in her firm's Seattle office. Even Julia's feelings were mixed about that, although the marriage had been shaky from the start.

More brightly, "Oh, I forgot to tell you," she said then: "I asked this computer-friend of mine at work about that date-default business? And he said that normally the default would be to the date when some gizmo called the BIOS chip was manufactured, which couldn't be before 1980. BIOS means Basic Input-Output System? But this guy's a PC aficionado who sniffs at Macintoshes. Anyhow, he's putting out a query on the Net, so stay tuned."

I was still getting used to some of Julia's recent speech habits: those California-style rising inflections and flip idioms like "stay tuned" that she picked up from her younger office-mates and that to me sounded out of character for people our age. But I suppressed my little irritation, told her sincerely that I appreciated her thoughtfulness, and withdrew to set up the charcoal grill before the subject could return to Things Left Out.

On 8/27/56, yet another bit of software informed me next day, the Dow Jones Industrial Average had been 579, and *Billboard* magazine's #1 pop recording in the USA had been Dean Martin singing "Memories Are Made of This." Whatever other desk-projects I had in the works—and my "retirement," mind, had been only from daily go-to-the-office journalism, not from the profession altogether—were stalled by distraction as the Big Date's anniversary drew nearer. In "the breakaway republic of Chechnya," as the media called it, a smoldering stalemate continued between rebel forces and the Russian military, whose leaders themselves were at odds over strategy. In Bosnia a sour truce still held as election-time approached. Julia found another possibly interested corporate co-sponsor for her college's fiber-optic upgrade. The queerly calm weather hung over tidewater Virginia as if Nature were holding her breath. There would be a full moon, my desk calendar declared, on the night after 8/27/96; perhaps we would celebrate the passage of my recent lunacy. On Sunday 8/18, trolling for bluefish aboard *Byline* with pals from the *Post,* I snagged my left thumb on a fish hook; no big deal, although the bandage hampered my computer keyboarding. My "little obsession" had become a standing levity since Julia (without first consulting me) shared it as a tease with our friends and children. George Jr., who worked for the National Security Agency at Fort Meade, pretended to have inside info ("We call it the X-File, Dad") that extraterrestrials were scheduled to take over the earth on 8/27/96. Picking up on her brother's tease, his academic sister e-mailed me from Michigan that the first UFOs had secretly landed on 8/27/56; their ongoing experiments on our family—in particular on its alpha male—would be completed on the fortieth anniversary (as measured in Earth-years) of that first landing. We'll miss you, Dad.

"So guess what," Julia announced on Friday, August 23. "I had lunch again today with Sam Bryer—my computer friend? And he found out from some hacker on the Net that all Macintoshes default to 8/27/56 when their logic-boards die because that's Steve Whatsisname's birthday—the founder of Apple Computers? Steve Jobs. A zillionaire in his thirties! Sam says everything about Macintoshes has to be cutesy-wootsie."

Aha, and my thanks to . . . Sam, is it? Sam. To myself I thought, Lunch again today with the guy? and tried to remember when I had last lunched with a woman colleague. The bittersweet memories then suddenly flooded in: a certain oak-paneled restaurant in downtown Rochester, far enough from the office for privacy but close enough for the two of us to get back to our desks more or less on time; a certain motel, inexpensive but not sleazy, on the Lake Ontario side of town; the erotic imagination and enviable recovery-speed of a healthy twenty-six-year-old on late-summer afternoons when he was supposed to be out checking the latest from Eastman Kodak or the University. It occurred to me to wonder whether it might have happened to be exactly at 3:45 P.M. EDST on August 27, 1956, that a certain premature and unprotected ejaculation had introduced a certain rogue spermatozoon to a certain extramural ovum: "Our imperious desires," dear brave Marianne had once ruefully quoted Robert Louis Stevenson, "and their staggering consequences."

For the sake of the children, as they say—but for good other reasons, too—Mr. and Mrs. had chosen not to divorce when the matter surfaced; and except for one half-hysterical (but consequential) instance, Julia had not retaliated in kind. The Nieman Fellowship year in Cambridge, not long after, had welcomely removed us from the Scene of the Crime as well as testifying to my professional rededication; its prestige enabled our move to St. Louis (the *Post-Dispatch*), thence to D.C., excuse the initials—and here, forty years later, we were: still comrades, those old wounds long since scarred over and, yes, healed.

Tell your pal Sam, I told my wife, that Eight Twenty-Seven is Lyndon Johnson's and Mother Teresa's birthday, too, though not their upcoming fortieth, needless to say. Virgos all. Birthstone Peridot. What's Peridot?

Julia, however, was communing with herself. "My pal Sam," she said deprecatingly, but smiled and sipped.

Who knows what "really" happened when the Big Day came? The explanation of my computer's default date, while mildly amusing, was irrelevant to the momentous though still vague significance that it had assumed for me, and in no way diminished my interest in its anniversary. By then my fishhook wound, too, was largely healed. Julia and I made wake-up love that morning—she had been more ardent of late than usual, and than her distracted husband. I cleared breakfast while she dolled up for work and then, still in my pajamas and slippers, lingered over second coffee and the Tuesday paper before going to my desk. Another sultry forecast, 30 percent chance of late-afternoon thundershowers. Second day of Democratic National Convention in Chicago; Hillary Rodham Clinton to address delegates tonight. Cause of TWA 800 crash still undetermined; Hurricane Edouard approaching Caribbean. I decided to try doing an article for the *Post*'s Sunday magazine—maybe even for the *New York Times* Sunday magazine—about my curious preoccupation, which by then had generated a small mountain of notes despite my professional sense that I still lacked a proper handle on it, and that those of my associated musings that weren't indelicately personal were too . . . philosophical, let's say, for a newspaper-magazine piece. I've mentioned already that the Really Important happenings, on whatever level, aren't necessarily those that get reported in the press: the undetected first metal-fatigue crack in some crucial component of a jet-liner's airframe; the casual mutation of one of your liver cells from normal to cancerous; the Go signal to a terrorist conspiracy, coded innocuously in loveseekers' lingo among the Personals. But my maunderings extended even from *What's the significance of this date?* through *What's the significance of the whole concept of date, even of time?* to *What's the significance of Significance, the meaning of Meaning?*

Never mind those. I quite expected 8/27/96 to be just another day, in the course of which we Americans (so said some new software sent by our Seattle-lawyer daughter) would per usual eat forty-seven million hot dogs, swallow fifty-two million aspirin tablets, use six point eight billion gallons of water to flush our collective toilets, and give birth to ten thousand new Americans. But I was not blind to such traditional aspects of Forty Years as, say, the period of the Israelites' wandering in the desert, or the typical span of a professional career—so that if, as aforesuggested, 8/27/56 had been for mine the end of the Beginning and beginning of the Middle, then 8/27/96 might feasibly mark the end of the Middle and thus the beginning of the End. I was even aware that just as my "little obsession" therewith had assumed a life of its own, independent of the trifle that had prompted it, so my half-serious but inordinate search for Portent might conceivably generate its own fulfillment—might prompt Julia, for example, this late in our story, to settle a long-dormant score by making, as she herself had more or less joked, "a few career moves" of her own; or might merely nudge your reporter gently around some bend, distancing me from her, our family and friends and former colleagues, so that in retrospect (trying and failing, say, to make a marketable essay out of it or anything else thenceforward) I would see that August 27 had indeed been the beginning of the end because I myself had made it so.

Just another day: the first for many, for many the last, for many more a crucial or at least consequential turning-point, but for most of us none of the above, at least apparently. I ate an apple for lunch; phoned Julia's office to check out *her* Day Thus Far and got her voice-mail message instead: a poised, assured, very-much-her-own-woman's voice. As is my summertime post-lunch habit, I then ran a flag up our waterfront pole from the assortment in our "flag locker," choosing for the occasion a long and somewhat tattered red-and-yellow streamer that in the Navy's flag code signifies Zero; it had been a birthday gift to me some years past from George Jr., who jokingly complained that I read too much significance into things and therefore gave me something that literally meant Nothing. After an exercise-swim I set out our crab traps along the lip of the cove-channel and patrolled them idly for a couple of hours from *Sound Bite,* our noisy little outboard runabout—inevitably wondering, at 3:45, whether my wife and Sam Whatsisname, Sam Bryer, might actually be et cetera. At that idea I found myself simultaneously sniffling and chuckling aloud with . . . oh, Transcendent Acceptance, I suppose.

Not enough crabs to bother with; they seemed to be scarcer every year.

At about 4:30—as I was considering whether canteloupe daiquiris or champagne would make the better toast to Beginning-of-the-End Day when Julia got home—the forecast thunderstorm rolled down the tidal Potomac, dumping an inch of rain in half an hour, knocking out our power for twenty minutes, and buffeting the cove with fifty-knot gusts, as measured on the wind gauge in our family room. Busy closing windows, I absent-mindedly neglected to fetch in the Zero flag before the storm hit; as I watched nature's sound-and-light show from our leeward porch, I saw the weathered red and yellow panels one by one let go at their seams in the bigger gusts and disappear behind curtains of rain. By five the tempest had rolled on out over the Chesapeake, the wind had moderated to ten and fifteen, and the westward sky was rebrightening. Our dock bench and pool-deck chairs would be too soaked for Happy-Hour sitting; we would use the screened porch. I reset all the house clocks and hauled down the last shredded panel of George Jr.'s flag, thinking I might mount it on a garage or basement wall behind that waterlogged clock as a wry memorial to the occasion: my next-to-last rite of passage, whatever.

Normally my wife got home from work by half past five; that day I was well into the six-o-clock news on television—Russians resume pullout from Grozny; Syria ready to resume talks with Israel; big hometown welcome expected for First Lady's convention appearance—when the garage door rumbled up and Julia's Volvo rolled in. Often "high" from her day at the office, she arrived this time positively radiant, forgetting even (I noted as I went to greet her) to reclose the garage door as usual from inside her car. Tugging her briefcase off the passenger seat with one hand while removing her sunglasses with the other, "Any champagne in the fridge?" she called. She kneed the car door shut—I pressed the garage-door wall button—gave me an exaggerated kiss hello, and exhilarated past me into the kitchen. Plopped down her briefcase; peeled out of her suit-jacket; yanked the fridge open; then stopped to grin meward, spreading her arms victoriously.

"Congratulate me! I *nailed* the guy! Fiber optics, here we come!"

· · ·

Well, I did congratulate her—wholeheartedly, or very nearly so. I popped the bubbly; toasted her corporate co-sponsoral coup; let her crow happily through half a glass before I even mentioned what I'd thought she would be celebrating, perhaps prematurely: the unremarkable close of what had proved after all to be just another day. When I did finally bring that matter up, it was via the heavyhanded portent of the thunderstorm and George Jr.'s flag.

"So here's to Nothing," Julia cheered, and although she topped off our glasses and bade us reclink them, her mind was obviously still on her successful courtship of that potential college-benefactor. Presently she excused herself to change out of office-clothes and take a swim, she announced, before hors d'oeuvres and the rest of the champagne. I wasn't even to *think* of starting the charcoals for the veal grillades and marinated eggplant wedges; she was flying too high to fuss with dinner yet.

So *I'll* fuss, I volunteered, but contented myself with merely readying the grill for cooking. Our pool is well screened from the neighbors, and we skinny-dip on occasion, though not as a rule—since who knows when a delivery- or service-person might drive up, or the lawn-mowing crew. But presently out she frisked jay-bird-naked, did my triumphant mate, and like a playful pink porpoise dived with a whoop into the pool's deep end.

"Come on in!" she all but ordered me after a bit. "Drop your drawers and take the plunge!" Not to spoil her fun, I did, but couldn't follow through when, to my surprise, she made to crown her triumph with a spot of submarine sex.

On 8/27/96 the Dow Jones closed up seventeen, at 5711. We ate late; watched the First Lady's convention speech on television (Julia raising her fist from time to time in a gesture of solidarity); decided not to wait up for the ensuing keynote address. Instead, nightcap in hand, we stepped outside to admire the moon over our cove—still officially one night shy of full, but looking already as ripe as a moon can look.

So, said I: That's that.

"What's what?" She truly had no idea what I was referring to.

Old Eight Twenty-Seven Et Cetera.

"Oh, right." She inhaled, exhaled, and with mock gravity said "You know what they say, George: *Today is the first day of the rest of your life.*"

How right she was.

———————

John Barth's novels, novellas, short-story collections, and essay collections have won various prizes and awards, including the National Book Award for Fiction. His new novel, *Coming Soon!!!*, will be published in November 2001.

"The Rest of Your Life" was suggested by the default of my computer's date-function to 8/27/56 (a characteristic of Apple computers, it turns out, for the reason given in the story) and my retrieval soon after, from the tidewater in front of our house, of a floating wall clock stopped at 3:15. What's to be done with such faux-portentous coincidences? "Of of what one can't make sense, one may make art."

TETURO MARUYAMA

APPENDIX

A list of the magazines currently consulted for *New Stories from the South: The Year's Best, 2001,* with addresses, subscription rates, and editors.

Agni
Boston University Writing Program
236 Bay State Road
Boston, MA 02215
Semiannually, $15
Askold Melnyczuk

Alabama Literary Review
272 Smith Hall
Troy State University
Troy, AL 36082
Semiannually, $10
Donald Noble

The Antioch Review
P.O. Box 148
Yellow Springs, OH 45387-0148
Quarterly, $35
Robert S. Fogarty

Arts & Letters
Campus Box 89
Georgia College & State University
Milledgeville, GA 31061-0490
Semiannually, $15
Martin Lammon

The Atlantic Monthly
77 N. Washington St.
Boston, MA 02114
Monthly, $17.94
C. Michael Curtis

Black Warrior Review
University of Alabama
P.O. Box 862936
Tuscaloosa, AL 35486-0027
Semiannually, $14
Christopher Chambers

Boulevard
4579 Laclede Ave., PMB 332
St. Louis, MO 63108-2103
Triannually, $15
Richard Burgin

The Carolina Quarterly
Greenlaw Hall CB# 3520
University of North Carolina
Chapel Hill, NC 27599-3520
Triannually, $12
Fiction Editor

The Chariton Review
Truman State University
Kirksville, MO 63501
Semiannually, $9
Jim Barnes

The Chattahoochee Review
Georgia Perimeter College
2101 Womack Road
Dunwoody, GA 30338-4497
Quarterly, $16
Lawrence Hetrick, Editor

Cimarron Review
205 Morrill Hall
Oklahoma State University
Stillwater, OK 74078-0135
Quarterly, $16
E. P. Walkiewicz

Columbia
415 Dodge Hall
2960 Broadway
Columbia University
New York, NY 10027-6902
Semiannually, $15
Kelly Zavotka

Confrontation
English Department
C.W. Post of L.I.U.
Brookville, NY 11548
Semiannually, $10
Martin Tucker, Editor

Conjunctions
Bard College
Annandale-on-Hudson, NY 12504
Semiannually, $18
Bradford Morrow

Connecticut Review
Southern Connecticut State
   University
New Haven, CT 06515
Semiannually, $12
Vivian Shipley

Crucible
Barton College
College Station
Wilson, NC 27893
Annually, $6
Terrence L. Grimes

CutBank
Dept. of English
University of Montana

Missoula, MT 59812
Semiannually, $12
Elizabeth Burnett and Keith Dunlap

Denver Quarterly
University of Denver
Denver, CO 80208
Quarterly, $20
Bin Ramke

The Distillery
Division of Liberal Arts
Motlow State Community
   College
P.O. Box 8500
Lynchburg, TN 37352-8500
Semiannually, $15
Inman Majors

DoubleTake
55 Davis Square
Somerville, MA 02144
Quarterly, $32
Robert Coles

Epoch
251 Goldwin Smith Hall
Cornell University
Ithaca, NY 14853-3201
Triannually, $11
Michael Koch

Esquire
250 West 55th Street
New York, NY 10019
Monthly, $15.94
Adrienne Miller

Fiction
c/o English Department
City College of New York
New York, NY 10031
Quarterly, $32
Mark J. Mirsky

Five Points
GSU
University Plaza
Department of English
Atlanta, GA 30303-3083
Triannually, $15
Pam Durban

The Florida Review
Department of English
University of Central Florida
Orlando, FL 32816
Semiannually, $10
Russ Kesler

The Georgia Review
University of Georgia
Athens, GA 30602-9009
Quarterly, $18
Stephen Corey

The Gettysburg Review
Gettysburg College
Gettysburg, PA 17325-1491
Quarterly, $24
Peter Stitt

Glimmer Train
710 SW Madison St., #504
Portland, OR 97205
Quarterly, $32
Susan Burmeister-Brown
    and Linda Burmeister Davies

Granta
1755 Broadway
5th Floor
New York, NY 10019-3780
Quarterly, $37
Ian Jack

The Greensboro Review
Department of English
University of North Carolina
Greensboro, NC 27412

Semiannually, $8
Jim Clark

Harper's Magazine
666 Broadway
New York, NY 10012
Monthly, $18
Lewis H. Lapham

Habersham Review
Piedmont College
P.O. Box 10
Demorest, GA 30535-0010
Semiannually, $12
Frank Gannon

High Plains Literary Review
180 Adams Street, Suite 250
Denver, CO 80206
Triannually, $20
Robert O. Greer, Jr.

Image
3307 Third Ave., W.
Seattle, WA 98119
Quarterly, $30
Gregory Wolfe

Indiana Review
465 Ballantine Ave.
Indiana University
Bloomington, IN 47405
Semiannually, $12
Laura McCoid

The Iowa Review
308 EPB
University of Iowa
Iowa City, IA 52242-1492
Triannually, $18
David Hamilton

The Journal
Ohio State University
Department of English

164 W. 17th Avenue
Columbus, OH 43210
Semiannually, $12
Kathy Fagan and Michelle Herman

Kalliope
Florida Community College
3939 Roosevelt Blvd.
Jacksonville, FL 32205
Triannually, $14.95
Mary Sue Koeppel

The Kenyon Review
Kenyon College
Gambier, OH 43022
Triannually, $25
David H. Lynn

The Literary Review
Fairleigh Dickinson University
285 Madison Avenue
Madison, NJ 07940
Quarterly, $18
Walter Cummins

The Long Story
18 Eaton Street
Lawrence, MA 01843
Annually, $6
R. P. Burnham

Lonzie's Fried Chicken
P.O. Box 189
Lynn, NC 28750
Semiannually, $14.95
E. H. Goree

Louisiana Literature
SLU-10792
Southeastern Louisiana
  University
Hammond, LA 70402
Semiannually, $12
Jack Bedell

Lynx Eye
c/o Scribblefest Literary Group
1880 Hill Drive
Los Angeles, CA 90041
Quarterly, $25
Pam McCully, Kathryn Morrison

Main Street Rag
P.O. Box 25331
Charlotte, NC 28229-5331
Quarterly, $15
M. Scott Douglass

Meridian
University of Virginia
P.O. Box 400121
Charlottesville, VA 22904-4121
Semiannually, $10
Ravi Howard

Mid-American Review
106 Hanna Hall
Department of English
Bowling Green State University
Bowling Green, OH 43403
Semiannually, $12
Michael Czyzniejewski

Mississippi Review
University of Southern
  Mississippi
Box 5144
Hattiesburg, MS 39406-5144
Semiannually, $15
Frederick Barthelme

The Missouri Review
1507 Hillcrest Hall
University of Missouri
Columbia, MO 65211
Triannually, $19
Speer Morgan

The Nebraska Review
Writers Workshop
Fine Arts Building 212
University of Nebraska at Omaha
Omaha, NE 68182-0324
Semiannually, $11
James Reed

New Delta Review
English Department
Louisiana State University
Baton Rouge, LA 70802-5001
Semiannually, $8.50
Andrew Spear

New England Review
Middlebury College
Middlebury, VT 05753
Quarterly, $23
Stephen Donadio

New Orleans Review
Box 195
Loyola University
New Orleans, LA 70118
Quarterly, $18
Christopher Chambers, Editor

The New Yorker
4 Times Square
New York, NY 10036
Weekly, $44.95
Bill Buford, Fiction Editor

Nimrod International Journal
The University of Tulsa
600 South College
Tulsa, OK 74104-3189
Semiannually, $17.50
Francine Ringold

The North American Review
University of Northern Iowa

Cedar Falls, IA 50614-0516
Six times a year, $22
Vince Gotera

North Carolina Literary Review
English Department
2201 General Classroom Building
East Carolina University
Greenville, NC 27858-4353
Semiannually, $17
Margaret Bauer

Northwest Review
369 PLC
University of Oregon
Eugene, OR 97403
Triannually, $20
John Witte

The Ohio Review
344 Scott Quad
Ohio University
Athens, OH 45701-2979
Semiannually, $16
Wayne Dodd

Ohioana Quarterly
Ohioana Literary Assn.
65 S. Front St.
Suite 1105
Columbus, OH 43215
Quarterly, $25
Kate Templeton Hancock

Ontario Review
9 Honey Brook Drive
Princeton, NJ 08540
Semiannually, $14
Raymond J. Smith

Other Voices
University of Illinois at Chicago
Department of English (M/C 162)

601 S. Morgan Street
Chicago, IL 60607-7120
Quarterly, $20
Lois Hauselman

The Oxford American
P.O. Box 1156
Oxford, MS 38655
Bimonthly, $19.95
Marc Smirnoff

The Paris Review
541 E. 72nd Street
New York, NY 10021
Quarterly, $40
George Plimpton

Parting Gifts
March Street Press
3413 Wilshire Drive
Greensboro, NC 27408
Semiannually, $12
Robert Bixby

Pembroke Magazine
UNC-P, Box 1510
Pembroke, NC 28372-1510
Annually, $8
Shelby Stephenson

Ploughshares
Emerson College
120 Boylston St.
Boston, MA 02116-4624
Triannually, $21
Don Lee

Prairie Schooner
201 Andrews Hall
University of Nebraska
Lincoln, NE 68588-0334
Quarterly, $22
Hilda Raz

Puerto del Sol
Box 30001, Department 3E

New Mexico State University
Las Cruces, NM 88003-9984
Semiannually, $10
Kevin McIlvoy

Quarterly West
200 S. Central Campus Drive
Room 317
University of Utah
Salt Lake City, UT 84112-9109
Semiannually, $12
Margot Schilpp and Lynn Kilpatrick

River City
Department of English
The University of Memphis
Memphis, TN 38152-6176
Semiannually, $12
Thomas Russell

River Styx
634 North Grand Blvd.
12th Floor
St. Louis, MO 63103
Triannually, $20
Richard Newman

Roanoke Review
English Department
Roanoke College
Salem, VA 29153
Semiannually, $9.50
Robert R. Walter

Santa Monica Review
Santa Monica College
1900 Pico Boulevard
Santa Monica, CA 90405
Semiannually, $12
Andrew Tonkovich

Shenandoah
Washington and Lee University
Troubadour Theater
2nd Floor
Lexington, VA 24450-0303

Quarterly, $22
R. T. Smith

64
Shine Publications, Inc.
1435 West Main Street
Richmond, va 23220
Monthly, $29.95
Lorna Wyckoff

The South Carolina Review
Department of English
Clemson University
Strode Tower, Box 340523
Clemson, sc 29634-0523
Semiannually, $10
Wayne Chapman and Donna Haisty
    Winchell

South Dakota Review
Box 111
University Exchange
University of South Dakota
Vermillion, sd 57069
Quarterly, $22
Brian Bedard

Southern Exposure
P.O. Box 531
Durham, nc 27702
Quarterly, $24
Pat Arnow, Editor

Southern Humanities Review
9088 Haley Center
Auburn University
Auburn, al 36849
Quarterly, $15
Dan R. Latimer and Virginia M.
    Kouidis

The Southern Review
43 Allen Hall
Louisiana State University
Baton Rouge, la 70803-5005

Quarterly, $25
James Olney

Southwest Review
307 Fondren Library West
Box 750374
Southern Methodist University
Dallas, tx 75275
Quarterly, $24
Willard Spiegelman

Sou'wester
Department of English
Southern Illinois University at
    Edwardsville
Edwardsville, il 62026-1438
Semiannually, $10
Fred W. Robbins

StoryQuarterly
431 Sheridan Road
Kenilworth, il 60043-1220
Quarterly, $12
M.M.M. Hayes

Sundog: The Southeast Review
Department of English
Florida State University
Tallahassee, fl 32311
Semiannually, $10
Miles Garrett Watson

Tampa Review
The University of Tampa
401 W. Kennedy Boulevard
Tampa, fl 33606-1490
Semiannually, $15
Richard Mathews

Texas Review
English Department
Sam Houston State University
Huntsville, tx 77341-2146
Semiannually, $20
Paul Ruffin

Third Coast
Department of English
Western Michigan University
Kalamazoo, MI 49008-5092
Semiannually, $11
Pedro Ponce and Chris Torockio

The Threepenny Review
P.O. Box 9131
Berkeley, CA 94709
Quarterly, $20
Wendy Lesser

TriQuarterly
Northwestern University
2020 Ridge Avenue
Evanston, IL 60208-4302
Triannually, $24
Susan Firestone Hahn

Virginia Adversaria
P.O. Box 2349
Poquoson, VA 23662
Quarterly, $15
William Glose

The Virginia Quarterly Review
One West Range
P.O. Box 400223
Charlottesville, VA 22904-4223
Quarterly, $18
Staige D. Blackford

West Branch
Bucknell Hall
Bucknell University
Lewisburg, PA 17837
Semiannually, $7
Robert Love Taylor

Wind Magazine
P.O. Box 24548
Lexington, KY 40524
Semiannually, $10
Charlie G. Hughes

Yemassee
Department of English
University of South Carolina
Columbia, SC 29208
Semiannually, $15
Lisa Kerr

Zoetrope
1350 Avenue of the Americas
24th Floor
New York, NY 10019
Triannually, $20
Adrienne Brodeur

ZYZZYVA
P.O. Box 590069
San Francisco, CA 94159-0069
Triannually, $36
Howard Junker

PUBLISHER'S NOTE
The stories reprinted in *New Stories from the South: The Year's Best, 2001* were selected from American short stories published in magazines issued between January and December 2000. Shannon Ravenel annually consults a list of one hundred nationally distributed American periodicals and makes her choices for this anthology based on criteria that include original publication first-serially in magazine form and publication as short stories. Direct submissions are not considered.

PREVIOUS VOLUMES

Copies of previous volumes of *New Stories from the South* can be ordered through your local bookstore or by calling the Sales Department at Algonquin Books of Chapel Hill. Multiple copies for classroom adoptions are available at a special discount. For information, please call 919-967-0108.

NEW STORIES FROM THE SOUTH: THE YEAR'S BEST, 1986

Max Apple, BRIDGING

Madison Smartt Bell, TRIPTYCH 2

Mary Ward Brown, TONGUES OF FLAME

Suzanne Brown, COMMUNION

James Lee Burke, THE CONVICT

Ron Carlson, AIR

Doug Crowell, SAYS VELMA

Leon V. Driskell, MARTHA JEAN

Elizabeth Harris, THE WORLD RECORD HOLDER

Mary Hood, SOMETHING GOOD FOR GINNIE

David Huddle, SUMMER OF THE MAGIC SHOW

Gloria Norris, HOLDING ON

Kurt Rheinheimer, UMPIRE

W. A. Smith, DELIVERY

Wallace Whatley, SOMETHING TO LOSE

Luke Whisnant, WALLWORK

Sylvia Wilkinson, CHICKEN SIMON

New Stories from the South: The Year's Best, 1987

James Gordon Bennett, DEPENDENTS

Robert Boswell, EDWARD AND JILL

Rosanne Caggeshall, PETER THE ROCK

John William Corrington, HEROIC MEASURES/VITAL SIGNS

Vicki Covington, MAGNOLIA

Andre Dubus, DRESSED LIKE SUMMER LEAVES

Mary Hood, AFTER MOORE

Trudy Lewis, VINCRISTINE

Lewis Nordan, SUGAR, THE EUNUCHS, AND BIG G. B.

Peggy Payne, THE PURE IN HEART

Bob Shacochis, WHERE PELHAM FELL

Lee Smith, LIFE ON THE MOON

Marly Swick, HEART

Robert Love Taylor, LADY OF SPAIN

Luke Whisnant, ACROSS FROM THE MOTOHEADS

New Stories from the South: The Year's Best, 1988

Ellen Akins, GEORGE BAILEY FISHING

Rick Bass, THE WATCH

Richard Bausch, THE MAN WHO KNEW BELLE STAR

Larry Brown, FACING THE MUSIC

Pam Durban, BELONGING

John Rolfe Gardiner, GAME FARM

Jim Hall, GAS

Charlotte Holmes, METROPOLITAN

Nanci Kincaid, LIKE THE OLD WOLF IN ALL THOSE WOLF STORIES

Barbara Kingsolver, ROSE-JOHNNY

Trudy Lewis, HALF MEASURES

Jill McCorkle, FIRST UNION BLUES

Mark Richard, HAPPINESS OF THE GARDEN VARIETY

Sunny Rogers, THE CRUMB

Annette Sanford, LIMITED ACCESS

Eve Shelnutt, VOICE

NEW STORIES FROM THE SOUTH: THE YEAR'S BEST, 1989

Rick Bass, WILD HORSES

Madison Smartt Bell, CUSTOMS OF THE COUNTRY

James Gordon Bennett, PACIFIC THEATER

Larry Brown, SAMARITANS

Mary Ward Brown, IT WASN'T ALL DANCING

Kelly Cherry, WHERE SHE WAS

David Huddle, PLAYING

Sandy Huss, COUPON FOR BLOOD

Frank Manley, THE RAIN OF TERROR

Bobbie Ann Mason, WISH

Lewis Nordan, A HANK OF HAIR, A PIECE OF BONE

Kurt Rheinheimer, HOMES

Mark Richard, STRAYS

Annette Sanford, SIX WHITE HORSES

Paula Sharp, HOT SPRINGS

New Stories from the South: The Year's Best, 1990

Tom Bailey, CROW MAN

Rick Bass, THE HISTORY OF RODNEY

Richard Bausch, LETTER TO THE LADY OF THE HOUSE

Larry Brown, SLEEP

Moira Crone, JUST OUTSIDE THE B.T.

Clyde Edgerton, CHANGING NAMES

Greg Johnson, THE BOARDER

Nanci Kincaid, SPITTIN' IMAGE OF A BAPTIST BOY

Reginald McKnight, THE KIND OF LIGHT THAT SHINES ON TEXAS

Lewis Nordan, THE CELLAR OF RUNT CONROY

Lance Olsen, FAMILY

Mark Richard, FEAST OF THE EARTH, RANSOM OF THE CLAY

Ron Robinson, WHERE WE LAND

Bob Shacochis, LES FEMMES CREOLES

Molly Best Tinsley, ZOE

Donna Trussell, FISHBONE

New Stories from the South: The Year's Best, 1991

Rick Bass, IN THE LOYAL MOUNTAINS

Thomas Phillips Brewer, BLACK CAT BONE

Larry Brown, BIG BAD LOVE

Robert Olen Butler, RELIC

Barbara Hudson, THE ARABESQUE

Elizabeth Hunnewell, A LIFE OR DEATH MATTER

Hilding Johnson, SOUTH OF KITTATINNY

Nanci Kincaid, THIS IS NOT THE PICTURE SHOW

Bobbie Ann Mason, WITH JAZZ

Jill McCorkle, WAITING FOR HARD TIMES TO END

Robert Morgan, POINSETT'S BRIDGE

Reynolds Price, HIS FINAL MOTHER

Mark Richard, THE BIRDS FOR CHRISTMAS

Susan Starr Richards, THE SCREENED PORCH

Lee Smith, INTENSIVE CARE

Peter Taylor, COUSIN AUBREY

NEW STORIES FROM THE SOUTH: THE YEAR'S BEST, 1992

Alison Baker, CLEARWATER AND LATISSIMUS

Larry Brown, A ROADSIDE RESURRECTION

Mary Ward Brown, A NEW LIFE

James Lee Burke, TEXAS CITY, 1947

Robert Olen Butler, A GOOD SCENT FROM A STRANGE MOUNTAIN

Nanci Kincaid, A STURDY PAIR OF SHOES THAT FIT GOOD

Patricia Lear, AFTER MEMPHIS

Dan Leone, YOU HAVE CHOSEN CAKE

Karen Minton, LIKE HANDS ON A CAVE WALL

Reginald McKnight, QUITTING SMOKING

Elizabeth Seydel Morgan, ECONOMICS

Robert Morgan, DEATH CROWN

Susan Perabo, EXPLAINING DEATH TO THE DOG

Padgett Powell, THE WINNOWING OF MRS. SCHUPING

Lee Smith, THE BUBBA STORIES

Peter Taylor, THE WITCH OF OWL MOUNTAIN SPRINGS

Abraham Verghese, LILACS

NEW STORIES FROM THE SOUTH: THE YEAR'S BEST, 1993

Richard Bausch, EVENING

Pinckney Benedict, BOUNTY

Wendell Berry, A JONQUIL FOR MARY PENN

Robert Olen Butler, PREPARATION

Lee Merrill Byrd, MAJOR SIX POCKETS

Kevin Calder, NAME ME THIS RIVER

Tony Earley, CHARLOTTE

Paula K. Gover, WHITE BOYS AND RIVER GIRLS

David Huddle, TROUBLE AT THE HOME OFFICE

Barbara Hudson, SELLING WHISKERS

Elizabeth Hunnewell, FAMILY PLANNING

Dennis Loy Johnson, RESCUING ED

Edward P. Jones, MARIE

Wayne Karlin, PRISONERS

Dan Leone, SPINACH

Jill McCorkle, MAN WATCHER

Annette Sanford, HELENS AND ROSES

Peter Taylor, THE WAITING ROOM

NEW STORIES FROM THE SOUTH: THE YEAR'S BEST, 1994

Frederick Barthelme, RETREAT

Richard Bausch, AREN'T YOU HAPPY FOR ME?

Ethan Canin, THE PALACE THIEF

Kathleen Cushman, LUXURY

Tony Earley, THE PROPHET FROM JUPITER

Pamela Erbe, SWEET TOOTH

Barry Hannah, NICODEMUS BLUFF

Nanci Kincaid, PRETENDING THE BED WAS A RAFT

Nancy Krusoe, LANDSCAPE AND DREAM

Robert Morgan, DARK CORNER

Reynolds Price, DEEDS OF LIGHT

Leon Rooke, THE HEART MUST FROM ITS BREAKING

John Sayles, PEELING

George Singleton, OUTLAW HEAD & TAIL

Melanie Sumner, MY OTHER LIFE

Robert Love Taylor, MY MOTHER'S SHOES

NEW STORIES FROM THE SOUTH: THE YEAR'S BEST, 1995

R. Sebastian Bennett, RIDING WITH THE DOCTOR

Wendy Brenner, I AM THE BEAR

James Lee Burke, WATER PEOPLE

Robert Olen Butler, BOY BORN WITH TATTOO OF ELVIS

Ken Craven, PAYING ATTENTION

Tim Gautreaux, THE BUG MAN

Ellen Gilchrist, THE STUCCO HOUSE

Scott Gould, BASES

Barry Hannah, DRUMMER DOWN

MMM Hayes, FIXING LU

Hillary Hebert, LADIES OF THE MARBLE HEARTH

Jesse Lee Kercheval, GRAVITY

Caroline A. Langston, IN THE DISTANCE

Lynn Marie, TEAMS

Susan Perabo, GRAVITY

Dale Ray Phillips, EVERYTHING QUIET LIKE CHURCH

Elizabeth Spencer, THE RUNAWAYS

NEW STORIES FROM THE SOUTH: THE YEAR'S BEST, 1996

Robert Olen Butler, JEALOUS HUSBAND RETURNS IN FORM OF PARROT

Moira Crone, GAUGUIN

J. D. Dolan, MOOD MUSIC

Ellen Douglas, GRANT

William Faulkner, ROSE OF LEBANON

Kathy Flann, A HAPPY, SAFE THING

Tim Gautreaux, DIED AND GONE TO VEGAS

David Gilbert, COOL MOSS

Marcia Guthridge, THE HOST

Jill McCorkle, PARADISE

Robert Morgan, THE BALM OF GILEAD TREE

Tom Paine, GENERAL MARKMAN'S LAST STAND

Susan Perabo, SOME SAY THE WORLD

Annette Sanford, GOOSE GIRL

Lee Smith, THE HAPPY MEMORIES CLUB

NEW STORIES FROM THE SOUTH: THE YEAR'S BEST, 1997

PREFACE *by Robert Olen Butler*

Gene Able, MARRYING AUNT SADIE

Dwight Allen, THE GREEN SUIT

Edward Allen, ASHES NORTH

Robert Olen Butler, HELP ME FIND MY SPACEMAN LOVER

Janice Daugharty, ALONG A WIDER RIVER

Ellen Douglas, JULIA AND NELLIE

Pam Durban, GRAVITY

Charles East, PAVANE FOR A DEAD PRINCESS

Rhian Margaret Ellis, EVERY BUILDING WANTS TO FALL

Tim Gautreaux, LITTLE FROGS IN A DITCH

Elizabeth Gilbert, THE FINEST WIFE

Lucy Hochman, SIMPLER COMPONENTS

Beauvais McCaddon, THE HALF-PINT

Dale Ray Phillips, CORPORAL LOVE

Patricia Elam Ruff, THE TAXI RIDE

Lee Smith, NATIVE DAUGHTER

Judy Troy, RAMONE

Marc Vassallo, AFTER THE OPERA

Brad Vice, MOJO FARMER

New Stories from the South: The Year's Best, 1998

PREFACE *by Padgett Powell*

Frederick Barthelme, THE LESSON

Wendy Brenner, NIPPLE

Stephen Dixon, THE POET

Tony Earley, BRIDGE

Scott Ely, TALK RADIO

Tim Gautreaux, SORRY BLOOD

Michael Gills, WHERE WORDS GO

John Holman, RITA'S MYSTERY

Stephen Marion, NAKED AS TANYA

Jennifer Moses, GIRLS LIKE YOU

Padgett Powell, ALIENS OF AFFECTION

Sara Powers, THE BAKER'S WIFE

Mark Richard, MEMORIAL DAY

Nancy Richard, THE ORDER OF THINGS

Josh Russell, YELLOW JACK

Annette Sanford, IN THE LITTLE HUNKY RIVER

Enid Shomer, THE OTHER MOTHER

George Singleton, THESE PEOPLE ARE US

Molly Best Tinsley, THE ONLY WAY TO RIDE

NEW STORIES FROM THE SOUTH: THE YEAR'S BEST, 1999

PREFACE *by Tony Earley*

Andrew Alexander, LITTLE BITTY PRETTY ONE

Richard Bausch, MISSY

Pinckney Benedict, MIRACLE BOY

Wendy Brenner, THE HUMAN SIDE OF INSTRUMENTAL
    TRANSCOMMUNICATION

Laura Payne Butler, BOOKER T'S COMING HOME

Mary Clyde, KRISTA HAD A TREBLE CLEF ROSE

Janice Daugharty, NAME OF LOVE

Rick DeMarinis, BORROWED HEARTS

Tony Earley, QUILL

Clyde Edgerton, LUNCH AT THE PICADILLY

Michael Erard, BEYOND THE POINT

Tom Franklin, POACHERS

William Gay, THOSE DEEP ELM BROWN'S FERRY BLUES

Mary Gordon, STORYTELLING

Ingrid Hill, PAGAN BABIES

Michael Knight, BIRDLAND

Kurt Rheinheimer, NEIGHBORHOOD

Richard Schmitt, LEAVING VENICE, FLORIDA

Heather Sellers, FLA. BOYS

George Singleton, CAULK

NEW STORIES FROM THE SOUTH: THE YEAR'S BEST, 2000

PREFACE *by Ellen Douglas*

A. Manette Ansay, BOX

Wendy Brenner, MR. PUNIVERSE

D. Winston Brown, IN THE DOORWAY OF RHEE'S JAZZ JOINT

Robert Olen Butler, HEAVY METAL

Cathy Day, THE CIRCUS HOUSE

R.H.W. Dillard, FORGETTING THE END OF THE WORLD

Tony Earley, JUST MARRIED

Clyde Edgerton, DEBRA'S FLAP AND SNAP

Tim Gautreaux, DANCING WITH THE ONE-ARMED GAL

William Gay, MY HAND IS JUST FINE WHERE IT IS

Allan Gurganus, HE'S AT THE OFFICE

John Holman, WAVE

Romulus Linney, THE WIDOW

Thomas McNeely, SHEEP

Christopher Miner, RHONDA AND HER CHILDREN

Chris Offutt, THE BEST FRIEND

Margo Rabb, HOW TO TELL A STORY

Karen Sagstetter, THE THING WITH WILLIE

Mary Helen Stefaniak, A NOTE TO BIOGRAPHERS REGARDING FAMOUS
   AUTHOR FLANNERY O'CONNOR

Melanie Sumner, GOOD-HEARTED WOMAN